SONG OF THE FALLEN
BOOK II

RACHEL HAIMOWITZ

Riptide Publishing
PO Box 6652
Hillsborough, NJ 08844
www.riptidepublishing.com

Crescendo (Song of the Fallen, Book II)
Copyright © 2011, 2014 by Rachel Haimowitz

Cover Art by Simoné, www.dreamarian.com
Editor: Tal Valante
Cover Design, and Layout: L.C. Chase, lcchase.com/design.htm

ISBN: 978-1-62649-238-7

Second edition
September, 2014

Also available in ebook:
ISBN: 978-1-62649-237-0

SONG OF THE FALLEN
BOOK II

RACHEL HAIMOWITZ

For Dad and my evil stepmom; mazel tov, and may your Ever After be as happy as Ayden and Freyrik's.

And for Tal, always.

TABLE OF *Contents*

Chapter One

reyrík had long ago come to realize that the gods rarely intervened in the lives of men, no matter what prayers or sacrifices were made. Yet only recently had he come to see their indifference as a blessing, for when the gods' great shadow fell upon you, it might well blot out the sun.

Which was how he found himself in the darkness now, tucked down in the canopy bed of his traveling tent with the man—the *elf*—he loved. The elf he'd sworn to see safely home. The elf he was now escorting to the one place more treacherous than even the darker forests: the High Court of Aegea.

"Maybe—"

"No," Ayden said, and none too gently at that. "How many times do I have to say it? I'll not run away without you."

Freyrík rolled to face him, glad for once of the elfglow in the dark tent, wondering if Ayden could see him back in a light that was not—according to the elf—actually there. "You know I can't leave."

"Then neither can I. Go to sleep."

Before Freyrík could try a new tack, Ayden rolled away. For a moment he thought the elf angry, but then Ayden pressed his bare back to Freyrík's chest and tugged Freyrík's arm over his waist. He held to it with both hands as if he suspected Freyrík might take to pacing. Which, admittedly, was tempting.

"I can hear your thoughts roiling," Ayden grumbled. "*Sleep.*"

As if he could with the dangers of the morrow looming so. "Not until you've heard me out."

Ayden sighed but then pressed up tighter against him, his arse grinding against Freyrík's groin. "Fine. Speak." Another wiggle that would have ended all conversation were Freyrík not so anxious. "But know my thoughts are not on your words."

Freyrík clenched his fist, his forearm flexing beneath Ayden's grip. 'Twas all he could do not to push the elf away and shake some sense into him.

He startled when Ayden's other hand snaked between them, probing. "Perhaps *your* thoughts aren't, either?"

And gods befanged, but those questing fingers raised evidence to support Ayden's theory. A moment's trying to coax more from him, then another. Freyrík grunted and pulled Ayden's hand away before he lost all will to stop him.

Ayden *hmph'd* and did not try again.

Freyrík sighed. Had he hurt the elf's feelings? What he wouldn't give for the power to hear them as Ayden could. Mayhap then he'd know the right words to make him understand.

He settled for nuzzling his face into the back of Ayden's head, nudging tufts of hair flat with his cheek. "You have sacrificed so much for me already," he whispered. "I would not see you sacrifice more. Were you my subject, I would order you home. But I cannot, so I beg of you: Go. Now. Allow me to decline your selfless offer."

Ayden shook his head, squeezed Freyrík's arm. "'Tis selfishness, you idiot, not comity." A marvel, how Ayden could make such harsh words sound so fond. "I could not bear to see you executed for treason. But I *can* bear High Court. We've been through worse together already and come out the other side."

'Twas true, and yet . . . He pulled back, dropped a kiss on Ayden's shoulder and ran fingertips down the fine web of scars on his back. "You nearly died. What if—"

"I'm *fine*, Freyrík."

"But will you still be, even when they bind your magic?"

Freyrík winced as Ayden tensed in his arms. 'Twas a cold, cruel thing to have said, but he'd say it again and again if it would breach Ayden's stubbornness. And mayhap it had, for Ayden remained stiff and silent.

"Tomorrow we ride upon the Splendor," he pressed. "Once we cross the first gate, there will be no turning back. You have to go *now*. The ambassador's escort—"

"Will think you complicit!"

"Beat me, then. Bind me. Make a show of it."

"It would not work," Ayden said, and gods but the weariness in his voice stabbed at Freyrík's heart. "You have intervened for me too often in the past to escape suspicion now."

Then make *it work*, Freyrík wanted to say. *Break me. Kill my escorts.*

But he couldn't betray his men so. Besides, deep in his heart he knew Ayden was right. None of it would suffice in the eyes of High Court.

He ground his head against the pillow in frustration. "Let them blame me, then. You have paid in blood for me; I would do the same for you."

Ayden's elflight flared so bright that Freyrík, startled, snatched his hand back to shade his eyes.

When he could see again, Ayden was standing. Pointing.

Furious.

"'Tis not *blood* they would take," the elf growled. Not shouting, no—too aware of men who might overhear—but his words were no less sharp for it. His anger pricked at Freyrík's skin like a thousand blowdarts. "'Tis your *head*. I have seen the cages strung like lanterns along the outer wall, displaying what remains of slaughtered commoners and kings alike. Do not try to tell me you would be exempt!"

No, he supposed he wouldn't, nor did he think it would come to—

"Wait, you've *seen* the cages?" He sat up, swung his legs over the side of the bed. "You've been to the Splendor?"

Ayden lowered his jabbing finger and nodded. "As a child, with my father. Things were different then."

Despite himself, a smile crept upon his lips at the thought of Ayden as a diplomat's son, dressed to the chin in finery and standing still and mannerly at his father's side—likely with that mop of unruly hair to ruin the impression—

"What?" Ayden demanded, folding his arms across his chest and scowling.

"Apologies," Freyrík huffed, laughter coloring his words. "I'm just"—he shook his head, scrubbed a hand across disobedient lips—"I'm just imagining you being polite, is all."

"Well, stop it." Ayden's scowl deepened, but Freyrík needed no elven magic to hear the smile behind it. "I'll have you know I was a terror, even then."

"I do not doubt it," he said solemnly. His grin cracked through again and he held his arms out, inviting. Ayden stepped into his embrace, the warmth of him soaking right through Freyrík's skin as hands slid round his shoulders and one smooth cheek came to rest against the top of his head.

Freyrík closed his eyes and let himself revel in Ayden's shelter.

But only for a moment, for though he'd surrendered the argument, the danger still loomed. He gave Ayden's arm a tug, guiding the elf to sit on the bed beside him. They angled toward each other, knees touching, hands laced together between them. Ayden gazed upon him, eyes questioning.

"You must not be a terror this time," Freyrík said.

Ayden squeezed his fingers. "I know."

"The Crown Prince will greet us at the gate to the inner ward. You must seem to him a slave broken and trained."

"I know."

"And gods pray, do not wander off. *Ever*. I cannot protect you if you leave my sight."

"Yes, yes, I *know*." He pulled his hands free and cupped them to Freyrík's cheeks with just a bit too much pressure to be tender. "Now if you've finished fretting, human, I would you still your tongue that we may put it to better use."

He could fair *taste* the elf at those words, and next he knew he was on his back, a hot, heavy weight across his hips, his manhood straining against Ayden's arse. Hands on his cheeks again, drawing his eyes up to Ayden's hungry, focused grin. When Ayden leaned in to claim him, he didn't fight it, just slid his hands round Ayden's hips and splayed his legs, opening up beneath him.

After all, 'twould be ungentlemanly to refuse an invitation so sincere.

Ayden woke before dawn to the sounds of rousing in their little camp, hand reaching by habit for the dagger at the bedside table. He doubted these men would harm him, but such instincts could not—*should* not—be quashed.

Freyrík stirred against his side, and Ayden let his hand slip back beneath the blanket and across Freyrík's chest. His fingers toyed with the sprinkling of coarse hair there, brushed once over a nipple, then settled atop his lover's heart.

Freyrík's hand came up to cover his own, squeezing lightly. It seemed neither of them felt much in the way of excitation this morn.

Freyrík lifted Ayden's hand to his lips and kissed it, then threw back the covers and rolled out of bed, calling for his groom, who appeared so swiftly he must have been standing just outside the flaps. Had he heard their argument last night? They'd kept mostly to whispers, even at the height of their anger, but Lord Vitr was never far from his master's side.

Ayden pushed the worry from his mind—he trusted Lord Vitr, and 'twas too late in any case if someone else had overheard—and went about his morning ablutions. They dressed in silence, then ate in silence. What little they had to say had been said far too many times already.

The moment they left their tent, four attendants swarmed in, packing it and its contents away. Ayden too was packed away, for they'd never allowed him a horse. He let two guards escort him to the supply wagon and give him a none-too-gentle shove onto the unforgiving bench where he'd spent the last three weeks, resigning himself to yet another day of watching the countryside rattle by.

In any event, 'twas easier to focus on his bruised backside than what might lie in store for him at journey's end. He'd not been to the Splendor in some five centuries, and could have gone another five without regret. Whatever pleasant memories he'd had of the place had been fouled beyond repair. His father had died there, murdered at treacherous human hands.

Gods alone knew what he might endure at the same hands to keep Rík safe.

The sun was just beginning to burn away the frost when a massive wall came into view—a stone structure that stretched on seemingly for leagues, curving round toward the horizon and back on itself. Fallen gods, where had *that* come from?

As it loomed larger and larger, farmland and the occasional wood-frame home yielded to the fieldstone country manors of the landowners. Here and there a small copse of trees stood out from the flatlands like a group of forlorn survivors. And survivors they were, Ayden realized with a start—the last beaten remnants of the elven forests, long since annexed by the humans whose defilement of the woods had driven his people away. Ayden's hand clenched round the wagon's rail as he turned from the sight of the wounded land.

The taint on his mood must have translated to the humans, for all round him they grew wary. Freyrík glanced back, and his *concern-alarm-love* washed over Ayden's mind-ear in a clamor of drums and cymbals.

Then Freyrík reined in, drawing even with the wagon, and leaned sideways in his saddle. "Whatever you have just done . . ." He looked away a moment, off toward the city, song abuzz with nervous hesitation. "Frightening men of the Splendor may get you killed. I know it is not easy, but I would you hide your elflight when we ride upon the city."

Ayden nodded. "I will be careful, I promise."

He only hoped it was a promise he knew how to keep.

Just as the humans had spilled into the old elven enclaves, the city had spilled into the country. A league or two from the first wall came the noise and stench of an impoverished settlement that had not been there last Ayden had: shoddy wooden homes along narrow, winding alleys, waste flowing free in the gutters where children played. Even from this distance, notes of hunger and weariness cut the air.

'Twas almost with relief that Ayden silenced his song, wishing he could dim his sense of smell along with it.

Their party skirted round the city with clear distaste, the noblemen pressing perfumed cloths to their noses when the road forced them between its outer edge and the steep southern bank of the Góz River. There tradesmen and small-plot farmers hawked their wares to travelers from rickety wagons and booths. Ayden huddled down into his own rickety wagon, more uncomfortable at the tight press of human disharmony than he cared to admit.

He was as glad as his "companions" to leave the squalor behind for the first of the Splendor's gates, an artful creation of wrought iron and carved oak as tall at least as four of him. He swallowed hard at the sight of the Aegean crest halfway up the gate, elf-sized and stamped in gold upon the wood. Swallowed again, this time with nausea, at the sight of the little cages hanging to the left and right of it, each marked with a sign—"Traitor," "Murderer," "Deserter"—and holding a severed head.

He forced down his dread as the gates parted to let them pass, splitting the sword and crown on the crest down the middle.

Once we cross the first gate, there will be no turning back . . .

He turned his gaze from the heads in the cages to the one on Freyrík's shoulders, wavy auburn hair distinct even from a half-dozen paces ahead. Gods help him, but the image that flashed through his mind could never be unseen, not even if he lived another ten thousand years.

Perhaps Freyrík sensed his distress, for the man turned in his saddle, locked eyes with Ayden and nodded slightly. *All will be well*, his expression said. But the off-key quiver of his song belied him.

On they rode through the league-wide wheel of land between the third wall and the fourth. He'd played there as a child, racing horses through pasture and farmland with the other diplomats' sons, swimming and fishing in the maze of streams that swelled the Góz as it flowed west from the Splendor.

Little remained of that flourishing life now. The land bore more semblance to the squalor they'd just passed: narrow streets crammed full of wooden houses and shops and their human occupants.

Closer though it brought him to High Court, he was almost relieved when they reached the next gate.

This one, leading into the Third Ward, was achingly familiar. He'd passed through it hand in hand with his father, awed by the sounds and sights and smells so different from all he'd known before. Long-forgotten scents enveloped him—midland spices and baking bread, roasting meat, woodsmoke and tallow and leather—bringing back memories full of wonder and mischief along these cobbled streets.

Even the guards seemed familiar, though in his youth, their ancestors had not regarded him with such malice.

Up the hill through the Third Ward, then another inspection at the gate, more thorough than the last. As they entered the Second Ward, he spotted archers on the parapets of the final wall and, beyond that, the spired roof of the castle keep. 'Twas a fortress as sure as any border outpost and just as heavily guarded.

At length, they approached the Splendor's inner sanctum, and this time the gates remained firmly closed as the guards studied first the ambassador's papers and then each of the men in turn. Ayden felt their eyes linger long and harsh upon him, but he kept his own stare affixed to the gates lest the guards find a pretext for violence. At last they seemed satisfied with him, moving on to inspect the contents of the wagons before waving their party through.

Ayden kept his head down and made himself small as the High Court nobility would expect him to be.

The gates parted to reveal a drawbridge lowering across a moat, and a second gate and guardhouse on the other side. This they crossed through without inspection, and Ayden peeked up through his eyelashes as the bailey unfolded before them, enormous and bustling as a city and breathtaking in its . . . well, *splendor*.

But where was the Crown Prince? Why had he not met them at the gate?

Why had *nobody* met them at the gate?

He turned his eyes and mind-ear to Freyrík and immediately spotted the tense set of his back, heard the insult and anxiety in his song. Yet the man rode on, shoulders squared and head up.

Perhaps the Crown Prince would meet them at the keep itself. The air was quite chilly today for a soft midland fop, after all.

They passed by a stable and training rings as large as Freyrík's entire bailey, a reflecting pool that seemed to capture the whole of the sky along its lilied expanse, a topiary, and a hedge maze Ayden had spent long days getting lost in as a child. Somewhere beyond a hothouse full of South Islands orchids and untold acres of manicured lawn, their party reached the staging ground before the castle keep, where a noble officer stood at the head of an honor guard.

Ayden had little experience with human royalty, but surely this plain-looking man could not be the Crown Prince of Aegea.

The officer—Prince Náliga, by Freyrík's greeting to him—stepped forward to welcome them, and the pages rushed to secure the party's horses and assist the riders. Ignored, Ayden tilted his head back and squinted against the sun, following the convoluted roofline with his eyes, tracing spires as tall as redwoods and nearly as magnificent. From atop the parapets, guards peered back.

"Elf!" Freyrík barked, and Ayden startled at the impatient tone, kicking himself for the lapse in attention.

He ducked his head with a mumbled "Master," then slunk from the wagon and to Freyrík's side, hands folded behind his back. Freyrík's hurt and anger echoed like a shout in Ayden's head, so loud he itched to study the scene before him with his eyes as well as his mind-ear. But he daren't risk eye contact with the Aegean officer. Instead, he sidled half a step closer to Freyrík, so that their shoulders nearly touched. He wished he could do more, wished he knew how to help. Crack it, he'd settle for knowing what was wrong.

"Follow these men," Freyrík said, pointing toward two pages and a handful of guards. "Do as they say. *Behave.* Do you understand?"

No, he did not. Had not Freyrík just lectured him the night before about the importance of staying together? Where did these men mean to take him, and what for?

And why was Freyrík allowing it?

He risked meeting Freyrík's eyes, saw within them a reflection of the maelstrom he heard in Freyrík's song. Fear, anxiety, carefully controlled panic . . . And love, gods, such love. *Trust me,* his gaze said.

Always, he thought back, even seeing clear as water that Freyrík didn't trust himself.

Ayden bowed and said, "As Master wishes." And if his voice shook a little, well, it wasn't as if he feared he'd never see the man again, right?

Right?

Freyrík clutched Ayden's chin in one hand, lifting his head and pulling him in for a bruising kiss. 'Twould surely seem absent of affection to onlookers—a taken pleasure, one-sided—but 'twas as reassuring to Ayden as Freyrík had meant it to be: all would be well, and they would be together again soon.

Chapter Two

reyrík followed Prince Náliga through the grand front entrance of the castle keep, his face aching with the effort to keep his smile in place. 'Twas bad enough the Aegis had sent one of his youngest brothers, far removed from the crown, to greet Freyrík, rather than the Crown Prince or even Berendil. True, they'd been friends—even occasional lovers—through their Academy years, but despite Prince Náliga's status as a Son of Aegea, he wasn't Freyrík's equal and never had been—at least not since he'd been placed into the line of succession eighteen men from the throne.

Worse still, this second-rate welcome party hadn't even met them at the gate.

Had he underestimated the Aegis's anger so greatly? Gods pray none here thought him a traitor. His own death might be swift, but Ayden's . . .

Prince Náliga waved him down the gilt marble entranceway with an abbreviated bow and a smile that looked as pained as Freyrík's felt. "I trust your journey was not too arduous, Your Highness?"

He ground his teeth and forced his smile wider—a feat as valiant as slaying a darker bear when his only desire was to rage at the man before him, demand his elf be returned *this instant* or, gods, even fall to his knees and beg. But 'twould be cross-purposes at best, further evidence of betrayal at worst. He could neither afford to pretend ignorance of his misdeeds nor seem overly repentant of them.

Prince Náliga paused, laid a hand on Freyrík's arm and offered him another hesitant smile. "Your Highness?"

Oh, yes, they were prattling, weren't they? At least Prince Náliga's concern seemed sincere. "'Twas long, Your Highness, but no hardship at all, for I knew your father's glory awaited me at journey's end."

Prince Náliga nodded at that as if 'twere no other reply he might comprehend, but said no more. Distancing himself from Freyrík, then? Or simply taciturn as he often was, given his rank?

"And the Aegis Exalted? He is well?"

Another nod. "Indeed."

"And my brother?"

"Also well, Your Highness."

He waited for more details, but the prince remained stubbornly silent. "I have gifts for the Aegis . . ."

"Of course," Prince Náliga said, expecting nothing less. "His secretary will be most pleased to receive them at the feast tonight on his Eminence's behalf."

Gods befanged! Freyrík froze in the middle of the tapestried corridor, his escorts pulling up short beside him. Was he truly to be slighted from the presence chamber too? Even the lowliest subject at audience was entitled to such courtesy.

Freyrík laid a hand on Prince Náliga's forearm—an old familiarity, long buried. "Is he truly so angry as that?"

Prince Náliga laid his own hand atop Freyrík's, worried at his bottom lip for a time. "He loves you as a son, Freyrík. I think 'twas why your . . . *negligence* cut so deep."

Freyrík nodded, feeling the fist round his stomach unclench, if only a little. At least Prince Náliga had not said "betrayal."

"He seats you at the dais tonight." Prince Náliga began to walk again, Freyrík's hand still pressed between his hand and arm. "You will find his favor again, I doubt it not."

More corridors, more tapestries. Stained-glass windows, opened upon gardens and courtyards, spilled crisp air and sunlight upon the marble floors. They moved toward an outer wing—a newer wing, its walls the bright white of fresh, fine plaster. Was this an insult too? An exile of sorts? Or was he merely being granted the courtesy and comfort of rooms fit for a crown prince, sweet-smelling and draftless?

Mayhap he was overthinking.

No. There is no such thing as overthinking in this place.

Prince Náliga drew him to a stop before two carved oak doors near the end of the long hall. "Here we are, then, Your Highness. I trust you'll find these rooms to your liking."

A statement, not a question. Such confidence because Farr was the "barbarian province," uncultured and lacking in finery? Or because Prince Náliga recalled Freyrík's tastes and had taken care to indulge them?

Hmm. Mayhap he truly was overthinking.

Two pages opened the doors, and as befit Freyrík's station as Crown Prince of Farr and status as a guest, Prince Náliga waved him through. He crossed into the drawing room with the same sense of awe and irritation he always felt at High Court extravagance. The room's every surface glittered and shone, from the inlaid exotic-wood floors, to the silver- and gold-threaded wall tapestries, to the tiled mosaic ceiling. 'Twas fit for a king indeed, more precious than even the presence chamber at Castle Farr.

Gods, they could have funded an entire Surge campaign with the contents of this room alone.

"Is there anything more you require, Your Highness?"

Freyrík took another long look round the room, but he already knew he wouldn't find what he was looking for. He swallowed down his ill composure and gathered about him all the airs of a Crown Prince to say, "Yes. My slave."

Prince Náliga's mouth drew into a pucker. "He's in the baths with the others, being prepared for service as befits you, Your Highness."

"He *befits* me well enough, thank you. I would that he be returned to me now."

The prince's mouth pinched again, and this time his eyes along with it. He laid a hand upon Freyrík's back and guided him into the bedroom, where three male elves stood waiting, heads bowed. Freyrík's chest ached at the sight—not at their beauty, which was stunning, true, but at the gold-and-starfall chains round their necks and ankles and wrists. At their utter subservience. The one in the middle had black hair and green eyes, just like Ayden, and for an instant he actually *saw* him there, a mute broken creature robbed of all his precious gifts—

He ripped his eyes away and swiped at them with a trembling fist. He could not, could *not* afford to appear sympathetic to the "enemy" here.

"I'm afraid your elf is not yet fit to walk these halls, dear Prince. But as you can see, I've personally arranged for others to serve your needs in the meanwhile. Even a prince in poor grace is still a prince, after all, is he not?"

Prince Náliga chuckled, but quickly stopped when he saw Freyrík's scowl. He cleared his throat and said, "Yes, well, I recall your fondness for males"—the hand resting between Freyrík's shoulder blades stroked once, firm and warm—"and believe I have chosen well for you."

Freyrík bit back choice words and made himself say, "Indeed." He turned his gaze back to the pliant slaves, but 'twas all for show. There'd been a time once, in his youth, when he'd availed himself of such pleasures, but now even the fathoming of it sent bile burning up his throat.

"And if Your Highness would care for some . . . company?"

At first Freyrík thought the prince to be offering the services of the slaves, but then Náliga turned to him, hand sliding from his back to his shoulder and squeezing. "I would be most pleased, dear Freyrík, to pass the afternoon in dalliance."

Fond memories of their Academy years brought the word *Yes* unbidden to his tongue, but there it remained, held fast by love and worry and a lack of desire for any but Ayden. He laid his hand atop Náliga's where it rested on his shoulder, and gently lifted them both away. "You are a most gracious host, Náliga. But I am weary from my travels, and wish only to rest."

Náliga smiled, nodded once. If he felt slighted, his face did not show it. "I shall leave you to it, then. The elves will fetch you food and a hot bath, assist your groom, unpack your belongings. If by chance you should need something they cannot provide—"

"Merely send one off for aid, I know. I did pass many a year here in my youth, if you'll recall."

Náliga's gentle smile matched the one on Freyrík's own lips. "Indeed," he said. He clicked his heels and bowed his head, and Freyrík returned the courtesy. "A good afternoon to you then, dear Prince. I shall see you at the feast."

If 'twere any mercy among the gods, Freyrík would see Ayden at the feast tonight as well. And Berendil, and the Aegis, and all would be forgiven.

He shook his head, sat down on the bed and barely refrained from snapping *Stop that* to the elf who knelt at his feet to unlace his boots. He should know better than to wish upon seashells. Prince Náliga might yet think well of him, but there would be no forgiveness from the Aegis tonight.

And there had been no mercy from the gods for the last three hundred years.

The noise was the first thing Ayden noticed as he crossed the threshold into the castle keep. It hit like fists to both sides of his head, a clamor in his mind-ear like swords scraping on shields, swine squealing in the jaws of a wolf, the *wrong* of the Hunter's Call, all wrapped into one. 'Twas not so loud, fallen gods thanked, but even the softest whisper of such noxious din set his teeth to grinding. He clamped his hands to his temples without meaning to, and one of his "escorts" was so cracking skittish that he shoved Ayden hard between the shoulder blades. Ayden stumbled, thrust his hands out for balance, but gods, the *noise*—how could they not hear it?—drove his hands back to his temples. Whatever on earth could possibly shriek so?

Nothing earthly, after all, but *starfall*—cursed metal from the heavens, where the very gods themselves had once tread. He spotted its iris-like glint on a frieze: a hunting scene upon the corridor wall in silver and gold relief, touched through with the wretched stuff. Had its wailing driven the gods from the skies so many millennia past? Or had they crafted the starfall themselves as testament to their power, or to deter those who'd dare trespass in their realm?

Whatever its origin, 'twas powerful, rarer than red diamond, harmless to humans but near unbearable to elves. And no doubt that was why it was here. He hadn't realized humans possessed any—he'd only ever seen it in the Hall of Elders before, locked in a stone room where elite soldiers tested their mettle. Certainly the humans had never displayed it before the War of Betrayal.

Of course, there'd been no elven slaves to subdue here before the war. Only elven diplomats, fragile though the peace between their peoples had become in those final years.

His guards herded him past the frieze, down an endless hall, the screech of starfall fading and rising and fading and rising again, tiny drops of the poison element worked into sculptures, candelabras, doors, weaponry—a thousand trinkets decorating the keep, the wealth of an empire lining its halls. So too did dead Feral beasts, carefully preserved mid-strike or mid-snarl. Ayden scoffed. As if these soft midland nobles had ever faced a Feral in their lives, let alone slain one.

Yet if the Aegis meant to show his dominion over all things with these displays, he had done a cracking fine job of it.

At the end of yet another long hall, the guards pushed him through a gilt double door into a little marble-tiled anteroom lined with shelves on one wall and a bench on another. On the wall opposite the doors they'd entered were two more doors gilt with starfall, the mental noise of it so deafening that Ayden hardly heard the physical sound of a guard stepping forward and knocking thrice.

Some seconds after, the doors cracked open, spitting out a puff of humid air and two human males. One made a sort of humming-*tsk*ing sound, half leeringly appreciative, half disconcerted, perhaps at the messy state in which the road had left Ayden. The other asked the guards, "Is this Prince Freyrík's elf?"

"Yes." A shove sent him stumbling forward a step, nearly nose to nose with the two men. Servants, judging by their livery. But judging by their demeanor, they clearly thought themselves the lords of this little room.

One of them—the short one, sized like a human woman and soft as one from the looks of him—reached out toward Ayden's chest.

Freyrík had warned that people at High Court might wish to use Ayden, and had told him what to say if confronted. Ayden was glad of that foresight now; he smacked the man's hand away and growled, "On the prince's orders, nobody touches me but him."

The man seemed momentarily cowed, or at least alarmed. He turned to his companion, exchanged with him a wide-eyed glance . . .

And they burst, as one, into laughter.

"Oh yes," the second man said. He was taller, built like a wild asparagus stalk and just as unappealing. "I see the rumors are true. Perhaps you'd better stay," he said to Ayden's guards. "Just until he's bound."

A stutter of fear at those words, quickly swallowed. He would show them no weakness. The binding would only be temporary in any case. Only temporary.

"Ayden, is it?"

The short man again. Looking at the guards rather than Ayden, as if he were incapable of speaking for himself. 'Twas an oily sort of humiliation; he felt heat rising in his cheeks, clenched his jaw against ill-thought words.

"Yes," said one of the guards.

The short man nodded, then turned his attention to Ayden. "I am Master Laug. This"—gesturing to asparagus man—"is Master Húskarl. We are the Chief Grooms of the Slaves for the Aegis Exalted. It is our job to see you all properly prepared to serve your masters. You will obey us as you obey them. Do you understand?"

This pompous little man would be scandalized to learn how Ayden "obeyed" Rík. He bit back a grin at the thought and pasted on the blandest expression he could manage.

The tall, thin man—Húski . . . Húsker . . . *Hú-cares?*—produced an equally tall, thin stick and lashed Ayden's calf with it. Or tried to, anyway; Ayden sidestepped the strike with ease.

Alas, 'twas not so easy to sidestep the guards who flanked him at a nod from Laug. He could have fought them, thrown them, even burned them, but he'd promised Rík he'd behave, knew cracking well how important it was for them both that he maintain at least some semblance of submission. So he let the guards hold him, let the asparagus man swat him thrice with the switch. 'Twas not so painful over his breeches; he took the strikes with stony-faced indifference.

"Do. You. Understand?" Laug said when the laughable discipline had ended.

Ayden graced the man with another jerk of his chin.

It seemed to satisfy, for Laug nodded back, then waved a limp hand at Ayden and said, "Undress."

"I beg your pardon?" A mock beating Ayden could humor, but not whatever this human planned to do with him naked.

Laug sniffed, curled his upper lip. "I think you'll find begging is not much tolerated here. Nor is repetition. Do as you're told."

Asparagus man brandished his switch again, and 'twas all Ayden could do not to laugh at such a pathetic threat. Yet it made him wonder: Were the other elven slaves cowed by such nonsense? Had they softened so—or worse, been broken so—in their time here? 'Twas a sobering thought.

On the heels of that realization came a second one, equally troubling: *Anything* could happen to him here. Freyrík had promised to keep him close, to protect him—a promise broken mere minutes after their arrival. And now, despite promises that none would accost or violate him, he was trapped and surrounded, ordered to bare himself for gods knew what nefarious purpose.

If he conceded, would their next order see him arse up over a bench? He trusted Rík, truly he did. But enough to trust in Rík's trust of these men?

They'd not bound him yet. Four guards and two attendants . . . He could still fight.

Or he could try it Rík's way. Fight with words and wit instead of song and fists. Bide time, be patient, and stay healthy. If it came to it, he could (he hoped) invoke Rík's name as a shield. Surely even these self-important little men feared the anger of a crown prince.

With a grimace, he bent to unlace his boots.

Socks next, then vest, then shirt. Easier than he'd thought it'd be. He did not share human modesties, but they were watching so closely . . .

He turned his eyes and mind-ear resolutely inward as he untied his breeches. Before he could lose his nerve, he pushed them over his hips along with his undergarments, and stepped out of them when they dropped to the floor.

The grooms studied him as if examining stock for purchase. They seemed to approve, though Ayden had only expression and posture to go by, for he could barely hear their songs over that of the starfall, even as close as they were.

Approval or no, Ayden would not grant them the power to humiliate him. He possessed the body of a warrior, honed and skilled; he took no shame in it. Let them gaze upon him if they wished.

Just do not let their hands rove as surely as their eyes.

The guards gazed upon him too, though less with lust or judgment, he thought, than concern for potential blades hidden on his person—despite having searched him once already before letting him step foot in the keep. Fools, the lot of them. As if he'd need a weapon to kill them all.

Besides, where would he be hiding the cracking thing now?

Fallen gods pray they wouldn't insist upon checking. He didn't know what he'd do if they tried.

A good thing, then, that they did not. The tall groom turned his back to Ayden—*idiot*—and threw the gilt double doors open. He stepped through them, and the guards pushed Ayden forward as well into a vast, humid, sunlit room that smelled strongly of perfumed oils.

A bath. Though he didn't quite relax at the sight of it, he did at least uncoil a little. No wonder they'd stripped him of his muddied clothes and boots in the antechamber. 'Twas pristine in here. The ceiling stretched far above his head, sunlight pouring in through foggy glass panels at regular intervals. He spotted no doors but the ones he'd come through, no reachable windows, no objects to be used as weapons. Dominating the space was a massive communal pool, heated to steaming, a dozen or so men and women lounging within, another dozen being attended to at grooming tables round its edges.

Men *and* women bathing together? How could that be in this backward human realm?

The grooms had marched him all the way to the edge of the bath before the answer hit him so hard he stumbled: Because they were *not* human.

They were elves. Utterly silent, all of them. But elves nevertheless.

His fists clenched at the sight—so many, so naked and meek—and worse, at the songless quiet.

Before he could even begin to make sense of that, someone shoved him in the pool.

He hit the water less gracefully than he might have if the starfall all round him weren't screeching in his mind-ear, throwing him off-balance and out of focus. The pool was shallow, at least; his feet quickly found the bottom, and when he rose up, spluttering and whirling toward the unmannered beast who'd shoved him, the water only reached his waist.

Whoever had pushed him was gone. Not that it mattered; impulsive though he might be, he knew better than to pick a fight here over something so foolish, no matter how much he might want to.

He sat down on a bench beneath the water and let himself enjoy it, just for a moment, just long enough to calm down. 'Twas intensely hot but just the right side of comfortable, a powerful warmth that chipped deep at the chill and stiffness of travel. Scented water lapped at his throat and sweet steam curled round his face. A gentle current brought fresh water in and carried out the old. He licked at his lips, tasted faint hints of oil and rose hips but no mineral trace. 'Twas not a natural hot spring, then. A furnace, perhaps, beneath the floor?

No matter. He had more pressing things with which to concern himself—in particular, his fellow elves. He let his gaze rove round the bath, from one elf to the next, but none would meet his eyes. Were they not at least a *little* curious about the newcomer in their midst? He sang out to them—*greetings, peace, friendship*—but 'twas as if they couldn't even hear him.

Perhaps they truly couldn't? All round them was the screech of starfall, after all. Fallen gods, how could they bear it? 'Twas not just near them but *on* them—delicate shimmering chains of it fastened round their throats, looped decoratively round their ankles and wrists, biceps and bellies.

Maybe he just needed to get closer.

He ducked beneath the water, pushed off the wall and glided partway across the pool, surfacing beside a male half again the size of Ayden. A warrior, surely, all lean muscle and power. The elf was leaned back against the tile wall, arms spread, eyes closed. He did not acknowledge Ayden's presence, though Ayden had no doubt he'd sensed it.

"Greetings, brother," Ayden tried.

The elf opened his eyes, narrowed them at Ayden, then cast his gaze upon the water. Ayden could hear nothing above the starfall, but even a one-eyed elf could have read the feelings on his face: *You are trouble. Take it and yourself away from me.*

Ayden did as he was bid, lest he give in to the urge to scream, to shout at the elf to *do something, be the warrior you once were*, rip away the starfall with his bare hands. Not that he could have, alas, stronger than steel as it was.

Yet was not his people's will stronger than starfall?

He swam up to a young female, Ella's age or thereabouts, knelt before her and flashed her the smile that so often sent Ella's friends into blushing fits. But she too only darted her eyes at him before looking away. Why? Were they not permitted to speak to one another? And if so, why had nobody stopped him trying?

He sat down on the bench beside the girl but did not attempt to speak to her.

She swam away. He tried not to take it personally. It seemed everyone was ignoring each other just as studiously as they were ignoring him.

Perhaps they were merely biding their time. 'Twas on their side, after all, and wise always to let your enemy underestimate you.

Someone thrust a sea sponge in his face and said, "Wash."

Ayden startled—*Laug, fallen gods cracked, where had he come from?*—and snatched up the sponge. How had he not heard the human draw so close? The starfall shriek was constant, true, but such knowledge held no comfort. Called, in fact, for ever more vigilance and a great many fewer excuses.

Laug squatted down to place a segmented porcelain dish beside him, stacked high with bars of marbled soaps. "I know not what fragrances your master prefers. I trust you'll select with care."

Ayden made a show of sniffing them one by one until he found one he liked, then began to lather himself.

Laug and Asparagus Man watched closely. Did they think him a simpleton, unable to clean behind his own ears? Or were they merely aroused by the sight of it? Crack it all, he couldn't hear a thing! However did humans tell one mood from the next amongst their companions?

Whatever their secret, he would have to learn it, and quickly.

He finished washing. They made him wash again. When he stepped from the water at last, they inspected him like a horse at market. 'Twas all he could do to hold his tongue as foreign hands raised his arms, spread his legs, parted his hair. Gods only knew what they were looking for.

At last the hands fell away. Laug looked to Asparagus Man and said, "Now he is ready."

The words sent a shiver, quickly suppressed, up Ayden's naked back. He took a single step away and folded his arms across his chest. "For what?" he demanded. "You to fuck me?"

The grooms reared back as one, outrage stamped almost comically clear across their faces, their dismay so loud he could hear it even above the starfall. The moment stretched on long enough to be insulting.

Ayden thought to say something, but then Asparagus Man cleared his throat, squared his shoulders, and said, "We are eunuchs, of course."

Eunuchs? 'Twas not a word of the trade tongue, he didn't think, judging by the truncated vowels, the hard consonant. "Eunuchs?"

Laug scoffed, turned to Asparagus Man, and grumbled something behind his hand that made Asparagus Man laugh. Ayden couldn't quite make it out—something about backward border kingdoms breeding boorish slaves—but heard enough to bristle on Freyrík's behalf. He stepped forward, saw from the corner of his eye the guards step with him. "Will you not answer me?"

Apparently, they would not.

Laug shook his head as if condescending to a spoiled child, then turned his back on Ayden, utterly confident in his safety. "Come, Húskarl"—ah, yes, that was Asparagus Man's name—"we have spent too much time on this one already. Let us bind him and be done with it."

Ayden froze, heart and breath seizing in his chest. If he felt helpless now beneath the din of the starfall, how much worse would the binding be? How was it achieved? The child inside him wondered if it would hurt; the adult thought simply, *How could it not?*

His eyes darted round the room as Laug beckoned the guards closer and Húskarl unlocked a pantry door on the far side of the bath with a key chained round his wrist. Ayden felt eyes on him— so many eyes. Was *this* what it took to make his sisters and brothers acknowledge his existence? Anger flared at the thought.

Húskarl returned from the pantry with several slim, glimmering hoops draped from his fingers, one larger than the others: a collar and cuffs disguised as jewelry, starfall and gold twined like creeping vines, dotted with leaf-shaped emeralds.

Ayden stumbled back a step, then another. He would not wear them. He would *not*.

The starfall shriek intensified as Húskarl drew near. Ayden pressed his hands to his temples, backed away further. Right into the arms of two guards, who wrapped strong hands round his wrists and biceps.

"No," he said. "Let me go. Let me go, I mean it, let me—"

Laug rubbed him on the belly like a cracking dog. "It does not hurt for long."

Húskarl stepped near enough to strike, handed the four smaller circlets to Laug and opened the larger one on a well-disguised hinge. "Laug speaks true," he said, meeting Ayden's gaze with what struck him as real sympathy. "The worst of it will pass by morning. Do honor to your master now; stand brave."

Crack his sympathy and crack his "honor" and crack this gods-forsaken starfall! He sang out for a blast of scalding steam and pushed the cloud at Laug and Húskarl.

Alas, it came out a small thing through the starfall's interference, weak and annoying at best. The men stepped back, but seemed unharmed.

No matter; he needed no magic to prevail here. He leapt up within the confines of the startled guards' grips, thrust his heels at an angle into each guard's nearest kneecap, and used their weight as they collapsed to land them on their backs, his elbows planting hard into their diaphragms. He was on his feet an instant later, knives from the guards' belts in his hands, brandishing the weapons at the startled— nay, *petrified*—grooms.

"Stay away from me," he said, each word its own distinct sentence, threatening just as clearly as his knives.

The grooms held out placating hands, backed slowly out of cutting range. 'Twould be an easy thing to kill them anyway—a simple lunge or toss—but he'd stirred enough trouble already. He wished only to leave this room now, find Freyrík, and never let the man out of his sight again.

He backed toward the closed doors, stepping cautiously past the unconscious guards. He'd pummeled the breath from them in one strike; they'd fallen in silence. 'Twas likely no one yet knew he'd made trouble, and he could sneak away.

Ten steps from the doors now. Five steps. Two. He turned round at last . . .

And nearly ran headlong into another elf.

The elf touched a hand to his bare shoulder and said his name.

"Do I know you?"

Judging by the elf's reaction, he'd heard the words beneath the ones Ayden had spoken: *Get out of my cracking way before I kill you.*

But then he smiled, soft and sad. "You are the spitting image of Vaska," he said. "She was possessed of quite a fire, too."

Ayden's hands tightened round the hilts of his daggers. The urge to use them was strong, if for no other reason than to escape the nearness of the starfall round the other elf's neck. "Who are you," he demanded, "and why do you speak of my mother as if she's dead?"

The elf lifted a hand, placed the flat of it against Ayden's wrist and gently pushed Ayden's arm down to his side. Ayden let him, uncertain of why. "I am Jagall. I am—"

"You served with my father," Ayden whispered, distant memories of a face, a voice, rising to the fore at the elf's name. He'd worn a beard then, and a fine velvet cloak.

He left my father to die.

Jagall's smile widened as if he'd heard none of Ayden's anger, as if he expected Ayden to be pleased to remember him. "Indeed. I was First Secretary to the Ambassador. I did not mean to frighten you, child; I merely have not seen your mother in over three hundred years."

Child? Hardly. And anyway, better a child than a coward or worse. Jagall had been trapped here since the start of the war. Why had he been spared while Ayden's father had been slain? Why had he done nothing to free himself in all his borrowed time?

Ayden brought his knives back up between them. "Let me pass."

"And then what? Where will you go? How will you leave? Would you kill them all?"

"*I* would do whatever it takes."

If his insult wounded Jagall, the elf made no show of it. Instead he curled one hand back round Ayden's wrist, waved toward Húskarl with the other hand. "Come, child." He tugged Ayden a single step away from the doors. "I know you've half your father's mind inside you. Use it. He knew well—as would you if you'd only stop to think—that you cannot fight your way out of everything. Certainly not out of *this* city." He pulled Ayden close, leaned in to whisper sharply in his ear. "Now is the time to swallow your pride and take your licks lest you fail to outlive these fools, do you understand? What is done today can be undone when the time is right."

He let go of Ayden's wrist and stepped away. Ayden eyed the closed doors, the unconscious guards, the grooms, his fellow prisoners, the doors again. Jagall spoke true, he'd known that all along, and yet . . .

"I know it's hard," Jagall said. "We will hold you, if you wish it."

Ayden looked up sharply. Could Jagall hear his fears above the starfall, or had the elf simply learned the human trick of reading faces?

"I was among the first enslaved," Jagall added. "I'd have been most grateful for kind hands to bear me up through my own binding."

Gratitude? For *restraints?* Ayden grimaced. Nay, he would *never* sink so far. He shoved Jagall aside, closed the final distance between himself and the bath doors—

And drove both knives into the wood panels with a curse, turning his back on them before he could change his mind. Crack it all, but Jagall was right. There'd been many opportunities for Ayden to escape this fate before he'd crossed through a single one of the Splendor's wards. He'd *chosen* not to. For Rík. And he'd not come all this way to lose his nerve now.

Besides, the binding was temporary. Only temporary.

Jagall nodded at him, solemn and . . . relieved, perhaps? "Come, Ayden," he said, cupping a hand round Ayden's arm and guiding him toward the pool. It did not escape Ayden that Jagall had used his name this time, as if he'd earned the elder's respect with his decision. "Here. Lie on your belly; 'twill be easier that way."

Alas, Ayden's belly was rather busy just now crawling into his throat. But he sank to his knees, let Jagall guide him to the tiled floor. Two male elves approached; he heard not them but their starfall, a wail so near unbearable even at a distance that he could not fathom their calmness. He felt none of it himself, especially when one elf settled across Ayden's calves and pressed hands to his hips, and the other laid Ayden's arms along his sides and pinned them there. These elves had clearly been soldiers once. He could barely move in their grasps.

And now? Now they were naught but human puppets, restraining him for binding of their own accord. The pain Ayden felt at that had nothing to do with the tightness of their grips or the starfall round their necks.

"Master Húskarl, if I may?"

Ayden strained to lift his head, just enough to see what was happening. Jagall touched a hand between his shoulder blades—all reassurance, no force—and extended his other toward Húskarl. The groom nodded once and placed the starfall circlets in Jagall's palm.

Jagall knelt beside Ayden, ducked his head to catch Ayden's eye. "The song ails gravely, I know. But your mind-ear will soon numb, I promise you."

Though Ayden knew 'twas futile, he struggled anew against the hands that held him. "Are you saying I will be *deaf*?"

Jagall shook his head. "Not forever, child. What is done today can be undone, remember? Besides, have you not *been* deaf from the moment you stepped inside the keep?"

Ayden supposed he had, more or less, but such thoughts brought no comfort now.

"The pain will end. You must hold on to that, do you understand?"

Ayden nodded.

Jagall nodded back, and slid the collar round Ayden's neck.

Ayden woke to shattering screams. Dozens of voices, hundreds, thousands; males and females and Ferals alike, all wailing straight into his ears.

Only when his throat seized did he realize his own voice was a part of that tormented chorus.

Someone touched him . . . somewhere. His chest, perhaps. A hand through his hair. He opened tearing eyes and blinked a high ceiling into partial clarity. He could not focus any of his senses through the overload of the one most critical.

What had happened to him? Where was he?

Warm tiles beneath his bare back. The bath . . . he was in the bath. Naked, shivering despite the steam heat. Agony he couldn't even begin to comprehend festered in his skull like a rotten human tooth.

The *binding*.

He thought he might have screamed again, but only because he felt blades hacking at the inner flesh of his throat. He could not hear himself.

Or anything else, for that matter.

Deaf . . .

No. Worse than deaf. For all the beauty of the world's music had been shattered, stripped away, leaving only this broken wailing *wrong* in its place.

He tried to sit. Couldn't. Could barely even muster the control or strength to bring his arms to his head, dig the heels of his hands into his eyes, his temples, the top of his skull. Nothing eased the torment. He floundered onto his side and tucked his head to his knees. It didn't help; the shriek was a part of him now, locked round his ankles and wrists and neck. He couldn't even remember that happening, but clearly it had, for he saw the starfall circlets with his own eyes.

Fallen gods help him, however would he bear this? He should have listened to Rík. He should have run while he still could.

Now it was too late, and here he was the fool, a mere shadow of the elf he'd been but moments before.

He should have listened. Fallen gods cracked, he should have listened.

Chapter Three

"Chin up, Your Highness."

Freyrík tilted his head back so Lord Vitr could adjust the high collar of his dress shirt and fasten a broach at his throat. In his youth, he'd taken great joy in such preparations, for the wealth and pageantry of High Court had made his father's court seem miserly and staid by comparison. But tonight, with Ayden still missing and the question of his own status yet unanswered, he found himself begrudging even the time it took to dress for ceremony. Only a lifetime of diplomacy and hard-won patience stopped him from snapping at his groom to hurry.

At last Lord Vitr fastened Freyrík's collar of state round his neck, smoothed his hands down Freyrík's velvet-covered breast, and said, "There. Fit for the Aegis himself, Your Highness."

Freyrík was not immune to the reverence in his groom's tone at the mention of their King of Kings. He too felt it, always had. 'Twas no less heady now to step where the Aegis stepped each day, to be recognized even for a moment by such a man as he, than it had been in childhood. And he loved the man no less now than he ever had, no matter what might stand between them this night.

He let Lord Vitr escort him to the corridor, but insisted on walking to the banquet hall alone. He knew not what reception he might receive. If he were to be shamed, or worse, best it not happen before his own men.

Besides, he craved these moments of solitude, and a long quiet walk would help fortify him for the evening to come. Might Ayden await him at the feast, decked out in footmen's garb? And what of Berendil? And the Aegis? Would he smile at him, or scowl?

Whatever the situation, he would make it right. Trust lost could be earned again. Love could be reclaimed, reformed, reshaped with wisdom and time. Just as his love of this place had been. He trailed his fingertips across a silk tapestry, a marble bust of the ninth Aegis. Such splendor in these halls.

But the years had brought with them wisdom to see what lay beneath: arrogance, vanity, isolation, waste—of time, of coin, of political will, of learned men concerned more for ambition than their people. Too many here knew the dark beast scourge by word and story alone, and one could not take seriously that which one could not comprehend. Freyrík may have learned the art of war within these walls, but the *truth* of war, the harshness and the pain of it, he'd not understood until he'd left here.

The truth of politics, the harshness and pain of that, he was only beginning to understand now he'd returned.

He pushed those thoughts from his mind as he neared the doors to the great hall. Pages and heralds lined the anteroom on both sides, standing stiff at attention, while guests yet to be announced lounged upon settees and cushioned chairs. A page bowed and pulled a seat out for him, but he'd be sitting soon enough, and for far too long. He shook his head, and found an empty space in one corner to occupy.

The anteroom emptied quickly, guests escorted into the great hall one by one to be announced. As the guest of honor at tonight's feast—the barbarian champion, returned triumphant to the heart of the empire with conquered enemy in tow—he was led in last, escorted not by a lowly page but by Prince Náliga.

The great hall was crowded, the whole court seated and waiting. He didn't have the luxury of looking for Ayden as the herald announced his presence; he could only confirm the elf was not straight ahead, not at or near the dais. The Aegis was, of course, and—curiously— Berendil in the seat beside him, looking as well as ever.

The Aegis gazed calmly upon Freyrík as he walked down the long runner to the dais. He wished to take that as a sign of the Aegis's forgiveness, but knew better than to fool himself. Even a disfavored prince was still a prince, after all, to be treated in public with a certain accord.

Yet surely there was more to it than that. True, 'twas near unheard of not to honor visiting royalty with a banquet, but the Aegis had seen him snubbed of proper welcome, had kept him from Ayden and even Berendil. That the Aegis had inflicted these less visible punishments but still chose to honor Freyrík before all the court clearly meant something. 'Twas imperative he discover what, and quickly.

Alas, he couldn't exactly interrogate the man, nor even study his face for more than a moment at a time. As if 'twould reveal anything to him anyway, even if he stared for an hour. The man was a fortress, penetrable only by invitation or key.

He stole a glance as he neared the dais. Not the greeting smile he was hoping for, but nor the stony indifference he'd feared. Something between, indecipherable.

A footman greeted him at the base of the dais stairs with a sharp salute, then led him round the table and pulled out his chair. 'Twas only two seats from the Aegis, in between Berendil and Rodull, Crown Prince of Aegea.

He followed, but did not sit. 'Twould be a waste of the moment, while all eyes were still upon him, while the Aegis thought him docile in his shame. Surprise would serve him better now; while this wasn't the time or place for formal greeting—no, that honor had been denied him this afternoon—he strode right past his chair and dropped to one knee before the Aegis.

Silence, stark as a shout. He couldn't see the Aegis's face with his head bowed, but he could hear the startlement of the court in their sudden stillness. From beside him, the sound of clothes rustling, the Crown Prince shifting or stiffening in his chair. None such from the Aegis, of course; he was far too skilled a diplomat for that.

Yet not so diplomatic, mayhap, as Freyrík had gambled, for the man had yet to extend his hand for Freyrík's kiss.

"Your Eminence," he ventured, breaking the persistent silence. A slight turn of the head toward the Crown Prince, gaze never leaving the floor. "Your Highness." He turned his eyes back to the Aegis's feet. "You honor me with this feast and this place at your table."

At last, gods thanked, the Aegis's hand inched into view. Freyrík barely refrained from seizing it in his eager relief, took it gently instead and pressed a kiss to his knuckles.

"As you do us, Prince Farr," the Aegis said before pulling his hand away.

'Twas perhaps not what Freyrík had hoped for after prostrating himself at his own banquet, but surely better than nothing.

"Now do take a seat," the Aegis said, "and let us celebrate your safe and triumphant return to the heart of the Empire."

Gentle applause throughout the great hall, fingertips tapping against linen-covered trestle tables. Freyrík stood, bowed deep at the waist and backed the two steps to his own chair, held waiting in a footman's hands. One last glance at the Aegis as he straightened from his bow revealed a shadow of a smile on the man's face. Not a happy smile, but nor a cruel one either. Pride, mayhap? Nay, respect. *Well played.*

He took his seat, feeling marginally more secure than he had a moment before.

But only marginally.

Berendil watched him as he sat, smiling curiously. "Your Highness," his brother said, bowing his head with a grace uncommon to a man as large and powerful as he.

"Your Majesty," Freyrík replied, trying—and no doubt failing—for the same grace in his own bow. "How fare thee, brother?"

He seemed well enough, hale and sharp-eyed, certainly not the troubled ruin Kona had made him out to be upon her return from High Court. Freyrík longed to draw him into an embrace, feel for himself the strength of those well-loved bones, but he'd already breached more than enough etiquette for one night.

Berendil inclined his head, and his smile curled wider. "I am joyous and well as always in the presence of the Lord Protector, may the gods bless him ever strong and wise."

Freyrík knew, even before cataloging the too-bright smile or the subtle lines of strain round Berendil's eyes, that the man was feeding him a bale of straw. But before he could think up some clever way to inquire about it in such a public space, his brother asked, "Kona, is she well?"

Freyrík thought Kona a great many things, but "well" was not the first to come to mind. Still, 'twas not his place to pass judgment on his king's wives, so he said merely, "She is ever strong. But she worries for her king." He paused for a moment as all the footmen at the dais leaned in to place the first course before their lords, then added, "Are you sure she has no reason, brother? A cold, perhaps, or bout of winter melancholy?"

Berendil met his gaze, and his smile fell away. "I have been kept awake a night or two with gout these past weeks."

Gout. An old lord's affliction, uncommon in a man Berendil's age. Freyrík grinned tightly and nodded: *Message received. We'll talk later.*

Just as well. He'd not forgotten about Ayden, not for one second, and at last he had the opportunity to search for him. Alas, a long look round the great hall revealed many perfumed beauties waiting on their masters, but no glimpse of the only elf Freyrík cared for.

As he was contemplating the risks and merits of asking after Ayden, the Aegis stood to speak a blessing over the food, and he and everyone else hastened to their feet. Freyrík raised his chalice, held it aloft until the Aegis had spoken his prayer, then drank deep. Honeyed wine of the finest order, stronger than he was accustomed to. He would need to take care.

The Aegis sat; everyone else followed. Berendil dug into his food with the appetite of a warrior but the manners of a king. Freyrík ate mayhap less politely, or at least far too quickly, even knowing there was no point; the banquet would not end until the Aegis declared it so, and he daren't leave before then. As much as he'd missed and fretted over Berendil, 'twas torture to sit still and prattle with him of wives and harvests and laying in for the winter, yet worse to regale the whole hall—at the Aegis's behest, of course—with tales of victory over the latest Surge. He laughed when he knew he should, smiled until his cheeks ached, and ate whatever was put before him, though he could not have named his food after swallowing it, even on pain of death. Between worry of his brother and worry of Ayden, his mind held no space for the pleasures of a fine meal.

Halfway through the second dessert course, Berendil leaned in and whispered, "My apartments, at moonrise. Bring no one." Then he went back to his custard, the very picture of serenity.

Freyrík wondered if he hadn't simply imagined the whole thing.

Ayden jolted awake and instantly wished he hadn't. Hissing insects were still burrowing through his brain, trailing noise and venom in their wake. He knew not where he was—a bed, he thought, from the warmth and softness of it—nor how long he'd lain here, vulnerable and insensate beneath the starfall's barrage. The urge to vomit competed with the urge to scream. He indulged neither, but only because his exhaustion was stronger.

"The sickness passes, Ayden *barn* Vaska."

Ayden scrambled upright, head turning toward the unexpected voice, one empty hand shooting out in belated reflex. But the man who sat beside him—wrinkled, gray, draped in linens and furs and silks—appeared to harbor no such intent; he was merely studying Ayden, brown eyes incongruously sharp and youthful in a face that seemed to be nearing its useful end.

Ayden let his hand drop back to his side. "Who—" His voice broke over a raw throat, and with it any hope of feigning strength . . . as if such hope had ever existed with him slumped, naked and sweating, in a foreign bed.

"I am the Aegis Exalted, Divine King of Kings, Man's Ear to the Gods and the Gods' Mouth to Man, Holy Ruler of the Empire and Binder of the Sixteen Realms."

The man cast out his titles as carelessly as stones into a river. Their import sank into Ayden's mind just as surely—*this man is Freyrík's master. Every human's master.*

But not mine.

The Aegis did not seem to mark Ayden's indifference, but the four attendants (guards?) hovering nearby seemed quite affronted on his behalf. Ayden couldn't bring himself to care, asked the only question that mattered to him: "Where is Freyrík?"

The Aegis quirked an eyebrow at him. "*Your master* is yet feasting. I thought to come while he was occupied, to learn for myself what manner of creature infatuates him so."

Creature? Ayden raised an eyebrow right back, stared the human down. But he clearly failed to intimidate the man in his pathetic state, for the Aegis merely smiled and reached out, touching cool fingers to Ayden's bare chest.

Ayden tensed, but lacked the strength to push the hand away. Probably for the best, anyway; he might well be separated from his arm if he raised it against this Aegis. He gritted his teeth and bore the touch.

The Aegis's hand moved from his chest to his hair, stroking as if he were a cracking lap-cat.

"Truly lovely," the human said. "But I've known Rík his whole life. This"—a wave from head to hip, presumably encompassing Ayden's person—"would not find him so lost as to keep you from me. So tell me, Ayden *barn* Vaska. What sorcery did you weave to woo my *fóstri*?"

Sorcery? He'd certainly not sung Rík to him, nor wooed him. Had been awful to him, in fact—a state he'd be perfectly happy to demonstrate to this human.

He spared the man a moment's glare, then pulled the bedcovers up to his shoulders, laid himself flat, and turned his back.

And realized the moment he did so—he'd forgotten, how could he have forgotten?—that he was deaf now to human feelings, his keenest senses curtailed. The empty silence behind him sent a shiver down his spine. He dismissed it. What could the Aegis do to him that hadn't already been done?

Still, when the man at last responded to the insult—with a laugh, of all things!—relief washed over Ayden, drowning even his anger.

"Ah yes," the Aegis said. "Yes, I see indeed."

A hand clapped Ayden's shoulder; he jumped, cursed himself for startling like some cowering human woman, and clenched his teeth against hasty words.

"Rest now, Ayden *barn* Vaska. We shall greet your master together soon."

At long last, Freyrík managed to disentangle himself from the banquet. The Aegis had left some half hour past, but Prince Rodull still remained, and as the guest of honor, so too did Freyrík. 'Twas late by feast's end, and he was weary, and wanted nothing more than to lie with Ayden and sleep. Assuming he could even find Ayden, of course. Assuming the Aegis didn't mean to keep them yet apart.

Gods, what if the Aegis meant to keep Ayden for himself? He need only imply he desired Ayden as a gift, and Berendil would see the thing done despite Freyrík's entreaties. As for what would happen to him if he tried to gainsay the Aegis . . .

No, such thoughts could do him no good. The gods knew he had enough to worry over without conjuring evils in his mind.

'Twas a long march back to his rooms with weary feet and a wearier heart. His relief upon arrival soured when he spotted the unfamiliar attendants at his doors. Why they put him on his guard, he could not say, but there was no denying the way his heart pounded as he stepped into his drawing room.

He calmed only after the attendants had closed the doors behind him.

And then panicked anew when his groom met him three steps into the drawing room and announced, "The Aegis Exalted, Your Highness. He waits in your bedroom."

Gods befanged! "Why was I not summoned!"

Lord Vitr made an abbreviated bow that seemed half nerves, half placation. "I do not think he wished it, Your Highness."

Whyever not? The Aegis waited for no man.

Unless . . . Gods, please do not let it be so . . . "Ayden," Freyrík asked, hesitant to hear the answer. "Is he with His Eminence?"

His groom nodded, dared touch a hand to Freyrík's forearm. 'Twas exactly what Freyrík needed, for he felt both frozen and unsteady upon his feet. "You mustn't keep him waiting, Your Highness."

Freyrík nodded once, sharply, more to himself than Lord Vitr, smoothed a hand down the front of his doublet, and strode into his bedroom with entirely more confidence than he was feeling.

"A good evening to you, Your Highness."

Freyrík heard the greeting and dropped to one knee before he could observe the scene. "Your Eminence," he said to the top of his boot. "To what do I owe this honor?"

He heard the creak of furniture, muffled footsteps on a silk-and-wool rug, felt a hand touch his bowed head. "Does one need a reason to see his *fóstri*?"

Of course he does, when one reigns supreme over humankind.

"Rise, Freyrík. Come and sit with me."

Freyrík permitted himself the luxury of a single moment's indulgence in his relief—eyes closed, breath escaping softly through pursed lips—before he stood on shaking legs and followed the Aegis to the couch opposite the bed. When the Aegis waved him to a cushion, he sat first, though the impropriety of it unsettled his stomach anew.

The Aegis sat close beside him, familiarly close, leaned back and draped his arms across the cushions.

"So," the Aegis said, waving carelessly toward the bed, where a dark, messy shock of hair peeked out from the navy and gold bedcovers.

Ayden. 'Twas a fortunate thing Freyrík was sitting, for the world tilted one way with the force of his relief, then the opposite way with the force of his concern. *So quiet, so still. Is he even alive?*

If the Aegis noted his distress—and surely he did; he noted *everything*—he made no hinting of it. "*This*," he said, "is the treasure you meant to keep secret from me?"

There was no anger in his words or gesture. He seemed, in fact, quite at peace with the idea that he'd been sidestepped. Yet Freyrík knew him well enough to take no solace in that.

"I—"

The Aegis cut him off with another waving hand. "Elf!" he called. *Not dead, then, gods thanked.* "Elf! Come here."

Ayden stirred, but did not seem to waken. Freyrík watched as Ayden's hands inched out from beneath the bedclothes to clutch at his head. Freyrík couldn't see Ayden's face, but he need not to know something was terribly wrong.

He feigned his best indifference and asked, "Is he well?" He kept his gaze somewhere round the Aegis's chin, but studied Ayden from the corner of his eye. 'Twas hard to tell from this distance, but he thought he heard Ayden panting.

"The binding does not sit well with his kind."

"What? So soon?"

He realized he'd raised his eyes—was, in fact, staring at the Aegis—only when the Aegis scowled at him. His next question, *Why was I not summoned for it?* died upon his lips at the sight of the Aegis's narrowed eyes.

"Not soon enough. You played with fire. 'Tis a marvel you were not burned."

No marvel at all but love. But of course he dared not say that, dared do nothing but bow his head and say, "I pray you forgive my foolishness, Your Eminence."

The Aegis patted Freyrík's knee—such uncommon generosity, Freyrík nearly startled from it. "You worry for his health. I understand."

Freyrík nodded, grateful eyes upon the Aegis's hand still curled round his knee.

"But you need not. He will be more himself by morn—quite charming, no doubt." The sarcastic amusement was impossible to miss, and Freyrík could not help but wonder—and worry—what Ayden might have said to cause it. "I thought to speak with him, but he shows no interest in polite discourse this eve. Perhaps *you* would be more inclined?"

"I would speak of whatever pleases His Eminence," Freyrík said, though the thought held none of its usual appeal. Ayden was suffering and needed him.

The Aegis smiled. "It would please me if you were not so formal, dear Rík. We have no audience here to impress."

He ducked his head again. "Of course, *náungi*."

"How fared your harvest?"

Surely he already knew the answer, for Freyrík had signed and stamped accounting reports in his brother's absence, had sent them to Aegea as always. There was no tithe this year, of course—had not been for three centuries. Farr grew soldiers for the empire now, not crops.

"'Twas disappointing this year, for the Surge crested at the worst possible time." His eyes drifted to Ayden, restless beneath the covers in the grip of night terrors—or worse, waking pain. "I fear the winter may be trying."

"The winter is always trying," the Aegis said, "for 'tis the season of politics." He laid a hand upon Freyrík's forearm, pulling Freyrík's wandering focus back from Ayden to his liege. "Fear not for your people's bellies. The Empire will guard them from hunger as surely as they guard the Empire from the darker scourge."

Freyrík nodded; he already knew that, and surely the Aegis knew he knew.

"Did you know your brother seeks a seat on the Council of Eight?"

"Nay," Freyrík said, eyes meeting the Aegis's in his surprise. The Aegis returned his gaze, long and probing, as if to judge Freyrík's sincerity. Freyrík added, "I know two seats come open at year's end, of course, but never has he spoken of such intentions, nor shown interest beyond the battlefield."

The Aegis nodded once and squeezed lightly with the hand still resting on Freyrík's forearm. "He does indeed excel at war. The

Empire carries a great debt of gratitude toward his sacrifices and yours, and toward the people's of Midr and Kali, as well. We would be lost without the bravery of our border province generals."

But . . . ?

"But some would say the political battlefield is even more treacherous than the world of dirt and sword."

Clearly, "some" had never *seen* the world of dirt and sword.

"I would that you remind your brother of this," the Aegis continued.

Ah, so this is what they'd been dancing round these last many minutes. 'Twas times like these he remembered why he'd never been sorry to leave High Court for Farr.

"Gently, of course. There is no need to speak of private words."

"Of course," Freyrík said. And then, to confirm he understood the chance for redemption this was, "I shall see him well reminded of where he's needed most. Surely if I plead my own inadequacy to sit the throne, he will see wisdom and return home."

The Aegis laughed, squeezed Freyrík's arm again. "Oh, my dear *fóstri*, you've not a single inadequate sinew in the whole of your body. King Farr's eldest is of age, yet still he places *you* first in line for the throne. Do not impugn your king's judgment by calling it into doubt."

He stood up before Freyrík could reply; Freyrík rushed to his feet as well, mindful of the tenuous forgiveness he'd earned. "Now tend your *gróm*, *fóstri*, for I could hear your bleeding heart beating from the outer ward. But do mind your own judgment as well, yes? I trust I can depend on you in that regard?"

Freyrík dropped to his knee once more, took the Aegis's hand in both his own and pressed his lips to the man's knuckles. "Always, my liege. May you ever find comfort in my loyalty and love."

The Aegis freed his hand to stroke Freyrík's head, his left cheek. As he had in childhood, Freyrík leaned into the touch, basking in its warmth. "Indeed, may the gods see it always so."

"Is he gone?"

The words, rough and plaintive, snatched Freyrík's attention from the doors through which the Aegis had just disappeared and to the bed. He half expected Ayden to toss back the covers and bounce to his feet, shaking off the airs he'd assumed to keep the Aegis at bay. But Ayden lay unmoving still, eyes closed, elflight dimmed near to nothing.

"Yes," Freyrík said, padding over to Ayden's side—walking, not running like a man taken leave of his senses, however much the effort cost him. "Did he— What did he want with you? What's happened? Did someone harm you?"

Freyrík sat upon the mattress, and Ayden rolled over, curled himself round Freyrík's hip and rested his head in Freyrík's lap. Freyrík moved to stroke Ayden's hair without thought.

"It's gone, Freyrík," Ayden said into Freyrík's thigh, and whether the tightness in his voice was from sickness or threatening tears, Freyrík could not tell.

Either way, it broke his heart. "What's gone?"

"Song. They have silenced all the world's song and replaced it with screaming. I hear naught but the starfall's wail. It is . . ."

Ayden's voice hitched. He sniffed, rubbed at one eye with the heel of his hand, a gesture so vulnerable and childlike that Freyrík's heart broke all over again. 'Twas bereavement *and* pain, he realized, that were stealing Ayden's voice.

"I'm so sorry," he said, wincing at the words' inadequacy even as he spoke them.

"It is *ugly*. Wrong." Ayden's arms snaked round Freyrík's waist and squeezed tight. "It *hurts*. I cannot sleep. I cannot *hear* you. And I cannot sing out. I have tried. I have—"

He cut off on a hitching gasp, and the one eye Freyrík could see squeezed shut. The arms round his waist tightened, and he felt a spot of wetness soak through his breeches beneath Ayden's cheek. He laid one arm round Ayden's shoulder, carded his other hand through Ayden's sweat-damp hair. Gods befanged, surely there was something more he could do?

"Take them off, Rík," Ayden whimpered against his leg. "Tell me you can take them off."

Take what off? he was about to ask, when one of Ayden's hands released its death grip on Freyrík's waist and went to the fine jeweled circlet round Ayden's neck, tugging with near desperation. A matching bracelet decorated Ayden's wrist, and beneath the thin band of gold and starfall, Freyrík saw chafing, bruising, even a cut at the back of the thumb where Ayden must have tried to pull the bracelet off. Why hadn't it healed yet?

"Is this how they do it?" Freyrík ran one finger across the bracelet. They both knew what "it" meant; no need to elaborate.

Ayden nodded, a slight and weary gesture. "Imagine the whole of your kingdom shouting in your ear day and night. How would you tell one voice from the next? How could you think above the din? Might as well put a dagger to your ears and stab through."

Freyrík grimaced at the thought of such suffering. Though he rather thought 'twould be more like blindness than deafness to him, for sound was not the sense through which he observed the world. It *was* Ayden's, though; he'd seen the elf fight blinded by scrim of smoke and never miss, seen him judge the identity and mood of a person at his back by what he called "song" alone. To be deaf to it of a sudden . . .

Freyrík bent forward and inspected the lock on Ayden's collar, grimaced again at what he saw. "'Tis soldered shut. Even if I had the key, I could not remove it."

He knew this not to be the case with all elven slaves in the Splendor, for some worked as craftsmen, forging fine weapons and armor or spinning clear perfect panes of window glass. Yet others heated baths with a mere thought, called animals close for the hunt, healed the sick and wounded. Did the Aegis still trust him so little as to bind Ayden's magic with permanence? Or did the Aegis mistrust Ayden so, think him responsible for Freyrík's actions and feelings with regard to the elf? Or was this something altogether different—a test, perhaps, or a warning of some kind? Something he could not yet puzzle through?

"Rík?"

Freyrík realized he was leaning heavy over Ayden, his forearm braced across Ayden's shoulder, his eyes still fixed upon the soldered collar.

"I'm sorry," he said, sitting up and running a tender hand through Ayden's hair, down the line of his jaw. He picked up the hand Ayden had rested on his thigh and examined the bracelet there, saw the same solder at the lock.

"I'm sorry," he said, even though he'd said it just moments before, and again before that. "These cannot be removed without proper tools. I shall appeal to the Aegis, but it may take time. He is already suspicious of my feelings toward you. And, I fear, of my loyalties."

Freyrík's hand stilled upon Ayden's head as realization sank in. "Oh gods forgive me," he whispered. "This too is *my* fault. He did not trust me not to remove your starfall."

"A wise choice," Ayden said. The words were matter-of-fact, lacking bitterness. In fact, Freyrík heard a distinct hint of amusement when Ayden added, "Do you think you might stop blaming yourself long enough to hold me?"

A grin clawed its way through Freyrík's distress. He *was* holding Ayden, of course, but 'twas clearly not what the elf meant. So he stood, shed his garments, and crawled into bed. He pressed his chest to Ayden's back, bare skin to bare skin, curled round him and held him tight.

Ayden sighed and inched closer to him, head pillowed on Freyrík's arm, fingers laced through the fingers Freyrík had draped across Ayden's belly. He pressed the soles of his feet to Freyrík's shins, the cleft of his muscled arse fitting hard and hot against Freyrík's groin.

Despite his worry and Ayden's distress, Freyrík felt his manhood swell, and his desire along with it. Surely Ayden felt it as well, though he made no comment or motion, did not press against or shift away. 'Twas not Ayden's usual eager permission, but nor was it denial, and *gods* but Freyrík wanted him, wanted to soothe and comfort him, to remind them both that they would survive this as they'd survived all else—together. He freed his hand from Ayden's, stroked gentle fingers over Ayden's flank, down the curve of his buttock, back up his hip and round to his thigh.

Ayden sighed—a contented little sound, Freyrík thought, but still the elf did not move: did not open himself for Freyrík's touches nor hide himself from them. Hesitant, Freyrík let his hand dip lower, down the flat of Ayden's belly and to his groin.

Ayden's member lay flaccid in its soft nest of curls.

Freyrík blew a breath out through his nose and pressed a chaste, lingering kiss to Ayden's shoulder. "Is the pain so very bad?" he asked, free hand still stroking up and down Ayden's thigh.

Ayden nodded once against his arm. "I am told it will pass."

Freyrík stilled his hand, felt it clench into a fist of its own accord. Ayden laid his hand atop it, gave it a little nudge. "Please, don't stop."

A command gladly, if gently, obeyed. Freyrík kissed Ayden again—his biceps, his shoulder, the downy soft nape of his neck just below the collar—and set about exploring with his hand once more, caressing every bit of flesh he could reach.

Ayden sighed, content again, and drifted into sleep beneath Freyrík's loving attentions.

Freyrík watched him awhile, content simply to hold him, to keep stroking him in sleep, for it seemed to soothe the elf, who on occasion would toss or moan in Freyrík's arms.

Yet his mind wandered far from Ayden as he lay there. Toward Berendil, toward the Aegis, toward the upcoming appointments to the Council of Eight, and most of all toward whatever secrets Berendil meant to share with him at moonrise. He wished he had the faintest hinting of what was passing through his brother's mind. He wished he knew what else the Aegis wanted of him.

He wished he knew when he would be allowed to take Ayden and go back home.

Chapter Four

T hough his tiredness seeped down to his bones, Freyrík lay
awake long into the night, waiting for the moon to rise.
Ayden slept a restless, clinging sleep beside him, heavy and hot against
Freyrík's chest.

Slowly, slowly, cold white light slivered through the uncovered
windows.

Freyrík disentangled himself from Ayden with as much care as he
could muster. The elf stirred but did not wake; this concerned Freyrík,
but 'twas nothing he could fix, so he smoothed a hand over Ayden's
hair, pressed a kiss to his temple and whispered, "I'll return soon."
He slipped a pillow into the space he'd vacated, smiling wanly when
Ayden curled round it, hugging it to his chest. With luck, Freyrík
would return before Ayden even realized he'd left.

He lit a single candle and gathered some clothes, simple things he
could don without assistance. Through the open door to the groom's
chamber, he saw Lord Vitr sleeping. Hopefully he too would remain
so while Freyrík was gone.

A last glance at the rising moon, and Freyrík slipped out of the
room.

The hall was sparsely lit, all gloom and flickering shadows that his
own guttering candle barely dispelled. He reached the first crossway
and only then realized he had no idea where Berendil was staying.
Right, left, or forward? Up or down?

He chose forward, and down, heading toward the center of the
keep, passing a drunken courtier here, a sharp-eyed guard there. He
daren't ask either of them for directions, nor the next man he passed,
sprawled on a bench in a shadowed niche between torches, breeches

round his ankles and an elven slave on her knees between his thighs. Freyrík looked away, not out of modesty but of a deeper, darker emotion he could not name.

At last he spotted two servant girls exiting the Great Hall with a massive bucket of water between them.

"You there," he called, and then cursed under his breath when the girls dropped the bucket with a great clatter, sloshing water across the marble floor.

"Apologies," he grunted, "I did not mean to startle you."

They curtsied hastily, heads bowed. "'Tis our fault, Your Highness," the older one said.

He brushed off the empty courtesy. "King Berendil of Farr, where is he lodged?"

They turned toward each other and conferred in hushed tones. For a moment it seemed they could not answer him, but then one giggled, blushing even in the torchlight, and said, "In the east wing, Your Highness. On the third floor, in the apartment overlooking the topiary. Shall I escort Your Highness?"

Freyrík eyed her through the gloom, and she turned her eyes to the floor. Pretty enough, he supposed, but Berendil would never . . . Not with a servant girl. "I know the way. Thank you."

He left them for the long walk to his brother's apartments, which were as far from his as they could be and still be in the keep. Another message from the Aegis? Or mere coincidence?

He ran into four tipsy courtiers in a tight clump near Berendil's apartments. They bowed, not quite as one, and cleared the way.

"Your Highness," said one of them, "I hope we've not disturbed you."

"Of course not," Freyrík said, reining in his impatience. "I'm merely overeager to meet my brother. I've not seen him in months, you understand."

A plausible lie, easily swallowed. He sent them on their way and reached Berendil's rooms without passing another soul save two patrolling palace guards.

The attendants at Berendil's doors bowed, and one slipped inside to announce him. Freyrík was ushered into the drawing room seconds later. Before the doors had even closed behind him, he said, "Truly, Berendil? The Coun—?"

And stopped dead at the sight of his brother sprawled loose-limbed and drunk across a settee. He was holding a goblet of wine in one hand, an elf's naked breast in the other. She was curled up against him, drawing lazy patterns on his thigh with the tip of her finger.

"Brother!" Berendil crowed, tossing his arms wide at the sight of Freyrík. Wine sloshed from Berendil's goblet, and his groom, curled sleeping by the warmth of the hearth, startled at the sloppy shout.

What beneath the shadow is this?

Berendil sat up, overbalanced, nearly fell to his knees. The slave caught him by the shoulders—how tiny she seemed beside his muscled bulk—and eased him gently back against the cushions.

"Would you like to try her?" Berendil asked, waving toward the elf. "No, no, of course you wouldn't," he added before Freyrík could respond—gods thanked, for he could not piece together an answer. He doubted he could speak without shouting. "Go on then, shoo."

It took Freyrík a moment to realize Berendil was talking to the elf and not him. But she understood, and off she went with a bow, leaving the room empty but for him and his brother and his brother's groom.

"You too," Berendil said, waving with his goblet toward his groom this time, spilling more wine upon the floor. "My brother and I have"—a pause, as if his next thought had fled his pickled brain—"*gossip* to attend. We've not spoken in months, you see."

"Yes, Your Majesty."

The groom left, dignified and nonjudgmental as all his lot. Freyrík watched him go, irrationally angry to be left behind, for of course it wasn't *proper* to rail at Berendil for dragging him from Ayden's side in the middle of the night for *this*.

"With your permission, Your Majesty," he said through clenched teeth, turning back to face his brother—

Only to find him standing, sharp-eyed and smiling, wiping spilled wine from his fingers with an embroidered napkin.

"Oh dear, I do believe I've stained a perfectly lovely tapestry."

Freyrík didn't know whether to hit him or laugh.

Neither, in the end. Berendil's air grew serious, and he stepped in to embrace Freyrík, then led him to a carved oak table on the far side of the drawing room with an arm round his shoulder. He sat upon a wing chair, waved Freyrík into the opposite one. All the servants had gone, but a tea service remained, and a plate of sweetmeats; Berendil bit into a date with relish—by the gods, wherever had the Aegis gotten *dates*?—and Freyrík tried very hard to be patient while his brother chewed.

Yet when Berendil, still silent, plucked a second date from the tray, Freyrík could not help but ask, "What is this, brother?"

"Delighted at your arrival, I have overindulged in wine and food and women, and gifted the servants an evening's rest that I might share these pleasures in privacy with my beloved brother."

"You clever knave." Freyrík grinned and took a date from the plate Berendil offered him. His eyes slipped closed at the taste of such a delicacy on his tongue, but he opened them again a second later. "So tell me, brother," he said, turning down the offer of a second date. "Why such a complex ruse?"

"Because we've much to discuss, and I would there be no prying eyes as we do so."

"Indeed. I hear you seek seat on the Council of Eight."

Berendil eyed him shrewdly, bit off half the date Freyrík had rejected and chewed as if he had all the time in the world. At last he asked, voice calm but gaze sword-tip sharp, "Where did you hear that?"

"From the lips of the Aegis himself."

"And did he also tell you to convince me of my folly?"

Freyrík hesitated a moment, torn between his promise to the Aegis—*There is no need to speak of private words*—and the duty to truth before his brother and king. At last he settled for, "You are needed in Farr, brother. You've been too long absent already. Your people cry for you."

Berendil laughed. "They do no such thing. Indeed, it is *your* name on every tongue. The war hero. The great victor." A moment's hesitation, and then, "The elf-lover."

Freyrík felt his cheeks heat, though from anger or shame he could not tell. "I'm sorry, brother, it was never my intent to impugn the Farr name—"

Berendil waved away his apology. "You may keep the creature for now."

For *now*? What did that mean?

"I've no interest in it, and Aegea funds our kingdom well. It clearly makes you happy, and does not seem to impede your judgment—"

Freyrík snorted.

"—despite what flapping tongues may claim. Besides, you have earned your spoils, brother, wouldn't you say? I am most proud of you."

Freyrík grinned beneath the praise.

Berendil returned the grin, bright as a hundred candles. "Come, I wish to hear of this creature who could turn my brother from his austere ways. Is he handsome?"

"Very much so. But he is so much more than fair face and form."

Berendil plucked another date from the tray. "Oh?"

"Does that truly surprise you, brother?" Berendil just raised an eyebrow, bit into the fruit. "He is . . ." Gods, where to begin? He could pass the whole night away speaking of Ayden, of what made him special—

Of course he could. And that, it seemed, was the point. "You clever knave," Freyrík said again, but this time he was scowling. "Brother, please, no more distractions. You cannot sit the Council. We are lost without you."

If Berendil was bothered by the insult or the foiled ruse, he made no showing of it. He merely popped another date into his mouth and said, "That is why I plan to seat *you* in my place."

Freyrík felt his jaw drop open, a jumble of words rushing forth and wedging tight in his throat. No, *no*, that was *not* where he'd meant to nudge his brother—

"You always were the clever one, and a prettier speaker than I could ever hope to be. I still maintain that had you been of age when father died, he'd have named you successor over me."

"Me? But I couldn't possibly— I mean, I am but a prince, an *outland* prince at that. I have no business on the Council."

"Of course you do, and more so than me, I daresay. Look at you: a scholar, a diplomat. What am I but a warrior? *You* are the great thinker among us."

"And yet father named you—a man of only sixteen years—over Uncle Feitr."

Berendil shrugged. "A father always chooses his sons over his brothers."

You *did not when you named me regent.*

Regent indeed . . . "Is my great thinking not needed at home? How would the last Surge have ended had I been wasting my days at the Council table?"

Berendil's eyes narrowed. "I *can* rule my own kingdom, brother."

Gods befanged. "I know, Your Majesty, that is not what I—"

"It's all right. I know."

Freyrík sagged in his chair, half relief and half desperation. "*Please,* brother. I do not wish it . . ."

Berendil's expression softened, but Freyrík did not make the mistake of believing his resolve had, as well. "I know," Berendil said at last. "But we must all make sacrifices for our people; that is what it means to be a ruler. This is the sacrifice *you* must make. I need you there, end of discussion."

Sometimes, Freyrík rather thought the gods had blessed his brother *too* strong and wise. But he was right, gods befang him; royalty was sacrifice. And even if 'twere not, Berendil was his king, and his king's word was law. He forced the grimace from his face and bowed his head. "As Your Majesty bids."

"Good. Now, I would have counsel from the mind I so admire."

Freyrík nodded. "I am ever at your service, brother; you know that."

The answering look he received, long and narrow, raised gooseflesh upon his arms and cast doubt upon his surety.

"Yes," Berendil said at last. "You have never once given me cause to think otherwise. So tell me, little brother, how long has it been since any province on the western front has held a Council seat?"

Freyrík knew this answer without thinking, but only because it had been a significant year for him: his twelfth winter, when he'd come of age for the line of succession. "Seventeen years ago, when King Skaut of Midr stepped down."

Berendil nodded as if he'd expected no less precision from his scholar prince. "And does that not seem the slightest bit unfair to you?"

He supposed he'd never given it much thought. After all, sixteen provinces, eight revolving appointments of six years apiece . . . *someone* was bound to be left out. Except Aegea, of course. But now that Berendil had drawn his mind to it, yes, it did smack of disparity. Nearly thirty appointments made in the last seventeen years, and not one to Midr, Kali, or Farr.

"No room for barbarian kings on the Council, you see," Berendil said when Freyrík remained silent. "What do we know of finesse, of politics? All they think us good for is raising a sword, breeding more boys to die beneath the darker menace."

He leaned forward in his seat, and Freyrík pressed back beneath the weight of his gaze. "I would see that remedied. We *all* on the western front would see that remedied."

And just how, exactly, did they mean to bring that about? Freyrík opened his mouth, closed it again. Did he really wish to know?

"Tell me, scholar-prince. How many soldiers died last year defending the Empire from darker invasion?"

"Just over eleven thousand across the three Surges."

"And how many died last time, when you took the fight to the darkers rather than wait like a lamb at the butcher's block?"

"Five hundred and eighty-four."

Berendil jabbed the tabletop with his index finger. "More than a tenfold drop in deaths, gained by taking a risk on a new stratagem."

Yes, and?

"Would you not see another sixfold drop if you could?"

"Of course, but—"

"As we speak, the princes and kings of the western provinces bend sympathetic ears toward another new stratagem."

For all Berendil belittled his statesmanship, his pause here was pure drama. He even poured himself a cup of tea.

When it became clear he would not go on without prompting, Freyrík said, "Pray tell, brother?"

"Year after year, we but sit and wait for the darker menace to overrun our lands, kill our sons, trample our crops. I propose we stop waiting; it is time to take the fight into darker lands, as you yourself did with such great success."

Is that all? Freyrík exhaled his relief, melting into the chair. "I do not think you need a Council seat to press that agenda, brother." The tea smelled lovely; he reached to pour himself a cup. "I'm sure our neighbors would embrace this novelty with little fuss, once they understand its true potential."

"Nay, you misunderstand. I propose we gather the whole of the Empire's army to find the dark elf beastmasters and kill them."

"*What?*" His cup clattered against his saucer; hot tea sloshed over his thumb and he shook it out with a curse. "You cannot be serious!"

"And why not?" Berendil stood forcefully enough to scrape his chair across the floor, and for a moment Freyrík thought he'd angered him with his insolence. But no, he'd merely stood to pace out his excitement. He strode to a bookshelf along the near wall, back to the table, raked a hand through his hair and pointed at Freyrík. "Did you yourself not do the same? Did you not return a victor? A hero?"

"Nay, brother, 'twas *not* the same. 'Twas only—"

"The first brave step on a journey long overdue. We will finish what you began, little brother." Berendil sat, leaned forward, elbows on the table and broad face inches from Freyrík's own. "With the beastmasters dead, there will be no more beasts. No more darkers. Can you imagine such a world?"

No.

Yes.

"May I speak, Your Majesty?"

The smile slid from Berendil's face, but he nodded, took his elbows from the table and poured himself more tea.

"I led our army but two leagues into the darker forest. 'Tis fifty more at least to the Meiri Sea, and another thousand from the South Sea to the northern border with the Elven Republic."

"I know. This is why we gather our *entire* force. Not nine thousand men, but *ninety* thousand. Infantry, cavalry, scouts. Our best trackers. Men in reserve, men in retirement still fit to march, young men grown strong enough to wield a sword."

"You would strip the Empire of *all* its sons and fathers?"

"Only for a short while. For one last time."

Freyrík shook his head. This was *madness.* Did the dark elves even exist? Or were they mere figments of battle-fevered minds, rumor passed like maids' tales to frighten children into their beds at night?

And what if they *did* exist? How did one go about ending creatures who held the whole of the forest's befanged beasts at their command? It seemed folly at best.

. . . And yet, Ayden's plan, when first presented, had seemed folly too. Mayhap he was being too quick to judge.

If Berendil's plan was possible . . . If they *could* end the darker menace forevermore . . .

His sons need never know such vicious war. Farr's tradesmen could learn to press fine wine as they once had, could board up the iron mines and the conscription yards and grow grapes again.

He could lay down his own sword and pick up his violin again.

'Twas such temptation that he felt it as pain high in his belly, just below his heart. He was breathless with it, lost in possibility, in dream.

"Little brother?"

Gods, the dream had been so strong he'd forgotten for a moment he was not alone. He cleared his throat, but only to gain time to clear his thoughts. "I daren't hope such a thing is possible," he said, "yet cannot help but imagine a world in which it were."

Berendil nodded, that old familiar smile curving his lips. "It dawns like the sun, this vision. I see its light in your eyes already. But some remain in the darkness, trapped in the caves of their stubbornness or fear. We must work especially hard to coax them forth into the daylight. Only then can they see it's for the best."

Alas, Freyrík felt quite certain to which men Berendil referred. "Did you . . ." He licked his lips, swallowed against sudden dryness in his throat. "Did you just call our Lord Protector stubborn?"

Or was it "craven"?

For the first time all evening, Berendil dropped his gaze from Freyrík's.

Freyrík's tenuous hope dropped right along with it, churning like soured wine in his gut. "Berendil . . ."

His brother held up a hand. "His Eminence is not the only voice on the Council. Three among them have already seen the light, and we need but five votes to place a border prince—or two, gods willing—in the open seats despite his protest."

"You mean against his will."

The look that earned him sent him shrinking back into his chair again. "If I had meant that, I'd have said it. I am well within my rights to maneuver for a Council seat. 'Tis certainly not the treason *you're* implying, brother."

Implying or *guilty of*? The accusation in Berendil's narrowed eyes suggested the second, but less perhaps out of judgment than simple leverage. Men in glass houses shouldn't throw stones, after all.

Freyrík conceded the point with an open palm, and Berendil, all smiles again, leaned across the table to thump Freyrík on the shoulder. "You trust me, little brother, do you not?" Of course he did, but Berendil pressed on before he could say so. "I have thought this through with the utmost care and counsel. And 'tis the Aegis's best interests I have at heart—and, of course, those of the people he is sworn to protect."

At last he fell silent, but this time, Freyrík could think of nothing to say.

"You will help me, then?"

He nodded. Of course he would help his king, even if he did not agree.

Another flash of teeth, the wide but wearied grin of the victor in a battle. "I am most pleased. Now . . ." Berendil reached into the chest pocket of his doublet and handed Freyrík a small folded slip of paper. "Here you'll find a list of friend, foe, and all between. I would you'd work your magic upon those undecided minds. We've but sixteen days to sway three men."

Freyrík unfolded the paper and read the names of the undecided: Crown Prince Skalli of Randvér, King Taf of Ingimárr, and King Gódr of Ofan. Wise leaders all, but far removed, in their inland provinces, from the darker threat. Between them they'd fought perhaps in two campaigns.

"They will not be easily won," he said.

"Ah, but I have faith in your eloquence, brother."

Freyrík bit back a snort. He rather thought 'twould be easier to find and kill the dark elves themselves than bring these men to his brother's cause. King Gódr was deeply religious, wary of magic; he'd fear the haunted woods more than most. Prince Skalli would be loath to make such a significant move without the consent of his king, which could not be had in time for the Council vote, even by fastest bird. And King Taf would wish to know Freyrík's opinion on this fanciful plan, a question Freyrík would not know how to answer.

Especially when all his senses screamed that he was seeing only half the game board, and even fewer of the pieces.

He looked up from the paper to his brother, who was studying him as Ayden so often did: as if to see right through to his inner thoughts, mayhap his very soul. If anyone at Court could do so, it was Berendil, who'd all but reared him in their dead father's place.

And yet . . .

Freyrík folded the paper, placed it in his own breast pocket, and said cautiously, "I am not a child anymore, Berendil."

Berendil nodded. "I know."

"Is there nothing more you would tell me?"

"Nay, brother. I speak the whole truth."

Freyrík pursed his lips, debated and discarded the idea of further probing. "Very well," he said. He slid from the wing chair and dropped to one knee at his brother's feet. "As always, my liege, I will do as you bid."

He kissed Berendil's hand, and Berendil stroked his hair with such stark affection that the ache returned high in Freyrík's belly, sharper even than before. "May the gods bless you ever strong and wise, little brother."

"You as well, Your Majesty."

But Freyrík felt quite certain Berendil would need more than strength and wisdom for what was to come. For whatever it might be, 'twas big enough for Berendil to have looked him in the eye and lied.

Ayden woke to blessed silence. Never had he conceived a circumstance in which he'd be grateful for deafness, but the absence of the starfall shriek was such profound relief he could have cried. Now if only he could rid himself of the vise which squeezed his temples, he might feel nearly himself again.

He opened his eyes to bright sun and an empty bed. He was unsurprised to find Rík gone, for he'd not heard his song, but then, he couldn't hear *anything* anymore, at least not with his mind-ear. How long would it take him to remember that?

Hopefully, he'd be gone from here and this wretched starfall long before then.

He sat up, massaging his temples as silken sheets pooled round his waist, and took a long look round the room. Massive—easily twice the size of Freyrík's bedroom at home—and appointed just as richly, if not more so. The doors to the drawing room stood open, as did the doors to the washroom. A single door beside that, presumably to the groom's chamber, was closed. A tray and tea service sat waiting on a little round table near the bed, along with his laundered traveling clothes.

He stood—too quickly, it seemed—staggered and fell back to the bed. The floor was not quite where he thought it should be, and his feet didn't quite respond to his mind the way he'd expected them to. The pain in his temples flared, though all the world remained stubbornly silent.

He stood again, eyes fixed upon the rug by the side of the bed. This time, his feet met the floor more or less as they should have. He crossed over to the table, fell into the nearest chair, set upon the food as if he'd not eaten in days. Everything tasted wrong somehow. The tea was cold and he could not warm it. He knocked over his cup by accident while reaching for a pot of jam; said jam lay on his tongue like a deadweight, songless and bland. 'Twas all so frustrating he gave up the moment he'd soothed the rumbling in his belly.

He dressed instead, then paced to a large window, discovering when he neared it that it was in fact a balcony door. He opened it, stepped outside. The air was sweet and clean and the midday sun warmed his face, even with a sharp chill on the wind. Two floors below, a garden sprawled for perhaps a quarter league: hedges and shade trees past their last fall colors, marble benches, a glass hothouse in the near corner with flowering plants and butterflies from all round the world. A small pack of hunting dogs roamed the garden paths, lunging after the occasional rabbit or squirrel. He'd not even realized they were there until he heard their barking; this outside world was as silent to him as the one inside the keep. 'Twas beauty fettered, and he felt as sick with the loss as he did with the pain in his temples.

At last he could bear no longer to gaze upon what was lost to him. He turned his back to the balcony, slid down to the floor, and rested his aching head against his knees. There he slept, wrapped in a cocoon of silence so complete he could not even hear the sound of his own sorrow.

"Ayden."

Ayden jerked awake, scrambling to his feet as his hand went to his belt in that old familiar reflex for a weapon. 'Twould not have helped him in any case; the world swayed, and he stumbled back against the balcony wall, only just resisting the instinct to clutch his head.

Freyrík's groom stood two paces away, out of reach of swinging fist or foot, an expression of . . . what? Gods cracked, he had no idea. Simple wariness? Or was it pity? Even the thought set him burning with desire to punch the man. The urge shamed him; Vitr had shown him kindness.

"Apologies," Lord Vitr said. "I did not mean to startle you."

"'Tis not . . ." *Your fault. I am deaf now, you see.* But such was too hard to say; Ayden left the thought unspoken.

Lord Vitr nodded anyway, as if 'twere he who could hear people's songs. "You have been summoned to the baths," he said. The balcony door opened, and a guard stepped out, startling Ayden all over again. The human had been but two paces distant and Ayden hadn't known he was there. Gods cracked, how did people live like this?

"You are free to walk the grounds unescorted now you're bound . . . at your master's pleasure, of course"—that last bit likely added for the sake of the guard, for Lord Vitr knew the true nature of Ayden and Freyrík's relationship—"but until you learn your way, this man will guide you."

Ayden gave the guard an appraising look, for inadequate as the sense was, 'twas all he had left to him. The man carried himself like a well-trained soldier, light on his feet despite his muscled frame, hands loose and ready, gaze sharp and mind likely more so. No doubt a palace guard in the Splendor was of the very best stock the humans had to offer. Ayden doubted he could best such a man in his current state. His cheeks burned at the thought, but 'twas folly pure and true to underestimate an enemy or overestimate himself.

Not, of course, that he'd be fighting anyone anytime soon.

He nodded at Lord Vitr, who—if Ayden was reading his face right—seemed a bit concerned, perhaps that Ayden might balk at his escort or his summons to the humiliation that was the slave baths. Well, the man needn't worry; eight hundred years of life and nearly six hundred years of armed service had taught Ayden to bide his time.

Yet he could not help but ask, "Where is Fr— my master?"

"Hunting with the Aegis," Lord Vitr said. "You'll attend him at dinner." Ayden nodded. Loath as he was to admit it, he'd gladly cut up Freyrík's meat and feed it to him one bite at a time if it meant he could feel the reassurance of that cool, solid body beside him again. Solitude had never much bothered him, but alone in this awful place, crippled and ill and far too defenseless for his liking, he wished only for Freyrík's company.

He gave Lord Vitr another nod and then stepped up beside the guard, letting the human lead him to the baths.

Though the way was long and winding, he took great care to memorize it—left out the door, to the end of the hall, down the stairs, right at the mounted body of a massive Feral wolf, right again at a collection of three life-sized human statues, down what he thought of as the tapestry hall, down another flight of stairs, across a marble inlay of the moon and stars twenty paces wide, and through the double doors into the bath. 'Twas more of a challenge than he'd care to admit to set the path to memory in his aching mind, but he might well need this knowledge someday. Fallen gods forbid Freyrík lost possession of him to King Farr or the Aegis; he would need every last advantage he could muster.

"Masters" Laug and Húskarl paid him little mind inside the bath, where it seemed every elf in the castle—not that Ayden knew how many were trapped here, but he prayed no more than the thirty or so he saw before him—was indulging in the luxury of their gilded cage. Laug pointed him toward the soaps and sponges, then left him to soak at his leisure.

He sat upon a low bench in the bath, eyes closed and head tilted back against the tiled rim. The steam heat eased the ache in his temples and the tension in his limbs he'd not even realized he'd carried until it faded. He thought perhaps to speak with some other elves once he could think round the pain in his head, but it seemed they all kept well to themselves, silent and downcast, as if 'twere against some rule to fraternize. Perhaps it was; gods knew if he were keeping such powerful prisoners, he'd not permit them the opportunity to plot escape together.

"Here."

Ayden startled away from a too-close voice and a hand in his peripheral vision. Fallen gods be cracked, would he ever learn to sense men at his back without his mind-ear?

He breathed deep, willing his heart to calm, and turned his attention to the outstretched hand. Long, bone-thin fingers. Húskarl's. The man was crouched by the side of the bath, holding a mug of tea that reeked of willow bark and some human concoction he could not place. Probably poison, if inadvertently so, given their ineptitude with nature.

"For your head."

Ayden turned said head away and stared down at his naked lap through the rippling water.

Húskarl did not withdraw his hand. "It will ease the transition," he said. Softly, kindly, as if Ayden's suffering somehow bothered him. Ridiculous, considering the man had beaten Ayden without hesitation just yesterday, even if he had only used a switch.

Ayden slid off the bench and ducked his head underwater. He stayed there until his lungs burned, unable as he was to tell if Húskarl had gone or not.

When he popped back up, gasping, that cracking cup of tea was still hovering by his head.

"Please," Húskarl said.

"'Tis foolish to be stubborn for the sake of it, child. Drink the tea."

Fallen gods be cracked! When had Jagall swum up beside him? He should at least have felt the disturbance in the water.

Unless . . . did the starfall do more than deafen?

"Your senses will return to you," Jagall said. To Ayden's shock, the old elf added, "And you will learn to compensate for that which is gone. You have never much paid mind to faces, I gather, but many speak as clearly as any song." He took the tea from Húskarl, who nodded and flashed Jagall a brief smile before melting back into the room. "'Tis foul, but will ease your pain. Drink."

Ayden took the mug, sniffed cautiously, felt his lips twist into a scowl. "Why does he do this for me?"

"He *is* here to care for us, you know."

"And does that not offend you? That these humans think you require care?"

Jagall shrugged, maddeningly calm.

"Is he friend?" Ayden asked.

Jagall shrugged again. Perhaps he didn't catch Ayden's true meaning—*Would he help or hinder an escape?* Or perhaps he did, and chose to ignore it.

"How many of us are in his *care*?"

Jagall gestured at the mug. "Drink your tea and I shall answer your questions."

Ayden sighed, pinched his nose shut, and downed the drink in one long gulp. He slammed the mug down on the tile rim of the bath, clutching at it tight enough to crack the ceramic until the urge to vomit had passed.

"There," he said, coughing once, ducking down to suck up a mouthful of rose hip–scented water to swish and spit. "Are you quite happy?"

Jagall smiled softly, immune—nay, *indifferent*, gods crack him—to Ayden's sharp tongue. "Fifty-three," he said, "including you. Ten or twelve come and go from High Court when their masters travel; the rest serve here always."

"All bound?"

Jagall nodded. "Of course."

"Always?"

"You've the only soldered locks among us now, if that's what you mean, although I have heard tell of same among the slaves who live away from here. And before you ask, I do not know who holds the keys. But I do know each lock is unique."

Jagall had been here over three hundred years and hadn't yet discovered where the keys were kept? Fallen gods cracked, what had he been *doing* all this time?

"And the humans? How many are they?"

Jagall leveled a hard stare at Ayden. At length he said, "You ask dangerous questions, child. Put foolish thoughts to rest before the humans beat them from your skull." His gaze shifted to Ayden's shoulder and flank, where a few fine scars from the *Blód Sekt* remained. "Have you not yet learned your lesson?"

Ayden's upper lip pulled back into a sneer. "Never," he said, then ducked beneath the water and pushed far, far away from Jagall, understanding full well just how long "never" might turn out to be.

Jagall didn't bother him again. Nor did anyone else. Ayden sat in the bath, watching the sun crawl across the sky through the glass-paneled ceiling, until thirst drove him from the water. He passed a plunge pool on his way to the drinking fountain against the far wall, held his breath and dived headfirst into the icy water. 'Twas a shock of the best kind after so long spent soaking in the heat; he broke the surface with a bark of laughter—more stunned than mirthful—and realized his headache was nearly gone.

'Twas hard not to be grateful for that, but he certainly did try.

Laug cornered him as he was toweling dry in a sunbeam by the fountain. Ayden had seen him coming, so the hand that came to rest in the small of his back did not surprise him, but it did offend. 'Twas too intimate a gesture when he was naked. He stepped away from it, and for his nerve, Laug swatted him on the arse.

Ayden hit him back.

Laug blinked up from his sprawl on the floor, one hand pressed to his bleeding nose. He seemed quite shocked, but to his credit, he did not run away. Although, nor did he rise to face Ayden.

Ayden turned back to the fountain to wash Laug's blood from his knuckles, waiting for more guards to appear. Everyone was staring at him, elf and human alike. Even deaf as he was, he could sense their surprise. All the wide eyes and open mouths likely had something to do with that.

Húskarl approached cautiously, switch in hand. He stopped several paces away, and said simply, "Are you quite finished?"

Ayden thought on it a moment. He knew he'd been foolish, acted impulsively. It might have been worth it, but then again, maybe not. 'Twas folly to call attention to himself now for any number of reasons.

So he ducked his head and said, "Yes, Master Húskarl." And when Húskarl bent him over the fountain and whipped his arse and thighs until he shouted, he took the punishment without argument, clutching bloodless fingers round the cool stone to keep himself still.

"You are stubborn, even for your kind," Húskarl said when he was done. He ran a gentle hand over the burning coals of Ayden's welted flesh. "You're sweating. Go back to the plunge pool. Come to the far table when you've dried, and I will teach you how to prepare yourself for service."

He ducked his head and said again, "Yes, Master Húskarl." The words came surprisingly easy. Was this how it had begun for the other prisoners? A lie at first, perhaps, but any words repeated often enough—even your own falsehoods—held power to turn true in time.

Eyes were still upon him as he returned to the plunge pool, stayed until the cold water leached most of the fire from his skin, toweled gingerly dry, and went to the grooming table as directed. They were subtle gazes, indirect, but he'd clearly captured the attention of his fellow elves. Mayhap the pain had been worth it after all, if he'd begun to rouse his brothers and sisters from their lassitude.

Best not to seem *too* pliant, then, while all were still watching. He stepped up beside Húskarl and nodded once in lieu of bowing. He did not avert his eyes, but nor did he openly challenge. 'Twas a reasonable compromise.

"Ayden." Húskarl met Ayden's gaze and nodded back.

Ayden said nothing.

"Stand thusly, if you would." Húskarl spread his arms and legs and tipped his head back in demonstration, waiting until Ayden—with as much delay as he thought he could get away with—copied the stance. Tension corded his muscles when he realized he could neither hear *nor* see very much round him now.

Húskarl fetched up a tin of powder from the grooming table and applied it to Ayden's skin with a sensuously soft-haired brush. It smelled of fine talc and sandalwood, left a sheen upon Ayden's skin— gold dust, perhaps?

"There," Húskarl said, sweeping the brush up under his chin and across his forehead and cheeks. "All alight again. Almost as lovely as before."

It took Ayden a moment to realize he meant *before the binding.* They'd silenced his song but still wanted him to glow for them like some cracking firebug? Some pet doing tricks?

Well, this pet would bite if they kept taunting him.

"Tomorrow you will apply this yourself," Húskarl said, deaf as ever to Ayden's fury. "Only the lightest touch is needed. You may call another slave to assist you with your back, or they you in return. Do you understand?"

"I am deaf, not addled," he snapped. "Of course I understand."

Húskarl seemed quite unbothered by his tone. He merely gestured toward the chair before the grooming table and said, "Please, sit."

Ayden's welted arse and thighs did not appreciate the thought of the wicker chair before him. "I would prefer to stand."

From three tables down, he heard Laug mutter to the elf he was tending, "*He* prefers, *he* prefers. He will soon learn what *he* prefers does not matter."

The clogged, broken-nosed sound of Laug's voice was the first pleasure Ayden had found in this place since his binding.

Húskarl snorted, soft and fondly exasperated, as if he and Laug were old lovers who'd humored each other's eccentricities for millennia.

"Fetch a cushion if you wish it," Húskarl said. "But then you must sit."

Another reasonable compromise, Ayden supposed, though in the end he was still obeying Húskarl's orders. Perhaps 'twas the kindness with which they were issued that lulled one into a false sense of fairness.

He fished a small silk cushion from a nearby pile, placed it on the chair, and sat gingerly upon it. Húskarl tugged a comb through Ayden's damp hair to work out the tangles, but made no real effort to tame it. Once finished, he selected a wrapped charcoal stick from a cup full of such things and crouched in close. "Close one eye and watch the other in the mirror," he said. "You will try this yourself tomorrow."

Ayden did as bid, though 'twas hard not to flinch away when he felt the tip of the stick touch his eyelid. Húskarl drew a line along his lashes top and bottom, then painted the lashes themselves with a tiny brush covered in gold dust. The eyelids he dusted with a subtle metallic green powder to match his eyes, then dusted the same powder across his cheekbones. To his lips Húskarl applied a thin coat of waxy dye only one or two shades redder than his own natural color. Ayden studied himself in the mirror when the painting was finished; he felt absurd, but supposed he could see the appeal of such a look had it not been inflicted upon him.

He thought the grooming finished when Húskarl stepped away, but the man was merely reaching for new tools: a wooden strip of tiny paint pots and a set of artist's brushes. He gestured Ayden to his feet—an order happily obeyed—and then proceeded to paint one continuous, twined wisteria vine in full bloom from the back of Ayden's right ankle to the top of his left shoulder. Where the vine crossed over his belly, Húskarl added two bright hummingbirds, one on his chest and one on his hip. From what Ayden could make of the work, 'twas masterful, but he was no canvas, and 'twas hard to appreciate any skill brought to bear to debase him.

At last Húskarl seemed finished. He dusted the whole design with the golden talc, then stepped behind Ayden to paint something large across his back. There followed another eternity of waiting—surely an hour or more had passed since Húskarl had first lifted his brushes.

When the human was done, he held up a hand mirror for Ayden to see the design upon his back: a bright bird of paradise—though the fallen gods knew where Húskarl had ever seen one—its wings stretching wide along Ayden's shoulder blades, its long tail feathers running down his spine. Ayden marveled at it despite himself, looked at Húskarl and said, half in jest, "Please tell me I will not be expected to do this tomorrow as well."

Húskarl cracked a wide grin and shook his head. "'Tis ink. The design will endure the baths for a week, perhaps two."

Ayden looked round at his fellow elves to see what art Húskarl had rendered upon their flesh, and realized almost none of them were painted.

"My welcoming gift for your master," Húskarl said, reading Ayden far too easily for his comfort. "I may paint another later if the mood strikes, but I confess it rarely does these days."

He put down the mirror, wiped his hands on a rag, and picked up yet another small clay pot. "Now if you'd kindly brace your hands upon the table and spread your legs, I shall make final preparations and fetch you new clothes." He took the lid off the pot—oil, of course; Ayden had seen that coming from a league away—fully expecting to be obeyed.

Ayden could endure many things, but some strange human's fingers up his arse was beyond all forbearance. Fallen gods only knew how his brothers and sisters could submit to such indignities.

Better that than raped dry, you judgmental fool. Surely not everyone's "master" is as kind or patient as Freyrík.

"My, uh . . ." His voice cracked round humiliation and nervous fear. If he could not dissuade Húskarl, he knew he would fight the man, and surely two assaults in one afternoon would bear poorly, if not dangerously, on Rík. He ducked his head, grateful for once for the heat that flushed his cheeks; 'twould work well to his advantage here.

Fallen gods, Rík, forgive me . . .

"My master prefers me dry," he mumbled to his feet.

Húskarl came round to grab his chin, looking into his eyes as if for the lie. "Truly?"

Ayden nodded, averting his gaze lest it give him away.

"Hmm," Húskarl said, returning the oil pot to the grooming table. "I did not imagine Prince Freyrík among the ranks of men who revel in the pain of their slaves."

There are many things you cannot imagine about him, Ayden thought. And all the fallen gods thanked for it.

Chapter Five

A hot bath awaited Freyrík upon his return from the day's sport hunt, but no Ayden. His groom came to undress him, and a servant scurried behind them on hands and knees, wiping mud from the floor. Freyrík made a beeline for the steaming water, not least because of the long damp chill of the day. He stank of blood, and death—the stench of war to his mind, not recreation.

Lord Vitr, gods bless him, hid well his distaste as he picked at a filth-crusted knot on Freyrík's sleeve.

"I hope the hunt was not too unpleasant, Your Highness?"

Freyrík grunted, noncommittal. If he started complaining now, he'd never stop.

The knot came loose at last, and Lord Vitr worked the lacing from the top of Freyrík's sleeve with blood- and mud-stained fingertips. "Were the rumors true? A darker beast in the midlands?"

Freyrík nodded.

"A bird?"

"Nay. Cougar." Freyrík breathed deep, eyes closed. Weary as he was, Lord Vitr nearly knocked him off his balance with a single hard tug to a stubborn knot. He threw a hand up against the wall to brace himself.

"Apologies, Your Highness."

Freyrík said nothing.

"However did the beast evade three provinces' worth of soldiers?"

Freyrík shrugged. He wished Lord Vitr would stop asking questions but did not have the heart to say so. "It happens sometimes. Anyway, the midland princes do not mind. What's a dozen dead commoners in the face of their grand sport?" He snorted, realized his fist was clenched when Lord Vitr tried to pull his sleeve off and couldn't. 'Twas a conscious effort to relax his fingers. "As if twenty men and a pack of dogs against a single dark cougar is *sport*."

As if it even should *be.*

"Indeed," Lord Vitr said, dry as sour wine, and set to work on the other sleeve. "But still, 'tis one less beast to terrorize the children and women. I suppose that's something?"

"And one more darker corpse to parade through the streets," Freyrík spat.

Lord Vitr said nothing to that, gods thanked, turning his full focus to Freyrík's filthy clothes. They could be washed, no doubt, but Freyrík would just as soon see them burned. He would think of today's farce of a battle every time he wore them.

And if such was the face of the war in the midlands, 'twas no wonder Berendil felt so frustrated, so in need of change.

"Your Highness?"

Freyrík opened his eyes. He'd been stripped bare without noticing, and Lord Vitr, bereft of further duty, hovered close. He gestured toward Freyrík, toward the sponge and soap sitting untouched on a tray beside the tub. Freyrík felt unspeakably weary, of a sudden, just looking at them.

"Shall I wash you, Your Highness?"

Freyrík nodded. 'Twas not the touch he longed for, but it would suffice.

He stepped into the tub, eyes closing at the steaming heat of it. Lord Vitr steadied him at the elbows as he settled down into the water, stretched out his legs and leaned back until the water lapped at his chin. The tub was big enough for two. Lonely with only one. "Where is Ayden?"

"At the slave baths, being prepared for tonight's dinner."

Freyrík would have grimaced at the choice of words, were even the muscles in his face not so tired.

"How fares he?" he asked, leaning into the soft touch of a sponge against his nape.

"He is much improved, Highness."

Freyrík wished to ask more, but could not bring himself to face the answers. He would see Ayden shortly. It could wait.

His arm was plucked from the water and laid across the lip of the tub. He was content to let Lord Vitr maneuver him, lulled by the touch of sponge and soap and fingers, gentle and unhurried as always. The man washed him in silence, gods thanked.

When Lord Vitr was finished, Freyrík hauled himself out of the tub. The man toweled him dry and dressed him for the evening meal as if a life-sized doll. Freyrík was content to allow it, and Lord Vitr seemed content to indulge him so. For those moments in Vitr's care, Freyrík felt becalmed. At peace. 'Twas almost too easy to ignore the danger they were in.

But then his groom was shoving him out the door, and the world of High Court came crashing back. He braced himself against it, chin up, shoulders squared. Dinner with the Aegis tonight, in His Eminence's private dining room, and Gods knew who else would be there. Ayden, at least, if Lord Vitr had spoken true. And Berendil, he hoped, lest he be left to face the Aegis's scrutiny alone.

He walked slowly, using the time to compose his thoughts and features into some semblance of neutrality. It had not escaped him that his promise to the Aegis and his promise to Berendil conflicted gravely. Was he to convince Berendil to abandon political aspiration, even as he curried favor for him with King Taf, King Gódr, and Prince Skalli?

Worse, 'twas favor for himself rather than Berendil, as Berendil meant to seat *him* on the Council. The thought burned more deeply than he'd expected.

But at least 'twas a path he could cut through both promises, narrow though it might be. He could look the Aegis in the eye and swear Berendil would not—did not want to—sit the Council. Never mind the wounded disappointment he'd see in that gaze when at last the Aegis became aware of Berendil's ploy.

But oh, he dreaded causing the Aegis such hurt even more than he dreaded sitting the Council.

"Your Highness."

He startled at the greeting. Two pages, bracketing the doors to the Aegis's private dining room, bowed deep. 'Twas worrisome he'd come all this way without realizing. More worrisome still how ill-prepared he felt when the pages opened the doors and ushered him inside.

He first laid eyes upon the Aegis, of course, seated at the head of the carved oak table and toying with his goblet. The Aegis possessed a gravity that drew all eyes and minds to his person, even when he seemed to idle. Even more so when he turned to Freyrík, and his eyebrows rose a fraction over a thin smile, as if awaiting a reaction.

To what?

A polite chorus of "Your Highness" reminded Freyrík of the other guests, and he took quick stock of all present: Berendil, curiously seated in a place of honor on the Aegis's left; King Taf of Ingimárr Province on the Aegis's right; and further down the table, Prince Skalli of Randvér opposite King Gódr of Ofan.

Freyrík's gaze snapped back to the Lord Protector as a shard of ice twisted in his guts. This was no private dinner; this was a warning, a show of power, of veritable omniscience on the Aegis's part. He knew what Berendil had asked of Freyrík. Mayhap he even knew what Freyrík had promised Berendil.

Or mayhap Freyrík was twitching at shadows, and this gathering was but the Aegis taking an educated guess.

"Pray be seated," the Aegis said, calmly as if Freyrík had not been staring. "We are all quite famished on the heels of our hunt, and a grand supper awaits us."

Freyrík bowed, blood heating his cheeks as he wondered if he'd truly heard the wry emphasis on the word "seated." He took the remaining chair—all the way at the arse of the table, as it happened.

"A blessing," the Aegis said, holding up his goblet.

Footmen rushed forth to pour wine that smelled of honey and herbs. Freyrík was tempted to cover his cup, but he daren't give such an insult to either the gods or the Aegis who ruled by their grace.

The servant somehow managed to poke him in the back as he poured. Freyrík nearly snapped at the man, but the faint scent carrying over the wine—glorious, blessedly familiar, autumn leaves and clipped grass and a hint of honeysuckle—stopped him cold. 'Twas not a *man* at all.

He turned round and nearly breathed, "Ayden"—part surprise, part relief to see him standing—but then caught himself and merely gave the elf a nod. He turned back, lifted the cup for the blessing—

And whipped his head round again, eyes wide. By the gods, what was Ayden *wearing*?

A scowl, for one. He was backing up to the wall with the other servants and slaves, pitcher of wine in hand and a familiar glare on his face: *Not a word, Rík, or I'll end you.* Clearly he was feeling better if he could loose such reprobation, though the look was softened by powder and paint. Freyrík stifled a grin—and the sudden image of licking a long broad stripe down the wisteria vine painted across Ayden's torso—but could not quite stop himself staring.

"Dessert is the *last* course, brother."

The smile fell from Freyrík's face in an instant, but he pasted it back as he turned round to nod at his brother. Beside Berendil, the Aegis sat smiling as well, but his was a knowing thing rather than a crudity.

An indulgent smile too, it seemed, for the Aegis raised his goblet before Freyrík could give apologies.

Freyrík lifted his own with clumsy fingers as the Aegis recited the evening's blessings, took a long draft when the prayers were at end. Footmen swooped in with a savory-smelling pottage, but Freyrík found himself without appetite.

The Aegis suffered no such lack; he finished half his dish before Freyrík had worked down his second bite. The stew stuck in his throat. Had Ayden gotten to eat yet today? Would it be too unseemly to feed his elf here?

From the head of the table came a deliberate tinkling of spoon on porcelain. All eyes turned to the Aegis.

"You will forgive me," he said, "if I spoil the night's supper with discourse of grave matters, but I would that Freyrík indulge me."

Freyrík bowed his head. "I am ever at your service, Your Eminence." And gods blessed for the excuse to leave his food alone.

"I would very much like, Your Highness," the Aegis said between one spoonful of pottage and the next, "to hear your opinion on the upcoming vote."

"On the Council seats, Your Eminence?" Freyrík said for wont of a better reply, but gods, what a foolish question. Of course, the Council seats; there were no other votes.

On Freyrík's right, King Gódr snorted, but the Aegis merely nodded with the sort of patience one reserved for small children and fools. "And the merits of each candidate's ideas, of course."

Berendil, may the gods bless him ever strong and wise, jumped to his rescue. "We spoke but just last evening, Your Eminence, of my thoughts to lead the army into darker lands. A man as deliberate as my brother no doubt requires more time to consider the benefits of the plan."

Awfully pretty words for a man who thought himself weak on the political battlefield.

The Aegis hardly spared Berendil a glance before settling his eyes upon Freyrík once more. "But surely you have *some* thoughts on the matter? Time is short, after all; the Council vote is but five days hence."

"Indeed." Freyrík lifted his spoon, put it back, forced his hands into his lap. *By the gods, do not* fidget *before the Lord Protector.* "I think . . ."

Gods, but how to say anything without upsetting one man or the other? He could feel Berendil's gaze as surely as the Aegis's, could see clear as running water the eager attention of his fellow princes. Surely his opinion could not matter so much? Or had his recent victory against the Surge bought him new respect as both prince and strategist?

"I must admit, Your Eminence, that the thought of a world without the darker menace is nearly beyond my meager comprehension. Such a dream . . ." He shook his head. "I almost daren't hope. And mayhap the rest of us daren't either, and so we do not take seriously the possibility that Berendil's plan could work."

Berendil snuck him an approving glance as servants refilled their wine. This time, Rík did cover his cup.

"You support your brother's folly, then," King Gódr said round a half-chewed mouthful of stew.

And he calls my *people uncivilized?*

"I pray you not place words on my tongue, Your Majesty," Freyrík said.

To his left, King Taf set his spoon in his bowl with a delicate *clink*. "Do let the prince speak, Gódr. Like our Lord Protector, I would hear him."

The Aegis too placed his spoon in his bowl, and the servants took their cue to swap out the pottage for a selection of roasted meats. Freyrík pointed at the proffered tray without looking; a cut of venison and a beef flank were placed on his plate. When the servant backed away, Ayden leaned in, ostensibly to refill Freyrík's half-empty goblet. His free hand, firm and warm, alit on the back of Freyrík's neck as he poured.

Gods, how Freyrík loved him.

Berendil's eyes honed in unfailingly, his smirk making it clear he'd not missed the subtle exchange. "You were saying, brother?" he prompted, picking up fork and knife to cut into his meat. "You find merit in my plan?"

"I do," Freyrík conceded. "Then again"—and like an elf, he could almost *hear* Berendil's eyes narrow—"the stakes are high, and the odds of success no doubt slim. The darker woods are vast, mountainous—"

"Cursed," King Gódr cut in.

"And yet Prince Freyrík led an army there and returned triumphant," Prince Skalli said.

For a moment, Freyrík watched as the men traded battling stares across the table. He cleared his throat and continued before the tension grew too thick. "True, but only two leagues. Deeper in, 'tis no fair territory through which to march an army. How would we search for the dark elves? Where would we begin?"

"And what would you do if you find them?" King Gódr said, stabbing his fork at the air. "Or worse, if they find you?"

"Kill them, I should imagine," King Taf murmured.

Gódr slammed down his fork and shoved away his meats with a disgusted snort. "You assume they can be killed. You assume—"

"Enough," the Aegis said softly, but the room plunged into silence as if he'd roared.

Freyrík dropped his gaze to his plate, watching the Aegis from the corner of his eye. The others were no doubt doing the same. But 'twas Freyrík alone the Aegis was watching back, and 'twas Freyrík he gestured to continue.

"Your Eminence," Freyrík said, "I know not if the dark elves can be killed. But if they *can* fall to mortal blade, I believe the threat of the dark beasts would indeed die with them."

He felt more than saw Berendil beaming at him from across the table, which made the words yet on his tongue even sourer. But 'twould be a dereliction to the Aegis and his own people to leave them unsaid.

"There is another matter," he began cautiously. His next words would anger both Berendil *and* Ayden, mayhap—gods help him— even alienate them. "To take enough men over hostile ground and fight what we hope to find there, I cannot help but think we need deplete our northern garrisons. The danger inherent is dire." Behind him, he heard Ayden stir, could fair sense the furious glare burning into his skull. The expression dawning on Berendil's face was no kinder; Freyrík stared resolutely at the Aegis to avoid them both. "We must acknowledge the possibility that the elven generals will take advantage and attack."

Silence all round, as if no one had yet considered this point. Berendil opened his mouth, closed it again. If his scowl was anything to go by, he was trying—and failing—to form a rebuttal more weighty than *No they wouldn't*. Or mayhap, *Gods crack you and your flapping tongue, brother.*

Berendil's ire he could face, but Ayden he daren't even peek at right now.

The servants, it seemed, knew not what to make of the lull. They stepped forward, hesitant—did they mean to swap out dishes already?—but the Aegis held up a hand and they froze, backed away again. "Insightful as always, Prince Freyrík. Yet still we do not know how your mind sways."

Freyrík's gaze slid from the Aegis to Berendil and back again. He saw no love in their faces, and gods forgive him but he couldn't help a silent curse against the Aegis for placing him in such a difficult position. Even if 'twas punishment for withholding Ayden—even if such punishment was well-deserved—'twas an especial cruelty to pit brother against brother before all the court when Freyrík had done naught to lend doubt to his loyalty.

"I beg His Eminence would forgive me if my mind yet sways in all directions, for the wind blows strong from each side, and carries with it scents of both victory and defeat."

The Aegis said nothing to this, merely waved the waiting servants in to bring the next course. This time, Ayden offered him no comfort; instead he elbowed Freyrík in the back as he leaned in, putting Freyrík's plate down with such force that fish sauce splattered on the tablecloth.

Quiet reigned for a time as they turned focus to their meal, or attempted as much anyway. 'Twas strange to eat in such company with no music in the background, no entertainers of any sort. 'Twas stranger still that the Aegis had let the matter of Freyrík's indecision drop. Freyrík prodded at his fish with a piece of bread and tried not to look half as miserable as he felt.

'Twas almost a relief when King Taf broke the silence again, even if it was to interrogate Freyrík further. "Do you not think, Your Highness, that your recent success against the Surge is strong argument for waiting, at the very least?"

"For waiting?" Berendil demanded, far too loud. "Nay, 'tis proof as sure as any we should press our attack—"

The Aegis touched his fingers to Berendil's forearm. Hardly a brush, but Berendil fell silent, looking every inch the scolded child.

Freyrík rather felt the same, between Berendil and the Aegis scowling before him and Ayden radiating disapproval behind.

When 'twas clear the Aegis did not wish to speak, King Taf picked up where he'd left off. "Your stratagem, once applied up and down the western front, will give us a new edge over the darker beasts. We may have no need of pursuing more difficult and dangerous solutions."

'Twas a shame to anger yet another man tonight, but alas, there was nothing for it. "If I may, Your Majesty, I think perspective has been lost in your reasoning. For though we've earned a victory indeed, 'twas bought at the cost of six hundred dead and a thousand injured, some never to fight again. At heavy expense to the Empire's coffers, as well, and a feat not so easily reduplicated in all weather or geography."

"Besides," said Prince Skalli, "'Tis not even two months past, and already we hear reports of darker movement in Midr. The dark elves resent their failed bloodletting. They come back for more too soon."

"Truly? I had not heard—" Freyrík began at the same time King Gódr said, "'Tis not so uncommon—"

"You were traveling," the Aegis said overtop them all, eyes upon Freyrík once more. "It may yet be but a few stray beasts such as the one we killed today; it is too soon to know. But if a second Surge does crest so quickly, we may take comfort at least in the knowledge that our troops have garrisoned the winter on your western front. Their march to Midr ought not be too taxing."

King Gódr seemed quite pleased to hear that. "You will try Prince Freyrík's plan again in Midr, Your Eminence?" he asked.

"I've made all due recommendations to Prince Ulfr. If terrain permits and the cold has not killed our source of poison, I do believe Prince Freyrík's stratagem will serve us well in the event of another Surge. And if the dark elves truly do strike again so soon? I say let them, for they cannot destroy us a mere six hundred soldiers at a time."

Easy words for a leader who need not look those men in the face as they die.

'Twas clear as water his brother thought the same—Berendil's fists were clenched so tight round fork and knife they were trembling—but gods thanked, the man held his tongue.

Their third dish was swapped out for a fourth, and strained silence yielded to strained small talk, which in turn yielded to cautiously pleasant recountings of the day's hunt, the fine meal, the many and varied pleasures on offer at High Court.

Which, of course, led to talk of Ayden as if the poor thing weren't standing right there, filling their wineglasses when they emptied.

"A fine trophy," Prince Skalli said, skirting fingertips across the flowering vine painted up Ayden's bare belly when Ayden leaned in to pour him more drink. Ayden's muscles rippled away from the touch, and beneath the table, Freyrík fisted his hand into his breeches lest he pound it into Skalli's face.

"Mmm," King Taf said round a mouthful of meat pie, "I care little for the males, but even I can see this one's appeal." His gaze shifted from Ayden's stony face to Freyrík. "Is it true you had him flogged at Harvest Fest? He seems so well-behaved."

The urge to laugh at the words "Ayden" and "well-behaved" in the same sentence was quite thoroughly quashed by the mention—and the memory—of the flogging.

"Fallen gods help us," said King Gódr, grimacing over his wine as if 'twere horse piss. "Do you still hold that barbaric ritual?"

Freyrík's hand fisted in his breeches once more, and he knew without looking that Berendil's had done the same.

"But I admit it seems to have worked," Gódr continued, holding up his goblet for Ayden to refill. It seemed impossible that no one else saw Ayden's clenched jaw and shaking hands as he moved to obey, but mayhap they'd simply not bothered to look. King Gódr sipped his wine, mock-saluted Ayden with his cup. "Such a docile creature now. I should rather like to . . . know him better."

Before Freyrík could speak dangerous words, Berendil replied. "I do believe it is pacified only in my brother's presence, Your Majesty."

King Taf snorted a laugh. "Indeed, it takes a wild hand to tame a wild beast."

Berendil slammed down his silverware, but the noise of it, gods thanked, was lost beneath the laughter of the midland princes. It seemed impossible they not recognize the insult of such words, and yet they spoke them again and again without shame. Boors, the lot of them.

"Speaking of the elf," the Aegis said when the laughter had died away, "I should like to take my evening with it, if you'd not object, Rík."

Freyrík had to grit his teeth against a resurgence of what little of the fine meal he'd managed to consume. The thought of Ayden passed along like some common whore . . . The Aegis couldn't possibly think he'd *not mind*. Must have known he'd mind very much, in fact. Another test of fealty, then, or further punishment?

Either way, there was nothing for it but to say, "Of course, Your Eminence," and try to pretend he'd not forced the words through a swell of hatred so thick and shocking he could scarcely credit it himself. He dared not so much as glance at Ayden's shadow as he added with false conviction, "You've my word he'll obey your hand and mouth as if they were mine."

The Aegis nodded, as sure in this as he was in all things. "Then if my lords will excuse me," he said—pure manners; he needed no one's permission to go anywhere or do anything, "I shall take my leave."

He stood, and all the men with him according to custom. Freyrík stared resolutely at his plate as the Aegis walked round him to take hold of Ayden—a wise move on his part, for Ayden would not have come if called—but he could well imagine his lover's fear, desperation, even hatred for Freyrík's acquiescence as he was taken to gods only knew where and for what.

He only prayed that Ayden would not rouse the Aegis's ire, and that the Aegis would do no harm—physical or otherwise—to his *fóstri's* dear "pet."

Ayden followed the Aegis from the dining room, glancing at Freyrík only long enough to understand—even deaf as he was—how devastated the man was. He tried to send him a reassuring glance, but Rík would not meet his eyes. Crack him, did he not realize Ayden knew he'd had no choice? He'd have given Rík an earful there and then if it weren't for the Aegis pulling him along, and his preoccupancy with his own impending fate.

The Aegis led him into the corridor. Ayden walked two paces behind the man but held his head defiantly high. Four palace guards closed in round them, liveried in ostentation—the Aegis's private guard, no doubt.

A short walk later, he was led into the grandest chamber he'd ever beheld. Every surface was polished or sparkled or shone: rare hardwoods as old and full of character as Ayden's great-grandmothers, silks and furs inviting touch, hundreds of scented candles casting a flickering sheen upon it all.

Beyond lacquered double doors on the far wall no doubt lay the bedchamber, and Ayden braced himself to be ushered in. But the Aegis made no move toward it. He sat instead upon a padded wingback chair, and waved at its twin in invitation—or rather command—for Ayden to sit as well.

A pretense of hospitality, then, before they turned to the business at hand. Ayden hid his grimace as he took his seat.

"Simi!" the Aegis called, and from the double doors emerged a woman moments later—no, a female elf, judging by the collar round her neck—who glided up behind the Aegis and draped her arms round his neck in a gesture that smacked of true affection. By habit, Ayden strained to hear the falseness and disgust that must have underlain it. But his mind-ear remained deaf.

However, the kiss the elven woman placed upon the crown of the Aegis's head, the way her lips curled against his skin as she rested her chin upon his shoulder, spoke volumes to the eyes.

"This is Ayden, Simi. He is new here."

She looked up and smiled, though her eyes, a startling blue, seemed faded. She'd clearly been beautiful once, stunning even, but now she only looked weary. Or maybe 'twas her silence that made her seem so.

"Hello, Ayden," she said, and in those words, in that sweet and lilting birdsong of a voice, he heard a tragic echo of the music long denied her.

He nodded in acknowledgment, but she'd already turned her attention back to the Aegis. She walked round the human's chair, sat down at his feet and laid her head upon his knee.

He stroked her absently, as if a house cat.

Ayden gripped the arms of his wing chair so tightly the leather creaked.

"He's pretty," she said into the Aegis's lap, as if Ayden weren't sitting a pace away. "Will he stay with us tonight?"

The Aegis chuckled, even as shock stole Ayden's breath from his chest.

"Would you like that, Simi?" he asked, running his fingers through her hair. When she merely shrugged, he added, "You know I have eyes only for you."

Ayden blinked, and blinked again, relief warring with confusion and illness in his brain. What was he doing here, then?

"Ayden doesn't want to stay with us," the Aegis continued. "He wants to go home."

"Why?" she asked, still staring off into the distance, her cheek on the Aegis's knee. "It's nice here."

"Is that what you brought me here for?" Ayden demanded. The urge to launch from his chair, to pummel this human's face beyond recognition, was as strong as—

"She will protect me," the Aegis said, calm as a windless day. "Do you want that? To fight your own kind?"

Ayden realized he was standing, and sat back down. His heart had grown too heavy for his legs to hold, anyway.

"Does she even remember home?"

The Aegis shrugged again. "This is her home now. You will learn in time there is peace in such knowledge, Ayden. Comfort. Ease. I would that you not disrupt the peace here. 'Tis upsetting to the others."

"And to you?"

The Aegis nodded. "And to me."

Ayden climbed to his feet again, but kept his distance from the Aegis. He would not fight Simi, and could not fight the many guards a mere shout away. "If that is all . . ." he said, turning toward the drawing room doors.

"Sit." A single word, softly spoken, yet possessed of so much power that Ayden found his arse back in his chair as if compelled. Was that how beasts felt when he called them to slaughter with song? Fallen gods help him.

"Do you love Rík, then?"

Ayden's head snapped up. Had he missed some key part of this conversation? The Aegis was looking at him with calm curiosity, as if they'd been speaking of nothing else.

"He is my master," Ayden said carefully. "I am obedient." His eyes flicked to the elven female, and he could not keep a trace of poison from his voice. "If that is how you define love . . ."

Still the Aegis stroked Simi's hair, though his gaze was firmly fixed upon Ayden. "You wound me, elf," he said in a voice utterly absent pain.

Thirty seconds alone, and I would wound you indeed, human.

"Does your master love you?"

Yes, he thought fiercely, even as he shook his head no. And to distract the human, "Would you claim to love Simi?"

He realized the question was a mistake the moment it left his lips. The Aegis confirmed this with a simple, "Yes."

"And yet you keep her chained."

"And in doing so protect us both from whatever primal urges may yet drive her. The gut does not always want as the mind and heart do; surely even you know that."

Ayden said nothing.

"In any event, this is not why I brought you here. I wonder, has your master told you of his brother's plans?"

Ayden shook his head. "We've not had opportunity to speak since our arrival. Even if we had, why would he discuss the workings of kings with the likes of me?"

The Aegis laughed, a condescending sound that grated upon Ayden's ears as surely as the starfall. "Simi here knows all the secrets of my kingdoms, don't you Simi."

She gazed up at the man and smiled, but said nothing. Ayden suspected she rarely did, and doubted she had much opportunity to repeat what she heard besides—the makings of a fine sounding board. He shifted in his chair, fighting down nausea.

"Did you heed our talk at supper?" Before Ayden could deny it, the Aegis said, "Of course you did. Rík would not care for you if you let such opportunity pass you by. You realize, then, that if Berendil sits the Council, he will hold enough sway to change the course of our war. He will muster the army and lead it into the darker forests to find and slaughter all dark elves."

Something in the human's shrewd eyes kept Ayden from laughing at such absurdities.

"But you and I know there *are* no dark elves, don't we, Ayden."

Unwelcome familiarity aside—*finally,* words of reason! "They are indeed a human confabulation," he said, unexpectedly relieved. "And a ridiculous one, at that. 'Tis Nature herself who molds the Ferals and sics them upon you, and for good reason." His sharp smile felt just the wrong side of bitter. "But of course such truths are too harsh for your people, and so instead they blame mine."

The Aegis lifted his hand from Simi's head to wave it dismissively at Ayden. "We shall not debate the root of this untruth—"

"Or the reason you've chosen to perpetuate it when you know it for a lie?"

Movement at the hall doors—guards readying weapons. Ayden tensed, surprised. His elfsong could not have flared under the screech of the starfall; surely the guards had perceived no threat from him. Was the Aegis so fragile, then, that his guards stood trained to silence the slightest question? Or was he merely above tolerating interruption?

Even Simi had tensed in upon herself. She expected violence, but the way the Aegis curled a protective hand round the curve of her head told Ayden she expected only to witness it, not endure it.

Let the guards come, then. He would not apologize for speaking truth.

"Stand down," the Aegis said, and Ayden resisted the urge to sink lower in his chair. But apparently the man had addressed the guards, who were sheathing their weapons, if not their malice.

"I let the rumor live because it serves me," the Aegis said, his eyes yet affixed to Ayden's. "You seem a clever elf—certainly a warrior, perhaps even a strategist. Surely you can understand this."

Ayden pursed his lips.

"But I think you do not understand just how ill it serves you. Ah—" He raised a hand to silence Ayden's protest. "I speak not of the old prejudices between our peoples, Ayden. Think: If Berendil gets his way and leads our army into the darker forests, what will happen when they find nothing? Dark beasts aplenty, no doubt, but no dark elves, for they cannot find what does not exist. Where do you think they'll go then? Who do you think they'll blame next?"

Sudden, deafening clarity set the room spinning, candelabras and oil paintings and gilt hardwood furnishings all whirling out of place above the silken South Sea rugs. *Us,* he realized, clutching to his chair amidst the maelstrom. *Fallen gods help me,* us.

Over the roaring in his ears, he barely heard the Aegis's self-satisfied, "Ah. I see you understand now."

Ayden's mouth was open. He shut it, swallowed hard, nodded.

"Then you know how well it serves you when I ask that you speak to the master you do not influence and whose love you do not hold about convincing his brother of the folly of this plan."

Ayden nodded again, fingers yet clawing for purchase in the arms of the wing chair. "But do not ask me to betray him. I will carry your words to his ears, but not his to yours. Do you understand?"

Again the guards shifted forward, but the Aegis merely shrugged as if to say, *I need not the likes of you to know your master's thoughts.* He flicked his hand toward the hall doors. "Good night, Ayden."

With that cold dismissal, the Aegis rose, then helped Simi to her feet. They slung arms round each other's waists and strolled into the bedroom together without sparing him another glance.

Chapter Six

Supper dragged through two more courses after the Aegis took Ayden away. Every bite, every clink of silver on porcelain grated on Freyrík's nerves. He stayed only because the alternative was to fret in the solitude of his rooms, and the mere thought of that all but drove him mad. At least here he might find a chance to repair the damage done to Berendil's trust.

But Berendil said nothing, only ate in a silence that struck Freyrík as more contemplative than angry. Even Prince Skalli and Kings Taf and Gódr limited themselves to empty comments on the food. As if they were afraid to ask more questions without the Aegis present. As if they feared he'd know.

Strange, to think of the Lord Protector and feel . . . fear.

At last King Gódr declared an end to the meal, no doubt deeming himself the ranking sovereign. Freyrík readily forgave him that for having released them of this wretched tension. King Taf stood next, and then Berendil. Freyrík watched his brother with raised eyebrows, wordlessly offering service, but Berendil only bid him good-night and left.

This left Freyrík with no further excuse to eschew his rooms.

He dragged his feet down sumptuous corridors, dreading what he'd find there. Ayden wounded? Ayden angry and accusing?

Worse, no Ayden at all?

And fallen gods be cursed, *of course* his rooms were empty but for his groom.

A quick washing, two drinks, and many failed attempts at a volume of poetry later, he startled upright in bed at the opening of his bedroom doors. Ayden slipped through them, looking blessedly whole and unharmed.

Freyrík threw the covers off and fair leapt from the mattress. "Are you—?"

"I'm fine," Ayden said, waving him back. "The Aegis wished only to speak with me."

Relief, pure and clean, left Freyrík sagging back against the headboard. "Nevertheless, I am sorry. I wish I could have—"

"Refused him?" Ayden snorted, sat upon the bed by Freyrík's hip. "Don't be an idiot."

"It's just that you have every right to be angry—"

Ayden squeezed Freyrík's shoulder and looked him dead in the eye. "I'm not angry with you."

"Not even for what I said about your people?"

Ayden paused a moment, teeth worrying at his lower lip. "I was," he said. "But I cannot claim not to understand such frame of mind."

Hard to comprehend such perfect forgiveness from this hot-blooded elf when Freyrík could hardly forgive himself. He touched hesitant fingertips to Ayden's cheek.

Ayden leaned into the caress and closed his eyes—his glittering, gold-dusted eyes.

"They have painted you like a woman," Freyrík said, smiling for the first time all night as he brushed his thumb over Ayden's reddened lips. "You are *sparkling*."

Ayden snatched Freyrík's thumb between his teeth and bit down not quite softly. "Do you no longer desire me, then?"

"I rather like it, actually." Freyrík worked his thumb free, scraped the nail down Ayden's chin, his throat, then splayed fingers across the painstakingly painted hummingbird on his chest. "'Tis pretty. It suits you."

Ayden grinned wide. "I would tell you to undress me, but they have not left much to remove."

True that. Ayden was bared above the hips but for trailing green silk sashes tied round each bicep. And below the hips . . . Freyrík let his hands dip, tracing the painted vine down to the waist of Ayden's hose, gauzy green satin so thin as to nearly be seen through. The hose were split up the sides, tacked only at the ankles, knees, and hips; 'twas an easy thing to slip his hands inside, to smooth palms and fingers round the firmness of Ayden's thighs and up toward what treasures lay between.

Ayden shuddered, leaned in and claimed a kiss, clutching hands round Freyrík's bare shoulders and neck and pushing him back against the headboard.

"No undergarments?" Freyrík murmured against the elf's lips. "How uncouth."

"Mmm. How *convenient*, more like."

Freyrík hummed his agreement. He tugged Ayden onto his lap; Ayden readily straddled him but kept a frustrating distance from his manhood, which stood yet at only half arms. Strange, that, but fatigue and worry had long gnawed at unexpected hollows in his being.

Then Ayden was up on his haunches, looming close. Ayden's scent filled his nostrils, Ayden's teeth worried at the lobe of his ear, and he forgot all about gnawed hollows—except for those being gnawed on by Ayden, of course.

He clutched at Ayden's back, slid hands down to his waist. Tangled fingers in the drawstring of those ridiculous hose, eager to strip Ayden bare of these High Court trappings, to touch and feel and reassure.

'Twas rather hard to concentrate, though, on complexities like square knots when fingers were worming 'twixt the cheeks of his bare arse, shivering across that tender patch behind his stones. He jerked at the tickling touch and cracked his head against the headboard. Barely even felt it above that questing finger circling his opening.

"Wait," he panted—or thought he did, for 'twas difficult to tell with Ayden's tongue lapping so against his throat. "Clothes."

Not so eloquent, perhaps, but Ayden always could divine his thinking.

Yet the elf, gods curse him, merely smiled against the hollow of Freyrík's shoulder. "Yes, 'twas thoughtful of you not to wear them."

The mattress dipped as Ayden rose on his haunches to scrape all ten fingernails down Freyrík's shoulder blades, and Freyrík gasped, arched into the touch . . . and gave Ayden's arse a hard swat.

"Cheeky imp," he growled, and Ayden threw his head back and laughed.

"Very well." He pecked Freyrík's left cheek, then the right, then the tip of his nose. "I shall put me out of your misery." He climbed from Freyrík's lap just long enough to shed his hose, then settled back again, closer this time, pressing chest to chest and finally, *gods*, groin to groin. Such delicious contrast, the furnace-heat of the elf at his front and the cool smoothness of the headboard at his back.

He wrapped arms round Ayden's waist, moaned into the elf's chest. His mouth brushed across a nipple and he parted his lips, pressed them to raised flesh, teased the nub with tongue and teeth until Ayden was writhing in his lap, beating at his head and shoulders in a clearly conflicted bid for freedom.

"Please," Ayden managed between shuddering breaths. "Please . . ."

Freyrík paused his tongue in its torture, but did not release the nipple from between his teeth. "Please what?" he asked round the hardened nub, enjoying the elf's desperation perhaps a little too much.

It seemed Ayden didn't know either, for he merely growled and clutched at Freyrík's head, half shoving him away, half holding him in place.

Freyrík took mercy and switched nipples.

Ayden bucked afresh, hips grinding against Freyrík's manhood until Freyrík's blood churned as wild as the elf's, the pain of Ayden's fists in his hair the only thing stopping him from spilling over.

The world tilted and spun, and Freyrík found himself suddenly on his back, Ayden's bulk hot and heavy on his chest, Ayden's hands pinning his own above his head. Like a woman, this, held steady for claiming, and yet he felt no fight—only desire.

The elf stared down at him—and stared some more, green eyes burning bright as ever he'd seen them, boring straight through his own. 'Twas worrisome, such motionless intensity *now* of all times, and gods but what he wouldn't give to understand it, to know what Ayden was seeking in this silence passing between them.

He lay still instead, chest heaving between Ayden's tense thighs, wrists limp beneath Ayden's clutching hands, and met that gaze with everything he had to offer.

The skin round Ayden's eyes tightened, just for a moment, and his upper lip along with it, flashing teeth. Then he was tearing at the strip of silk round his biceps, fingers and teeth making work of the knot in seconds. He unwound the cloth as if doing battle with some long green beast, and next Freyrík knew it was wrapped round his own wrists, cinched tightly, looped somehow round a bedpost with the loose end in Ayden's hand.

Ayden settled back against Freyrík's hips with a strange, almost painstaking gentleness. He was panting, flushed, openmouthed, as if he'd just run a horse into the ground and could hardly comprehend his negligence. Studying him as if *Freyrík* were that horse. The silk, like a rein, was still wrapped round one tight fist.

His manhood had drooped to half arms. Was he, like Freyrík, thinking on the last time he'd clutched at bindings in Freyrík's presence? How he'd trusted Freyrík?

How much grief it had brought them both.

But whatever their past, 'twas *past*. And this . . . This would bring them bliss, he was sure of it.

Yet still Ayden stared, breathing hard, fist round the silk resting light on Freyrík's breastbone. Slowly, never breaking their stare, Freyrík drew his knees up behind Ayden, until the tops of his thighs pressed firm against Ayden's lower back. "It seems," he said, tugging just hard enough at his bonds to feel Ayden's hand, still at his chest, tighten round the silk, "that I am at your mercy, oh great elven warrior."

Ayden looked down at his own fist, then to Freyrík's bound wrists, Freyrík's face. His tongue peeked out from between parted lips, moistened them. His eyes seemed suddenly black in the candlelight.

Freyrík tugged again, harder this time. Still Ayden held fast to the silk, unmoving . . . but for one small part of him, growing less small, like Freyrík's, by the moment.

"I wonder, what will you do with me now?"

A wicked grin broke slow and wide across Ayden's face. He surged forward and latched his teeth to Freyrík's neck, scraped his free hand down Freyrík's flank in a manner clearly meant to induce squirming. And squirm Freyrík did, laughing despite himself, trapped beneath Ayden's weight and skill and the silk round his wrists that held him open, exposed, no matter how he struggled. Powerless, helpless in Ayden's arms.

Strange, what a thrill he found that to be.

He was at full arms again, standing so tall he hurt. Ayden, gods have mercy, reached round behind him, wrapped callused fingers round the root of Freyrík's manhood, and pulled. His eyes never left Freyrík's, but a smile grew within them to match the one curling his lips, playful and deadly serious all at once. The silk round Freyrík's wrists pulled taut, stretching him near to discomfort, but even that strain seemed transformed somehow by that perfect pleasure at his core, by the elf's devilish grin, and he wanted more of it, struggled back and made Ayden work for it, force him, match him strain for strain.

Freyrík lost, of course. He could hold on to nothing in Ayden's hands. Didn't want to, anyway.

And gods, but those hands gave no quarter. Ayden worked him with all his considerable skill and finesse, fingers gripping, squeezing, sliding, twisting, forcing Freyrík to the barest edge and holding him there—a deathblow pulled at the last instant, confident and steady.

And absolutely *maddening*.

The silks pulled tighter still. He followed the shimmering line of them with his eyes, watched Ayden wind the loose end once, twice round his hand. The burn in his belly joined the stretch in his shoulders, and his manhood twinged. Strained, eager. 'Twas almost as if the silk were wrapped round it and not his wrists.

Ayden's smile faded from his lips but never left his eyes, which remained affixed to Freyrík's own as if by tidal force. "Will you beg me," he asked—said, rather, as if he already knew the answer.

Freyrík licked dry lips and nodded. "If you wish it."

Ayden leaned in, and his lips met Freyrík's own with softness utterly striking in contrast to all that had come before it. A sweet sweep of tongue against tongue, a gentle press of lips, less exploratory than savoring, no more claiming than a parting caress.

"I do not," he whispered against Freyrík's mouth, and then his hand was out behind him again, reaching to meet Freyrík's straining manhood. Firm, deliberate strokes and murmured endearments against his skin set him squirming once more, pleading despite Ayden's words—*please* and *harder* and *oh gods, Ayden, yes*—and with a final tight twist and squeeze, a final soft bite to the cord of his neck and a final hard pull to the silk at his wrists, Freyrík bucked and shuddered and burst against Ayden, crying out his pleasure fit for the gods to hear.

Nothing for a time save the buzz and tingle of his flesh, and then a slow awareness of the chill of the room, the dampness of his skin, the strange liquid quivering of his muscles. And, best of all, the tickle of

Ayden's hair at his chin and the soaking warmth of the elf pressed up tight beside him.

His hands had been freed, and at some point he'd curled one arm round Ayden's shoulder. He reached across himself with the other, only skimming Ayden's hip before Ayden stopped him with a simple touch, then leaned up on one elbow to kiss away Freyrík's concern. "I have already had my pleasure," he said.

A quick, confused glance down the bed told Freyrík otherwise. Had Ayden not enjoyed their play? Surely he had shared, if not surpassed, Freyrík's own excitement. Surely the thrill of *taking* control had been just as complete as the unexpected thrill of relinquishing it—

Oh.

Freyrík sat up against the pillows, stroked Ayden's cheek. "Do you truly feel so helpless here?"

Ayden's gaze snapped up to his, sharp and . . . surprised? Angry? Gods befanged, had he *shamed* the elf?

Ayden sighed, captured Freyrík's fingers in his own, placed a kiss across the pads. "No," he said, but then hastened to add, "I mean yes, of course, but that's not . . ." He flopped down on his back, gestured at his collar as if swatting a persistent gnat. "I cannot *hear* through this. It's . . ." More swatting, his hand flapping this time between Freyrík and himself. "*This.* Intimacy. With elves, it's . . . harmony, a twining of songs, of . . . of *everything*. Not just bodies. And I don't— I can't— Not without—"

Freyrík caught Ayden's waving hand and clutched it in his own. "I'm sorry," he said, and gods but he hoped Ayden knew how much he meant it. "But perhaps . . . Perhaps, while we are bound here, we might seek a new way?"

Ayden said nothing for a long while. Contemplating Freyrík's offer? Or merely mourning what he'd lost?

At last the elf nodded. "But not tonight. Tonight I am weary."

"As am I," Freyrík said, and though 'twas true, he'd gladly have wiled the night away in search of Ayden's pleasure if the elf had let him. "What wits I managed to retain through supper I lost quite thoroughly to your hand."

"My apologies to the people of Farr."

Freyrík barked out a laugh. "Your insincerity astounds."

"No more than my prowess, I hope."

"Or your modesty."

That earned Freyrík a poke in the side, setting off a brief but vigorous tussle that ended in exhaustion rather than victory. They gave up as one, Freyrík relaxing the arm slung round Ayden's neck and Ayden's death grip round Freyrík's waist easing into a simple hug. Ayden laid his head upon Freyrík's shoulder and tucked a knee between Freyrík's legs; Freyrík wrapped his arm round Ayden's shoulder and nuzzled his cheek against the sweet-smelling scatter of Ayden's hair.

"Feeling better?" he murmured.

Ayden nodded against Freyrík's chest. "I am . . . mostly numb now. My head still aches, but no more than it ever might when dealing with humans."

Freyrík chuckled. 'Twas a mark of how far they'd come together that Ayden's insult held no venom, mayhap even no sincerity—spoken more in jest than hatred or even habit.

"Did the Aegis bend your ear to the point of pain?"

"No. He spoke more sense than most humans combined, actually. I'd fear his shrewdness, were I you."

"He is not my enemy, Ayden."

Ayden shifted in his arms until they could look each other in the eye. "Perhaps not. But neither should you call him friend."

The urge to push Ayden from his embrace—mayhap even strike him—was nearly overwhelming. But he beat it down, tightening his grip round Ayden's shoulders and measuring five careful breaths before chancing to speak.

"I call him *náungi*," he said.

Ayden's brow furrowed; Freyrík could practically see him riffling through his eight hundred years of memory and gods knew how many languages, searching for the meaning of that word.

At last Ayden tried, "Uncle?"

Freyrík bobbed his head from side to side. "And guardian, and mentor, and advisor. There is no one word for it in Trade. But no matter, as long as you understand his importance to me and to the empire at large. His life holds no purpose but to guide and serve all mankind, so his shrewdness could no sooner be a threat to the empire than it could to his own flesh, do you understand?"

A moment's silence—had he offended Ayden?—before the elf sat up and said, "Would you like to know what your guardian of all mankind said to me?"

Clearly something of import, to mention it now. Or for the Aegis to have mentioned it to Ayden at all, for surely the Lord Protector had no reason to concern himself with who warmed Freyrík's bed.

And yet, that he *had* concerned himself meant he was counting on Ayden to repeat it to Freyrík. If his news were so important, why not simply tell him directly?

Why else? Because he thought you would not listen.

He blinked up at Ayden and said, "He wishes you to sway me."

If Ayden was surprised by Freyrík's insight, he did not show it. He said merely, "Indeed."

"And will you?"

"What, sway you?"

Freyrík nodded.

"I would have tried even without prompting, had I known earlier of Berendil's plan. It will not work."

"It might."

"It *cannot* work, Freyrík. There are no dark elves to be found."

"How can you be so certain?"

"Because I know! Not a single one among us holds the power to transform the beasts into Ferals. Not a single one among us can sway them from their course for so much as a moment. Even singing as a group, we could not warp nature so."

Freyrík sat up and took Ayden's pointing hand in both his own. "Look, I'm not laying blame on your entire people—"

Ayden tugged his hand away and stood from the bed, thumping his open hand against his chest. "*We* are not the shapers of this world! We have never tried to turn it into something it's not! We could not if we wanted to. Your brother thinks to march your army against Nature herself—how do you think that would end for you?"

He had thought of nothing else since the moment his king had confided his plan.

"And what about *my* people? When yours find nothing, whom do you think they will blame next?"

"We are already at war, Ayden. We already blame each other. This would change nothing." He snatched up a pillow and stuffed it behind him, expending his anger on silk and feathers in lieu of Ayden's glowering face. "And as for *nature*, we have marched our army against it for the last three hundred years. We have lived this long. And thanks to your contribution, we ought live longer yet."

Ayden stared down at him, glower fading to a scowl, but still he was shaking his head. He dropped back down to the bed, nearly sitting on Freyrík's thigh. "No, you have *held the line* against Nature. Barely. Defending your walls is in a whole different key than what your brother proposes. You have new tools now for your defense—use them. Do not squander your men."

I did not realize you cared so much for my men teetered on the tip of Freyrík's tongue. But he owed Ayden honesty, not jest. "I cannot help but wonder," he said, "how the world might be if— There must be *something* to fight, surely. Mayhap not dark elves, but *something*. Some kind of beastmaster, some will behind the striking fist. Is it not worth the effort to seek it?"

Ayden licked his lips, drew them between his teeth. He seemed . . . apprehensive, of a sudden—a look most unsettling on this cocksure spirit.

"It is not worth your life," Ayden said at last, lying down beside Freyrík once more.

And though Freyrík wrapped arms round him and kept his silence, he utterly disagreed.

Freyrík's next day was an endless stretch of private gatherings—morning prayer with King Gódr before even the sun had woken, three lunches, two suppers, and four chats over wine. Not just with the councilmen, either—oh no, such would be too simple. No, to sway these men, he must also influence those who held their ears.

And so followed not only a second day of prayer with King Gódr, but also a pledge of his fourth son to the priesthood and a donation of pre-Empire scriptures from his own private library. He still had little chance of competing against Man's Ear to the Gods and the Gods' Mouth to Man, but a promise to support extending the Góz canal through Ofan Province might yet sway King Gódr to believe the gods had spoken to Freyrík as well.

As for the rest of the councilmen, well . . . he'd seen the difficulties from ten leagues back. Bad enough he could scarcely bury the urge to snatch up Ayden and run screaming from court each time he considered the possibility of winning this vote. Such distaste was hard to hide from Prince Skalli, even harder to hide from King Taf.

At least all the wine kept him loose and smiling.

Though he rather thought the hour before noon was a bit early to be feeling quite so at ease. Ah well, no doubt tea with Berendil would dispel it promptly.

A fire was raging in Berendil's hearth when Freyrík stepped into his drawing room, warm and inviting after the chill of the temple and the afternoon's long walk with the high priest through the frozen bailey. Berendil took one overstuffed chair before the fire and gestured Freyrík toward the other. A servant pressed a mug of hot cider into his hands.

"How many hearts have you yet captured, dear brother?"

Freyrík hid his frustration in a long draught of cider. "It's been but a day and a half, brother. Not even. Swaying minds takes time."

Berendil huffed. "And coin. And a son, I hear?"

Gods befanged, word traveled by swiftest bird round High Court, it seemed. "What else would the fourth son of a second son have done anyway, but enter the priesthood or fight? At least now he will live to sprout gray hairs."

"They will *all* live to turn gray if we can only take seats on—"

The drawing room doors flew open and through them dashed a page, who dropped to his knee several paces from them. "Apologies for the disruption, Your Majesty," the page said to his boot, "but the Aegis Exalted has sent an urgent message."

He held a note in both hands, folded and wax-sealed. Berendil raised his chin at the page and said, "Go on then. Read it to me."

The page cracked the seal and studied the note a moment. He seemed fretful to Freyrík, but mayhap 'twas the constant state of a man in his position.

"The Aegis Exalted calls an urgent meeting, my lords. Both His Majesty King Berendil and His Highness Prince Freyrík are to join him in the council chamber at once."

A moment's panic, tamped down by the utter stillness radiating from his king. It could be nothing at all—more likely lunch than, say, an invasion from the north. And yet it seemed nothing in his life had been so simple or easy in a great many months.

'Twas folly to assume now would be any different.

Ayden's stomach rumbled as he poked at his lunch tray, piled high with cold meat pies and braised fish. Had they never heard of a vegetable in this cursed place? There was good brown bread, but he'd had it this morning, and the morning before, and every other morning besides. He'd little appetite since the starfall, anyway. A footman stared at him as if he were shitting on a temple altar when he dug the filling from a pie with a teaspoon and ate the crust.

He smiled with far too many teeth and waved at the footman with the little plate he'd dumped the filling on. Gods, but it actually *looked* like shit on porcelain. "Hungry?"

'Twas no small feat of self-control not to hurl the plate at the footman's answering sneer.

And no small relief when Freyrík burst into the drawing room some moments later.

Deaf as he was, it took him a second to realize something was terribly, terribly wrong. Freyrík was just standing there, two paces past the doors, looking as if he couldn't remember where he was or why he'd come here or what was chasing him down the halls.

"Rík? What is it?" Ayden pushed from the table and rushed to Freyrík's side, wrapping one arm round his shoulder and guiding him toward the nearest chair. Freyrík fell into it as if he'd been sliced at the knees.

"The Council vote," Freyrík whispered.

Ayden hunched down to eye level before Freyrík and gripped his forearms. "What? What of it? Are you well?"

"The Aegis has moved the vote. It happens *now*, two weeks early. Two *weeks*."

That was why Freyrík seemed so shaken? "But is that not good for you? You dreaded winning anyway."

Freyrík pulled his arms free of Ayden's grip, folded them across his chest, dropped them to his lap, then finally laid them back on the armrests, clutching tight. "It is not—" One hand came up to rake through his hair before returning to the armrest again. "It is not about what *I* want. *I* am not king of Farr. And now surely I have failed my king."

Ayden rubbed his open palms up Freyrík's thighs, squeezed at the tension there. "He will understand."

"He will be *furious*! He will— I fear he will speak foolish words. Accuse the Aegis of abusing his power . . ."

Freyrík dropped his gaze to his lap and slumped forward, touching his head to Ayden's. Ayden reached out by reflex for the complex melodies of Freyrík's mind and heart, for the path through Freyrík's distress, but of course he heard nothing. Even so, he was not so deaf as to miss the glaringly obvious here: 'twas *Freyrík* who felt betrayed by his *náungi*.

Freyrík sat up straight, cleared his throat, and smoothed a hand down the front of his doublet. "I must see to my king now."

Ayden nodded.

"I'll return when I can."

"All right." That worked just fine for Ayden. With the vote pushed forward, he had some things of his own to take care of sooner rather than later. For if somehow Freyrík *did* win, he'd need to bring warning to his people. Which meant escaping—and hopefully taking the whole lot of the elven slaves with him.

He'd explored the grounds briefly already: the castle, the gardens, the forest, the fields, the low barracks, the stately dowager homes— the whole of the Splendor's inner ward. For bound as he was, these soft midland fools thought him no danger. And 'twas true perhaps he wasn't right now, but each day he relearned his body a little more, regained a little more of the equilibrium and skill and instinct of which the starfall had robbed him.

His first day out, he'd left through the front doors—an offense the guards and pages had warily tolerated, though their faces had twisted something fierce—he'd not been surprised when Freyrík asked him that night not to repeat it. Next he'd gone out through the guest kitchens, and then through a dusty passageway and storeroom that held coal for a series of water pumps and furnaces.

Today he once again sought a circuitous route outside, adding detail to the map in his head. Similar to the city wards themselves, the keep was made of three massive concentric squares round an inner tower so tall as to touch the sky. Each curtain was connected to the next by a warren of passageways that cut through inner courtyards ten to twenty paces wide. The courtyards were lush, carried fresh air and sunlight to the hundreds—perhaps thousands—of inner rooms. Many of them he could only study through a window, for they seemed private spaces: herb gardens, sitting gardens, training grounds, play yards for children.

He passed a courtyard between the middle and outer curtain filled with washerwomen, steaming buckets, sheets piled like shifting dunes in the white-sanded deserts of the deep south. A young washer, barely more than a child, caught him staring through the window. Ayden smiled at her, though he couldn't fathom why. Her answering smile was as bright as the bleached cloth in her hands.

Someone scolded her, and she bent back to her work. Ayden moved along. There'd been no clotheslines in the courtyard—not enough sun and wind for drying in the enclosed space—which meant there must be lines nearby, likely right on the other side of the outer curtain. Indeed he found the door but moments later, watched like most servants' entrances by two stiffly vigilant guards. They let him pass without comment into the maze of billowing sheets.

For just a moment as he walked among them, he felt small again and carefree. Could almost hear his sister's giggle and his mother's fond vexation as she tried to herd them in for supper.

Then a wash maid clipped him hard in passing, knocking the smile right off his face.

"Filthy *gróm*," she snapped. "Get outta here. Don't you got duties to be doin'?" She eyed him once, up and down, and added, "Like as not on all fours."

"I mostly do them lying flat, actually," he said with a calm he did not feel, more angry at the fragile memory she'd shattered than at her bigotry. "But only in the mornings and evenings."

He flashed her his most unctuous *Get cracked* grin and walked away before she could reply. When she was out of eyesight, he snagged a sheet from a line and wrapped it snug round his shoulders. He felt the cold these days as he never had before, unable as he was to sing for heat through the starfall.

He shed the sheet some half hour later, out by the north corner of the great wall where it disappeared into some hundred-odd acres of ancient wood. A hard run had seen him overwarm, and he wiped sweat from his face with the sheet's edge before tucking it under one arm. Who knew, perhaps it might come useful in his explorations.

And with two thousand acres at least to explore, he'd need all the help he could get. He'd spent over an hour his first day walking the length and breadth of the great wall.

Fortunately, 'twas full of weakness, older than him and wearing poorly among some of the less-inhabited stretches, especially here through the old forest. Of course, beyond this wall lay three more, each newer than the last, so 'twas not as if his people would be free even if they did slip from the inner ward undetected.

'Twould be foolish to think they could achieve such stealth in any case. If he could convince Freyrík to show him the other wards, he could concoct a safer plan for what lay beyond.

Ayden picked his way through the forest, a task made easy by the smothering canopy of old-growth trees. A bit like the forests of his home, also lacking in underbrush. Even without a red cedar in sight, 'twas enough to ail him with longing.

He passed through mixed stands of oak and maple, poplar and sumac, the occasional dogwood struggling toward the sun. Some minutes later, he broke through to the clearing between the wall and the woods, fifteen paces of grassland meant no doubt to protect the wall from falling trees or skilled climbers.

He made a dash from the tree line to the wall, hoping to avoid the attention of the tower guards some hundred paces distant. He doubted they would question his presence here, but he knew for certain they'd balk at what he was about to do.

The wall had begun to crumble in places, mortar worn loose with time and neglect. Such arrogance, when repairs would have been so simple. All the better for him, though; he worked loose a single stone, then another and another, placing them carefully upon the ground at his feet. The loose mortar he mixed with dirt and smeared across his clothes and skin. (And oh, what glee shivered through him at the thought of Master Laug's horror to come!)

Done playing in the mud, he glanced right and left, to the guards in the distance. They were vigilant, but unlikely to pick him from the color of the earth and the wall in his current state; he was no light-bending scout, but he did not lack for stealth.

He peered through the hole he'd made in the wall. Beyond it lay a narrow ledge, a sheer drop, and far too much wind for such a precarious perch. Heart pounding, he stepped carefully through, easing onto his hands and knees.

He'd never been bothered by heights, but the crumbling ledge and the tearing wind set his stomach to twisting as he looked out over the edge. Some hundred paces below, at the bottom of the cliff, lay the Góz river valley. The water was broad and calm, but of unknown depth. Could he survive it if he jumped? Unlikely with the cracking starfall round his neck, but a down-climb looked possible. For him, anyway. He was not so sure about his sisters and brothers. And if they were spotted? Gods help them all, for soldiers would have all the time in the world to muster at the riverbank.

'Twas with relief that Ayden climbed back through the hole and replaced the heavy stones exactly as he'd found them, plugging the empty spaces between them with the mortar fragments lying in the dirt. He could not remove his footprints entirely, but did his best to disguise them with some sweeps of a fallen branch. A token precaution; he'd seen no signs of men visiting this place.

He wiped dirt from his hands and face as best he could with the sheet, then stuffed it in the hollow of a tree thirty paces due south of the patched hole in the wall. If he collected enough of them, the weaker elves could use them as a climbing aid. In the dead of night, no one might be the wiser 'til morn, by which time they could ride the river several leagues away and begin their overland escape.

Fallen gods pray at least one of his sisters or brothers still possessed the necessary skills to lead this venture. He did not want to go with them, at least not yet. Freyrík might suffer for his absence, a thought he could not abide. But if his sisters and brothers needed him . . . Well, he'd always put the needs of his people over the needs of his heart. This time would be no different.

Freyrík would understand.

Ayden jogged back to the keep as the sun hit full zenith, detouring round the garden sprawled out beneath Freyrík's window. The hunting dogs sniffed him out near the hothouse, and he stopped and squatted to pet the pack leader. It bared its teeth; Ayden withdrew his hand, then averted his eyes when the growling continued. A shiver of fear, anticipation: he didn't want to hurt this animal, knew cracking well he couldn't fight them all. And he couldn't sing them calm. Was this how the humans felt, facing down the Ferals?

"Peace, friend," he murmured, voice soft, hands loose but at the ready as he backed away. The dogs held their ground but made no chase. At last he felt it safe to turn round, and made for the nearest door, trying very hard to ignore the image of slinking away with his tail between his legs—a task made no easier by the guards who halted him at the entranceway.

"You're filthy," one said. A statement of fact, for once blessedly absent passion or cruelty. "Use that door." The guard pointed to a protruding entrance some dozen paces down the curtain.

Ayden nodded and left. No point in arguing. Besides, he'd not found that door yet from the inside, so 'twas one more hall to add to the ever-sprawling map in his head. Too sprawling; he was having trouble remembering it all. Time to raid Freyrík's chest of writing supplies, perhaps.

The hall he traversed was barren of both hiding places and cross-corridors, and bustling with servants besides. Not so useful, then, as a means of escape. He cataloged it anyway, and found his way to the baths with but a single wrong turn.

Master Laug stormed toward him as he walked through the doors, trailing mud in his wake. The human was indeed as comically shocked and angry at Ayden's soiled state as Ayden had imagined he'd be. Less comic was the beating Laug inflicted for it, twenty hard lashes across his back with a rod as thick as his pointer finger. But he took it without argument, reminding himself with every strike of the importance of seeming docile before these fools. He didn't even have to fake the wetness in his eyes, or the urge to behave when it was over.

'Twas quite the struggle, though, to fake his indifference to his fellow elves' pitiless, broken stares.

Before he even managed to unpeel his fingers from round the whipping post, Master Laug grabbed him by the collar and shoved him toward the hot bath. No stairs; the human just pushed him in, grabbed a fistful of his hair, shoved him underwater, and held him there.

Ayden reached for the threat by instinct but then forced himself still, remembering only as his lungs began to burn that he could no longer draw air from the water. He could *drown* now, a fear he'd not felt since sail training in the open sea.

Laug dragged Ayden's head from the water just as his vision began to fade, and then attacked his flesh with a barely damp sponge, scrubbing at the welts on Ayden's back until the water round him swirled with the first hints of pink. The soap stung the shallow wounds like wasps. Ayden clutched the tiled rim of the pool with whitening fingers lest he give in to the urge to punch the man.

Yet cowering wouldn't help his cause. He lifted his gaze from his fingers and turned his eyes to the elf nearest him, who was watching him without sympathy . . . at least none that showed on his face. Then to the next elf, a young female, surely but a child when she was taken, a diplomat's daughter perhaps.

That could have been Ella.

The thought struck him so breathless 'twas as if Laug were holding him underwater again. How often she'd traveled here with their father. How young she'd been when he'd died.

As young as this female sitting naked in the bath before him, watching a human scrub him clean.

The male beside her sat close, protective, one hand resting on her thigh beneath the water. Were they lovers?

Ayden needed to learn these things if ever he hoped to lead them from High Court. *Wanted* to learn these things: their names, their passions, their family histories, their dreams beyond these walls . . . if such things yet survived. He'd never been much good with that, but if *he* thought of his sisters and brothers as individuals, then they too might start to see themselves as such again. And perhaps if he knew *what* to call them, he could determine *how* to call them—how to rally them to their freedom.

Laug finished scrubbing, followed it with another punitive immersion that went on far longer than necessary to rinse him clean. The little man was already walking away when Ayden resurfaced, coughing and spluttering in the steam-choked air. He tasted rose hips and bile in his sinuses. Whirled round at the touch of a hand on his shoulder, heart pounding as it had out on the wrong side of the cliff wall.

"Jagall." It was not his friendliest greeting. He just barely managed not to scold the elder for sneaking up on him when he couldn't hear.

Jagall was smiling that little smile of his, part knowing, part patronizing, wholly infuriating. His hand was still on Ayden's shoulder. "You made some work for the washerwomen today, I see."

"I fell in the woods," Ayden told him, just as he'd told Master Laug.

Jagall nodded. "I too have fallen thus."

The smile did not change, but Ayden found himself fixed upon it of a sudden. Was Jagall saying what Ayden thought he was?

"The others are wary of such accidents," Jagall added. "Perhaps together we might show them that it does not hurt so very much."

Ayden scoffed. "Perhaps you failed to hear my cries just moments past?" Yet he could not help but think of Freyrík's wise words— *"Trust must begin* somewhere*"*—as he spoke his own dismissive ones.

Jagall's smile grew larger, as if he knew precisely which thoughts were passing through Ayden's head. Maybe somehow he did. "Only a few at the end," Jagall said. "A fair price to pay. Besides..." He leaned in close enough to caress, touched his lips to Ayden's ear and whispered, "You cannot be punished if you do not get caught."

Jagall cupped Ayden's face in both hands, nuzzled his jaw, his ear. Ayden sensed no desire from Jagall, nor felt any of his own, despite the grand rush of excitement and hope flooding his heart; Jagall was merely hiding their whispers from prying eyes.

"Walk with me tomorrow," Ayden breathed into Jagall's ear. "Meet me at the butterfly house, one hour after sunrise."

Jagall nodded, so slightly Ayden didn't see it, only felt it against his cheek. A kiss followed, tender but chaste, and Jagall's hands tightened round his head as he jerked back.

He very nearly growled, *I'm not* your *whore, too,* but he understood the need for this, truly he did, and so he closed his eyes and kissed Jagall back, committing to the role they must play to blind the enemy to their treachery. Then he swam away, toward the stairs, letting his fingers linger on Jagall's outstretched arm as long as possible before exiting the bath for the plunge pool.

He felt only the smallest stab of guilt at sharing such intimacy with another. The cause was just. Freyrík would understand.

Chapter Seven

reyrík spent the entire long walk to the Great Hall wrestling a polite smile onto his face. Gods, but he'd grown weary of High Court suppers, and tonight he felt naught but a sick, roiling fear, for the Aegis would be announcing the results of the Council vote at the conclusion of the meal . . . once all the players had been liberally pacified with honeyed wine, of course.

In the Great Hall, Ayden was waiting for him behind the long table of the outland emissaries, eyes narrowed, posture rigid. Tonight's outcome would affect his people just as it would Freyrík's own. In that, as in many things, their fates were linked.

Ayden bowed and pulled Freyrík's chair out. Freyrík nodded back, ever so slightly, and sat, eyes lingering upon the elf. He was wearing an open green vest tonight—the first he'd been allowed to cover himself above the hips since their arrival. None of the other elves were dressed thus. A sign of respect? Unlikely. Which left . . .

Freyrík reached for his wine glass and drained it in one long swallow, fortification and ploy all at once. He slammed it back down on the table and barked, "Elf!"

When Ayden leaned in to pour, Freyrík grabbed his wrist and slung a rough arm round his waist. Ayden winced—beaten by the harem masters, then?—but went willingly enough when Freyrík pulled him into his lap.

"You're hurt," Freyrík mumbled against his jaw.

Ayden leaned in to nuzzle his neck and whispered, "Stop worrying, I'm fine." A sweep of tongue, a nip of teeth at the lobe of his ear, and for a moment Freyrík forgot why he'd pulled Ayden over in the first place.

Dangerous, that. And nor was this the time or place, no matter how many of the other courtiers were thus engaged. Surely Ayden did not mean to sink to his knees and undo Freyrík's breeches in public, but just in case, Freyrík nudged the elf off his lap and shooed him back with the other footmen.

"You're blushing, little brother."

Freyrík's head whipped to his left, where Berendil had sat while Freyrík had been . . . otherwise occupied. His brother was smiling, though it struck Freyrík as strained. Likely not over the elf, though. No, Berendil had much bigger beasts to hunt tonight.

Berendil's gaze drifted toward Ayden, and his smile faded. "I can see why he affects you so, but perhaps now is not the best of times."

Freyrík swallowed his resentment and nodded, though he could not help but add, "The matter is already settled, brother. There is nothing more anyone can do now but wait to hear the outcome."

Berendil held his gaze, a strange dark intensity sparking in those light blue eyes. The look said *This matter will* never *be settled*, even as his lips formed concession: "Indeed."

Their meal progressed in strained quiet. Anticipation had quashed the usual ebullience of manor lords indulging in their wealth and power—for power especially was at stake tonight, and even the masters of diplomacy amongst them could not pretend otherwise. Two seats . . . two seats every two years. Why then did it feel as if all the world hinged upon this year's choice?

Mayhap this year it did. Mayhap this year would see the war ended forever. Which side would reign victorious, well . . . that was a truth only the gods could see.

At least the Aegis did not leave them hanging too long upon their tenters. Four short courses tonight. A great deal of wine and a near absence of casual chatter. A crier calling for silence halfway through the dessert course. The Aegis rising from his chair. The councilmen following suit, four on either side of him, like rivers of power with the Aegis at their confluence.

"My lords," the Aegis said. Though he'd aged some in the years of Freyrík's absence, his stance had lost none of its strength, his voice none of its splendor. 'Twas moments such as these Freyrík felt the gods moving through the man, felt his faith redoubled. No matter the outcome tonight, the empire would soldier on, the Lord Protector as its sword and shield.

The Aegis swept both arms out at the councilmen. "Tonight we give our gratitude to King Taf of Ingimárr and Crown Prince Happ of Prír-Vatn, whose six years of service to the Council end now."

Applause as King Taf and Prince Happ took bows, four hundred fingertips drumming on tabletops. Berendil's nearest hand slid beneath the table and found Freyrík's wrist, clinging tight.

He would have me pinned here. Trapped for six long years.

Freyrík laid his free hand atop his brother's, felt the trembling tension in the flesh beneath his fingers and prayed he'd not need to restrain the man.

The Aegis silenced the applause with a single wave. "Tomorrow we seat the 287th Council of Eight to convene beneath the banner of a united Aegean Empire. And we celebrate those who shall begin their six years of service to the Council on the morrow."

The Aegis paused, long and cruel, his gaze raking the room. "Celebrate with me your newest councilmen, King Heili of Dalr and King Foss of Forn-Nes! May the gods bless them ever strong and wise."

Berendil's hand tightened round Freyrík's wrist far past the point of pain, but at least he made no move from his chair. A fortunate thing, since Freyrík's own relief left him dizzy and weak-kneed, even seated as he was. More applause—of which Freyrík partook only gently, for Berendil's sake—buried the faintest of murmured reactions. 'Twas clear not all present were pleased with the outcome, but none would dare display it. No—Kings Heili and Foss now held the fates of everyone in their hands, and even the clumsiest among the courtiers knew amends must be made, bribes paid, deals brokered, interests secured. Already a smile graced his brother's stiff lips—painful and insincere, but only to those who knew him best.

King Taf and Prince Happ stepped down from the dais, and Kings Heili and Foss took their places. The applause went on. The murmurings ceased. When the Aegis silenced them again to read the accounting of each councilman's vote, the room fell so silent Freyrík could pick out the sound of a throat clearing, the scrape of a chair leg, the soft clink of teeth against a goblet half a table away. Berendil was still squeezing his wrist fit to snap it—in lieu, mayhap, of the dagger at his hip.

The accounting of votes barely filtered through the pain and the cloying silence. Of the eight votes Berendil could have won, he'd garnered only three, two of which he'd secured before Freyrík's arrival. Only one, Prince Skalli, had been swayed by Freyrík's efforts. And no wonder, given Freyrík's own uncertain convictions.

Freyrík made to pull his arm free, but Berendil's grip tightened further, forcing a hiss from Freyrík loud as a thundercrack in the ponderous silence. Gods praised, no one gave any sign of hearing it. Was Berendil seeking his own comfort, or simply Freyrík's suffering?

No matter. Freyrík owed him both.

All around them, men stood and approached the dais to congratulate the new councilmen, some quite genuine, others wishing merely to ingratiate themselves. Freyrík was neither. Nor, he thought, was Berendil. But still he stood, urged his brother to stand as well with a hand upon his elbow. Berendil rose without argument; surely he saw the wisdom in it, or perhaps merely the futility of resisting. 'Twould be the death of all his hopes to cause a scandal here.

Gods praised, he let go of Freyrík's wrist. Hopefully his hand would be too tired to inflict such force upon the new councilmen when they grasped forearms.

The crowd around the dais felt larger than it was—hot, pressing, far too loud. Freyrík wished only to take his elf and leave, find some quiet space to make sense of the evening's turns and plan for the morrow. But he could do no such thing until dismissed, so he trailed behind Berendil, obedient as a bloodhound in the presence of his king. He pasted on a smile as broad and flattering as Berendil's, if perhaps a little less false, grasped forearms and bowed his head before the night's victors. They bowed back in turn, as falsely gracious in their victory as Berendil was in his defeat. Freyrík spoke true with his well-wishes, but 'twas hard to feel happiness in his heart when his beloved king's weighed so very heavy.

Berendil made his excuses shortly after, and Freyrík, still close on his heels, waved Ayden over and made to follow his brother from the hall.

Three paces beyond the towering front doors, Berendil rounded on him so abruptly that Freyrík threw his hands up and braced against a blow. It never came, of course; Berendil had never once struck him outside the practice field. He felt quite foolish as he lowered his arms under his brother's narrowed gaze.

"Go, leave," Berendil ordered. "Do not be seen with me now."

"But brother—"

Freyrík cut himself off, or perhaps 'twas the incredulous twist of Berendil's storm-ravaged features that silenced him. What beneath the shadow had possessed him, to challenge a direct order from his king? And in public, no less?

He dropped his gaze, nodded once, then ducked his head. "Apologies, Your Majesty."

By the time he dared look up, Berendil was gone.

"So what now?"

Freyrík turned to Ayden, who'd made a line straight for the tea table the moment they'd crossed into his drawing room. Already the elf was tearing into an apple, but he seemed to chew without taste or pleasure, merely satisfying hunger. His whole focus was on Freyrík.

That gaze, that expectation, held too great a weight for Freyrík's weary mind to bear; he slumped down on the nearest furniture and scrubbed his hands across his face. "I don't know. Berendil will try to ingratiate himself with the new Council, no doubt, but to many he is seen as an outsider. A barbarian. And now, I fear, an overreaching fool."

"Yet three of eight gave him a vote."

"True, but each man voted thrice; three votes of twenty-four are hardly impressive. King Heili received seven votes. King Foss, six. And one of Berendil's supporters stepped down tonight—two councilmen do not an agenda make."

Ayden said nothing, nibbling his way down to the core of his apple. He looked as if he wished to speak, but didn't.

Freyrík let his head loll against the sofa back, took the glass of he-didn't-know-what that a footman pressed on him. It was warm in his hand. "Does he blame me, do you think?"

Ayden look up from his stripped apple core as if startled. "Why should he? You did your best."

"Did I?"

The elf shrugged. Clearly he was no more convinced than Freyrík. "He seemed so angry . . ."

With a sigh, Ayden set aside the remains of his apple and joined Freyrík on the sofa, leaning in against him. "I may be deaf," he said, "but I am not blind. If 'twere anger and not fear he showed—which I do not think the case—"

"Fear?" Freyrík sat straight, grasped Ayden by the shoulders. 'Twas a gentle grip, but the elf winced. Freyrík frowned, jabbed his chin at the green vest. "What is this? What's happened?"

Ayden shrugged Freyrík's hands from his shoulders. "It's nothing. The slavemaster did not approve of me playing in the mud, is all."

Freyrík slid the vest from Ayden's shoulders. For a moment it seemed Ayden would fight him, but then he nodded once and turned round on his own.

Gods befanged! He'd been beaten black and blue from neck to waist.

"I will have *words* with this slavemaster," Freyrík growled.

Ayden spun back round, his left knee banging into Freyrík's right, and clasped Freyrík's hands. "You will do no such thing. Direct your energies at what matters and do not draw attention to me."

Freyrík snorted—Ayden seemed to have done a fine job drawing attention on his own—but he held his tongue. He'd respect the elf's wishes, even if he himself wished to break the slavemaster's nose.

"For what it's worth, I do not think Berendil angry with you," Ayden said. "I think him afraid for his kingdom, and angry, perhaps, with all the world right now. If it concerns you so, speak with him and see your mind eased. For I need it clear for what I'd ask you next."

Whatever beneath the shadow . . .? Ayden's hands were fists round Freyrík's fingers, his eyes boring into Freyrík's as if straining to hear him through the starfall. Freyrík could think of no reason for such dire focus, nor comprehend what Ayden might ask him. But gods pray, make it simple. *Please, one battle at a time.*

"My mind is clear already," Freyrík lied. "Ask what you will."

The elf hesitated. 'Twas so unlike him not to speak outright that Freyrík's stomach clenched. He had to suppress the urge to flee before Ayden could voice his question.

"You know I've sisters and brothers in bondage here."

Please do not let him take this where I think he will . . . "Yes."

"Fifty-two besides myself, to be precise."

"And?"

"And they have been here some time. Many since the Great Betrayal. Rík, this is no life for them—"

"Stop." Freyrík untangled his hands from Ayden's, put one out between them. "I cannot hear this, do you understand?"

"Freyrík—"

"I said *no!*"

Freyrík was on his feet somehow, halfway across the drawing room. The loss of Ayden's nearness stung, but one look over his shoulder made it clear he'd not be welcomed back. He strode to the hearth on the far wall, put his back to warm slate and folded his arms across his chest.

"*You* brought me here," Ayden said, voice raised to carry cross the room, one finger pointed square at Freyrík's chest.

"And I will bring you home, too, I swear it on my life! But the others are not—*cannot*—be my concern. What would you have me do? Buy them all? Solicit the Council on their behalf? Because you saw how well my efforts worked for Berendil."

Ayden regarded him a long moment, the tension easing from his muscles in the silence. At last he said, "I ask for nothing of that sort."

Freyrík blinked, hesitantly let his arms drop to his sides. "Then what *do* you ask?"

"A mere stroll."

Freyrík frowned. 'Twas like their beginning all over again, Ayden begging to go outside. Except now he was free to roam the yard; why would he need Freyrík?

"A tour of the other wards," Ayden continued. "Surely you would not deny me something so small?"

He thought *that* small? Freyrík raked the hair from his face, fisted his hand at the base of his skull until he felt himself grounded. "No, I cannot make excuses for taking you beyond the gates. Already the Aegis's eyes are upon me."

And again, just like their beginning—Ayden scowling, narrow-eyed and bitter. "I'll make my own excuses, then," he said.

"You do what you must, Ayden; I will not stop you. But ask me nothing and tell me less. Only—" His lips pursed, and he shoved away from the hearth, too hot of a sudden despite the shiver through his spine. "Only kiss me before you go, for it would kill me not to have farewell, even if I do not know it at the time for what it is."

Ayden nodded, eyes fierce and fixed upon Freyrík's face. He looked as sad and somber as Freyrík felt, and angry besides, but he held his tongue.

"You should go," he said at last. "To Berendil, I mean. He needs you now, no matter what he said."

In other words: *I do* not *need you.* Or perhaps, *I need you badly, but you've failed me.* Or maybe just, *I cannot stand to look at you right now.*

With a heavy sigh, Freyrík turned on his heel and left.

Strange to feel as if he were skulking round his childhood second home and Lord Protector's castle, but that's precisely what Freyrík was doing. Why he felt such caution necessary to begin with, he knew not—visiting one's brother was hardly a crime. Only his own subterfuge made the act suspect.

The castle had grown since he'd mastered its back passages and secret chambers in his academy years on stolen forays for wine or food or company. This foray was hardly alike, but still he remembered enough to wend his way toward Berendil's apartment without passing a soul.

Freyrík eased out from a narrow corridor behind a massive old tapestry that smelled of dust and cedar. The hall outside Berendil's apartments was empty, not even pages flanking the drawing room doors. Most likely Berendil had dismissed his staff to nurse his defeat in privacy.

Freyrík raised his hand to knock.

And stopped, a hairsbreadth from the thick polished wood.

Do not be seen with me now, Berendil had said. Strange words, spoken with such force and conviction that Freyrík could not help but fear them. He would not be welcome here.

Yet Ayden thought *Berendil* afraid, and Freyrík had long learned to respect the elf's instincts. He could not desert his own brother.

He took a deep breath and braced himself, pressing his palms to the double doors. *You'll refuse me permission, brother, but I hope you will not deny me forgiveness. Add trespass to my list of transgressions if you must.*

He threw the doors open wide, striding in with all the bearing and confidence Berendil had taught him.

"Forgive me, brother, I have come to—"

He ducked to the ground before his conscious mind had even made sense of the blade coming at him, drawing his own weapon as he slid between his captor's legs, twisting to aim the dagger for the man's groin.

"*Stop it*! Both of you."

The command stayed his hand before the rest of him caught up. An order heard and obeyed, without question or pause, times beyond counting in his youth. Berendil.

"It's all right," his brother said from across the room. "He may stay."

Freyrík sheathed his dagger, barely registering the myriad men in the room before an open hand entered his field of vision. He looked up at its owner and realized, with some horror, that he'd nearly emasculated the Midr ambassador. He gripped the man's hand and let him pull him to his feet.

"Apologies," said Lord Trúr. "I was ordered to guard the door."

"A task perhaps less risky from the hall," Freyrík said, but he was grinning, giddy with the aftermath of battle too short and poorly consummated. He clasped forearms with the ambassador, then turned to take in the rest of the scene.

And a scene it was indeed. Seven men not counting himself or Berendil, powerful all: ambassadors, royalty, secretaries to kings. Three were from Midr and Kali, but four came from midland and far-east realms. All mingled as if equals, tense and staring from their perches on sofas and chairs. Yet most surprising was the man sitting by the hearth, Berendil standing beside him with a forearm draped across the back of his chair: Prince Máni, heir presumptive to the throne of Aegea itself. Freyrík couldn't fathom what these men might share in common at all, let alone what had driven them to discard rank and custom or what secret they felt the need to protect with steel.

"Brother?" he asked, slow and cautious, unable to quash the note of reproach in his tone. "What is this?"

Seven sets of eyes turned toward Berendil, the reaction so synchronous Freyrík swore it made a sound: soft and wet and wondering. As for Berendil's gaze, it landed square upon Freyrík, and remained there with the weight of a smothering hand . . . until at length something seemed to *give* in the man, some critical seam split in two.

And from it spilled the batting that gave this gathering shape:

"A meeting of like minds, of men who grow weary of burying their sons."

Silence then. Another smothering gaze. Every man in the room was at the ready. For what, Freyrík knew not, but he could *smell* the danger. And he wondered, of a sudden, if he might die here tonight.

Berendil's words churned like water over rocks in his mind. The river forked—one path smooth, the other fraught with danger. He yearned for the safer path. Tested it: "You still plot favor with the Council?"

Nobody moved, yet the tension redoubled. Fingers tightened round knife hilts. Freyrík forced his own to stay loose by his sides.

"We plot," Berendil said. Nodding slightly, brows raised. His eyes darted to Prince Máni and back again.

Freyrík's throat tightened. The floor swayed, deep currents tugging at his feet, but he would not let it trip him down. "You would kill him," he said. Flat, hard, not a question.

Berendil grimaced, but nodded. "If we must."

Freyrík took a single step forward, toward Prince Máni, before Lord Trúr halted him with the tip of his blade. Freyrík froze, breathless. "Your own father?" he said to the prince. "You would see him dead?"

No regret at Freyrík's words, no love, no weakness upon Prince Máni's face. A master soldier, a master diplomat. Whatever he felt, Freyrík would never know it.

"He leads us into ruin," the prince said. "He is old, overcautious, even addled perhaps. I would he step down for the good of the Empire."

Freyrík's lips twitched into a snarl, but the warning press of Lord Trúr's blade at his sternum saw him quickly tamed. "And you would help him do so, if he falters."

Infuriating, how calm the prince remained. He leaned back in his chair, crossed one leg over the other. "I will do what I must for the Empire. As will we all." A pause, a glance to the men on the couches, to Berendil still standing at his side, back to Freyrík. "And what of you, Prince Freyrík? What will *you* do?"

"He is my brother," Berendil answered quickly. "He will stand with me."

Freyrík smiled even as the others shook their heads. 'Twas not as simple as that, and they all knew it. Otherwise Berendil would not have excluded him from this meeting.

King Villtr, as old and fat and sun-worn as all the nobles of the far-east coastal provinces, lumbered up from the sofa. "Berendil . . . We've come too far to let—"

"I know." Berendil's features were as granite, unyielding and grim. Nowhere in those blue eyes, that red-blond hair, that thrice-broken nose, did Freyrík see the love of a brother. Only the heavy resolve of a king.

Freyrík licked his lips, shifted warily against Trúr's blade still pressed to his chest. "You would kill me as well, then?"

"I would have protected you from this!" Berendil slammed his fist against the top of Máni's chair with enough force to shatter the prince's smug calm. "You with your gods-befanged intellect! Your righteousness! Your curiosity! What am I to do with you now, brother?"

Freyrík ever so slowly tossed his hands, half *I'll not draw blade* and half *I don't know.*

Berendil growled, frustrated or disgusted or maybe both. "You would not claim complicity even to save your own neck, would you."

"No. Nor would you believe me if I did."

"I suppose not." At last Berendil stepped out from the shadow of Prince Máni, drawing near to Freyrík. He seemed fragile without the chair to lean upon. "But would it *be* a lie? You know the merits of our plan, you know it must be done. The Aegis leaves us no other option. Surely you can see it."

Freyrík closed his eyes against the hope on his brother's face, opened them again when the bite of steel against his ribs grew too insistent. "Truly? I do not know. I would hear more in the face of such a choice."

"You can't tell him—"

"Silence, Villtr."

Such calm authority from Berendil, such confidence. The king he'd just hushed obeyed him as if he were the Aegis himself. Freyrík looked at his brother with new eyes, thoughts awhirl. Perhaps Berendil could lead these men to victory in High Court and the darker forests. Perhaps 'twas right to do so. Perhaps, perhaps . . .

Berendil sighed long and deep. "Leave us, brother. Return to your chambers for now."

"But, Your Majesty—" King Villtr began, even as the others joined in, as the tip of Lord Trúr's blade bit hard in warning.

"He will not betray us tonight," Berendil said. "Nor could we explain away his death or disappearance. At least not yet." He plucked a goblet from a side table near Prince Máni's chair, took a calculated sip. His calm might fool the others, but Freyrík knew better. "Go," he said over the rim of his goblet. "You and I shall talk alone on the morrow."

Lord Trúr lowered his sword reluctantly, and Freyrík stepped back at last. He bowed, both out of habit and because he could think of nothing to say, and retreated for the doors.

"Rík," his brother called after him, and when he paused, said, "use this night to steel yourself for what must be done."

Freyrík ducked his head and bowed again, this time to hide his expression. As if he could idle away this night, when come this time tomorrow, he'd be either a traitor or dead.

Just as Ayden was truly starting to worry over Freyrík's midnight vanishing, the man trudged into the drawing room, looking pale as a grub in a rotting tree and not a whit fitter. He'd also brought company—*such a foppish guest at* this *hour?*—and looked none the more pleased by it than Ayden was to have their sanctuary invaded.

Ayden stood from the rug before the fire, held his half of a silent conversation with Freyrík—*Who is this man? Where did you go? Are you well?*—and turned toward the bedroom.

"I will join you in a moment if you'll have me," Freyrík said.

Ayden tried on a smile, found it tight but suitable to his purpose nevertheless. "I am not so angry with you as to cast you from our bed."

He'd hoped to bring a smile to Freyrík's face, but alas, the man remained somber. Worse, the fop beside him cast a look that clearly said, *What manner of prince are you to permit such liberties from a* slave?

Freyrík ignored him and shuffled toward the bedroom, looping an arm through Ayden's as he drew abreast.

"Your Highness," the fop called as they stepped into the bedroom and turned to close the door.

Freyrík froze, hand on the knob, and eyed the man sourly. "What," he demanded.

The fop shifted his weight from one foot to the other and back again. "I just— Rather, don't you think it wise to sleep with your door open this night?"

Freyrík slid his arm round Ayden's waist and pulled him tight to his side. "Why, my lord? Are you so desperate for entertainment? No elf of your own?"

Even from across the long drawing room and in the dimness of the firelight, Ayden could see the fop blush. 'Twas so satisfying, he was happy to dismiss Freyrík's coarseness in its service.

Freyrík slammed the door.

Out Lord Vitr came from his little groom's chamber, candle in hand. He looked still half-asleep, but he approached at Freyrík's nod and began to undress the man with all his usual skill and haste. Freyrík stood silent, not meeting Ayden's eye as he moved this way and that under Vitr's guidance.

"Who is that man?"

Freyrík sighed and said merely, "A friend."

Ayden snorted. *And I'm the First Minister of the Elven Republic.* A change of tack, then.

"Listen, I'm sorry. I should not have asked you to compromise one loyalty for another." And under his breath, because he could not help it, "Even if the one loyalty is so clearly in the wrong."

Freyrík grunted, vaguely affirmative. Mostly distracted. Lord Vitr had to tap his calf three times before he thought to lift his foot from the hose pooled at his ankles.

Ayden sighed, put aside his agenda for the moment. "Please, Freyrík. Tell me what's happened?"

This, at last, caught Freyrík's attention. "I went," he said quietly, glancing back at the closed doors, "to visit my brother."

Ayden raised an eyebrow at the dramatic delivery, but Freyrík merely crawled into bed, propped his back against a stack of pillows, and closed his eyes.

Ayden crawled into bed beside him, mirrored his posture against the headboard. " . . . And?"

Freyrík slid under the covers, settled back against the pillows again. He'd moved closer in the process; he wasn't touching Ayden, but nor was he all the way to one side of the big bed. "Ask me, Ayden. Ask me again what I found."

Ayden rolled his eyes but obliged him. "What did you find?"

A moment's silence, crack the man. Then, "A nest of connivers, out for the Aegis's crown."

Instant wariness. Ayden slipped his fingers round the dagger under his pillow and threw open his senses, straining eyes and ears for lurking danger.

"Be at ease," Freyrík said. "I am safe for the moment."

"You've thrown in with them, then?"

Freyrík shook his head and recounted the evening's events, the politics leading up to it, the pros and cons of the coup, the information yet missing that he hoped to learn on the morrow. He spoke as if a spectator: dispassionate, undecided. Ayden cursed his own deafness, but he suspected Freyrík's song would make little sense even with his mind-ear open: 'twould be two opposite melodies, clashing and disharmonious.

"So you see," Freyrík said, draping one arm over his eyes, "No matter how I choose, someone I love will die."

You might die, too.

Before Ayden could voice that fear, Freyrík barked a strangled laugh. "Listen to me. I'm wallowing. Of what consequence are the people I love when 'tis the fate of all mankind I must consider?"

Not all *mankind,* Ayden almost said, but surely Freyrík wasn't interested in peoples so far across the ocean their very seasons were reversed. "Such a burden," he said instead, and was surprised to mean it, especially since Freyrík had just called him inconsequential. If he could even count himself in that statement.

But of course I can. Freyrík loves me as much as Berendil or the Aegis. And he'll throw us all—himself included—to the Ferals if it will save his people.

There was no anger in this thought. How could there be, when he would no sooner let his love for Freyrík—no matter how precious or hard-won—stand in the way of duty to his own sisters and brothers?

But which path would serve that duty better? The chaos of a coup would form a perfect screen for Ayden's escape plans, but afterward . . . Afterward, Berendil's new puppet Aegis would send their armies in search of the mythical dark elves, and the whole of the Elven Republic would be at risk. The humans would invade, and the banked flame of war would reignite. The cost would be terrible. Unthinkable. Not just for his own people, but for Freyrík's as well—it took but one skilled cloudsinger to kill a hundred men with a whirlwind.

'Twould be irony most unpleasant if none remained standing in the aftermath but the cracking Ferals.

But if Freyrík warned the Aegis and stopped the coup . . . The executions sure to follow would provide ample distraction for escape. And 'twould ensure no invasion into Feral lands. No witch hunt, no war.

"Ayden?"

"Hmm?" He turned his head to find Freyrík blinking at him, brows furrowed, eyes shimmering with more than just the candlelight. Such desperate need—what could he possibly tell him? He sighed, found Freyrík's hand beneath the covers and touched pinky finger to pinky finger. "You would have my counsel?"

Freyrík bit his lip, inched his hand a fraction closer to Ayden's, yet he said nothing. No matter; 'twas clear as water he wished to be absolved. To have his choice made for him.

Ayden nodded. He could give Freyrík that much.

"I think—"

His next words froze upon his tongue. For he'd *not* thought. Freyrík was being watched—that fop in the drawing room was as sure a sign as any of that—and would likely be killed if he reported to the Aegis. 'Twas doubtful he could name all the players in the coup, and those who remained would seek revenge. His best chance to live was to join the conspirators, not betray them.

"I think—" he said again, and again could make it no further. The air seemed thick of a sudden, scalding and dead. So much death, no matter what path they chose. "I think you should join your brother."

"I thought—"

"But only in words," Ayden pressed on. If he held his tongue now to let Freyrík speak, he might never find the strength to free it again. "Buy his confidence. Then, as soon as you can, go to your Aegis."

His words lay in the small space between them, heavy and mysterious as an echo. Freyrík's pinky twitched against his own.

"You still think his plan doomed to failure."

"Yes." Ayden seized Freyrík's hand, turned onto his side and touched his free hand to Freyrík's cheek. "Freyrík, you must believe me. There are no dark elves."

Freyrík curled as if that pained him, turning away from Ayden, withdrawing from his touch. "I am sworn to serve my king!"

You're sworn to serve your Aegis first, Ayden thought of saying, but could not bring himself to push so. Then again, no need—

"But I am sworn to serve my people above all." Freyrík sighed and rolled onto his back again. Their knees touched. "Would that I knew how."

"You know how."

Freyrík said nothing, only turned away again. For a moment Ayden thought him furious—and rightfully so, perhaps—but he'd only moved to blow out his candle. When the room fell dark, Ayden felt the press of him against his side, knee and hip and shoulder. 'Twas a feat of control fit for the gods to stop himself from rolling into the man, clinging on with arms and legs and cracking *teeth*, but he'd no right to that anymore.

Not after what he'd just done.

A sigh from beside him, dark and wet and heavy as the ocean's cold depths. "He's my brother, Ayden."

And you're my lover. "I know."

Nothing else to say for it. Ayden reached beneath his pillow, wrapped fingers round the dagger he kept there, and resolved to keep watch against the night, against the fop in the drawing room and all the dangers he might bring to the man he loved.

Easier that than keeping watch against the night terrors sure to come—of Ella and Mother and all the elves he loved, trampled to blood and dust by Berendil's invading force.

His eyes stung, and he wiped at them as quietly as he could, fingertips coming away moist. One death, or thousands? The choice was easy.

No. 'Twas *clear.* But not easy, never that.

Not when he'd already forgotten how to live without the man beside him. Or if he'd even want to, once Freyrík was gone.

Ayden had barely pulled himself from bed the next morning when Berendil paid visit to their rooms, dismissing the guards and servants as Freyrík had the night before and sending Ayden along with them. Freyrík didn't argue to keep him, but that bothered Ayden little; he understood the need for appearances.

Besides, that cracking fop had been banished to the hallway as well, and Ayden damn well planned to keep an eye on him.

And a blade, if I have my way.

Ayden loitered in the hall with the fop and the servants, waiting to be useful again.

Or, fallen gods forbid, waiting to be needed—to intercede should Berendil do Freyrík harm.

In the end, the wait was short and uneventful. Berendil opened the drawing room doors and strode through the little throng of servants as if he owned them all. What Ayden wouldn't have given then to hear his song, for he could read little on the strangely familiar face, and likely none of it true in any case. The face of a politician, all bland smiles and false confidence.

The smile remained firmly in place, even as he pulled the fop to the far side of the corridor and whispered in his ear.

Ayden watched them as long as he was able, but when Berendil looked up at him with raised eyebrows—the sort of *Well? Go, shoo!* look one might reserve for a child or an overaffectionate dog—he followed the servants back inside Freyrík's rooms.

Freyrík awaited him in the drawing room, whole and unharmed, looking neither relieved nor shaken. He laid a hand on Ayden's shoulder and walked him into the bedroom, closing the doors behind them. They were alone; even Lord Vitr remained in the drawing room.

"Well?" Ayden asked, trying nobly not to sound quite so worried as he felt. "You are safe?"

"For now."

"He believed you?"

"He wanted to. I am his blood, after all. And I have never given him cause to doubt before." Freyrík's gaze slid uneasily away from Ayden's, then back again. "That there is cause now, his heart overlooks. He knows it is foolish, knows I have doubts. He even told me so. But still he's put his life in my hands." Freyrík did not look away again, though Ayden almost wished he had. He was blinking too much, his eyes shining too bright. When he bit his lip, Ayden caught himself leaning in to kiss the mark away. "I would care for it, if I can."

Ayden shook his head. He could certainly understand Freyrík's desire, but couldn't afford to indulge it. "But you cannot."

Freyrík shrugged.

Ayden took him by the shoulders and gave him a single hard shake. "When, Freyrík? When will you tell the Aegis?"

The man just stood there, brows drawn and lips parted, and let Ayden shake him again.

"I don't know," he said at last. "You have seen for yourself, I am being watched."

I have seen for myself you are being washy, as well. What a convenient excuse not to choose, that fop in the drawing room.

At last Freyrík plucked Ayden's hands from his shoulders, held them in his own. The hardness of . . . well, perhaps not surety, but resolve, at least, was back in his eyes. "Three days, a week—no more. Many of the Aegis's supporters return to their castles this next week, now that the year's politicking is done. The Aegis must know before they leave that he may keep them here; the more who remain as obstacles, the smaller the likelihood of Berendil's success."

"So you do not know for certain?"

Freyrík shook his head, but then froze, eyes narrowed, and asked, "Why is it so important you know?"

Crack the man's sharpness anyway. "These will be dangerous days for us all. I merely wish to know how long I need remain vigilant, and when to expect the earth to shift beneath our feet."

Not a lie, but neither the whole truth, and gods but he hated to keep things from Freyrík. Still, 'twas at the man's own behest—nay, insistence.

"I will tell you as I know it," Freyrík said, then clasped him on the shoulder and said, "Come, let us eat. I'm afraid all this scheming builds quite the appetite."

Ayden joined him, but downed the sparse meal quickly and without talk. After all, he had some scheming of his own yet to do this morn.

Jagall was waiting for him on a marble bench inside the glass-walled butterfly house, a riot of warmth and color among the dormant landscape of early winter. Ayden slipped inside, but only long enough to say, "Walk with me." He did not wish to be comfortable here, even for a moment.

Jagall followed him into the cold, pulled him into an embrace and then pulled back for a kiss. Ayden accepted readily enough, for all he disliked the ploy. He doubted they had audience for their little performance, but 'twas not the time for unnecessary risks when so many unavoidable ones hung over his head.

They strolled across the grounds, hand in hand like lovers, wending toward and then through the woods that would take them to the damaged wall. There they removed the loose stone and stepped through to the other side. Ayden pressed back flat against the wall, away from the sheer face, but Jagall started climbing down with all the surety and nimbleness of a mountain goat. He stopped some half-dozen paces down the cliff face and then climbed back up again, panting and scraped but grinning hard. Together they made short work of replacing the stones and erasing their tracks, and Ayden led him to the tree where he'd hidden the sheet.

"For the weaker among us," he said. "I'll bring more. Maybe some rope if I can find excuse."

"And what of the guards? All the rope in the Empire won't save us if armed men await us at the riverbank."

"I will have distraction. You must trust me on this."

"What sort of distraction?"

"The effective sort. As I said, you must—"

"Trust you, yes. Even though," Jagall added, eying him shrewdly, "you clearly do not trust me."

Ayden touched fingertips to his collar. *Can you blame me?*

Jagall propped his back against a tree and slid down to sit in the duff, dusting off his palms. 'Twas as clear a sign as any that he planned to remain there until his questions were answered. But this secret was not Ayden's to share. Brother or no, he would not put Freyrík's life in Jagall's hands.

He sat down beside Jagall, legs crossed, and picked up a fallen leaf. Sugar maple, bright red. If Freyrík were here, he'd know all the right words to rally Jagall, to pacify and assure him.

But Ayden was no diplomat, no speechmaker. The only words in his arsenal were honesty. "Forgive me, brother, but I do not know you."

A hand on his shoulder, kind, firm. Words to match: "And yet you've told me enough already to cost you your life."

"It is mine to spend."

"Ah." Jagall leaned forward, and Ayden had to turn away to avoid his stare. He did not trust his face to keep secrets from this elf with human guile. "You protect someone."

"This distraction"—Ayden swallowed, tore a thin strip from the leaf and balled it between his fingers—"will come sometime this week. 'Twill be quite the spectacle. All the court will speak of nothing else. Think and do nothing else. We will be forgotten. Be ready."

He traded the leaf for a stick, cleared a swath of duff down to the soil beneath and sketched a rude outline of the inner ward. "There are many exits from the keep. 'Tis likely we'll have limited time to sneak away before the walls are shut up tight. We must use all that time, and many doors, to avoid undue suspicion. We can meet up at forest's edge and proceed from there. By then all eyes will be inward; no one will see us."

"We cannot leave under cover of darkness, you know. Most of us will be . . . otherwise engaged."

"I know." 'Twas the part of the plan that worried him the most, but he could see no remedy for it. "But we can outwait the daylight in the forest. Climb the trees. Even if they realize we're gone, they may not search for us. And even if they do, they will not look up. Humans never do."

"What of the dogs?"

Ayden shrugged. "They find us or they don't. We can set traps while we wait—bury wooden stakes and snares—but if their handlers know how to hunt more than game, our plan may fail." It might well fail anyway, and not just for the dogs; Ayden gave half odds at best that the humans would ignore his people in the turmoil of the upended coup rather than blame them for it and hunt them down. "But tell me, are we all free to walk the grounds when our masters do not require us?"

Jagall nodded. "As far as I know, though some of us live in locked stone rooms, never left to wander. Healers and metalworkers and the like, freed of starfall that the humans might harness their song."

Ayden grimaced. Poor souls, locked away forever from the sunlight, the fresh air. He'd borne it but weeks in Freyrík's court; three hundred years of it would surely drive him mad.

"Do you know where they are kept?"

"Nay, child. I know you wish to save us all, but it simply may not be possible. They would understand. You are a soldier; I know you understand too."

"I do not like the thought of leaving any of us behind."

"You do not have to like it. Only accept it. Unless you have a better idea?"

Ayden shook his head. Jagall clapped him on the shoulder again, then took the stick from his hand and began to draw Xs on his map. "I know where most of us stay. Let me spread the word; they trust me. We can leave in ones and twos from these doors without arousing suspicion."

"You are certain?"

Jagall rose to his feet. Ayden followed, carefully brushing leaves from the seat of his pants; his back still throbbed from yesterday's beating and he'd no intention of courting a second one.

"Yes," Jagall said. "I am certain."

Ayden cared not for the old elf's long delay in reply, but there was nothing to be done for it now. In the end, he would simply have to take this, like so many other things, on faith. And for an elf like him, that was perhaps the biggest challenge of all.

Chapter Eight

They parted ways at the butterfly house, exchanging heated embraces for prying eyes. 'Twas too early for the baths, so Ayden set to hunt for supplies to lay by. They would need dry clothes for their escape, food, weapons, tools. Until the collars came off, everything would be hard: hunting, staying warm, keeping watch. He'd not even lit a fire without song in almost six hundred years.

He wandered round the keep toward where the sheets were hung, but the drying lines were too busy for much pilferage. He managed only one sheet, which he folded down small and wrapped round his waist beneath his shirt, before a woman brandishing a large wet washing bat chased him away.

The stolen sheet was damp against his skin, and the winter wind leached all warmth from his body with hungry fingers. He circled the keep toward the north face, where the other sheet was stashed, setting a brisk pace against the cold.

Shouts and grunts and the clang of wood and steel informed him long before his eyes did that he'd soon reach the training grounds of the Royal Academy students. Here Freyrík had grown into the fierce warrior he now was; two of his sons were now doing the same, if Ayden recalled correctly. He slowed to a halt by the stone wall of the keep, wrapped arms round himself to keep from shivering too hard, and surveyed the scene with his own warrior's eye.

Some hundred-odd half-grown humans were playing soldier in the yard, minded by seven—no, eight—clearly skilled officers. Few looked up from their training to pay him any notice, even though he'd spent long moments tallying them up. Those who did dismissed him with a glance. Ayden snorted. Would that all human guards were so unobservant; escape would be easy then.

He watched a while longer, leaning his shoulder against the wall with a carefully casual air. Most cadets were training with wooden weapons, but a few worked with live steel. Pity that they were good enough not to kill or maim each other. But they were not good enough to hold their own against him for more than a few seconds, even with his song restrained.

'Twas not their fighting skills that kept him here in any case, but rather the chance of laying hands on proper weapons. The cadets would have to rest eventually. If their habits were as sloppy as their skills, perhaps he could filch a sword or two. He would even settle for the wooden blades.

Alas, when the teachers called for a meal break, the whelps revealed unexpected discipline. Wooden weapons were racked, live steel locked away. All this in under two minutes, students scrambling from their tasks and into neat lines, standing tall for inspection before being dismissed.

He took that as his cue as well. No point lingering here when their weapons were clearly out of reach; best to hide away his sheet and return to the keep before he froze to death.

Not ten paces from the wall, he heard footsteps and laughter behind him, drawing near. A quick glance round revealed four older boys, staring at him and jostling each other in that rough and tumble manner of pubescent males planning trouble. Crack them, he had no time for whatever foolishness they intended. But nor could he continue on as planned with them following him.

He ducked through the nearest door into the keep—some empty corridor he'd not yet explored—and set out in search of familiar halls. Behind him, the door opened and closed again. Heavy footsteps and chatter and laughter set the space between his shoulder blades to itching. He walked faster. Those cadets seemed young and foolish enough to ignore his status as a prince's attendant—oh, who was he fooling, a bed slave—and the last thing he needed was another encounter with Laug's hickory rod over self-defense they'd no doubt call assault.

He heard voices in the distance ahead, and lengthened his stride for the vague promise of safety in more populated hallways. Still the boys closed in behind him. He would not run—fleeing from predators only incited their killer instinct—but even at his brisk pace, they would catch up to him in a moment. Clearly they meant to have their altercation.

Fine. He would give it to them.

"What?" he asked, cold and flat, whirling on his heel to face them.

The one in the lead reared back, stumbling into the boys behind him. 'Twas almost comical, the surprise on their faces. Not so comical the way they straightened up an instant later, sneering contempt. Ayden tensed as the four of them fanned out, closing in beside and behind him in a well-practiced flanking move.

He clenched his fists but allowed it.

"You're quite ill-mannered for a slave," said their leader, who'd clearly riled dangerous prey before: the scar across his cheek seemed the handiwork of an angered falcon.

"And you for a cadet of noble blood," Ayden returned.

The boy to his left chuckled, but fell silent under Cheekscar's glare.

Cheekscar unsheathed his dagger with a long slow hiss of steel on leather. "Impudent *gróm* . . . You need a lesson in respect."

Ayden huffed, gestured toward the knife. "And you in close armed combat. You watch my hands but forget my feet, and your own are spaced too close for balance should I choose to sweep them out from under you."

He cursed his unruly tongue a heartbeat later. Even deafened, he could feel their easy confidence subsumed by outrage. Knives appeared in all their hands. He braced himself, cold and dispassionate. They were young, arrogant, overconfident—no doubt their bladework was unimpressive.

At least he hoped it would be. Freyrík would be displeased if he was forced to kill them.

He put his hands out with a sigh—a submissive gesture that would also buy him half a second's advantage should he need it—and forced himself to say, "Apologies, my lord, I meant no disrespect. But my master expects me, you see, and I daren't keep him waiting."

"And yet you wasted half an hour watching us train," Cheekscar returned. He deliberately sheathed his dagger, his lips stretching into an unpleasant smile. "Are we so captivating to you, *gróm*? Is your master so old and ugly that you seek reprieve in the vision of fit young men at work?"

Ha, big words from a boy who held none of Rík's allure, even if he'd not lost a fight with his own falcon. And of course, *of course* his thoughts would swing this way, for when did humans ever not?

The ghost of a touch shivered over his throat, his lips, his ear, and for one breathless heartbeat, Kona's perfume clogged his nose.

He forced the thought from his head, the sense memory from his flesh. He'd survived that wily harpy; these boys were nothing.

"I assure you, my lord, I had no thought but of fresh air and exercise this morn. Now if you'll excuse me . . ."

By some silent signal, the boys tightened ranks, though they'd thankfully all sheathed their daggers. They crowded him, close enough to touch; Cheekscar actually took the liberty, laying a splayed hand upon Ayden's chest.

Again Ayden allowed it . . . for now.

"You must be new here, *gróm*, to think that a slave might dismiss a lord and not the other way round. You are *not* excused. Surely your master won't begrudge us a short delay." The boy's hand slid down Ayden's belly, then dipped beneath the waist of his breeches.

Ayden knocked his hand away and said through gritted teeth, "No one touches me but the prince."

Cheekscar smiled that sly smile again and put his hand back on Ayden's belly. "I'm a prince."

"Me too," said the boy on Ayden's left.

"And me."

"And me as well."

And then the four set upon him.

What happened next passed without conscious thought. One moment, eight hands were ripping at his clothes; the next, four boys were lying bruised and moaning at his feet. One boy was sobbing and clutching at his face, blood from his broken nose spilling through his fingers and down the back of his hand. Cheekscar was curled round an arm bent visibly out of shape. The other two were out cold.

Ayden could smell their blood, taste their fear on the back of his tongue, that same metallic tang that set his senses to sharpening, his limbs to tensing. He felt no pain, dismissed it for a moment as battle high. But as his breathing calmed and the sounds and scents and colors of the world faded back to normal, he realized 'twas because he'd escaped injury altogether. Simply remarkable, and gods but what relief to see proof his deafness was not so crippling as he'd feared.

"Idiots," he muttered, shaking out his stinging hands. He stepped over sprawled limbs and bodies, peeked round the corner of the hallway. The adjoining corridor was blessedly empty; he slipped into it and hurried away. No doubt one of the princelings would soon collect enough wits to cry for guards. He had no intention of being anywhere near this mess when that happened.

By the time he reached Freyrík's rooms, the full import of his actions had begun to sink in. He'd struck down four human boys— soldiers—princes. Their humiliation might drive them to secrecy, but what excuses could they make for their injuries?

Never mind *they* had sought him out. Never mind he'd merely been defending himself.

In the eyes of this tone-deaf court, he was doomed.

Freyrík's quarters were empty, even of Lord Vitr—a surprising discovery he both relished and regretted. He was not ready to face Freyrík's anger . . . Yet at the same time, some part of him wanted the comfort of Freyrík's arms. The illusory protection of his presence, though he doubted Freyrík could save him now.

Perhaps he should have let those princelings have their way. He was no stranger to pain *or* humiliation; he could have endured it. At least then he would not have compromised his plans so.

He stalked over to the settee and kicked it hard enough to knock it over.

Then, temper appeased, he regathered his wits. Best to make what strides he could while he was still able. He unwound the pilfered sheet, all but forgotten, from round his waist, and hung it out to dry over a chair in a little-used corner of the bedroom. Back to the drawing room for the ever-present fruit bowl, whose contents he hid beneath the sheet. After a moment's consideration, he took the bowl as well. 'Twas solid gold, which the humans so valued; perhaps they could barter it on their long journey home.

He rummaged next through drawers and trunks, finding two woolen winter jerkins and matching fur-trimmed cloaks stored in a cedar chest. Two extra pairs of boots as well, fallen gods thanked, for not all of his brethren appeared to own shoes. Stealing from Rík did not sit well with him, but he'd never seen the man wear any of these things, and Rík owned more than enough. Besides, the cause was just.

Ayden gathered all the items into a cast-off satchel and hid it in an empty trunk. If he could still walk tomorrow, he'd take it to the hollow tree by the northern wall. And if he couldn't . . . Well, he'd pass the supplies to Jagall somehow. The old elf would carry on in his place.

Now if only he could find a weapon or six . . .

There was of course the dagger at his bedside, but it belonged to Rík, and Rík would notice. He'd mind, too, for he'd know why Ayden had taken it and what target it might find. So Ayden turned back to the drawers and trunks, shelves and dresser tops. He found a hand-sized eating knife in the drawing room, on a leftover tea tray; an old silver hairpin behind a corner trunk, nearly the length of his hand and sharp enough to pierce flesh with but small force; a hardened oak cane with a heavy silver knob in the shape of a hawk's head; a finger-sized blade on Freyrík's desk for the slitting of envelopes and wax seals. He worked quickly and silently, stowing each tool as he found it, knowing the palace guards might barge in at any moment.

He almost wished they would hurry up and arrive, just to have it done with.

But Freyrík came instead. The banging doors gave Ayden just enough notice to cease his hunt for weapons and try for a penitent look, or perhaps a pathetic one—anything to engender sympathy in place of hostility.

No such luck.

"What happened to not drawing attention to yourself?" Freyrík demanded as he strode into the bedroom.

His anger came as no surprise, but it stung more than Ayden had expected. He backed away until his calves bumped into the chest at the foot of the bed. "That's not fair, Rík. All I did was defend myself."

Freyrík pinched the bridge of his nose, left his head bowed upon his hand for a long moment. The muscles in his jaw were twitching. "You had to hurt them so?"

"They pulled blades on me! Four against one. What would you have me do? Let them cut me?"

The hand at Freyrík's nose moved to scrub his face. "And I suppose you'll tell me you did nothing to provoke them."

"Gods cracked, Freyrík, they would have *raped* me!" He surged forward so suddenly Freyrík flinched and tripped away. "And no, I did not incite or invite their attentions. It is *your* people who paint me like a harlot and parade me round half-naked, *your* people who find it amusing to use my brethren like toys, *your* people who teach their children such high art of disrespect that boys think raping in packs a pleasant pastime!"

Strange, how exhausted that little tirade left him. He slumped down on the nearest thing to hand, the cedar chest at the foot of their bed. Freyrík's bed. The one all the court—his own sisters and brothers included—thought Ayden lived only to warm.

From the corner of his eye he watched Freyrík watch him, by all appearances struck speechless, though Ayden had no idea why. The man wore the slack expression of a run-through soldier whose mind had not yet caught up with his body.

Freyrík took a single step forward, froze. Then said something so soft and terrible Ayden could scarcely fathom it: "Would it truly have been so unbearable?"

Ayden leapt back to his feet, fists balled at his sides—never mind he'd asked himself the same question. "How *dare* you!" he roared. "Would you ask the same of your brother? Your sons?"

"No, I—"

"Have you so much concern for your High Court machinations that you fear the attentions I'd bring by not going arse-up for everyone who eyes me?"

"*No*, I didn't mean—"

"Next time I shall simply *kill* them, would you like that?" Ayden advanced a step. Another. Freyrík backed away as if from a Feral beast—Ayden rather felt like one just now. "I spared their lives in consideration to *you*, but clearly I should not have, gods crack my soft heart! At least the dead cannot tattle!"

"Gods befang it, Ayden, I just want you to *think*! What were you doing at the Academy in the first place? You should have known better than to tempt fate so—should have been prepared to face whatever consequence when you chose to act against all better judgment."

"Are you saying I *deserved* it?"

"I'm saying you must use your head lest your temper get you killed, for I cannot protect you here!"

"When could you *ever* protect me!"

Freyrík recoiled as if punched. Ayden stood his ground, breathing hard, watching with faint horror as Rík's eyes filled with tears. He'd spoken to wound, of course he had, but he felt no satisfaction when faced with the unexpected force of his blow. Only a strange tight hollowness beneath his breast, a weakness in his legs. He turned away, cursing himself for a coward on top of it all, and slumped back upon the cedar chest.

This place was killing them.

Freyrík's ragged breathing cut through the silence. Then the sound of clothes rustling, soft footfalls on the rug. A body settled beside him, cool and solid, almost touching.

"I'm sorry," Freyrík said, so soft 'twas nearly a whisper. Voice thick, worked carefully round the tears. He reached out, then stopped himself, hand hovering over Ayden's thigh.

Ayden sighed and covered it with his own, guiding it down across his leg. "I am too."

"I should never have said—"

"No, you should not have."

"And you're right that I never could protect—"

"But you have *tried*. That means something." He stroked his thumb across the back of Freyrík's hand where it rested on his thigh. "A lot, actually. That means a lot."

He turned to face Freyrík, and Freyrík met his gaze with moist eyes. He cupped Ayden's cheek with his free hand, slid his fingers round the back of Ayden's neck and bowed his head, touching forehead to forehead. Ayden brought his own hand to Freyrík's stubbled cheek, a blinder blocking out the world of all but mingled breath and scent and heat. How long they remained so he could not say. Only that it ended far too soon, with a gentle press of lips upon his own that nearly pained him in its sweetness.

"The palace guards will be here any moment," Freyrík whispered against his lips. The hand at his neck reached up, stroked through his hair. "I asked for time to collect you that we might avoid a second fight."

Ayden nodded, pulled himself away from that precious little cocoon of peace they'd woven round themselves. 'Twas no easy feat; he felt bound as if with traces, lines between them spreading the burdens they each carried. The moment of separation brought all that weight crashing down upon his shoulders once more.

"What will happen?" he said.

Freyrík held his gaze a moment longer, then looked away. "I don't know."

"Can you not tell them you'll mete my punishment yourself? I'd scream fit to carry to the central tower."

At that Freyrík almost smiled. "Nay, they'll not be so easily fooled. Besides," he sighed, "you had to go and break the arm of one of the Aegis's own sons; he seeks personal redress."

Gods cracked! Of all the whelps in this castle, he'd had to tangle with a prince of Aegea itself?

Ayden let his eyes close, wrenched them open an instant later when all he saw in the darkness was his own broken body on the pavilion at Castle Farr, dangling by shackles atop a bloody heap of dirt.

"Will you be there?" As close as he could come right now to admitting his fear, even to himself.

"If they let me. 'Tis no great secret I care for you. I will tell the Aegis you acted on my command, that I ordered you upon pain of death to lay with no man but me."

"And will he care?"

Freyrík speared him with a glare. "He is a good man, Ayden. A *great* man. He is not a dark beast; his heart is not so cold as you would paint it. Stand humble and speak true, and I have faith he'll treat you fairly."

Perhaps. But it seemed unlikely that fairness toward an elf in this place bore any resemblance to that which a human would engender.

Well, nothing to be done for it now.

When the guards came some minutes after, Ayden went to them without having to be told. Freyrík tried to follow, but the guards stopped him at the door.

"Apologies, Your Highness," one of them said, "but His Eminence wishes to speak with the elf alone."

Ayden squeezed his eyes shut. *Of course he does. He wouldn't want to upset his* fóstri *by breaking his toy in front of him, now would he.*

He was led to the Aegis in chains. He didn't fight that; he knew he'd proven himself plenty dangerous this morn, despite the starfall. And shackles and hobbles were much preferable to being beaten into submission—a service the guards looked quite eager to perform at the slightest provocation. Ayden took care not to give them one.

They led him to a study that seemed somehow oppressive for all its vast spaces and grandeur. 'Twas the floor-to-ceiling bookcases, perhaps, or the dark wooden paneling, or the massive furniture. The desk alone must have taken eight men to move.

Behind it sat the Aegis Exalted, looking unimpressed as Ayden shuffled in, chains rattling with every awkward half step. Someone shoved him to his knees and he went sprawling, unable to brace his fall with his hands cuffed behind him.

"It seems to me," said the Aegis, placid as a lake on a windless day, "that keeping you is rather more trouble than it's worth."

So focused was Ayden on righting himself—but not all the way to his feet; best to stay kneeling before this man—that his mind lapsed in its control over his tongue, which took advantage of the moment to say, "Then the simple solution is to set me free."

That was not at all the apology he'd intended, so he was quite relieved to hear the Aegis laugh at it, rather than, for instance, order his death.

"Oh my, no. For one, I do not think Freyrík would agree. And besides, I believe you may yet be of use to me. Leave."

It took Ayden a moment to realize that last bit was aimed at the guards and not him, but the guards had gone out and shut the door before he could get even one shackled foot underneath him.

He gave up trying with a mixture of relief and anxiety. Surely the Ruler of the Sixteen Realms didn't stoop to meting out his own corporal punishments . . . And yet, staying alone with this powerful man was disturbing all in itself.

He licked his lips and summoned the words of apology he'd practiced. "If I may, Your Eminence. About this morning—"

"We shall speak of it soon enough. Right now, I'm more interested in the other day. My message, you delivered it to your master, yes?"

Ayden nodded, then nodded some more to buy time. How had he not foreseen this? "I did."

"His response?"

"Nothing." The Aegis stared him down, clearly not believing, so he added, "I am just a slave, Your Eminence."

That laugh again, deep-chested and blithe. "Do not lie to me, elf," he said, still grinning broadly.

Well, Ayden could play at such confidence too. "I am not. He said nothing to me."

The human's smile faded a touch. He leaned back in his chair, laced his hands over a chest still broad and firm despite his body's aging, and nodded to himself. "Yes, if memory serves, you did say you'd not carry his words to my ears."

Ayden nodded back. "I did."

The Aegis's smile faded clean away. "And if I had you tortured, it would make no matter, would it."

"It would matter very much to *me*," Ayden said, "but you would not find what you're seeking. You are hunting for dark elves," he added, hoping to draw upon their mutual understanding. "There is nothing to find."

The Aegis regarded him for a long moment, and finally nodded. "I believe you." He sat forward, leaned his elbows on the desk and flapped a hand at Ayden, whose expression must have betrayed his surprise. "Not about what your master said, of course. Only that you would not repeat it even under the strictest duress. Which leaves me in a quandary, for I find myself quite interested in the things you could tell me. This business of the Council, for example . . ."

"Is settled, is it not? The votes were cast."

Ayden's attempt at naiveté earned him only a thin smile, sharper than any of the weapons he'd found and hoarded. He shifted uneasily on his aching knees.

It occurred to him, of a sudden, that this was the perfect chance to warn the Aegis of the coup, what with Freyrík under constant watch and unable to do so himself. It might even earn him absolution for the morning's debacle.

But coming from him, the words would implicate Freyrík no matter how he denied it. Coming from him, now, they would also set off a distraction his people would be helpless to exploit.

Silence, then, whatever the cost.

The Aegis shook his head as if to clear it—a deliberate move, no doubt—and said, "No matter. I'll forgive your silence if you continue to speak my wisdom in his ears. What's done is done; no good can come now from stirring conflict in the new Council. 'Twould be a shame of the highest order to see anyone come to harm over petty disagreements. Do we understand each other?"

Ayden nodded.

"Good. Now about this morning . . ."

"I assure you, Your Eminence, I did not mean to—"

"Oh, I've no doubt you didn't. And do you know what that tells me?"

Ayden waited for him to continue, trying subtly to work the kinks from his strained shoulders. But the human kept silent—apparently, his was not a rhetorical question. "No, Your Eminence, I don't."

The Aegis tipped his head. "It tells me that you're so very skilled at what you do, you needn't think about it anymore. And clearly you have *not* been thinking, or you'd never have raised so much as a finger to my son."

"I was only trying to—"

"Protect your master's property? A likely tale."

Ayden said nothing, lest his tongue betray his true feelings on the matter.

The Aegis seemed unbothered by his silence; the man was probably well accustomed to people being tongue-tied in his presence. He merely leaned forward over the massive desk and waved a benevolent hand. "You are quite fortunate, Ayden. For your brethren saw to it that what little harm you'd wrought was quickly undone. And I would grant you 'twas a lesson swiftly learned for careless boys."

Before Ayden could wrap his mind round this backhanded approval, the Aegis added, "In fact, I think you've a gift for swift lessons, which I shall make use of. For the remainder of your days here, you will teach these cadets every move and skill with which you so effortlessly felled them this morn."

He would do *what*? No, gods be cracked—the *Aegis* be cracked—he would not teach those spoiled whelps a single cracking thing!

The Aegis folded his arms across his chest and arched an eyebrow. "Would you rather I have you flogged? Or will you take the harmless punishment that does fair service to the aggrieved?"

"No, I . . . Wait, how many?"

His eyebrow arched again. Strange trick, that, to raise but one so high while the other remained drawn. "Cadets?"

"No, lashes."

The Aegis laughed, but Ayden could find no humor in this. A flogging would at least be done and gone, borne with pride and defiance. But teaching his skills to the spawn of the enemy day after day . . . an ongoing blow to his pride and his people, yet another subjugation he could ill endure in this cloistered place: a lesser but infinitely longer torment.

"I see why Freyrík likes you so. But I myself do not care for such spirit in my slaves. So let me speak plain, elf. You will do as you're told, or I'll see you lashed so hard the *Blód Sekt* will seem merciful in comparison. Then I'll have you healed and do it all again. Are we clear?"

Much to his disgust, Ayden flinched at the images those simple words tore from the locked compartments of his mind. He was panting, crack it, even trembling as he glared up at the knowing sparkle in the Aegis's eyes.

No choice, then. If he'd learned anything in his time in human hands, 'twas not to strike at stone walls with brittle sticks. He'd not be here much longer anyway, one way or another.

"Yes," he ground out.

Besides, this punishment would draw him that much closer to a whole vast array of weapons. 'Twould be irony most delicious if the verdict meant to subjugate his spirit were in fact the very thing that saw it freed for good.

Freyrík paced the drawing room, trying very hard to think of nothing. Not of what Ayden might be going through, not of the incriminating note from Berendil he'd just burned, not of the choice he still had to make, not of how his life would soon be turned on its ear either way—assuming he actually managed to outlive his choice—not of how that choice might forever alter the course of his people's history, not of how Ayden's fate at the Aegis's hands might well cement or change Freyrík's mind toward said choice . . .

Gods, but he was bad at not thinking.

Which made his relief all the stronger when Ayden strode in, unshackled and seemingly unharmed, and said before Freyrík could ask, "I'm fine."

Freyrík closed the distance between them in three long strides and drew the elf into a crushing hug.

"At least I was until a second ago," Ayden said, though his arms came up round Freyrík's back and squeezed just as hard. "Ow."

Freyrík laughed as he released Ayden, though he had no idea why; he'd carelessly forgotten Ayden's bruised back, could see in Ayden's face that he'd hurt him. Ayden did not seem to fault him for it, though. He merely stepped back, hands resting on Freyrík's shoulders, and said, "And what of you? Are *you* all right?"

"I am now." He took Ayden by the hand, led him to the sofa and sat him down. "But you must tell me what happened."

"Your *náungi* is a cruel man."

So serious, his tone. So hateful. Had Freyrík been too quick to relief? "Has he declared your punishment, then?"

Ayden's lips peeled back from his teeth in a gesture quite *not* a smile. "I am reduced to arming the enemy with tools for my own oppression."

Whatever did *that* mean?

"The academy students. I am ordered to teach them unarmed combat each day until we depart."

Relief returned, strong as ever, and with it the urge to laugh again. He squeezed Ayden's hand in his. "That is all?"

"It is enough!" Ayden shouted, wresting his hand away.

"Surely it won't be *that* bad? I was once an academy student here, remember. I'd have been most grateful for an opportunity to learn from a master such as yourself."

"You flatter," Ayden said, dry as sour wine.

"I do no such thing. You and I both know that among my people, your talents are unmatched."

"My talents! These students seem to think my only talents are demonstrated on my knees, or worse, my belly."

Freyrík winced at the thought of that—the disrespect, the humiliation. How would he have felt in Ayden's place? Shamed, no doubt. Unmanned. For such a proud warrior . . .

"Well," he tried by way of consolation, "you certainly proved them wrong this morn, much as I prefer you hadn't. Perhaps these lessons will serve as opportunity to prove them even wronger."

". . . I suppose."

"And my two eldest will be among your pupils. They'll be quite eager, no doubt."

Ayden blew out a sigh, slumped back on the sofa and pressed his hands to his head as if trying to keep it from shattering. Mayhap he was. "Can we just . . . not talk about this, please?"

Freyrík nodded, laid a hand on Ayden's knee. "All right."

He waited for Ayden to change the subject to one he preferred, but there came no such relief. And the silence was not pleasant; still Ayden sat slumped against the sofa cushions, head back, palms pressed firmly to his temples. Little black tufts of hair poked out through the gaps between his fingers.

"Actually," Freyrík said, mayhap a little too loudly, "I was wondering why you have a wet sheet full of apples."

"Huh?" Bleary eyes shifted toward Freyrík in an otherwise unmoving head. "Oh." Ayden's hands flopped down into his lap, landing with a dull smack. "Never you mind that."

No talking of that either, it seemed.

"They mean to poison him."

At this Ayden turned to face him fully, his startlement a mirror of Freyrík's own. Befang it, he'd not meant to share this burden with Ayden. Enough that he was implicated, enough that his own life was forfeit—though mayhap it was better this way; now if the elf were questioned, he'd have answers with which to barter for his life.

Ayden prompted him with a soft, wordless sound.

Freyrík shook his head . . . then sighed and relented. "Him and all his sons, his brothers, his uncle. All his potential heirs.

And one particularly troublesome councilman. Fourteen men in all, exterminated just as we did the dark beasts this last Surge. A message—a showing of our power."

Ayden listened without judgment or pity. Or comment.

Say something. Anything. Please.

But the elf could no longer hear his need, any more than Freyrík could interpret the machinations behind Ayden's closed expression.

"When?" Ayden asked at last.

"Two days hence."

"That leaves you little time to warn the Aegis."

"I can't!" Freyrík stood from the sofa, paced a tight circle and dropped back again. "My every step is dogged, my every word outside these rooms overheard. If I go to him now, I'll be dead before I reach his doors."

"Then you must find another way."

Gods befanged his dispassionate demand. As if 'twere so simple to sign his own brother's warrant. But he could not bear to reignite that argument, so he said nothing.

At length Ayden nodded, but to himself—a closed, distant gesture. Mayhap he did not even see Freyrík, so inward his focus had turned.

"Ayden, I—"

—need you. Am frightened. Cannot do this alone.

But he could say none of those things, not now, when Ayden might not even hear them. Or care. Gods knew he had every reason to be angry with Freyrík, but Freyrík could not stomach the thought of his rejection. If he spoke it, 'twould be *real.*

It seemed the elf sensed none of this, either, for he said simply, "I should sleep," and rose from the sofa. Freyrík reached for him without thinking, and Ayden brushed a single absent touch across Freyrík's outstretched arm as he walked past and entered their bedroom.

Through the open door, Freyrík watched Ayden snuff the light dead, one candle at a time.

Morning came far too early. Ayden thought to ignore it, but 'twas hard what with all the throat clearing going on just outside the bed curtains. He cracked a bleary eye open and watched Freyrík pull the curtain back, saw Lord Vitr lean his head in and whisper to him. Freyrík grunted. His groom retreated and began the long task of tying back the window shades, letting in the first dawn light.

"You are summoned," Rík said. He was sprawled on his back, eyes closed, still half-asleep. He made no move to touch or even look at Ayden. Upset, then? Or just tired?

Ayden felt so raw himself the distinction hardly mattered. "Where?"

"Training grounds. Cadets rise before the sun."

Gods, cruelties upon cruelties. He indulged a long, loud groan, but it failed to soothe his temper. Nor Freyrík's, though the man might once have found humor in such hyperbolic displays.

"Your escorts await," Freyrík added. Crack "escorts"; surely they were guards. "There's bread and tea in the drawing room. Dress warm. They train outside."

Ayden slid out from beneath the covers, careful not to let cold air into Freyrík's half of the bed. Though for a second, he felt sharp the temptation of flinging back the covers and forcing Rík to share at least a measure of his punishment.

Two days, Freyrík had said. Only one more, now.

Ayden let him rest.

Beyond the bed curtains, he heard servants prodding the fire back to life, smelled the first fresh curls of woodsmoke. Freyrík rolled onto his side, into the warm spot Ayden had just left, face slack but somehow restless. Naked, trusting, wounded. Ayden felt an overwhelming urge to touch those sleep-smooth features, and indulged it.

"Mmm." The tiniest hint of a smile cracked through the tension that clung to Freyrík even in sleep, but his eyes remained closed.

"You know I love you, don't you, Rík?"

Freyrík nodded, and his hand snaked up from beneath the down comforter to capture Ayden's fingers. At last his eyes opened, and they were shining as he said, "And I you. Promise me you'll be safe today."

Ayden smiled, a desperate, almost bitter thing. He was an elf of his word; he did not make promises he couldn't keep. "You too," he said instead, leaning in to kiss Freyrík before stepping out to face the day.

He dressed and ate beneath the watchful eyes of two human behemoths, stern and disciplined and bristling with weapons. The mere sight of them extinguished his appetite. He forced himself to finish breakfast—no doubt he would need his strength today—and followed them out into the morning chill like a good little slave.

Fallen gods, but it was bitter outside, all wind and hoarfrost and the thin, mocking light of dawn. 'Twas times like these he missed his elfsong most acutely, for still his first instinct was to sing for warmth, no matter how futile the effort. Did Jagall still do the same after three hundred years? Part of him hoped so; he could fathom no yielding of spirit more complete than to simply stop trying. Yet another part of him hoped not, for the binding was an open wound and always would be, scored afresh with each reminder of what he'd lost.

He could hold on to pain, though. Use it. And as he crossed the practice field like a lone deer through a wolves' den, set upon by some hundred-odd hostile stares, he gathered it round him— every indignity, every injustice, every abuse he'd suffered here—and forged with it the truest of elfsteel armor. As Ayden approached the instructor at field's edge, the man sneered like the alpha wolf he was. But if he meant to bow Ayden's back, he'd be sorely disappointed.

Ayden stopped a pace away, and the human eyed him as if a plucked chicken in the marketplace. "*You*?" the instructor said. "*You're* the one they call Ayden?"

Ayden drew himself up to full height, still a handspan shorter than this towering human instructor. "I am."

The man huffed his amusement, then placed a fine wooden whistle between his lips and blew three short, sharp bursts that carried cross the field. Instantly, the cadets ceased their chatter and assembled into lines organized roughly by height. Or age, more like—the youngest whelps on the far right, the eldest on the far left.

"We've a guest instructor today," the man shouted. Every last bit of him, from voice to face to flapping hand, made clear his disdain of the proposition.

Ayden rather agreed, though surely for different reasons.

"He is here to teach you how not to end up like those four." The man pointed to the boys who'd accosted Ayden yesterday, lined up side by side near the left edge of the field. Now that he knew what to look for, Ayden saw a hint of the Aegis in Cheekscar's visage. A pale shadow, more like.

Strange: they were still bruised, the lot of them. Had the elven healer been charged to leave reminders of their folly upon their flesh?

"Who wishes to go first?"

Ayden half expected silence, but quite to the contrary, every hand in the field shot out high. All eager for the chance to put the elf in his place, no doubt. To avenge their colleagues. Or perhaps just to outshine them.

Whatever the motive, these boys would be quite disappointed. He might not wish to draw attention to himself, but he still possessed enough pride not to fall before a pack of untrained children.

The instructor grinned a peculiar little grin and waved forward a cadet already well on his way to manhood, tall and muscled and full of the swaggering confidence of noble youth.

He saluted the instructor and said, "I am ready, Grandmaster."

Then he turned to face Ayden, and Ayden didn't know whether to laugh or panic. There was no mistaking that wavy red-blond hair, those blue eyes, those strong, open features. This boy was Rík's.

The boy met Ayden's eyes and inclined his head, politeness or acknowledgment or both. Calm, possessed. Just like his father.

Then the instructor—the so-called "Grandmaster"—turned to Ayden and said, "Begin with the disarming and felling you exercised yesterday. Demonstrate—*slowly*. Explain each step so all may hear."

It all sounded so reasonable Ayden could almost imagine he was tutoring his own people's green recruits. Perhaps in a way, with this boy, he was. He focused on the child to the exclusion of all else. "Your hand," he said. "Hold it out as if attacking with a knife."

No "as if" required; Rík's son pulled a dagger from the sheath at his hip and gripped it in reverse, laying the blade tight to his forearm. It wasn't how the four boys had done it yesterday, and it certainly complicated matters, but Ayden could work round it. In fact, he knew just the right technique—a challenging maneuver that these boy-soldiers might master on the practice field but never accomplish in battle.

He took position opposite the boy, measuring him. 'Twas hard to be objective with this one, but the child was *not* Rík—could not possibly possess his father's strength or skill or experience at his tender age. "Strike slowly, if you would."

Ayden was prepared—was half-expecting, despite the boy's parentage—a full-force blow in defiance of his order, but the boy struck quarter-speed at best. Obedient, polite, attentive. Rík had likely been the same at this age.

"You cannot parry the underhand grip without a vambrace, so you must duck or counterstrike," Ayden explained as the knife made its slow way toward his chest. He brought his own hand up, fisted tight, to connect with the underside of the boy's wrist just behind the blade. "Step aside as you strike," he said, shifting his weight in demonstration, "in case you miss, and aim well away from the blade. If you land your strike true, your attacker will drop his weapon."

The boy rather thoughtfully complied by letting his dagger fall to the dirt.

"As you're already touching, just twist your hand round to grip the wrist—like so—then twist once more to bring the arm up under the shoulder. If your opponent does not wish a broken arm"—here he applied gentle upward pressure 'til he had the boy bent so deep at the waist his head nearly touched the ground—"he must fall. At full speed and power, you may pull his elbow or shoulder out of joint. If you've a gauntlet on, you may also break his wrist or forearm in the process."

Ayden released the boy and looked round at the sea of faces fixed upon him. Rapt to the last. Even the Grandmaster, who asked, "And after the fall? Can you keep control?"

"You can straddle him, yes." He pictured slamming the Grandmaster face-first into the dirt and landing hard enough atop him to snap his spine. The thought raised a smile to his lips. "Shall I show you?"

Sadly, the Grandmaster merely waved toward the boy, whom Ayden rather thought he might like too much for such violent displays. "Do not harm him," the Grandmaster warned.

To the boy's credit, he picked up his dagger and swung into Ayden without hesitation.

Ayden demonstrated the counterattack at full speed, albeit at less than half power, sending the boy to the dirt and following through with a straddle, the boy's wrist pinned up between his shoulder blades.

"If you did not break the arm on the way down," Ayden called out to the group, "you can do so now with a simple application of upward force."

This he refrained from demonstrating. Instead he rolled to his feet and offered the boy his hand.

The boy acknowledged Ayden's outstretched arm with a nod, but climbed to his feet on his own, rubbing surreptitiously at his elbow.

Prideful as his father, then.

"Good," the Grandmaster said. "Now you, Leikr."

The boy—Leikr—squared off with Ayden again. Except this time he handed Ayden the dagger. Or rather, tried to; the Grandmaster barked a sharp, "No," and punctuated it with a cuff to his ear. Leikr took the blow without flinching and resheathed the knife, looking sheepish.

"Now, slowly. Elf, talk him through it."

But Leikr needed no talking. Ayden struck at quarter-speed, and Leikr stepped to the side and counterstruck with perfect form. A quick study—just like his father. Ayden grinned at the thought, though he felt rather a sentimental fool for it.

"Very well done," he said, and for a second, Ayden thought the Grandmaster might cuff *his* ear too. Were the man's toes so very large to be stepped on so easily? How absurd.

"Well enough," the Grandmaster said, "for quarter-speed. Try at full."

"Yes, Grandmaster." Leikr nodded to the instructor, then to Ayden, signaling his readiness.

Ayden made to strike, and the boy slammed his fist into the soft inside of his wrist. Pain spiked up his elbows and down to his fingers, which promptly went stiff and tingly beneath a hot wash of hurt. Then a hand was on his wrist, driving it out and under his armpit with enough force to rip him off his feet. There was no way to land well in such a hold, but he did his best, bracing with his free arm a split second before Leikr sat atop him as if dropped from a cliff and yanked his hand up nearly to his neck. The pain in his wrist spread like fire on pitch to his elbow and shoulder, and he clawed into the dirt with his free hand, just barely holding back a cry and the urge to turn tables on the two-faced little cur.

"There," Ayden gritted into the dirt. "You've done it. Let me up."

Leikr jerked his wrist up higher, and Ayden coughed as if kicked in the chest. Any more pressure and his elbow would break. What did the cracking whelp *want*?

A polished pair of boots stepped into his field of vision. The Grandmaster. He squatted down in front of Ayden, calm as could be, and said, "On this field, the loser yields to the victor or he does not stand."

Yield. The thought set Ayden's teeth on edge; had he not yielded enough to these humans already? And yes, Leikr was clearly among *these* humans, not deserving of the blood he carried or the face he wore. 'Twould be so easy to roll Leikr off him; the boy's grip on his wrist was faulty, his weight not properly anchored or balanced. But for Rík's sake he'd not hurt this boy, no matter Leikr's lack of compunction about hurting him.

Leikr gave his arm another jerk that made his eyes water. He knew he should play by their rules; he jeopardized all with injury, or worse, imprisonment. Besides, just one more day now . . . one more day and he'd be free of this.

"I yield," he said, and said it calmly, though it felt as if the words had been ripped from his guts and pulled up through his throat.

Leikr leaned in close across Ayden's back, lips to his ear, and whispered, "Stay away from my father, you filthy *gróm*." Ayden bit back a cry as the pressure on his elbow increased, certain of a sudden the boy would break it despite his yielding. But then Leikr sat up and let him go.

Ayden curled onto his side and hugged his arm to his chest, hoarding a moment to himself even as the Grandmaster called the next boy forward. He must say nothing of this to Rík—nothing at all. 'Twould hurt the man in ways no elven healer could fix.

Chapter Nine

Freyrík had spent the whole of his adult life making difficult choices. Strange, then, how this one choice looming over his head made all the world seem gray and lifeless. 'Twas all the worse for the lordling circling round him from morning prayer to breakfast, from the library to the garden, from the open Council session to tea with the ambassador to Midr. The man watched him like a hawk, and was no doubt as ready as one to swoop down with beak and talons if he so much as drew within shouting distance of the Aegis.

Freyrík gave the Lord Protector wide berth all day.

He returned to his rooms after supper—and with perverse pleasure, shut the doors on the lordling's nose—fully expecting to find Ayden, feet up on the furniture and food in hand, eager to complain about his day. Yet the elf was not in the drawing room. Nor was he in the bedroom. Surely he wasn't still at training? The cadets would have adjourned for the evening by now . . .

"He's in the washroom, Your Highness."

Gods! He spun about, but 'twas only his groom. Freyrík removed his fumbling hand from his dagger.

Lord Vitr, bless his discretion, pretended naught was amiss. "Shall I undress you?"

Namely: *Would you like to join him?* And oh, how he did, though not in the manner his groom implied. Rather, to soak away his tension in hot water, to ease the kinks in his shoulders and neck . . . "Yes, my lord. Thank you."

Lord Vitr untied and unbuckled and tugged and pulled at layer after layer of winter dress. Gods befang these court trappings anyway; Freyrík had half a mind to put his dagger to good use on them. But then he was down to his warm winter underclothes, which not even the massive hearth fire could convince him to shed until he reached the tub proper.

He walked into the wet warmth of the washroom. Vanilla-scented steam curled like dawn mist in the candlelight, blurring the room and clinging to his underclothes and hair. Every now and then, a long hiss came from the corner, where an attendant sat ladling water over a grill of hot coals. No other sounds disturbed the peace: no greetings, no splashing, not even deep breathing.

Freyrík ventured through the steam, waving it from his face to no avail. When he reached the giant tub, he found Ayden seemingly asleep, leaned back against the sloped walls and submerged to his chin. He did not acknowledge Freyrík. Mayhap did not realize he was no longer alone.

"Ayden," Freyrík said by way of greeting, not wishing to startle the elf. 'Twas hard to remember Ayden could no longer sense presence by song.

Ayden turned his head and cracked his eyes open. One looked black and blue in the candlelight.

"How was training?" Freyrík asked.

Ayden rolled his head back to stare at the ceiling.

Strange, the wash of panic lurking in the silence, the way the air choked with more than just humidity. "Will you not speak?"

Apparently, he would not. Nor did he meet Freyrík's eyes again.

Freyrík stooped down beside the tub, knees cushioned against the sheepskin pelt there. In the dim light, the wash water seemed opaque. He skimmed the surface with his fingertips and snatched them back, surprised—the water was ice cold.

The chill went down right to his guts.

"Ayden . . ."

"I've broken ribs," the elf said, still to the ceiling, his voice small and roughened as with sand. "It hurts to speak."

The cold deepened, seeping into all his body's dark crevices and hollows. He clenched his teeth, dipped his arm into the water and searched for Ayden's hand. His fingers brushed skin.

Ayden gasped, jerked as if struck. "Don't," he rasped.

Freyrík withdrew, fingers clenching into a fist. Ayden's face was a mask, but behind it, Freyrík saw pain of more varieties than he cared to count. He offered his hands again, but did not touch. "Come, please. I must take you to a healer."

Ayden seemed to think on that a while, gaze lingering long and languid on Freyrík's extended hands. At last he grimaced, dragged his left hand from the water and grasped Freyrík's forearm. His right hand—the dominant one, the one Freyrík had hurt with a simple touch—lay yet limp beneath the water.

Freyrík tried to be careful, but Ayden fell right into him when he pulled the elf to his feet. The attendant draped a towel over Ayden's shoulders as Freyrík lifted him from the tub. He was cold beyond shaking, soaking Freyrík's underclothes with frigid water and hugging to him with his left arm hard enough to bruise. When Ayden's legs gave out from under him, Freyrík simply scooped him up and carried him to their bed. He didn't know what worried him more: that Ayden couldn't stand, or that he wasn't protesting being lifted like a child.

Lord Vitr looked up from tidying Freyrík's clothes the moment he stepped from the bathroom. "Is he—" his groom began, even as Freyrík said, "Warm clothes. Now."

Lord Vitr nodded and hastened off to a chest of drawers, returning but moments later, clothes in hand, to draw back the bed curtains and pull down the blankets. Freyrík nodded his thanks and laid Ayden upon the mattress.

Free of the steam and in the brighter light of the bedroom, he could see why Ayden had collapsed. The elf seemed one big bruise from head to toe, front and back, as if he'd been set upon for hours with sticks. Freyrík cast his eyes to the painted ceiling and sent up a quick prayer. *Please, please don't let Ayden have provoked the Grandmaster . . .*

"You judge me?" Ayden asked, calling Freyrík's attention back. He sounded wounded in a way that had naught to do with his breaks and bruises.

"Nay." Freyrík forced a smile to his lips. He pulled the covers up to Ayden's chin to keep him warm while he sorted through what Lord Vitr had brought him. "I understand."

A huff, followed by a coughing cry. "You understand nothing. I obeyed—I *yielded*—like a good little slave, let them all disarm and fell me in turn. Each and every one of them." Strange, so much venom in words so softly spoken. And as an afterthought, "I think they broke my arm."

Freyrík froze in the act of shaking out a pair of heavy woolen hose, handed them back to Lord Vitr and pulled the covers down just far enough to examine the mass of bruising above Ayden's right wrist. It was much darker than the rest, though he saw no deformity and little swelling. The latter, at least, had likely been kept at bay in the icy bath. Now if only Ayden could be warmed before he caught a chill and died . . . "Why did they not see you to a healer?"

Ayden squinted at him with a depth of derision he'd not unleashed upon Freyrík in months. "I served my purpose, Rík. Why should they care beyond that?"

Such wretched words . . . He stopped them the best way he knew how: with a soft kiss upon the elf's chilled lips. "I care."

Ayden shuddered beneath him, but he seemed mayhap a feather's weight less miserable than before. Now if only Freyrík could chase out the chill.

He thought to strip down, crawl into bed with the elf, and cradle him warm, but bruised as Ayden was, it might do more harm than good. So too might the clothing—he'd not appreciate having layers tugged on over broken ribs.

A robe, then. He went to fetch one himself, the fur-lined heavy silk he wore on cold mornings abed. Between he and Lord Vitr, they propped the elf into sitting and wrapped the robe round his shoulders. Then Freyrík made work of his own wet clothes, pulling on breeches and a simple shirt in their stead. He waved away Lord Vitr's attempts at anything more. Indecency be damned.

"Come," he said, returning to Ayden's side. The elf had laid himself flat again, legs dangling off the side of the bed, head and shoulders on a heap of pillows. "If you cannot walk, I will carry you."

Ayden made no move. Just closed his eyes and lay there, tremors racking his body now he'd regained some measure of warmth.

"I would fetch a healer here if I could, but they're not allowed outside their work chambers. We must go."

Ayden blinked, blinked again, and again. Far too fast. *Please gods, do not let those be tears.* Physical wounds could be healed, but Freyrík lacked the strength and wit just now to tend those hurts he could not see.

"I want to go home, Freyrík."

Freyrík's legs cut out from under him as surely as his breath. He fell to his knees beside the bed, clutched at Ayden's left hand and pressed it to his forehead, his lips. Tasted the salt of his own tears upon the still-cold skin. "Soon," he whispered. "Soon."

Empty words. They brought no comfort to anyone.

He cleared his throat and laid Ayden's hand back on the bed. "Come," he said again. He climbed to his feet, shook out a throw from the foot of the bed and wrapped Ayden in one more layer of warmth before gathering him up in his arms. The elf was no sack of feathers, but still Freyrík turned away Lord Vitr's help. This was his own burden to carry.

Careful, so careful, he maneuvered Ayden through his rooms and out into the corridor.

Down one hall, then another. He paused a moment to adjust his grip on Ayden, trying not to jostle him along the way. Ayden blinked up at him, and he looked back down and smiled thinly.

"Ayden . . ." he began without meaning to, indulging the curiosity—nay, the fear—that had been niggling at him since he'd found Ayden. He knew not quite how to phrase it. "My sons . . .?"

Ayden blinked, eyes clouded with . . . what? And at last said, ever so softly, "They did only as the Grandmaster told them."

Freyrík blew out a breath. "That is . . ." Good. A relief. But neither mattered to Ayden, so he held his tongue.

Freyrík stayed half the night with Ayden in the little stone cell where the elven healer lived and worked. She could barely hear over the starfall locked round Ayden's flesh, but Freyrík held no power to remove it.

The befanged stuff distressed and distracted her, made her work painstaking and difficult. Freyrík begged her for anodyne to no avail—'twas locked in a sturdy cabinet for which she had no key—so he held Ayden's hand instead, let Ayden squeeze until his bones felt ground to powder. The pain made it easier to block the elf's whimpers and cries as the healer went about her starfall-hobbled work.

Four ribs, two arm bones, and one damaged kidney later, she sent them on their way. She'd not bothered with the bruising; not a one among them thought it worth the pain.

By the time they returned to their rooms, Ayden looked so wrung out that it came as no surprise when he mumbled, "I pray you make excuses for me tomorrow," crawled beneath the covers, and fell dead asleep.

Freyrík watched him awhile, sitting beside him on the bed and letting his thoughts wander. He'd been distracted by Ayden's needs, but now, in the silence of the night, 'twas impossible to hold the world at bay. Tomorrow was the day of reckoning, and afterward, nothing would be the same. And still he'd not found a way to warn the Aegis.

Nor was he certain 'twas the right thing to do.

The more time he spent with his brother poring over attack plans and testimonies of dark elf sightings, the more hope he held for a world free of the darker threat. True, Ayden had said there *were* no dark elves, but Ayden's first agenda was protecting his own people. Freyrík did not begrudge him that. But nor could he doom the whole of mankind for his love of Ayden.

And dark elves *had* been sighted—'twas not a rumor, he was certain of that. This last day he'd read through record after record of such instances: sometimes one being, sometimes two or three or even ten, the darkers circling thick round them as if foot soldiers round their generals.

And if indeed the dark elves could be destroyed, if their deaths would mean peace at last for the humans, then Freyrík could not doom the whole of mankind for his love of the Aegis.

Beside him, Ayden stirred in his sleep. Freyrík stroked a hand across Ayden's hair, its softness gone beneath a layer of dirt and sweat.

Ayden . . . what would become of him? If Freyrík threw his life on a desperate attempt to warn the Aegis—if he failed—no doubt Berendil would see Ayden silenced, or else truly claim him as a slave, an heirloom for House Farr. Centuries upon centuries of cruel servitude . . .

It would kill him. If not in body, then even worse so: in spirit.

And even if Freyrík succeeded in warning the Aegis, he might not be pardoned for his involvement. Again, Ayden would share in his fate or be claimed as reward for all time.

Only if Freyrík threw in with Berendil and saw the coup through . . .

He couldn't do it. Couldn't do any of it. Best if he'd never reached this cursed place, if he'd taken a fall off his horse on the road to Aegea and broken his neck, if he'd—

His heart tumbled over a beat. This, he could do. This might secure some future for Ayden, not to mention Lord Vitr and his sons. After all, their only crime in the eyes of the court was their association with Freyrík; if he freed them of that burden, would he not be giving them the best chance at life, perhaps even at freedom?

His gaze wandered of its own accord from Ayden's familiar features to an equally familiar dagger, resting on the bedside table just beyond the open curtains.

He leaned over to take it. Strange: his hands had stopped trembling. He picked it up and tested the blade against the pad of his thumb. Sharp, well kept. A gift from the Aegis when he'd graduated the academy—an honorable blade for an honorable death.

He pressed the tip to his stomach, then stopped. Better the throat. And not on the bed; he couldn't bear the thought of Ayden waking up beside his corpse.

"Rík?"

Gods befanged! He jerked his hand away, quickly reversed his grip on the dagger. In the moonlight he saw Ayden sit up, saw the whites of his eyes fix on the blade.

"Rík . . . What are you doing?"

Freyrík lowered the dagger but did not put it down. "Guarding your flank," he said, touching his free hand to Ayden's cheek. "Go back to sleep."

Ayden stared, unblinking. "Not tired." A lie so absurd he might as well have said it round a yawn. He reached for the dagger, pried it from Freyrík's fist, and placed it on his own bedside table, well out of Freyrík's reach. "I will stand guard with you."

This time when Ayden reached out, it was to give, not take. He gathered Freyrík into his arms and pulled him down, tucked round him like a second skin and held on as if for life.

Ayden was ripped from sleep with the sudden realization that he might never see Freyrík again. He'd known this always, in that abstract, far-off certainty that all human things must die. And he'd known lately that Freyrík was tangled in perilous, ever-constricting webs—*Tomorrow, all would change tomorrow*—that might claim the man's life no matter which way he twisted.

But to know something and to *understand* it—to wrap one's heart and mind round its consequences—were not at all the same. And gods, but this understanding *hurt*, left him choked and gasping and curled round a ripping pain in his gut. Like being stabbed—hollowed, cored. Like bleeding out right here beside the man he loved.

It was still night, perhaps an hour since he'd woken to find Freyrík toying with that gods-cracked dagger. The bedroom was dark but for a mute glow from the banked hearth. Even with the bed curtains drawn back against unknown dangers, the air was warm, and heavy with Freyrík's scent. Still Ayden was curled tight round the man, pressed naked to that cool solid bulk so deceptive, so humanly fragile. But in the wake of his new understanding, it wasn't enough. Didn't stem the bleeding or stop the pain or bring him any solace.

Was this how Freyrík had felt the morning of the *Blód Sekt*, clinging terrified to Ayden and praying, praying he'd survive the day?

Ayden needed Rík now as then, as if air, as if sunlight. Needed the sound of Freyrík's voice, the power in Freyrík's hands, the pulsing warmth at Freyrík's core. He needed to *live* now, right now, this instant, lest he find himself adrift in the next.

"Freyrík, wake up." He pressed hungry lips to the nape of Rík's neck, bit softly at the flesh there as his hands set to roving. "Rík."

Freyrík stirred like a bear in hibernation, cranky and reluctant to leave the warmth of its cave.

Ayden slid his hand from hip to groin and took firm hold of Freyrík's cock, which sprang awake much more promptly than its owner.

Freyrík moaned, a sultry low vibration Ayden felt clear down to his toes, and pressed back tighter against him, shimmying *just so* until Freyrík's arse cheeks pressed firm round Ayden's erection. The fit was perfect, *maddening*, but if Rík thought to buy Ayden's patience while he worked himself awake, he was well and sorely mistaken.

Ayden latched teeth to the jointure of neck and shoulder and bit down hard enough to leave a mark. Freyrík moaned and went rigid in his arms.

"Prepare yourself," Ayden growled into his ear, licking and sucking at the lobe.

He'd but a second to indulge thus before Rík broke from his embrace and lunged across the bed to snatch up the oil on his bedside table.

By reflex Ayden tried to light the candles there with song. But he couldn't anymore, of course he couldn't. He could, however, not allow it to upset him.

Not tonight, at least.

While Freyrík pulled the stopper from the oil, Ayden struck the firesteel to light the candles nearest him. Five tries to catch the wick, but it was worth it. He needed to watch, needed to see Freyrík's face as he—

Oh good gods. Freyrík had risen up on spread knees and was plunging two oil-slicked fingers inside himself. One stroke, two, a third, thighs flexing, head tipped back, mouth open round a moan . . .

Ayden stared, breathless, at the tight shadowed space where Rík's fingers disappeared, reappeared, disappeared again, taking Ayden's wits along with them. For some untold time, his every thought, his every control was gone to those fingers, to the small secret moans they wrung from Rík. Moans he longed to tear from Rík himself.

The thought of sheathing his cock to the hilt in Rík's eager flesh restored his wits in a flash, and then he was on Rík, knocking the man's hand away and tackling him down to the pillows, flat on his back, knees pressed to Ayden's sides. The look in his lust-darkened eyes— begging, trusting, open—nearly undid Ayden there and then.

A hand down between them, fingers touching to his own cock, to Freyrík's eager flesh. Ayden buried himself stones-deep in a single thrust and then froze.

'Twas near overpowering, the urge to *move*, his body shaking with restraint, his nerves thrumming so loud 'twas nearly like hearing song again.

Rík hooked his heels round Ayden's arse and dug nails into the small of Ayden's back—coaxing, demanding, begging—but Ayden would not be swayed so easily. He leaned forward, buried his face in the hollow of Rík's neck and tasted, breathed him in: salt and a hint of honeysuckle and that masculine human essence, all the more precious for its fragility, its transience. Like this moment, like their shared passions, too soon spent.

Rík thrust up beneath him with a wanton moan, his cock pressed hard and desperate along the line of Ayden's hip. Ayden smiled into his skin. The next thrust he stilled with a whispered, "Shhh," a soft bite to his collarbone, a lick to soothe away the mark. He wished to make this last. To savor.

It seemed Rík understood, for he settled down beneath him, his hands unclenching from Ayden's waist to slide up his ribs, ghost over his flanks, his shoulder blades, up into his hair. There they tangled and tugged until Ayden lifted his head from the cradle of Rík's shoulder and met him lips to lips and tongue to tongue.

A single rocking thrust of his hips, and Rík moaned into Ayden's mouth, grabbed at Ayden's hair as if to ground himself. The pressure on his scalp shot little bolts of pleasure down Ayden's spine and tightened his stones. He deepened their kiss, mouth possessive as Rík's hands clutched round his head, breathing Rík in and breathing himself out into Rík all at once. A second thrust, slow and shallow, and Rík pulled back, gasping, pressed forehead to forehead and begged, "Touch me, please."

Ayden propped himself up on one forearm and worked his free hand down the space between them but passed by Freyrík's cock, trapped as it was between their bodies. Enough friction there. He touched fingers instead to the stones hanging hot and heavy beneath it, and then further down, to the flesh stretched round his own cock, outlining their joining with his fingertips. Slick and pulsing, alive, eager . . .

It took but barest force to slide his middle finger in alongside his cock straight down to the third knuckle, and there beneath the pad of his finger he felt the hard little nub of Rík's pleasure and pressed.

The sound this ripped from Rík was of a dying man—raw, animal, utterly helpless. Rík's eyes closed tight and his head arched into the pillow, body taut from toes to hair.

Ayden wiggled his finger and Rík half shouted, mashed his mouth to Ayden's and bit his lower lip. Ayden smiled round Rík's teeth and did it again, rolling his hips along with it.

"I'm ... I'm ..."

Ayden froze, shifted his weight to lift the pressure from Rík's trapped cock. "You'll do no such thing," he growled.

Rík slumped beneath him, trembling and foaming like a hard-run horse and panting just as loud. His lips moved round the word "Please," but he could not seem to form it through his rasping breaths. Ayden grinned down at him and pumped his finger slowly in and out, trembling himself with desire to thrust unfettered into that desperate flesh, to sate his own need clawing forth from his stones.

Rík let his legs fall from Ayden's hips, splayed them wide and wanton—or perhaps just boneless, long beyond his ability to control. Like his lust-slackened lips, his fluttering eyes, his hands that clenched in the sheets at his sides. Slowly he regained his breath beneath Ayden's gentled attentions, and at last he used it to say, "If you withhold release another moment, I shall be forced to enlist outside assistance."

'Twas teasing of the gentlest sort, but it spurred Ayden beyond reason. To drive even the hinting of such thoughts from Rík's head. To drive *everything* from Rík's head.

He grabbed hold of Rík's knees, lifted and shoved them to the mattress near the man's ears and planted his hands upon them, using this new leverage to drive down into Rík with every ounce of force and speed he could muster. *Gods* but this angle was sweet, so easy to drive stones-deep into that fist-tight slickness.

Rík met his eyes—Defiant? Testing? Coquettish?—and took his own cock in hand, the fierceness of his pleasure shining clear on his face. His breathing sped, chest heaving like a bellows, pulse pounding at his temples and throat. Teeth bared, hand working at furious speed in time with Ayden's thrusts, and for all that it was crushingly silent it was raucous as well, a whole vast banquet of the five remaining senses, tangy and sharp and sweet near to pain.

As Rík shot his seed with a stuttering cry and a long hard spasm round Ayden's cock, Ayden's own climax ripped through him in reply, and suddenly it didn't matter that their songs could not twine when their bodies and hearts and minds fit so perfectly, harmonized so exquisitely well. He hung in the moment, a perfect crescendo, and wanted for absolutely nothing.

Ayden woke to the thin light of morning, still groggy but well beyond sleep. Strange how the dawn had washed away the peace in his heart. Was the sun not supposed to banish the darkness?

When he met Freyrík's eyes in the gloom of the early light, one word only hung unspoken between them: *Today.*

'Twas too stifling to stay abed in the presence of such a specter. Silently, Ayden drew back the covers and shuffled out, hearing Freyrík do the same behind him.

Lord Vitr emerged from his cubby at the sounds of their stirring and pulled fresh clothes from a chest of drawers. Ayden slipped on a robe and approached him, hands outstretched.

"I'll do it," he said. "Go back to sleep. Please," he added when Lord Vitr looked at him askance. "I have watched you often enough."

At last Lord Vitr nodded and turned over the bundle of clothes, then retreated back into his room. Perceptive human that he was, he closed the door behind him, granting Ayden a rare moment of privacy with Rík.

Now if only he could figure out all these straps and ties and buckles.

"Have you determined," Ayden asked as Rík approached, beautiful and far too tempting in his nudity, "how to warn the Aegis of the coup?"

Rík stopped in front of him, freed him of the mess of clothing he'd been turning this way and that, and plucked his underclothes from the pile. "Not yet."

Ayden looked up sharply as Rík stepped into his drawers. "Time runs short."

"I know," Rík snapped, and then, softer, aching, "I know."

He pulled his shirt over his head, turned round so Ayden could tie the laces at the neck. That, at least, he could manage easily enough. And though he needed Rík focused, he couldn't quite stop himself from brushing fingertips across Rík's nape, smiling when the man shivered.

"He breakfasts with the court after church," Freyrík said, pulling away and smoothing down his shirt. "I shall try then to catch his eye—"

A knock on the bedroom door had them both reaching for weapons. Silly—an assassin would not *knock*.

The door opened, and an unfamiliar page took one step into the room and bowed. "A message, Your Highness, from—"

The fop who'd become Rík's persistent shadow knocked the poor page aside, shouldering past him. Ayden quickly dropped to his knees, eyes down and Rík's breeches in hand, and Rík put a steadying hand to Ayden's head to step into his clothes.

"Yes, my lord?" Rík sighed, as if the fop bored rather than infuriated him.

A moment's silence as Ayden, still on his knees, laced up Rík's breeches.

"His Majesty King Berendil requests your presence for breakfast in his chambers, Your Highness."

Ayden fumbled with the laces, felt Freyrík jerk under his hands— and not because he'd brushed against the man's limp cock. The same bolt of anxiety had shot through them both.

Rík snatched up and fastened his belt on his own, turning away from Ayden. "My thanks for his gracious invitation," he said. "I shall be there shortly."

From the corner of his eye, Ayden saw the fop fold his arms across his chest. *Like a puffed-up rooster, all feathers, no fight.* "Now, Your Highness, if you would."

Ayden smothered a feral grin as Freyrík *slowly* buckled his weapons belt, making a show of checking the dagger at his hip. But then he eyed the fop and nodded, much to Ayden's disgust—and to Rík's own, no doubt.

Rík nudged him in the thigh with a socked foot, and Ayden realized he was waiting for his boots. He scrambled to fetch them, again offered his shoulder for Rík to balance upon and tugged the supple leather onto the man's feet. When he'd tied the last lace, he stood, smoothing hands over Rík's chest and sides in pretense of neatness. He gritted his teeth against the fop's eyes on him; surely 'twas no crime for a bed slave to show affection to his master.

Rík seemed to think the same, for he slid his own hands up Ayden's arms, to his shoulders, his neck, cupped his cheeks. "Do not fret so, elf," he said through a smile so thin it starved upon his lips. "I shall have you this evening."

Such a beautiful lie when they both knew Rík would like as not end this day parted from his head. And even if Rík somehow returned, Ayden would like as not be a dozen leagues down the Góz, guiding his people to freedom.

Ayden covered Rík's hands with his own and tried very, very hard not to cling to them.

The fop cleared his throat. With a final, faint smile Rík turned from Ayden, his hand sliding down Ayden's arm, loosening, letting go . . .

On impulse, Ayden's fingers tightened round Rík's wrist. Rík turned back round, eyebrows raised, and Ayden gave his arm a hard tug, pulling them chest to chest and crushing his lips to Freyrík's. He ignored Rík's little hum of surprise, let go of his wrist only to thread fingers through his hair, still tugging tight, holding Rík close as he could, parting Rík's lips with his tongue and tasting him, feeling him—

—*one last time.*

As he'd promised.

And suddenly Rík was returning the kiss, taking Ayden's face in both hands and marching him back, parted lips to parted lips, until Ayden hit a wall. There they stayed, tangled and breathless, until Rík pulled away, wiped glistening lips with the back of his hand and said, "There. Now be good while I am gone."

He turned and nodded to the fop, who was gaping at Ayden with wide eyes, chest heaving, tongue flicking over his lips. Ayden barely spared him a sneer, too busy watching Rík's receding back, aching with the loss of his touch.

Long moments after Freyrík had left, Ayden still stood slumped against the wall. His lips still tingled; he could still taste the man upon his tongue, smell Rík's soap, feel the silk of Rík's hair against his fingers. If he closed his eyes and thought hard enough, he could nearly convince himself his lover was still there in his arms, pressing him to the wall—

Which was why he must stop thinking and start acting. He wrenched himself away with a single self-indulgent cry, and forced his mind back to what lay ahead.

He dressed in more layers than were necessary inside the castle, then lingered over his half of the spare little breakfast in the drawing room. Slowly the chambers emptied of servants. When the humans had all gone, Ayden dropped his pretense and set about his work.

He moved his cached items into the trunk at the foot of the bed—safer there, and more quickly accessible—and added Freyrík's half of the breakfast tray and the freshly stocked fruit from the new bowl in the drawing room. Two satchels' worth now. Not nearly enough to feed and clothe and arm them all, but it would do for a start. It had to.

After a moment's consideration, he snatched up the firesteel and the dagger at his bedside and added them to his packs. If all went well for both of them, Freyrík would scold him for it later. He'd be too happy to see Freyrík alive to care.

Tasks completed, he left for the baths. For once, he was looking forward to them; between the Academy training and the night's exertions, he felt as if he'd walked mute into a bear cave and run afoul of a mother protecting her cubs. A long soak would ease his strained muscles and nerves.

The baths were nearly empty when he arrived, so he indulged his own pains awhile, reviewing the plan in his head. Spread the word to the others. Make excuses to the bath masters. Slip away one by one and gather at forest's edge. Down the wall, to the river. Ride the swift waters to freedom, or at least well into the countryside, where they might plan their next step safe from tracking dogs and prying eyes.

So simple . . . and yet so sickly thin in the cold gaze of a rational eye. But then, the best plans always were. Or so he tried to convince himself.

The arrival of his brothers and sisters, coming one by one from serving their masters in ways he did not care to dwell upon, spared him from dwelling upon sparse detail.

Jagall was one of the last to enter. Only when the tension drained from Ayden's body did he realize how anxious he'd been. So much of his plan depended on the elder elf, 'twas all Ayden could manage not to swim across the room and accost him right there in the doorway. He made himself sit still, head resting against the ledge, eyes half-hooded, until Jagall disrobed and sank into the hot pool. Then he glided over to Jagall, kissed his cheek, and whispered, "Today."

The rest was up to Jagall. 'Twas he the bath-masters trusted, so 'twas he who made excuses to Laug and Húskarl to see them all early dismissed.

And 'twas he the other prisoners trusted, so 'twas he who passed Ayden's message along.

Ayden tried not to watch him as he approached each elf in turn, slowly, so as not to arouse suspicion or the ire of the bath-masters. The morning turned to afternoon, and still Ayden most carefully did not watch as Jagall completed his rounds.

He also most carefully did not think about the healer locked in a stone cell, somewhere in the heart of the keep. She'd helped him, but he could not return the favor. How many were there like her, held away from the bed slaves and bent to useful work? How many would he be leaving behind?

At least when he returned to Vaenn, he'd carry with him much knowledge of this place. Its layout, its defenses, its guard posts. Perhaps the very best scouts, the ones who could bend light clear round them as they moved, could mount a rescue with such knowledge.

But now he could not think of such things. Now he must think only of the night to come.

He counted away every second and minute and hour. Watched with forced calm as an elf was called to service round noon. Another left an hour later.

Fallen gods please, let them return in time.

But the afternoon shadows grew long, and still they did not return. The remaining elves left the pools, napped away the afternoon on pillows, sought massages or engaged in gentle exercise. They took turns, as always, at the little mirrored tables, painting themselves for service. A waste of time, when soon they'd all be smirched with travel, but he saw the necessity of the ruse. He forced himself to do the same.

From the corner of his eye he saw Jagall seeking out Master Húskarl. Ayden picked up a charcoal stick and touched it to his eyelid, watching the elf and the bath-master in the mirror. They were leaned in close, whispering. Húskarl nodded; Jagall bowed, backed away.

"Your attention!" Húskarl called. "Finish quickly now and be on your way. You mustn't be late."

Ayden nearly snapped the charcoal stick in his excitement. He threw it down, filed toward the door with the others. Left the baths behind—for good, this time.

They were safely past their first obstacle now, and for the first time in what seemed hours, Ayden allowed himself to breathe. Even to smile. He fought to bury his grin and did not care that he lost.

Back to Rík's rooms, where nobody questioned his presence no matter the time of day. He found but a single servant there, scrubbing soot from the hearth. The sight of the empty rooms was a cold fist round his heart, and he realized he'd half hoped to find Freyrík there, for all it would have hampered his preparations. Even Lord Vitr was still gone—two days in a row, an oddity Ayden could scarcely credit. He gripped the doorjamb with numb fingers.

Was Freyrík still alive? Surely he'd have heard *something* . . .

The servant looked up from the hearth and said, "Is there something you need, elf?"

Ayden shook his head, realized he'd been standing motionless in the doorway for several moments. He moved into the bedroom and shut the door firmly behind him.

He retrieved his satchels from the cedar chest and headed for the bedroom doors, then paused. 'Twould be hard to explain the bags to any of the guards at the ground-level exits, especially if—fallen gods forbid—he were stopped and searched. About-turn, then, and out the balcony doors instead. He tossed the satchels over the railing and followed them, shimmying down the façade into the garden.

The whole move took but a matter of seconds, and then he was off at a loping run toward the trees.

He gained the forest and slowed to a jog, then to a walk. His sisters and brothers should have taken refuge in the treetops by now, pretty little birds perched on the verge of freedom. Humans never looked up; elves knew better. He scoured the treetops with a stare—

—and cursed his starfall deafness with all the vigor and hate he'd felt in the whole of his eight hundred years, for he saw not his fellow elves, but half a contingent of palace guards lying in ambush. They dropped out of the trees round him, too many and too heavily armed. Ayden's muscles tensed right down to his toes, seeking traction, seeking to lash out in a thousand directions, even as his mind knew there was no place to run.

He spread his hands out, let his stolen satchels fall to the ground.

The guards set on him anyway, the flurry of fists and pikes so fierce his legs gave way in seconds. All he could do was huddle on the forest floor, curled tight to protect his belly and head.

Gods thanked it was over fast, though even his bruises would have bruises by the morrow. The ground undulated beneath him, a sickening wave that crashed into his belly alongside the pain. Again the world swayed; something slammed into his middle and stayed there, pressing hard. He cracked an eye open and realized he was slung over someone's shoulder, carried none too gently away from the trees.

He knew where they were dragging him. No point in watching his chance at freedom recede; he closed his eyes.

And must have fallen unconscious, for he came awake to the bone-crunching pain of impact with a hard floor. When he could pry his eyes open again, 'twas to the sight of a rug against his face. He squinted up the runner and saw marble stairs, a pair of feet clad in boots so expensive and delicate they must surely be nonfunctional out of doors, the legs of a gilded chair. The Great Hall. The Aegis's throne. And, it seemed, the Aegis himself.

"On your knees, *gróm.*"

Some guard, prodding him with the blunt end of a pike. A veritable jest; he couldn't so much as lift his head proper off the rug. It must have shown, for hands quickly grabbed him at the armpits and dragged him up.

Strange how much this reminded him of those first hazy moments at Castle Farr.

"I do believe I mentioned once already," the Aegis said to him, "that I dislike such spirit in my slaves."

And there the semblance to Farr ended. But oh, what he'd give to be facing Freyrík right now.

"Have you nothing to say for yourself?"

Ayden spat a mouthful of blood—most carefully not in the Aegis's direction, for such spirit was not worth the pain he'd suffer for it—and said, "Is a slave banned from walking? Or is it a crime now to seek fresh air?"

"You would lie to *me*?" The Aegis paused a beat, but Ayden made no reply. "Your master may be an outland prince, but he was raised within these walls. *My* walls. I expected he'd have taught you better."

"Not his fault," Ayden said quickly, taking pains to enunciate round his swollen lower lip. He'd never meant Rík to be blamed for this. "I am a poor student."

"A poor instigator, as well, for you rallied not one of your fellow slaves to your cause."

Bollocks.

"It's true," the Aegis said, so self-satisfied that Ayden half expected to see a wet spot on the man's breeches. "Come, Jagall, tell him."

Jagall? A fist-sized stone settled hard and miserable in the pit of Ayden's belly as Jagall stepped from the vestibule behind the dais and knelt beside the Aegis's throne. Surely Jagall wouldn't support the human's lies? Surely he was being compelled—

"It's true," Jagall said. His face wore no sympathy, no hint of struggle or regret. At least none that Ayden could see.

"You betray your people," Ayden spat—literally—at Jagall's feet, saliva and blood and fury. He strained forward in the guards' hold, but they easily outmatched his rage. "For what, *svíkja*?" Jagall winced at that, a human insult for a human pet. "For *him*? For your gods-cracked human masters? You tone-deaf, pathet—"

A fist slammed into his bruised cheek, ripping him clear from the guards' grips. He heard the crack before he felt it, a fire below his eye as cruel and blistering as Jagall's duplicity. He lay where he fell, hand pressed to his fractured cheek, huddled against it all.

Yet no one struck him again, or spoke another word. No one even bothered to drag him back up to his knees.

Feet in his vision again. A hand on his shoulder. Ayden flinched from it, but there came no pain. At least not of the flesh, though what followed was somehow worse.

The *svíkja* ducked his head to meet Ayden's eyes. "My word means nothing to you now, I know, but I give it regardless. If but one—just *one*—of our sisters or brothers had thought running worth the risk, I'd have kept silent and let them cast their lot with you. But none thought it so. You're blind, Ayden, as well as deaf. Could you not see how your willful insistence upset them, reminding them time and again of all they have lost? I could not let you go on hurting my people."

His people? Ayden pushed up on one elbow—as close as he could manage to sitting just now—and knocked Jagall's hand from his shoulder. He might have to endure the *svíkja*'s lies, but not his touch. Not again, never again.

No lies, Ayden, and you know it. You were alone in those woods. You are alone here. None wished to join you.

Jagall held Ayden's gaze. His eyes were absent thought, absent will, absent even false sympathy. No, Ayden saw naught there but the deadened fear of a caged beast too weary to keep fighting. Beaten, sniveling at its master's feet, so intent upon avoiding pain that it failed to notice when its cage was left unlocked. He saw hopelessness, madness, the endless slow passage of three hundred years.

Worst of all, Ayden saw his future.

Chapter Ten

Lord Trúr made surprisingly good company when he wasn't tending to the post of sentry with dangerous zeal. The ambassador was clever, impassioned, and unafraid to speak his mind, even in the company of his betters. Nor did he begrudge Freyrík for nearly lopping off his stones. Berendil was wise to have trusted him, wiser still to have included him in this intimate gathering. Their numbers were rounded out only by King Villtr, whose mind was sharp as an elfsteel blade on the rare occasions he chose to wield it.

They were huddled in Berendil's drawing room, close round a table piled high with ancient scrolls—accountings of Surges from the very first to the very latest. Or rather, three of them were huddled close. King Villtr was leaned back in his chair, content to let the rest of them sift the wheat from the chaff.

And wheat they had found indeed, a faded account of a dark elf sighting some two hundred years back, and the Midr king's petition to track them down and kill them.

Berendil furled the scroll closed, absently tapped it to his lips. Brittle as the old thing was, a piece of edging flaked off at the contact.

"Brother, please," Freyrík said, reaching out to still him. "While Your Majesty's kiss is surely an honor, this scroll mayhap is too withered to survive such excitement."

Berendil huffed, half laugh, half irritation, and placed the scroll back on the table.

Freyrík slid it over with reverent fingers and scanned the ancient lines of text once more. "I wonder . . . If they had succeeded then, might we all have been born free of this war?"

Another huff. "We'd have wasted our youth away to boredom and idle leisure."

"Like some wealthy midlander, gods help us."

Berendil nodded. "Gods, you'd have become a *poet*. How utterly mortifying."

Freyrík laughed along with Berendil, and even Lord Trúr was smiling. King Villtr, on the other hand, was glaring daggers at them all.

Freyrík cleared his throat and kicked his brother under the table—respectfully. "Apologies, Your Majesty," he said to King Villtr. "We did not mean you, of course."

"Of course," Berendil added.

King Villtr merely grunted.

"Anyway," Freyrík said, fingering the scroll once more, "I wonder why we were not taught of this. An Aegis who planned to take the war to the darkers—"

"And was overruled by the Council. How ironic."

Berendil slid the scroll out from under Freyrík's fingers, tied its old ribbon back round it, and set it aside with a pile of others. "Do you see now, brother? The gods have whispered this plan in the ears of kings before. We have ignored them, and see how our people have suffered for our hubris! But no more. Tonight, but three hours from now . . ." Berendil's breath caught, and he dropped his gaze to his clenched hands. Overcome by excitement?

No, there was no mistaking the sudden shine of his eyes, the furrow of his brow.

"It pains me," Berendil said at last. "I too loved him as a father. But in that regard, he has failed me. Failed us all." Berendil looked up, but only at Freyrík. There his gaze remained, soft, beseeching. "Time now for the chosen son to step up and take control of his fate, can't you see?"

Oh, but he saw—through both the son's eager eyes and the father's cautious ones. If only those views were the same . . . But they were not, and wishing on a darker's claw would only see you wounded.

Freyrík nodded, turned his eyes from Berendil's stare. "I see, brother."

A hand squeezed his shoulder, the touch firm and familiar. There'd been a time he'd trusted that touch to protect him from all the world's ills.

"Good," Berendil said. "Good. Now go to your rooms. You must prepare. Have your elf lighten your spirit, for you'll need all your senses at supper tonight."

"And I shall have them, my lord." Freyrík stood, bowed at the waist as he backed from the table. So little time remained; he wished only to spend it in his rooms with Ayden, in the sweet silence of privacy. Might Berendil allow him that now?

... 'Twould seem not. That same befanged shadow of a lord fell in at Freyrík's heels the moment he left Berendil's rooms.

Strange how for the first time, the lack of trust stung. And gods but he wished to be alone, just for a moment, if only so he could ease his iron hold on his expression. He looked over his shoulder, narrowed his eyes at the man and bared his teeth darker-like, then turned round just in time to avoid crashing into a page.

The page drew up short and dropped into a hasty bow. "Your Highness," he said, panting as if he'd run clear across the keep, "the Aegis Exalted commands your presence."

In an instant, all the world came into shocking focus: the rasping breaths of the page, the slide of fabric from the lord behind—a hand moving toward his dagger?—the soft sound of voices some corridors distant, the slightest current in the air.

For surely it could not be this easy. Three days he'd spent turning and turning this stone in his palm, seeking the crack, the way inside. And now here 'twas handed on a golden tray, his for the taking, just hours before the coup's fruition. Had the Aegis uncovered their treachery, then? Did he wish to interrog—

"Please, Your Highness," The messenger said, bowing deeper still. "'Tis most urgent."

Freyrík nodded and followed the rushing messenger down the corridor. The pace left him little time to plan, and half his focus remained on the lord three steps behind, shadowing him still. Had the Aegis somehow found Berendil out? Why else summon Freyrík alone, and with such haste? To ask him to betray his brother? To extract from him the names of all involved? He coughed round a half-hysteric laugh; three days ago he'd have told the Aegis everything if only he'd been given the chance, but now ... now ...

They reached their destination all too quickly. Freyrík stood outside the Lord Protector's chamber door and simply breathed.

Shoved his hair from his face and wished 'twere so easy to shove back his rising gorge as well.

A glance over his shoulder revealed his shadow yet glaring from the corner of the hallway. Too late for the man to stop him now; all he could do was report back to Berendil. Report what, though?

If he truly were trapped now between one death and another, then at least he could do the right thing for his people before the end. He only wished he knew what that was.

One last breath, something less than half-panicked, and he knocked upon the closed door.

The attendant who opened it bowed him inside. There waited the Aegis, seated stiff upon a sofa and looking stern as Freyrík had ever seen him. The room tilted once, hard, and righted itself again; Freyrík grasped at the nearest thing to hand, the wingback of a heavy wooden chair. Hardly a politician's smooth response, but then, it seemed the time for concealment was over.

"Sit, Your Highness."

The Aegis gestured toward the chair to which Freyrík was clinging. He dropped into it more than sat, grateful for the invitation but terrified of its formality.

"Your Eminence," he said—or rather, tried to say. The words stuck in his throat until he cleared it, tried again. Nodded once, slow and careful, as if they were strangers.

Silence stretched long and thin between them. Freyrík fought the urge to squirm under his Lord Protector's cold, intense stare. His eyes darted to the nearby side table, where a carafe of wine and two cups stood, and he wished for some to wet his throat. Not without invitation, though—neither wine nor words.

So he waited.

Waited some more.

Let the sweat on his forehead drip into his eyes rather than wipe it away, for if he unclenched his hands from the armrests of the chair, they would start trembling and might never stop.

"You are concerned," the Aegis said at last.

Freyrík's relief at the waiting's end almost robbed him of breath. "Yes, Your Eminence."

"Why?" A single raised eyebrow, perfectly calm. So at ease, while Freyrík felt sweat trickling down between his shoulder blades.

Why? Because he'd not come forth sooner. Because he'd pretended to throw in with his brother. Because pretense had slowly taken deeper roots . . .

"I fear I have failed you," he said, hands yet tighter on the armrests, head bowed beneath the Aegis's regard.

"Yes. You have." Spoken softly, no anger in his words. Simply fact. *Water is wet. The sky is blue. Dark beasts eat our future.*

"Please, Your Eminence." Freyrík slid from the chair to his knees. "I beg of you—"

To forgive him? To spare those close to him, who had neither hand nor mind in the conspiracy?

He heard the shuffle of cloth against cloth, the jingle of the Aegis's jewelry, muted footsteps on the rug. One broad hand came to rest atop his head.

"Look at me, *fóstri.*"

Freyrík steeled himself, lifted his head, and met the Lord Protector's piercing brown eyes. He could not read the man's expression.

The Aegis's hand slid down to cup his cheek, his little finger alighting on the pulse at Freyrík's neck. Freyrík shuddered. How easily that finger could be replaced with a knife—how well within the Aegis's right, perhaps even his duty.

"Your elf," the Aegis said, and Freyrík's world tilted again.

"Ayden?" he said without thinking. "Wha— Has he offended in some way?"

The Aegis's hand clenched on his face, fingertips digging into his jaw. "You mean to say you do not know?"

Freyrík shook his head—or tried to, at least, against the steel grip on his face—and let every ounce of sincere confusion bleed into his voice. "I'm sorry, Your Eminence, I—I do not."

The Aegis's eyes bored into him with more force than those fingers at his jaw, but Freyrík made himself bear it. Only guilty men averted their eyes. A long beat, two, three, and at last the Aegis let him go, turned sharply and retook his seat.

The Aegis leaned back in his chair, watching, waiting. When he did not speak, Freyrík ventured, "Your Eminence, if I may—"

The Aegis waved at him—not to speak, but to get off the floor. Freyrík obeyed, but he cared little for dignity just now, only answers.

"Please, Your Eminence," he said as he retook his seat. "About Ayden . . ."

Anger flitted across the Aegis's face at the name, fighting against the man's iron control. "*Ayden* thought to whisk away all my elven prizes," he growled. "Plotted and planned. My guards found him heading for the north wall with two stolen satchels of kit and weapons. *My own dagger* among them, Freyrík, that which I'd gifted *you*."

Oh, Ayden . . . Freyrík dropped his face in his hands, but he could no sooner shut away his despair than he could shield himself from the betrayal in the Aegis's voice.

"And how is it you left him with such spirit? You were brought up in *my* house, Freyrík— Look at me. *Look at me*." Freyrík pried his hands from his face, curled them back round the armrests and forced himself, somehow, to meet the Aegis's eyes. "You know better."

He nodded. "I do, Your Eminence. Please, if I could just explai—"

"There is nothing to explain!" The Aegis punctuated his shout with an open palm to his thigh, hard enough to bruise. "Your infatuation with your plaything blinded you to the simplest truth— that he is yet the enemy. I will not have this discord in my court!"

"Your Eminence, I— You are right, of course, I was blinded. Please, let me correct my oversight. I will break him well this time, I swear it. I beg of you—"

"It is already done, Freyrík."

Stiff as death, of a sudden. An iron rod in his back, fusing his spine, his ribs. He couldn't breathe, couldn't move, couldn't wrap his mind round what horror those words portended. *Oh gods please, gods please do not let him be . . . We haven't even said good-bye—*

Except they had, hadn't they, this morning. That desperate kiss. He'd thought it for his own departure, his own risk. He hadn't known—couldn't have known—just as he'd asked of Ayden—

A sob ripped free of his chest, and he caved in on himself, trembling with the pain of it all. *Ayden, Ayden . . . I'm so sorry—*

A hand alit upon his head, and he jerked upright.

"Be easy, Freyrík. He is not dead."

Not dead? He tried to move, to lift his head and read the truth upon the Aegis's face. But the combined weight of that hand and his relief was too great, all his strength spent drawing air, merely breathing, and when had the Aegis stood and crossed the room anyway?

One shaky, shallow breath. Another. At last Freyrík could lift his head, if only a fraction, but hope, hope . . . "Not—?"

"No." The Aegis looked kindly down upon him. "Beaten half to death in capture, though." The Aegis ignored his wince, soft smile never faltering. "He is in the stone rooms; a healer examines him now."

Examines, Freyrík noted, and winced again. Not *tends*. A deliberate distinction on the Aegis's part.

He gathered up the tattered remains of his courage and asked, "May I see him, then?"

But the Aegis was already shaking his head, lifting his hand from Freyrík's hair. He turned away and walked back to his seat. "Gods above, Rík, you must not fly your heart on a pennant so. Not all among us will be as forgiving as I."

Forgiving? Freyrík choked on a bitter laugh, covered it with a cough. But too late, or too poorly done; the Aegis spun back with a slitted stare. "You think me harsh?" he demanded.

"N-no, Your Eminence, I didn't mean—"

"Enough! It is your own softness, your own weakness that forces my hand. Be consoled—I shall not take your slave's life. But since he cannot be trusted to know his place and keep to it, he will be hobbled tomorrow. A lesson made before the other slaves."

Hobbled. Ayden held down at the Aegis's orders as hammers shattered his ankles—

Freyrík launched himself from his chair, crumpled at the Lord Protector's feet. "I pray you, Your Eminence!" He reached for the Aegis's ring hand, but it was denied him. Panic swelled in his throat. He pressed his forehead to the Aegis's boots, kissed them fervently. "Spare him this, please!" A desperate gambit then: "Please, *náungi*, as a man who understands such feelings . . . you yourself admit your love toward Simi—"

"Be silent, boy." The Aegis extricated his feet from Freyrík's arms, stepped back. "And count yourself lucky I'll not have his tongue ripped out too. That, at least, he'll still have much use for."

Freyrík shuddered, a full-body tremor that rattled his knees against the floor. "You would have him . . . ?"

The Aegis chuckled, dry and low. "You bare your heart again, Freyrík. I only meant he must remain of use to *you*. But I warn you now, if you cannot keep him silent in future, I shall indeed see him gagged by every eager cock in my court. Am I understood?"

Freyrík nodded until he could force his leaden tongue to shape words. "Yes, Your Eminence."

"Good. Now compose yourself, *fóstri*. It pains me to my very soul to see you so unmanned by an elf."

"Yes, Your Eminence," he repeated, scraping himself off the floor. He dusted off his knees, grimaced as he swallowed the foul taste in his mouth. A goblet was thrust into his hands—he fumbled, nearly dropped it. Murmured his thanks as the Aegis returned to his seat across the room.

"Is there anything else, *fóstri*?"

Freyrík stared at the man he'd always loved like a father, his hand tight round the goblet's stem. Thoughts of Berendil and death and war and darkers swirled in his mind.

He drank deep and set the goblet down upon the side table. "No, *náungi*. Nothing."

For the first time all winter, the Great Hall felt empty at the evening meal. Many a visiting dignitary had left for home, particularly those of the southern and eastern lands whose return journey would not be hindered by blizzard or treacherous passes.

Berendil's contingent of conspirators still remained, of course, for it took sword arms to quarter a darker lion, even with its head cut off. The men were scattered up and down the table, on either side of Freyrík, who drowned his stare in his soup and tried very hard not to look at them.

"Eat, brother."

Berendil. He'd spoken from the side of his mouth, as if he too were afraid to make eye contact tonight.

Freyrík picked up his spoon and made himself swallow what was on it. Like every course so far, it tasted of poison on his tongue; a foolish thought, when *that* would come hidden in the fish sauce, and certainly not served to him. At least, so he hoped.

"I hear tell your elf besmirched our House today."

Freyrík's head whipped round, angry words eager to follow, but 'twas clear at a glance Berendil would brook no such outburst. Freyrík hid his glare in his dish once again, fingers tight on his spoon.

Berendil leaned in close enough to whisper. "I'm sorry it betrayed your trust, brother. But do not be disheartened by the Lord Protector's rebuke. He thinks you soft, but he is no better. Hobble the elf?" He scoffed, a hot puff of air against Freyrík's ear. "I would see him flogged to death before the others. A necessary cost. But *His Eminence* and all his simpering soft-bellied midland parasites do not understand sacrifice. And so we lose the war, as surely as we lost the slaves' respect."

The grim fury in Berendil's voice was not unfamiliar, though Freyrík had only heard it directed at darkers before. That, he could have understood. But this . . . Gods, he'd thought the Aegis cruel! Had a lifetime of fighting twisted his brother so? Or perhaps it was High Court itself?

And what else in Berendil was twisted? His ambitions? His dreams? His plans?

A footman cleared away his soup bowl, refilled his cup with wine. He touched neither.

A necessary cost . . . like the Aegis's life? Could he question one but not the other? He snuck a glance at the dais, where the Lord Protector was holding a wine goblet to Simi's lips. Her delicate face fair glowed with admiration for the Aegis Exalted. The same admiration Freyrík himself had once felt.

Berendil's hand squeezed his thigh, calling his attention back. Freyrík clenched his eyes shut. When he opened them, a dish of whole mackerel in tarragon sauce, iced fresh instead of salt-cured on the long journey inland, occupied the table before him.

A necessary cost.

Berendil's hand tightened on his thigh.

The smell of the mackerel turned his stomach.

He wanted to take Ayden home.

A screech of chair legs on the floor, the hiss of steel against leather, and then—

"Poison, Your Eminence!"

Silence.

The clatter of dropped silver on porcelain. Guards coming alive throughout the hall, weapons drawn. Murmurs of shock and outrage.

And Freyrík in the middle of it all, on his feet, dagger in hand, throat still sore from the force of his shout.

Gods help him, what beneath the shadow had he done?

The next minutes were a maelstrom of motion, noise, shouts, and jostling. Freyrík remembered only the twin gazes cleaving as if blades into his flesh: his Aegis and his brother, both struck speechless with surprise and betrayal.

Then the Aegis was whisked away, the dining hall locked down tighter than a convent. Guards pervaded the room, herding everyone away from the tables, stripping the men of weapons, enforcing silence. A burst of panic as one of the noblemen collapsed to the floor, convulsing. Freyrík watched with his heart in his throat. The man was but a secretary to an Aegean minister; as far as Freyrík knew, his death held no cause.

How little did he truly know, then?

He glanced at his own distant plate of fish and wondered.

Then the time for wondering was over, as a full contingent of the Aegis's personal guard separated him from the crowd and marched him away, forceful and callous even though Freyrík offered no resistance. He couldn't blame them. Nor could he shake the prickle of his brother's glare between his shoulder blades until the heavy doors closed behind him, cutting it off.

The cool corridors offered little comfort. The twenty guards closed ranks round him, both forestalling escape—which he did not so much as contemplate—and shielding his life. Still Freyrík expected to be struck down before they reached their destination. Every servant they passed, every bewildered-looking lord, could be one of Berendil's agents. Any one of them could slip a knife between his ribs, hoping to save the rest.

At least Ayden was secure in the stone rooms, gods thanked. And Freyrík's sons as well, escorted by Lord Vitr to their cousin's country estate.

As for himself, the guards delivered him unharmed to the Aegis's inner sanctum, but he held little confidence he'd remain so for long.

The room was large, lit bright as a furnace, absent windows or any doors but one, and bristling with armed guards. After the coolness of the corridors, the wall of warm air slammed into him with cloying force. He was instantly soaked with sweat.

Or perhaps that was due to the Aegis's unreadable stare, which pinned him as if a darker beast to a surgeon's table.

The Aegis waved him over to a single empty chair at the small ornate table where he himself was seated. Freyrík fair collapsed in it, as if he were wearing full armor rather than court finery. A footman poured him a cup of wine—strong stuff, unsweetened, unwatered—from a pitcher no doubt already tasted.

Freyrík drank it down in one long breathless go.

The Aegis himself leaned forward to refill his cup, looking far too calm for a man who'd narrowly escaped assassination. Freyrík downed half the wine again before he realized the Aegis wasn't touching his own full cup. He froze, eyes darting to the Lord Protector's face.

"Speak, *fóstri*," the Aegis said grimly.

Conquering his nausea—the wine, or just nerves?—Freyrík began his tale, painfully aware that every word dug deeper his own grave and Berendil's.

The Aegis listened well. So studious, in fact, that try as he might, Freyrík could read no emotion on his stone-hard face. Though betwixt the beginning and the end of his tale, the Lord Protector seemed to age years.

Quickly, before the questions could begin, Freyrík added, "I pray you remember their cause and be merciful, Your Eminence. They are not greedy men, nor arrogant for kings, nor lusting for power. They want only what is best for the Empire."

The Aegis raised a single eyebrow.

"As do you, of course," Freyrík rushed to amend. "You simply . . . do not agree on its nature."

The Aegis inclined his head, lifted his cup to his lips and sipped slowly. Some measure of tension dissolved from Freyrík's guts; he followed suit, draining his own cup dry.

Yet the Aegis's next words wounded him anew.

"You aim to make yourself a neutral piece on this chessboard," the Lord Protector said. "Have you forgotten there is no such thing?"

Freyrík began to answer, but fell silent at the Aegis's hand cutting through the air.

"You betrayed me, Freyrík. First, when against my wishes you promoted your brother's aspirations with the Council. Second, when you did not come to me immediately after you stumbled upon that darkers' nest."

"They would have killed me—"

"Then you should have died." The Aegis's face was an implacable mask, his fingers light and steady round the stem of his cup. "At least your death would have served to warn me where you yourself failed to do so. And third, but four hours past, when you looked me in the eye and lied. *You had nothing else to say*, remember?"

Indeed he did. His anger, his humiliation, his despair . . . "But I spoke at last, *náungi*. I spoke in time. Surely that holds worth? If not my life, then Berendil's at least, whose purpose was pure throughout—"

"Enough!" For the first time, the Aegis's face twisted with rage, and he pounded the table with both fists, knocking over their goblets and spilling dark red wine on the cloth between them. "Can you not see I value your life above theirs?"

Silence, thick and heavy, broken only by their breathing. Wine dripped like blood off the table into Freyrík's lap. He let it.

Finally Freyrík said, "Yet you would rip from my life all I treasure. Can *you* not see? I belong to you both with all my heart, and it bleeds to see you at odds."

The Aegis leaned back in his chair, face wiped clear of emotion once more. "And yet you chose to warn me," he murmured, seemingly to himself, gesturing for a footman to clean the table.

Gods, but Freyrík had forgotten all about the servants, about the guards that lined the walls at attention. He shrank down in his seat.

The Aegis seemed a giant by contrast as he rose from his chair. Freyrík hastened to follow lest he insult the man further, but the Aegis waved him back with a careless hand. He began to pace. Was this where Freyrík had learned the habit?

"You truly did see merit in their plan," the Aegis said.

"Yes." Freyrík followed with his gaze as the Aegis paced round the room. "The old accounts—"

"I am well familiar with the old accounts," he said, drawing to a stop before a guard and fingering the dagger at the man's hip. He unsheathed it, held it before his eyes and turned it this way and that.

"And yet," he continued, eyes still upon the blade in his hand, "to gamble everything on a single long shot in an endless night . . ." His eyes met Freyrík's again. "Would you have done it?"

Freyrík swallowed, wishing his goblet were still full. "'Tis not for me to say, Your Eminence. I am but a prince of an outland province—"

"No, child." The Aegis's voice glided as smooth and lethal from his lips as a darker water snake, even as he glided bodily round the room. "You do not get to play that game anymore; you've been denied it by your own hand. Now you must answer me as a king, nothing less."

King. He could grasp the implications of *king* no more than he knew how the seasons turned. The word meant nothing. He *felt* nothing.

Yet to *do* nothing was a luxury denied him. The muscles in his back bunched as the Aegis paced round behind him. He clenched his hand on his knee against the tingle at his nape, and braced to cast his lot in with truth, no matter the outcome.

"As king, I would steel my heart against the temptation. But I know well its pull and power, and would absolve those who succumb."

Silence—even the footsteps had ceased—then a bark of laugh from behind him. The Aegis's hand landed on his left shoulder, and 'twas all Freyrík could do not to flinch. Harder still when a second weight fell upon his right shoulder, cold and hard: the borrowed dagger, its tip just visible from the corner of his eye, hovering near his throat.

"Ah, *fóstri.* I should never have allowed your father to name Berendil over you."

Freyrík swallowed, so careful, shook his head but a fraction of an inch. "Nay, Your Eminence. Berendil is a good king, and I have never wanted the throne—"

"How little it matters what we want." Away went the knife, and the Aegis's hand along with it. Freyrík blew out a breath, relieved and bereft all at once. "But this one time," the Aegis said, pacing back into his sight, "I shall grant your wish."

Hope flared in Freyrík's chest, bright and powerful as elfglow unfettered. He met the Aegis's gaze, praying he wasn't merely hearing what he wished to hear—wasn't merely succumbing to temptation.

"Your brother's life," the Aegis said, then grimaced. "My son's life. The rest of the connivers', as well."

"Thank you, Your Eminence," Freyrík breathed, barely more than a whisper for all his conviction. "They will do your mercy proud, I am certain—"

"But there is, of course, a price."

Price. Such a simple word to fill him with such dread.

He watched closely as the Aegis retook his chair and tapped his borrowed blade against the table.

The Aegis stilled his blade and caught Freyrík's eye. "You argue well, Freyrík. In fact, you have convinced me of some merit in your brother's plan."

He had?

"You understand you will be king now."

He would?

"But you said—"

"I said I would spare their lives. Would you have me seat those darker vipers at my table, embrace them to my heart?"

He supposed not—indeed, he'd not have done so were he the Lord Protector. "No, Your Eminence."

The Aegis nodded. "I will allow them to repent—to be stripped of rank and title and sent to fight at the front lines of battle, never to return to my court or any other. An honorable life, some would say. An honorable death, when it comes. Does that satisfy you?"

Satisfy? To never see Berendil again? To know his proud brother, gods-chosen to lead, would serve as a common soldier under some boorish field commander?

Better than seeing Berendil's decaying head in a cage on the outer wall.

He bowed his own head, shook it once, but the image of those cages refused to leave. "Yes, Your Eminence. 'Tis very generous."

Even if said generosity came at a price.

The thin smile on the Aegis's lips suggested his thoughts flew parallel to Freyrík's. "Well, then, Your Majesty."

Your Majesty. A shiver ran up Freyrík's spine to the top of his head, where soon his brother's crown would sit.

"Your Eminence?"

"I would have a show of loyalty from my new king."

"Of course, Your Eminence. Name it and it shall be yours."

Only gods, please, do not name Ayden on top of everything else.

"Reports in Midr are confirmed—a Surge gathers. Three weeks at the earliest. You must leave on the morrow and may still be too late."

"You wish me to join the defense?" He frowned. "King Skaut of Midr is a capable leader. He's fended off as many Surges as King—as—" A bright hot flash of despair, like lightning to his heart. He wrestled it down, buried it until such time as he could confront it privately. "As my brother has."

He did not fail to register, through his faltering, the cold appraising look in the Aegis's eyes. Not join the defense, then . . .

"You would have me deploy the new stratagem? Lure the darkers into a trap of our choosing?"

Perhaps if he finally credited Ayden with the plan, the Aegis would spare him further harm . . .

But the Lord Protector still regarded him with unreadable eyes.

"Your Eminence?"

Slowly the Aegis picked up his borrowed dagger, set its tip on the table and turned it round and round with deft fingers. His stare, however, remained fixed on Freyrík.

"You will follow this Surge to its source, *fóstri.* Past the Crack, into the heart of the darker forests. You are not to lend aid to the settlements." A turn of the dagger. "You are not to engage the beasts in battle." Another. "Yours is but to find the source of this Surge."

"The dark elves?" Freyrík asked.

The Aegis shrugged. "Whatever it may be. Destroy it if you can. If not, send bird for reinforcements."

Freyrík nodded slowly, even as he scrambled to comprehend the enormity of the task. "And if we find nothing?"

The Aegis sat forward with a sour smile and leveled the dagger's tip at Freyrík's chest. "Then look again."

Chapter Eleven

etching Ayden from the stone rooms was one of the harder things Freyrík had ever done, and for more reasons than he cared to count—not that his treacherous mind obliged him.

He found Ayden curled on a narrow stone bench against the wall, shackled there with heavy irons by the ankles and wrists. At least someone had thrown a blanket over him, but still he was shivering, staring off at nothing through hooded eyes. One whole side of his face was bruised, and gods only knew what the blanket was hiding. It worried Freyrík that Ayden did not sit up when he approached, nor respond when he called Ayden's name.

He knelt beside Ayden, touched gentle fingers to his hair. He thought to kiss the elf but worried he'd hurt him; there seemed no inch of him unmarred by cruelty.

"Ayden?" he whispered.

Dull green eyes flicked up to his, lingered a moment, then flicked back to nothing.

Gods help him, what beneath the shadow had they done to him?

Freyrík rounded on the healer slave who hovered across the room, as far away from Ayden's starfall as she could. "What's wrong with him?" It came out harsher than he'd meant. Even well out of striking distance, she flinched.

Then she muttered, eyes firmly to the floor, "He is punished for his crimes, Your Highness."

Yes, he could see that perfectly well himself, thank you. "You are to heal him now. Every last cut and bruise. We travel at first light." When the healer made no move, he added, "On the Aegis's orders. Come now, do as I say."

She took a step. Another. Stopped, pressed the heel of one hand to her temple. "His starfall, Your Highness . . ."

"Cannot be removed."

And not for lack of trying. But no amount of begging or reasoning had won the Aegis's heart in this matter. It seemed a miracle Freyrík had even secured permission to take Ayden with him.

His back teeth hurt; he realized he was clenching his jaw and forced himself to relax. "Come," he ordered again, taking a large step to close the distance between them. He'd throw her over his shoulder if he had to.

The healer inched forward once more, a grimace on her fair face. She was hurting, he knew, but that did nothing to temper his impatience. Not when Ayden was hurting so much worse.

Perhaps she sensed this, for she came forward at last, half-knelt, half-collapsed at Ayden's side, and laid her head upon his chest.

The sound Ayden made at that pierced Freyrík just as surely as the starfall's noise pierced the healer.

Yet she did not seem to notice anymore. She was already gone to her healing trance, glowing fit to roll back the night. Freyrík moved beside her and brushed fingertips across Ayden's cheek.

Chains rattled as Ayden's hand inched out from beneath the blanket, clutched at Freyrík's sleeve. Freyrík bit his lip. Even his fingers were bruised, though he had no cuts on his knuckles; he'd not fought back, and gods but that made it all so much worse.

"Rík?" Ayden rasped.

Freyrík took Ayden's hand in his own. "I'm here."

A long, slow blink, like mayhap Ayden thought he was a dream. "I don't—" He winced, whimpered as the healer's elflight flared, fingers tightening round Freyrík's with but the strength of a dying child's. "How? They told me I could not see you."

His fingers tightened again, barely a whisper against Freyrík's own. Freyrík reached out to wipe a tear tracking its way down Ayden's temple, felt his own threatening to spill. "Circumstances have changed. We leave this place on the morrow."

"Home?" Ayden asked, and the hope his whisper carried nearly broke Freyrík's heart.

"Nay, I'm afraid not."

Ayden blinked, long and slow. He seemed to have trouble parsing even Freyrík's simple reply. "Where then?"

"Midr Province."

Another blink, and then finally, simply, "Oh."

His eyes slid closed again. No more questions, though there should have been dozens. Freyrík laid his hand upon the crown of Ayden's head and followed it with a gentle press of lips to one damp temple. "Just sleep, Ayden," he whispered. "I'll be right here."

Everything else could wait 'til morn.

Ayden slept like the dead. No dreams, no memory of how he'd ended up in Rík's bed, in Rík's arms, mind clear and body absent pain. 'Twas shocking, breathless relief, and he clung to it. Clung to Rík, who'd slept through Ayden's waking—the sleep of the unafraid. Perhaps 'twas justified, for whatever had happened, Rík had survived the day. Ayden clung to that too, and went back to sleep.

When next he woke, the room had lightened just enough to see by, and Rík was gone. Had someone come for him in the night? Surely not, else Ayden would never have woken. Left, then? Off to attend court business without so much as a farewell kiss?

A door opened, something thudded across the room, and Ayden bolted up in bed. Another thud. Footsteps. Voices. Rík. "Over there, please," Rík said.

A voice Ayden didn't recognize answered, "Yes, Your Majesty." More thudding. Drawers opening and closing.

Packing? He stuck his head out the bed curtains. Yes, definitely packing. Was Rík going on a hunt?

Midr. Last night, in the healer's room. He'd said something about Midr. Whyever would they be going *there*?

He meant to ask Rík, but the man was clearly busy, speaking in hushed and hurried tones with what seemed an endless stream of men in and out of their rooms, taking equally hurried bites from a hunk of brown bread he carried round from place to place. Besides, 'twas not a slave's place to question his master; Ayden daren't risk it in front of so many people.

He stood from the bed and dressed quietly as some dozen servants packed Freyrík's things beneath the watchful eyes of Lord Vitr—returned in the night, it seemed, from wherever he'd gone—and Freyrík's occasional order. Ayden knew him well enough now to see the excitement in his eyes, hear the eagerness in his voice. Had the coup succeeded after all, then? His brother's life spared? Would they travel through Midr into Feral lands now?

He tied the last lace on his boot, and straightened to find Rík standing before him, smiling wide. Rík seized him by the head and kissed him square on the lips. "Good morning, Ayden."

Ayden's return greeting was considerably less . . . frisky. "What's happened?" he asked. "Where are we going?"

Freyrík grabbed him by the wrist and led him to a table in the drawing room, set with simple fare. "Eat, and I shall tell you everything."

The sight of food turned his stomach, but he poured himself a mug of tea and listened close as Rík spoke. The failed coup. The Aegis's mercy. The crown of Farr. The test of loyalty to come.

This Feral goose chase sat ill with Ayden, yet never did he argue his inclusion in it. Of course he would go with Rík. *For* Rík, yes, but if he were brutally honest, he'd go out of fear as well. It was harder now to blame Jagall for what he'd done. Ayden didn't know what he'd do, what he'd say, what he'd promise these humans if they came for him again as they had yesterday.

Freyrík returned to packing with a final admonishment to eat. He did not, though he knew he should have. Healing took much from a body, and his was weak now. But his belly was weaker and would not have it.

As the commotion died down, Freyrík came back to the drawing room and handed Ayden a weapons belt—with weapons. A short sword, two long daggers, six small knives weighted for throwing, a dart gun, and a cache of darts. Ayden strapped it on and inspected each blade in turn. True quality. Elfsteel all.

Next came two lovingly carved sticks and a harness that slung across his back. They were just the right length and heft, tipped with etched steel on both ends. The blessing carved into the tempered wood was in the ancient tongue. These were elven, had no doubt been taken from one of the slaves here. A slave who might never see the world beyond the Splendor again. Who might never fight for his people again.

Who didn't *want* to fight again.

Ayden stowed the sticks in the harness. He didn't want to touch them.

The servants finished packing just as the sun was cresting the horizon. Freyrík rolled up the map he'd been studying and tucked it under his arm, looked up at Ayden from across the drawing room and smiled. "Are you ready?"

So excited, he seemed. Surely not for the task, which was cruel in dead of winter and impossible besides—they could not find that which did not exist. Perhaps just for the leaving of this awful place, then? Or for all the men Freyrík loved having survived the night?

Both, most likely. But neither mattered to Ayden. He did not smile back. His only answer was a sullen shrug.

It pierced his heart to see Freyrík's smile fade away and know he was the cause of it, but he could not find it within himself to undo things.

"Yes, well." Freyrík cleared his throat, crossed the room and placed a hand on the small of Ayden's back. "We'd best be going now. Don't forget your cloak. It's cold out."

Cold was an understatement. Frozen grass crunched beneath Ayden's boots, and the wind tore at his clothes like a Feral magpie. He drew his cowl down and clutched tight to his whipping cloak, hating starfall more and more with every moment. Fallen gods knew how humans ever survived a winter when they could not sing themselves warm.

A footman threw him a horse's reins, which dropped from his stiff fingers. He cursed, bent down to gather them with a hand against the beast's speckled flank. He nearly jumped at the twitch of muscles under his palm. Fallen gods, but these creatures were huge. Menacing, even. How had he never noticed before?

Ridiculous. They were horses, and he'd been riding them since childhood.

He wedged a foot in the stirrup and hoisted himself up, but nearly dropped back down as the horse sidled with a snort. Ayden gave it a sidelong glare, then quickly swung a leg over and found his seat. For a moment, anyway; the horse bucked once, twice, then cow-kicked, almost spilling Ayden from the saddle. Only his balance—and his death grip on the pommel—spared him the humiliation. He'd had enough of that lately, thank you.

At last the beast resigned itself to his presence, wandered off a few steps, and started ripping up grass with its teeth. It did not help Ayden's mood to realize he'd dropped the reins again.

Freyrík rode up beside him, looking torn between laughter and horror.

"You must control its head," he said. He leaned over in his saddle to take Ayden's reins, tugged hard and steady until the horse lifted its head. "Like this." He held both reins in a single overhand grip, fist loosely curled round the extra, palm facing the saddle.

Ayden took the reins and tried to copy the hold, but Freyrík corrected him, sliding his pointer finger between the two reins. "Otherwise they may drag or tangle when the horse need turn its head."

He did as told, and was corrected again. "Do not clench so tight. And don't wrap the reins round your little finger. If the horse pulls of a sudden, the bone may snap."

Great. Just great. He moved his finger, yet when he looked at Freyrík again, 'twas clear he was *still* somehow in the wrong.

"Less slack in the lines," Freyrík said. "If you give the horse leave, it will do nothing but eat. Like a certain elf I know," he added with a stifled grin.

Ayden glared the amusement clear off Freyrík's face.

"Anyway," Freyrík said, shifting in his saddle, "I believe you have it now. Come, follow me."

Ayden watched how Freyrík turned his horse round: leaning his weight and tugging both reins in the direction he wished to go. He copied the motion, but nothing happened. Gods cracked! Human children did this—how hard could it be?

"You must kick it," Freyrík said.

"I must *what*?"

"Kick it," Freyrík repeated patiently. "With your heels."

Ayden sat up straight in his strangely long-stirruped saddle and said, "I'd rather kick *you*."

Freyrík, crack the man, only chuckled. "You will not hurt it, I swear. Just tap with your heels, or squeeze with your thighs. A harder kick will set it running."

Ayden glowered and tried to sing the horse forward. Leaned over in his saddle and let his desire to move spill out of him in commanding waves.

The horse dipped its head in a forceful attempt at the grass, nearly ripping the reins from Ayden's hands.

Fine. Have it your way.

Ignoring Freyrík's encouraging smile, he took firm hold of the reins and tapped his heels against the horse's flanks.

Freyrík's soft laughter followed him as the cracked beast galloped away.

At last he reined the monster in, and it fell in line, peaceful as if it'd never fought him, behind Freyrík's horse. They rode out as they'd ridden in a week past, through each of the four gates in turn. By the time they passed under the last one and veered toward the Góz River, Ayden had come to terms with his horse. When they reached their waiting paddleboat, he felt confident enough to ride straight up the loading plank and to the animal pen: big as a stable, narrow but long, just like the boat.

A deckhand waved him still at the entrance to the pen and took hold of the horse's bridle. Ayden cast it a warning stare as he dismounted, never mind that the beast couldn't see it. Still, he made it safely to his feet, and patted the creature on the shoulder. It turned its massive head and snuffled once against his hand, then turned away as if disgusted he'd not brought it food. *It* . . . He made a point of checking its ducting as he left the stall. A female. Just his luck—a mare with the ego of a stallion.

He left the pen, stopping for a moment to glare at four soldiers leading horses into the enclosure. Lieutenants loyal to the Aegis, the lot of them, sent to nanny him and Freyrík on their mission. How Freyrík could so easily dismiss the insult was beyond Ayden's ken.

At the fore-end of the deck, he found Freyrík overseeing the unpacking of pigeons. Dozens of them. Rík looked up at him and tried on a smile, took one step forward and lifted a hand. Ayden nodded, but then turned away—not quickly enough to miss the hurt in Freyrík's eyes. Crack him anyway for making Ayden feel guilty for a moment's solitude.

He found a quiet stretch of rail upon which to lean and watch the workers finish loading the boat. Five minutes, perhaps ten, and then the boatmen were pulling up the plank. No other people had boarded—just Freyrík and Vitr and Ayden and the Aegean lieutenants. No footmen, no servants, no infantrymen. Just a military force of miniature proportions with the fate of the Empire on its shoulders. How typically, foolishly, *arrogantly* human.

The boat pushed off, and Ayden watched awhile as the Splendor grew slowly smaller. Strange, how little he felt at the sight of that receding horror. He touched the collar round his neck with half-numbed fingers, and realized, *No, not so strange at all.*

The bitter wind drove him belowdecks in search of his and Freyrík's quarters. 'Twas easy to find—it was the only room spanning half the boat and appointed like a floating palace. He drew the curtains over the thick little windows, stoked the fire, and snuffed the lamps; thus nestled in warmth and privacy, he shed his clothes and crawled beneath the covers, where he drifted off to sleep to the old familiar creak of wind and wood and the rocking slap of water against the hull.

Ayden had forgotten how small a ship could feel after several days aboard. Even the grand elven tall ships, triple-masted and sixty paces long, felt cramped and confining after a time. And this ship was no elven beauty.

Worse, the cold drove him belowdecks most days, with no distraction to pass the time. Not even those of the heart or flesh, for he and Freyrík shared a bed but nothing more. Freyrík's new crown sat as burdensome upon his brow as Ayden's collar sat upon his neck. The man mourned for his brother, wore his guilt wrapped tight like a cloak against the wind. Now that the excitement had faded and the drudgery of long travel had set in, Freyrík had too much time to wallow. It left him unreachable, untouchable.

Not, in fairness, that Ayden tried very hard, for he himself felt distant from the world. He spent his days thinking of Jagall, and of Simi, and of all the others he'd left behind. He thought of home. He thought of what would happen if Freyrík died searching for elven phantoms in the Feral woods.

And sometimes, lying in the dark so very near to Freyrík and yet so very far, he thought of running away in the night. But the world seemed a frightening place to the deaf; however could he survive the winter crippled so? And what would become of Freyrík in the cold Feral wood without Ayden to guard his flank?

So he practiced his human-style horsemanship, and took turns at the paddlewheel to stay warm and ward off boredom, and lit the fires by hand in every hearth until he could do it with ease. And when they left the boat for the snow-dusted Góz Highway some fifteen days later, he breathed a sigh of relief—not the least for a strange pang of homecoming as they rode hard for Farr Province.

Yet they never actually *went* home, for Freyrík wished to avoid all ceremony. News of the failed coup and Freyrík's ascension had traveled well ahead of them, so they did not even enter the castle proper. Freyrík made them camp in the game preserves a league off, and his Uncle Feitr, whom he'd tasked to warm the throne, came down to meet them. Ayden left to fetch firewood while the two discussed matters which did not convey well by bird.

He was met by one pleasant surprise, at least, when he returned: along with Feitr had come Freyrík's secretary, Lord Lini. A warm reunion, that, with embraces all round—even for Ayden.

The Lord General Vísi joined them as well, rounding off their party, and off they set again on fresh horses with fresh supplies.

And fresh misery, Ayden soon discovered. Without song, he had no way to escape the winter wind on horseback, and the pains of constant riding added to his wretchedness. The humans all looked so easy in their saddles that he felt a small cold spark of that old hatred rekindled. Even toward Freyrík. He was not proud of it.

Three days gone from Castle Farr, and never once had it warmed enough to thaw water. The air chilled even more as the sun sank toward the horizon, and General Vísi called a halt for the day. Ayden dismounted stiffly, gratefully, and set to work making camp.

He tended the fire, as he had each night since they'd left the boat. It kept him warm, and though it shamed him to admit it, he among them all needed it most.

Cooking also fell under his purview. He'd darted a particularly large jackrabbit early this afternoon, and he spitted it now, glad to avoid their dried rations. Admittedly, this wasn't much better. Though he did his best to dress up the hare with a pot of dried vegetables and rice, all but the hindquarters made for poor eating—and those choice bits would go to Freyrík, of course.

He glanced up at Rík, who was pitching his tent with the help of Lord Vitr. No grand canvas palace this time, just a small simple structure meant to hold the wind and snow at bay. A mockery for a king, Ayden thought. Not that Freyrík seemed to mind.

The others trickled in from their tasks as the night grew dark and the hare finished cooking. Nearly three weeks in on their merry trek from the Splendor, and Ayden hadn't bothered to learn the lieutenants' names. But they knew his, and the two not stuck with first watch greeted him cordially enough. Not camaraderie, but respect. He'd take it.

He shifted aside to make room for Freyrík—no downed logs or boulders here, so they rested on their saddle blankets on the frozen earth—who unsheathed a knife to carve the jackrabbit. The silence between them was colder than the night, but when Freyrík cut the back leg and groin from the hare, he passed the steaming plate to Ayden.

When Ayden eyed him, Freyrík shrugged and said, "You caught it," but Ayden thought he heard, *I don't deserve it.*

Or maybe he'd really heard, *I love you. Help me come home.*

Gods, how Ayden wanted to. If only he knew how to get there himself.

Freyrík lay on his hard field bed amidst a chilly pile of furs and watched the firelight play across the walls of their tent. A small, practical tent, as unfit for a king as he himself was unfit for the crown.

Was Berendil lying in a tent like this even now, nine common conscripts for company, huddled on his bedroll against the freezing night? Exhausted from a long day's fight? Wounded?

... Dead?

"You are quiet."

Ayden, lying beside him and shivering despite the heat he threw. He glowed no more beneath the starfall, but Freyrík could just make out his features by the light of the fire filtering through the tent walls. He was curled tight beneath the blankets, facing Freyrík. Studying him. So close that Freyrík could see his own reflection in the elf's green eyes.

And yet the handspan of void between them stretched as deep and dark as the Great Crack that had cut off his people forever from the Meiri Sea.

Freyrík rolled over to face him, tucking a hand under his cheek. "As are you."

"We are—" Ayden agreed, or perhaps started something new, but then fell silent again.

Freyrík slid his hand toward Ayden beneath the blankets, but did not touch. "We are what?"

"We are both of us mourning," the elf said, surprising him. Then nothing more for a time.

Freyrík inched his fingers forward until they curled all the way round Ayden's hand, and Ayden flipped his palm up, grasping back.

"And I think . . . I mean, I do not understand why we do not mourn together."

The plain, plaintive words brought tears to Freyrík's eyes. He did not fight them. Could not. No more than he could burden Ayden with all he carried when Ayden bore so much himself.

"This is all my doing," he said, pulling his hand from Ayden's.

Ayden's hand closed like a bear trap round Freyrík's own. He laced their fingers together, tucked them back beneath the covers. "You speak as if you had a choice."

"There are *always* choices!" Gods befanged, he'd shouted so loud he half expected the night watch to come running. "There are always choices," he said again, pretending at a far-distant calm.

"Such as?"

"I could have— If I'd approached the Aegis sooner—"

"You might have died. And your brother. And I."

"You cannot know that," Freyrík said sullenly, though he stopped twisting in Ayden's grasp.

Ayden smiled wanly. "Neither can you. We have each of us made the best choices we could. You did not unseat your brother; he unseated himself. You did not steal my music; I walked into it willingly. You did not send us on this wild chase, and you are not the one who—"

He heard of a sudden in Ayden's voice the same wet tightness he felt in his own. "Who what?" he asked, squeezing Ayden's hand. Gods, how he wanted to take Ayden in his arms. Why didn't he?

"When I—" Ayden swallowed, swallowed again. "When I tried to escape, it was Jagall who betrayed me. And I thought . . . I thought, he is but one elf. He is weak."

"He was," Freyrík whispered fiercely. "*Svíkja.* I would have skinned him alive—"

"No!" Ayden shook his head against his pillow, green eyes glittering in the spare light. "Do not curse him. Curse me if you must. He was right. He spoke for them all. And I was foolish and blind and arrogant to think I could somehow be different. Stronger. Better. And there *are* no dark elves in those woods, Freyrík, there is *nothing to find*, and the Aegis will never let you come home and you will *die* out here and I will be . . . I will be—"

Freyrík gave in to the urge and did pull Ayden into his arms, hugged him so tight they could neither of them breathe. Ayden clung back and cried into his shoulder, "I'll be *lost*, Rík. *Lost!* Promise me you won't—"

—let go.

"Shhh, I promise. I promise I won't. I won't let that happen, do you hear me? I *won't*."

Ayden burrowed somehow closer, and Freyrík welcomed him, twining legs through legs, looping arms round his waist. He pressed his chin atop Ayden's head, feeling him shudder and tremble as if weeping. All Freyrík could do was hold on. But he would do so with all his might. He would not fail another loved one.

Never again.

Ayden seemed cleansed come morn, much like Freyrík himself felt. The elf's tears had sealed the rent between them as sure as desert rains upon dry, fractured soil. Or perhaps 'twas Ayden's strength to shed them that had mended their bond.

Their troubles still weighed heavily, but for certain the day felt a little less cold, a little less dreary, and a lot less lonely.

They rode side by side for the length of it, Ayden's horsemanship yet a pale shadow of his skill before the starfall, but strong enough now not to hinder the party. Freyrík found himself watching the elf ride from the corner of his eye. His balance and seat had not suffered for his deafness, nor had his reflexes.

Freyrík's own, on the other hand, suffered for his watching of the elf. He nearly missed the two stone cairns on either side of the road: the border markers between Farr and Midr. Such an innocent landmark. Yet as Freyrík led his party beyond them into the neighboring province, he shivered bodily.

Midr, where even now a Surge was cresting, where his brother would be fighting, mayhap dying. Midr, where he and his men would pick up the track of some thousand-odd darker beasts and follow them back to their lair.

It seemed madness that his horse did not scream and bolt from under him, but rather strode on without care.

"I said, why so grim?"

He turned round in his saddle to find Ayden reined up beside him, so close their thighs nearly touched. The elf was staring at him, concern shining clear in his eyes.

"I'm fine," he said.

Ayden studied him some more, then nodded. "I thought you might be worried by that." He pointed ahead to a smudge on the horizon, some half a league up the road at the crest of a gentle hill. "What is it?"

"A watchtower," Freyrík answered. "From the days when Midr and Farr often warred."

He frowned, scratched one bristled cheek. Hard to imagine humans fighting amongst themselves now. Not when lives were so precious, ever dwindling in the jaws of the darker threat.

Though did not Berendil's attempt nearly drive us there once more?

He shook the thought from his head and kicked his horse into a trot. "Come," he called over his shoulder, "I don't know about you, but I plan to spend this night with a roof over my head."

Ayden kicked his horse into a gallop and drew ahead, just for a moment. As he passed, he yelled, "Not a chance, human; I claim this in the name of the Elven Republic!"

Freyrík stood in his saddle with a laugh and leaned low over Spyrna's neck. *My arse you will, elf.*

Spyrna knew him well, and he was ten times the horseman Ayden was in any case. He overtook the elf quickly and reached the watchtower first, but Ayden cared not. They all smelled the storm on the wind, and at least this night the snow would not entomb them in their tents.

The stone tower stood stable after all these centuries, but some of the chinking had gone, and the wind slipped sharp and cold through those spaces. Still, 'twas better than the tar-cloth by far, and just as private alone here on the second floor; and once Ayden had set the fire burning merrily, Freyrík was able to shed his winter cloak.

Ayden took one look at it and snatched it for himself, wrapped it atop his own and waddled round stiff and fat-looking as an old midland noble. Freyrík tried not to laugh at that—he scarce thought Ayden would appreciate it—but alas, the urge was stronger than he.

Ayden glared and thrust an elbow at him from across the room, though both look and rude gesture lacked venom.

At last Freyrík wrestled down his laughter enough to say, "I would speak with you, if you would."

"I would not." Ayden folded his arms across his chest and jerked up his chin, but Freyrík found this act no more convincing than the last.

"Very well. I shall simply have to share my fire with Lord Lini."

Ayden's glare returned. They both knew he wasn't talking about the kind of fire one might find in a hearth.

Freyrík took a single step toward the stairs, and Ayden gave in with a gusting sigh.

"Fine," he groused, though beneath it lurked the same smile Freyrík felt upon his own lips. Gods but he'd missed their raillery these last weeks. "We shall *have words*."

Ayden stretched out along their fur-lined field bed with a great, satisfied groan and toed his boots off, then pointed his socked feet at the fire and tucked his arms beneath his head. 'Twas an outwardly casual pose, but Freyrík knew the elf too well—he saw the tension beneath. He felt a curious urge to dispel it with tickling fingers to Ayden's flanks, but quickly quashed the impulse; Ayden would probably punch him in the throat.

He must have stood staring a moment too long, for Ayden turned a narrowed eye toward him and said, "We cannot have words if you have lost them." And then he did a wonderful and unexpected thing: he threw an arm out over the side of the bed, palm up, and wiggled his fingers.

Freyrík crossed the room in three long strides and laid his hand in Ayden's.

"Now?" Ayden asked, pulling their joined hands to his lips and kissing Freyrík's knuckles. 'Twas a gesture deeply fond but absent passion, which suited Freyrík just fine. It wouldn't do to be distracted now.

"Yes." He sat down by Ayden's hip on the sliver of bed the elf had left him. "Last night—"

The way Ayden's gaze shot to his, narrowed and guarded, told him just how fragile was the ground he treaded. But he had no intention of abusing Ayden's gift to him by belaboring it.

"Last night you said there are no dark elves."

Instead of the relief Freyrík expected, Ayden tensed, propping himself on his elbows. "Yes, and?"

"How can you be so sure? How do you prove the *absence* of a thing you cannot see?"

Ayden dropped onto his back again and folded his arms across his chest. "And if I said 'twas dark humans in the Feral woods? Would you concede the possibility of *that*?"

"I—"

"No. You would not. You would be *certain* it could not be. As am I."

Freyrík shook his head. "Nay. 'Tis hardly the same. Why would humans slaughter their own?"

"Gods forbid," Ayden drawled, arching an eyebrow up at Freyrík, then looking rather pointedly round the tower in which they sheltered. "Because they have *never* done that before."

Befang it. "Ayden . . ."

"Freyrík . . ." A perfect, mocking imitation. "Why can you not see what even your own Aegis sees? He himself says there are no dark elves!"

Liar.

He forced back that first cruel instinct—Ayden would *never* lie to him—and blinked down at the elf, waiting for Ayden to correct himself, take it back.

But he did not.

"Why— When did he say this?"

"The night after we arrived. When he"—a pause, a sneer—"*borrowed* me for the evening."

"Surely he was lying to gain your trust."

"Maybe, but I do not think he was."

"You were collared then?"

Ayden grimaced, nodded.

"Then how could you possibly know?" Ayden narrowed his eyes, opened his mouth. Freyrík cut him off before they could begin this same old argument again. "No, never you mind. Forget I asked. Let us . . . let us assume you're right. Then why has he sent me here?"

Ayden sat up, retook his hand—*not trembling, he was* not *trembling*—and stared him dead in the eye. "To close the barn door before all the horses have fled in the most politically expedient way possible. You are a hero, Freyrík; you've saved his life. He cannot simply banish you to the commoners' infantry. And yet he can no longer trust you, for you conspired with your brother, and came forth only soon enough to win his crown. So the Aegis sets you on a grand and noble quest from which—woe is he—neither you nor your problem elf shall ever return."

Such a sharp strategic mind the elf possessed to speak his toxic words so easily. The frightful potential of their truth burrowed slick and deep in Freyrík's chest, cramped his gut and speared his head. And yet they were but *one* possibility, *one* truth, when so many others made sense.

"No." Freyrík pulled his hand back. "No, he would not do it. He would never make so vulnerable the province that guards half the Empire's western flank. Who would sit the throne then? My uncle—brother to the sire of two traitors? Some distant cousin?"

"Or your son."

"A mere *child* on the throne? He would not. He would *not*."

"Not a child. A regent. Placed there by the Aegis himself."

Freyrík stood from the bed, paced once round the little room, twice. Surely Ayden was wrong. The Aegis—his *náungi*—would not do that. He would *not*. "No." He stopped before Ayden, hugged his arms to his chest. "I'm sorry, but I cannot believe it. Not of him."

Ayden blinked up at him, shaking his head, but said nothing more. The stubbornness faded from Ayden's eyes, compassion in its place. "No," he said, "I see you can't."

He held out a hand; Freyrík took it and let Ayden pull him onto the bed. Ayden slung an arm round his shoulder, tucked him tight into his side. "It's all right," Ayden said, and for one foolish moment, Freyrík clung to that, tried to believe it with every fiber of his being. "I see well enough for us both."

Hard as Freyrík pushed them the next two days, Ayden almost regretted having made him face the truth. No matter how fast Freyrík led them or how fiercely the man searched, he would not find the lie he was looking for. But Ayden held his tongue; there was so little left of Freyrík's heart, he cared not to shatter the remains.

Besides, Freyrík was no fool—he'd come round eventually.

In the meanwhile, Freyrík drove them ever on, through snow so heavy even the animals had camped away. 'Twas wet, sticky stuff, liable to gather in clumps on bare branches and drop upon their heads, shaken loose by vibration as they rode beneath. Even the pigeons seemed miserable, huddled and shivering in their covered cages. But the Surge could crest any day. If they missed it . . .

If they missed it, they might gain their lives. For a little while longer, at least. But Ayden knew better than to speak such thoughts aloud.

At last the snow turned to slush, then rain, then disappeared altogether. They were all of them ill-tempered by then, including the horses. Even Ayden was glad when they crested a steep hill and sighted the sprawling human camp awaiting the Surge.

No, not awaiting. Cleaning up from. The decimated remains of a scarecrow field stretched between the camp and the nearby forest. Men were striking tents, cleaning weapons, digging graves—a foolish pursuit in the frozen earth. Strange how silent it all seemed. How underwhelming. He had no sense of the survivors, couldn't sort with his eyes what his mind-ear would once have told him so clearly.

Freyrík turned round in his saddle, shoulders slumped. "We are too late."

General Vísi pulled even beside Freyrík and fished a familiar old farseer from his saddlebag.

"Hey—" Ayden began, but the general had already put the device to his eye.

"Not by much, I do not think," General Vísi said, scanning the field this way and that. "The wounded still bleed. Look." He passed the farseer to Freyrík, or tried to anyway—Ayden leaned in his saddle and snatched it from the general's hand.

"That's mine," Ayden said, inspecting the lenses for damage.

General Vísi had the decency to look sheepish; Lord Lini barked out a laugh.

Yet Freyrík merely put his hand out and said, "May I?"

Ayden thought to deny him, or tease him into begging, but Freyrík's mirthless face and the set of his shoulders put him off it. So fragile, he seemed, so easily shattered. Like the glass in Ayden's farseer. Ayden placed it in Freyrík's outstretched hand, but could not help adding, "I want it back when you're done." 'Twas his, after all. A piece of his old life. A piece of *home*.

"Of course," Freyrík said, airy, absent, as he raised the farseer to his eye. He peered round the camp for several long seconds. And then several more, and more still, until Ayden squinted down himself, trying to determine what had so captured Freyrík's attention. He saw nothing of note with his naked eye, yet still Freyrík looked, and looked.

At last 'twas Ayden who finally saw. He nudged his horse forward, curled a hand round Freyrík's taut shoulder. "He might not even be there, Rík," he said, soft enough for Freyrík alone. When the man said nothing, just swept the camp with the farseer again, Ayden added, "And he is a more than capable warrior, is he not?"

Silence. Tension rippling beneath his fingers. But then, at last, Freyrík lowered the farseer and nodded once, briskly, before offering it back.

Keep it, Ayden was tempted to say, but Rík was waiting, the moment passed. Ayden plucked it from his fingers and tucked it in his saddlebag.

Freyrík nodded again, sharp and firm, patted Spyrna twice on the neck, and squared his shoulders back. "Stay behind me," he said, presumably to Ayden. "'Tis likely none will know you for what you are here, but just the same . . ."

Ayden rather agreed with both sides of that assessment. "Fear not, Rík. I shall try not to break anyone's leg this time."

Freyrík turned round and flashed him a shaky little grin to match his own. "I knew I could depend upon you."

It was the closest thing to a real smile he'd seen from Rík in days, and it left him feeling light and strange in a hundred happy ways. He followed Rík down the hill with but the slightest echo of the angst he'd felt just moments before, Lords Vitr and Lini at his flanks and General Vísi at his back, the lieutenants far behind.

The future was no less tenuous than ever, but the present, at least, would not see them broken.

No fanfare to greet them this time. No announcement. Just a quiet party of ranking officers and a man Freyrík called Prince Ulfr who seemed vaguely familiar to Ayden from High Court. The prince was limping on a leg that clearly pained him, but he seemed to pay it no mind. Just like Freyrík would have done.

Freyrík, General Vísi, and Lord Lini followed Prince Ulfr to his tent to discuss their plan, while the rest of their party—Ayden included—were led to a guest tent. 'Twas blessedly warm inside, strewn with comfortable cushions and hearty food. They all took best advantage while they could, eating and resting round a central pit of hot rocks.

Freyrík returned perhaps an hour later, took a long—and longing—look round the tent, and said, "Mount up. Ayden, in front with me; I shall need your eyes."

Nobody complained as they hoisted themselves from their warm bed of cushions and out into their frozen saddles, but Ayden could see in their faces how much they wanted to. Even Lord Vitr, ever staid, looked weary and out of sorts.

"The Surge crested but nine hours past," Freyrík said as he checked the girth on Spyrna's saddle and then mounted. "Be vigilant. 'Tis almost certain stray dark beasts still stalk these hills."

General Vísi rode abreast of Rík and Ayden, looking very much like he wished to go first in the face of danger. He'd acquired a massive hawk, which perched serenely on the gauntlet on his left arm, taking in the scenery. "Perhaps I should—" he began, but Freyrík cut him off with a shake of the head.

"Nay, my lord. Just be vigilant." That was the last of the conversation, it seemed, for Freyrík kicked his horse into a gallop, and they all followed after.

'Twas harder this time for Freyrík to urge his horse past the great fissure in the earth. No battle fever to grip and carry him; only a sick uncertainty of purpose and the insidious doubt Ayden had planted in his head.

The very air seemed to change as they crossed into the darker forest. 'Twas an overactive mind, mayhap, that saw the sun fall behind the clouds, felt the air chill yet deeper than a moment before. He felt an evil here he'd not noticed the last time he'd dared to cross.

Spyrna slipped on the muddy glass round the crack and went down onto her front knees. Freyrík threw himself clear lest she roll, but she regained her balance and her footing and stood, waiting, for him to remount.

"Your Majesty?"

Several voices at once expressing their concern. Ayden's was absent from the chorus, but he was studying Freyrík from atop his mount.

"I am unharmed." He picked his careful way back to his horse, marveling at the anger of the gods to do such damage, to rent the earth in two and fuse the soil. 'Twas sharp and slippery beneath his feet.

He checked Spyrna's forelegs and hooves before remounting. She hadn't cut herself, but something told Freyrík this was just the beginning of a long line of difficulties in their future. They would not always be so lucky.

He wanted to turn round and ask the others, *Do you feel it?*, but he was their leader, their *king* now, may the gods bless them all ever strong and wise, and it was up to him to keep everyone on task. Even if that meant pretending at his confidence. Gods knew he'd done enough of that in his life already.

Ayden sidled close and touched a hand to his shoulder. He realized he'd just been sitting there atop his horse, staring off into the darker forest like some lost and frightened child. He caught Ayden's worried gaze, nodded once—*all is well*—and then nudged Spyrna forward at a cautious walk.

Once they cleared the barren mud-glass field, 'twas obvious from whence the dark beasts had come. They'd cut a path of destruction like a thousand wild boars, churning up earth, gouging bark, felling saplings . . .

"I do not think you need a tracker just yet," Ayden said. His tone was in jest but his face . . . his face was pure awe and no lack of concern, just like everyone else's. Just, no doubt, like Freyrík's own.

"Be vigilant," Freyrík said. Behind him, he heard men draw steel, and thought how very like children with toys they must seem to the evil within these woods.

They followed the trail for hours as it wound and steepened through the foothills and into the Myrkr Mountains proper, rocks and vegetation strewn like a shipwreck across a path that sometimes spanned half a league or more. They found on occasion a dead darker, trampled into anonymity by its fellow beasts. The horses shied from these corpses, as did his men, as if they feared some hostile spirit might remain. Gods knew it *felt* that way, felt as if the woods had eyes, and through them glared upon his trespass, biding their time to strike.

As the sun began to fall behind the mountains, Ayden said, "We should stop. It will be dark in an hour."

Freyrík's men seemed to find this an agreeable suggestion and took no particular mind to the fact that a slave had made it. Even among the Aegean lieutenants, Drengr and Rekkr were nodding. But Lieutenants Varnan and Herlid wore their distaste like livery, bright and unmistakable. Freyrík could not afford dissent in his ranks, but he would not win harmony at Ayden's expense—not again, *never* again—so he said rather louder than necessary, "Yes, a wise idea, Ayden, thank you."

Ayden eyed him sideways but then nodded, the barest hint of a smile playing at his lips. "If Your Majesty thinks it prudent"—and this, too, spoken a little more loudly than necessary—"I recommend sleeping aloft tonight for safety."

Aloft? Aloft *where*?

"I often make blinds in the trees on patrol, and bed the night in those. Best to have the high ground in a fight, and I'd rather not get trampled while I sleep."

"Indeed," Freyrík said. "Come." He clucked his horse into a walk toward the edge of the unmolested woods. "But let us leave the path. 'Tis far too exposed here for my comfort."

They picked their way through the forest some hundred-odd paces from the edge of the trail—a task made challenging by the steepness of the surrounding land; the dark beasts had taken the path of least resistance—and Ayden dismounted to scout for trees. Freyrík snagged his arm as he walked past, seized of a sudden with an image of Ayden's body slumped over a tree limb, neck broken, dead. Surprised from behind by . . . By what? This, he could not picture.

Ayden glanced up at him through raised eyebrows. "Rík?"

"Take Lord Vísi." He looked round at his fellows, still seated on jittery horses. "Travel in pairs. Until we leave these woods, no one takes a single step alone or unarmed, is that clear?"

A chorus of "Yes, Your Majesty," and gods but it still struck Freyrík like a staff to the chest to hear those words directed at him.

'Twas no more pleasant to watch Ayden and the lord general pace off into the forest. He could not shake the feeling he was watching them go for the last time.

"Your Majesty?"

Lord Vitr stood beside Spyrna, gently tugging the reins from Freyrík's hand. He was the last man on horseback. Back at the path, he saw Lord Lini and Lieutenant Drengr gathering deadfall for a fire. Lieutenants Rekkr and Varnan were scouting the area—not quite in a pair as he'd ordered, but well within sight of each other at least. Lieutenant Herlid was building a fire ring. The horses needed staking, brushing down. Someone needed to cook. There would be no more fresh meat—he'd sooner starve than eat an animal from *this* place—so they need portion from their stores. And gods but it was colder than a dark beast's heart, and felt surely as barren. The trees were different here: very few had needles, and most had lost their leaves. He saw only scarred, crooked branches and empty gray sky when he looked up through the canopy. Nothing stood between them and the wind.

"Your Majesty."

Poor Lord Vitr sounded even more worried now than he had a moment ago. Freyrík tried to grin at him, let go his reins and dismounted. "Tend the horses, if you would. Stake them near the fire for now. We'll move them later when we know where we'll sleep."

Lord Vitr nodded and set to task. That left only sorting through the stores to keep Freyrík's hands busy, though he fetched ink and paper before food, and wrote an update to the Aegis in the dying light. He had no confidence the pigeon would find its way home—it might just as easily fall into the curse of these woods and turn darker—but he had to try.

Ayden was halfway up a pinyon pine when he remembered he could no longer build blinds like he once had. Strange and stupid to forget such a thing when each day he tripped over his mute deafness, yet here he was, straddling a thick horizontal branch and trying to sing. The wind tore through his hair, stung his eyes, bit straight through his cloak and skin. For a moment, the tears prickling his eyes threatened to overspill.

He wanted to go home. They *needed* to go home before they died out here. 'Twould not be so hard to dispatch the Aegean lieutenants and leave. Rík wouldn't hear of it, but Lords Lini and Vitr trusted him, could be swayed. Even General Vísi might be made to see reason. Could help him make Freyrík see reason.

He tugged his hood down, snatching at the distant promise of warmth, and set his mind to more immediate concerns. They must have shelter. He could build the blinds by hand, surely. It would merely take longer. A second set of hands would not go amiss.

"General!"

General Vísi looked up from where he waited near the trunk and called back in the exact same tone, "Elf!"

By the gods, had he just made a *joke*?

Ayden smiled despite himself. "Climb up. I need help."

For a gray, wrinkled human, the general moved with shocking ease. He was up the tree in moments, unwinded. Ayden showed him what to do. "We must build five and sleep in pairs. This tree will hold two more, there and there." He pointed to two particularly amenable pairs of near-horizontal branches just a few feet overhead.

The general nodded. "Four will do," he said. "Two men will stand watch at all times."

Indeed. Perhaps he and the general would stand together. 'Twould be so easy for them to slay the lieutenants in their sleep. "General," he began, but when the old man met his eyes in the dying light, his next words stuck in his throat. This man had served Rík, served Farr, the whole of his life. He respected his king. Respected Rík's skill, Rík's knowledge, Rík's wisdom. Trusted him, too.

Perhaps I should do the same. He has earned that much.

Indeed, he might have thirty lifetimes on Rík, but if Ayden had learned anything by the man's side, 'twas that he didn't always know better after all. And after the horror of High Court, all the politicking and backstabbing and lying and secret-keeping to which not even he had been immune . . . Well, he never wanted to do that to Rík again.

"Ayden?" the General prompted.

Oh, yes. Blinds. He pointed to a greenwood switch he'd woven through the main supports and said, "You may need to harvest branches from further up for cross-pieces. Call me if you need help."

"I will," the general said—no derision, no foolish human pride— and climbed up ahead to set to work.

Ayden decided he liked the man.

Freyrík woke at the first hint of predawn with the sour fear of a night terror coating the back of his throat. He'd dreamed of cold—no surprise—and vicious wind, and a blowing snow forming an ever-shifting face. But whose? It felt important, somehow.

Ridiculous.

He was just uncomfortable, that was all. Sore and freezing, wedged between a tree trunk and an elf shivering so hard the branches shook. And the men hadn't woken him for watch, befang them all. He might be king now, but he'd damn well take his turn like the rest of them.

The urge to stay abed—hard and uncomfortable as it was—was near overwhelming, but he desperately needed to water the grass. He sat carefully, trying not to wake Ayden or fall out of the befanged tree. Pine needles scratched across his exposed skin. From somewhere above him, people began to stir.

Freyrík eased his way down the tree and puffed hot air onto numb fingers. As his feet touched the earth he heard rustling to his left and spun round, weapon already in hand. "Name yourself," he shouted, voice deceptively steady. If 'twere a darker, it'd already have smelled him, and the only humans in these woods were his. Surely it was safe to call out.

"Lieutenants Varnan and Herlid, Your Majesty!"

Watchmen. Just the watchmen. Freyrík resheathed his sword. Above him, two men came climbing down the tree. Lords Lini and Vitr; he could tell by their boots. A moment later, Lord Lini leapt to the ground with a grace Freyrík prayed he'd still have in fifteen years and gave Freyrík a little bow.

"Account for everyone," Freyrík said. A bit brusque, perhaps, but apprehension left little room for niceties. "And see us packed. We'll eat on the trail."

Freyrík went about his morning ablutions, and by the time he'd finished, the horses were saddled and munching grain. Ayden and the Lord General were returning from gods knew where with a horse between them, loaded down with waterskins. They were talking, and though he could not hear of what, it seemed amicable, if not downright friendly. Dark beasts, night terrors, and Ayden with manners? These woods were terrifying indeed.

Ayden handed the horse off to Lord Vísi and stopped before Freyrík. "You are happy?" he asked, eyebrows drawn and lips quirking with confusion.

Freyrík grabbed that perfect face in both hands and kissed him.

Chapter Twelve

*T*he trail grew steeper as the day dragged on, their little group's progress slow and nearly silent. They passed nearly a week of days thus in their quiet, wary miseries, the trees thinning as they climbed and climbed, endless stands of evergreens sprouting from the rocky soil.

The path of destruction zigzagged up and down and over peak after jagged peak, often so distant from the straighter path of water they'd lose an hour or more to fetching it. Never did the cold relent, and by the third day it settled deep in all their chests, bringing with it strange and startling symptoms as they climbed: crippling headaches, nausea, dizziness, fatigue. Lord Lini's nose began to bleed. They had to stop for the day when he pitched from his saddle, dizzy and blinded with pain.

Only Ayden seemed unaffected by the curse, and gods bless him, he tended the rest without complaint. Some days it seemed they traveled but two or three leagues. On the days the snow fell sideways, blinding them in stinging sheets, it seemed they traveled in circles.

They took to building large fires at night for warmth of soul as well as body. But not even the light could cheer them. Tonight he gazed across the fire at Lord Lini, huddled and shivering on a fallen log, ignoring the food in his hands. The others had gotten . . . well, if not *better,* exactly, then at least no worse, but 'twas as if poor dear Lini had taken all their miseries upon himself. He breathed wetly, in shallow pants. He'd not spoken a word all day.

Ayden sat down beside Lord Lini and offered him a mug of tea, something he'd made from gods knew what he'd collected along the trail. When Lord Lini didn't take it, Ayden held it to his lips for him, tilted it until the man drank.

Gods, how Freyrík loved them both.

The wind howled down the mountainside, and the fire guttered. Their big, bright fire. He drew his cloak down tighter about his shoulders and slurped at his porridge. 'Twas freshly cooked and already cold.

Another gust of wind, and a flaming log blew outside the ring and extinguished.

They all looked at one another, eyes wide and fearful.

Freyrík cleared his throat, swallowed, cleared it again. "Stake the horses windward," he said, and gods thanked for a youth misspent at poetry recital, for that practice kept his words steady even as his heart sought to thump through his chest. "They will protect the flame."

The wind gusted again, and out went their fire. Whatever beneath the shadow . . . ?

No. We are beneath the great shadow of the gods no longer. They cannot dwell here in this cursed land.

Lord Vitr and Lieutenant Rekkr went to fetch the horses, and Lieutenant Drengr rushed to relight the fire. The tinder was dry but their sparks would not catch. The wind blew Freyrík's hair in his face and he shoved at it, fearful. The sun had fallen behind the mountain. It was nearly dark.

Over the wind, Freyrík heard the scrape of flint on steel, the clomp of hooves on frozen earth. No insects chirping. No woodpeckers. No owls. No distant call of the coyote. These woods were dead.

And so are you, whispered the cruel voice of doubt in his head.

At last they re-staked the horses and relit the fire. It burned just long enough to set Lord Lini coughing from the smoke, but the wind blew hard and harder still, and out it went again. Lieutenant Varnan stood of a sudden as the last flame guttered, and pointed an accusing finger at Ayden.

"I know this is your doing, elf."

Ayden stood too, and across the dead fire, so did Freyrík.

"Do you think I am not as cold as the rest of you?" Ayden jerked a hand at his own throat, at the collar sitting there. "Or that I could have quashed the fire so bound, even if I'd wanted to?"

Lieutenant Varnan growled again, low and wordless, and Lieutenant Herlid rose to stand by his side. After a moment's hesitation, Lieutenant Rekkr joined them. Only Lieutenant Drengr remained seated, but Freyrík did not miss the way he watched his fellows, hand on the hilt of his sword.

Behind Ayden, Lord Lini doubled over coughing.

"What poison have you fed the king's secretary?" demanded Lieutenant Herlid.

Which, truly, was at least ten steps too far for Freyrík's patience. "Enough!" he snapped. "All of you! Not you," he clarified, pointing toward Ayden when the elf raised wounded eyebrows. "Sit down, and still your tongues. I'll have no dissent and no blind suspicion among my ranks, am I clear?"

The lieutenants, chastised, returned to their log with a chorus of "Yes, Your Majesty."

Shame Freyrík didn't believe them for a moment.

Freyrík spent the night in thrall of terrors. Teeth and claws and wind and fog, dark malevolent forces ripping through the forest like a whirlwind, killing everything in their path. Later, on watch with Ayden in the hours before dawn, he heard the others toss and moan, and wondered if they dreamed the same. If they'd *been* dreaming the same, as he had for days now.

The fire was dead, the logs still arranged neatly, unburned. Not even a bed of coals to warm themselves or see by. They stood watch in the wind-torn dark, pressed side by side.

"Your secretary is dying."

Freyrík startled, turned toward Ayden. But for the starlit gleam of eyes looking back at him, he might have thought he'd heard those awful words on the demon wind.

He sighed, scrubbed at his eyes with both hands. "I know."

"Yet you persist."

"We are soldiers. Soldiers die."

"For *good causes*," Ayden said.

And bad ones too. And pointless ones, and selfish ones, and foolish ones. It happened all the time. But he kept that to himself. Ayden already knew it, and would only throw it back at him anyway: *Which of those is* this *cause, do you think?*

"This is foolish, Rík." *You are foolish*, left unspoken but clearly heard. "We die for nothing."

No. Not nothing. He refused to believe that. He refused even to dignify it with acknowledgment. "I'll try the fire again," he said instead. He turned round and walked back to the cold ring of stones. Ayden let him.

The men began to stir at the first hint of predawn, just as Freyrík was relighting the fire for the fourth time. The gods-befanged wind rushed down the mountain and snuffed it again, sure as a smothering hand. Freyrík shuddered at a vision of fangs, fury, a storm cloud racing through the trees . . .

He shook his head with a gasp, dislodging the dream fragment, and prayed the sun would rise soon.

Rustling, a grunt, the scrape of boot soles on bark: men coming down from their blinds. Lord Vitr and Lord General Vísi came to stand beside him, looking as worn as they had when they'd gone to sleep. "No fire again, Your Majesty?" the lord general asked, then coughed into his fist, wet and breathless.

Freyrík eyed him through the gloom—gods befanged, was he too falling prey to the demon sickness here? "Nay, my lord, I'm afraid not."

More rustling, more scraping. Shapes scurried down the trees, though 'twas hard to tell who was who in the predawn gloom.

Lord Vitr glanced forlornly at the fire ring, but made no attempt to kindle it. He lit a candle instead, putting his back to the wind and guarding the flame close to his chest. The men gathered round him like moths and ate stale bread and pinyon nuts Ayden had pilfered from animal caches. An errant gust of wind snuck in sideways and blew out their candle. Even in the east, the sky remained stubbornly dark.

Halfway through the day, sun obscured behind a swirling gray wall of snow, on an uphill path so slippery and steep they were forced to dismount and steady themselves with their hands, Lord General Vísi lost his footing and slid down the mountain. Freyrík raced after him, found him facedown at the bottom of a gully and knelt beside him. The blood on his lips was pink. His heart lay still in his chest.

That did not stop Freyrík from shouting at him.

"Get up, gods damn you!" He rolled the man onto his back, saw blood pooling through a rent in his clothes and pressed both hands to it. Broken ribs grated beneath his fingers as warm blood ran down his wrists. Not spurting, just . . . draining.

Gods befanged, this wasn't *possible*. He'd been fine. Healthy. Strong. The old hawk should've outlived them all.

And he'd died of *lost footing*?

Freyrík stumbled back, wiped his hands in the snow. Strange how the cold numbed more than just the flesh. He stood, wondering how to bury the body in this frozen earth.

A hand clasped round his shoulder, and he started. Ayden, jaw set, staring grimly at the lord general. His hard gaze flicked to Freyrík, and he shook his head. "For what purpose, Rík?" he asked.

Freyrík shrugged out from under Ayden's grip and bent to pry a rock from the soil. A cairn—they would make the lord general a cairn. The dark elves may have claimed his soul, but Freyrík refused to let their beasts take his body too.

"Rík?"

"If we leave now, 'twill be for none at all. We press on."

"I have seen the same blood on Lord Lini's lips."

"*We press on.*" Befang the elf, why was he just *standing* there? "For all beneath the shadow that is good, grab a damn stone!"

Ayden scowled, but bent to work.

Later, after they'd buried the lord general and scrambled back up over the slope that had killed him and made their cold dark camp on the lee side of a cliff that still failed to block the demon wind, Freyrík watched as Ayden and Lieutenant Drengr built blinds.

He skipped what meager cold supper they had and crawled into bed before the sun had fully set.

Near dusk, Ayden crawled in beside him, smelling of cold and earth (*death*) and bright, sweet pine sap. He lay on his back, but not apart, and when Freyrík curled into his side and wept, Ayden was kind enough to hold him and lie with utter sincerity, "It's not your fault."

Freyrík woke as he'd fallen asleep: in Ayden's arms. Yet something was different, ominous, strange, and in the cold damp predawn it took him a moment to realize what. A dense, chill fog had settled over everything while they'd slept.

He half expected to see a face in it.

Ridiculous. 'Tis only night terrors. The fog wears no visage, has neither tooth nor claw.

So he might tell himself, and yet he could not shake the feeling . . .

No more lazing abed. Movement and purpose would dislodge his superstitions. His grief.

He climbed down from his blind and nearly tripped right over Lord Vitr and Lieutenant Varnan. Gods knew how they were keeping watch; the world faded into nothingness five paces away. Men milled round the edges of their camp, risen earlier than he had, but he couldn't tell who was who through the fog. Surely they were allies, at least.

Lord Vitr bowed silently as he walked past, shoulder to shoulder with Lieutenant Varnan. "My lord," Freyrík said, catching Lord Vitr by the arm as he went by. "Is my secretary yet awake?"

Lord Vitr nodded. "He seems much improved this morn."

Of course he does. The demons ate yesterday; they no longer hunger just yet.

"That is—" He cleared his throat, flashed a tight-lipped smile. "Good news. But let him rest. And have Lieutenants Rekkr and Drengr saddle the horses now. The fog"—*disquiets me*—"will slow us overmuch; we must waste no time this morn."

A gusty sigh from behind him: Ayden, who'd climbed down from the blind without making a sound, or mayhap 'twas just the fog obscuring it all. Lieutenant Varnan, near enough to overhear, whipped round toward Ayden, hand on the hilt of his sword. "Problem, elf?" he snarled.

Before Freyrík could even open his mouth to reply for Ayden—bad idea to let the elf speak for himself in this, after all—a fog-shrouded figure to his left said, "A man can sigh, Varnan. It doesn't have to mean anything."

"But he is *not* a man," Lieutenant Varnan replied.

The figure stepped forward, coalescing into Lieutenant Drengr. Pointedly ignoring his friend, he turned to Ayden and said, "I'd be much obliged if you'd help me with the horses."

Ayden sighed again, noisy enough to make known his displeasure all the way back in Midr, but nodded and went off with the lieutenant. Freyrík quashed a shiver of unease as they disappeared into the wind-churned fog. For a moment, just a moment, he'd have sworn they'd gone straight into the maw of some monstrous wet-gray beast, but then the wind gusted again and the illusion was gone.

Early that afternoon, the darker path came to an abrupt end. Or beginning, more like, in a high alpine meadow of churned earth and frozen scat just below the tree line. They rode once round the fog-choked perimeter, then round again, looking for signs. Tracks everywhere—hundreds, thousands, from all directions. Clearly the curse, the beastly transformations, had happened here.

But how? And why? He sensed no great evil here, no dark spirit, no more danger than he'd felt yesterday or the day before or the day before that. Was this soiled patch of earth the dark beasts' cradle always, or just this once? Did some unholy power source churn deep within the roots at their feet?

He guided Spyrna to the center of the clearing, then closed his eyes and simply sat there. Listening, feeling.

Nothing. Gods cursed, he felt *nothing.*

Mayhap there was simply nothing to feel. Nothing here. Nothing *anywhere.* Mayhap Ayden had been right all along.

Then the lord general died for nothing. Get off your horse, you damned siga, and find what you came for.

"We must search for clues," he said. When nobody moved or replied, he clapped his hands together once, sharp, an ominous thundercloud in the foggy meadow. The men as one removed arse from saddle.

"Pair up. Lieutenant Varnan, stay with Lord Lini and tend the horses. Ayden, with me if you please."

Off they went in their separate directions, scouring the meadow on foot for clues. Alas, 'twas all tracks upon tracks upon tracks, impossible to separate one from the next. And even if there were something to find, even if 'twere the size of a darker bear, finding it in this fog seemed nigh impossible.

Yet still they scoured. One hour, two, more, combing over the same ground again and again. Finding *nothing*. Muddled tracks came into the meadow from every direction, went back through the forest in every direction. No way to know which to follow.

As if 'twould matter anyway. They would only take us to some dead animal's den.

The light was fading, and Freyrík was tired, they all were, *beyond* tired. They would find no more. Not today.

Not ever.

Ayden, growing ever more adept at reading people, came to a stop beside him and slipped his hand into Freyrík's. "It's not your fault," he said.

That could have meant so many things, Freyrík hardly knew where to begin. "The lord general died because of me," he said.

"No. He died because of the Aegis."

But Freyrík was shaking his head before Ayden even finished his sentence. "Nay, he died because *I* refused to believe the Aegis sent us here for that express purpose. He died because I was so blinded by hope for peace that I could not see what stood right before me. And yet more will die if I cannot find a way to bring us home without ruin."

"There is peace and freedom in Vaenn. You and Lords Lini and Vitr could be welcome there; I would see to it." Was that a smile peeking through Ayden's studied features? "You could play violin, and write poetry. Worry no more."

Freyrík closed his eyes against such temptation. He was king now. He had no right to live for himself.

Yet you would die for nothing?

And were not the gods supposed to whisper in kings' ears? Guide them through to truth?

Will you not speak to me? Gods, please, tell me what to do.
The wind picked up, and from above, snow began to fall.

Ayden woke to the Hunter's Call, the first light of dawn suffusing their field tent. The Call disappeared the instant he opened his eyes—a dream fragment, nothing more—but the pain of it still lingered in his back teeth, his cheekbones, the space behind his nose and eyes. There'd been something else too, something sliding like sand through parted fingers. Blood and death and primitive fury. Shapeless, wordless . . . but not powerless. No, not by any means.

He slipped from bed and drew back the tent flap. The waking world was shrouded in fog and covered in fresh snow that was still falling, heavy and silent, like dust from old bones. He dragged himself into it to water the grass.

The cold had more teeth than a crocodile. He hurried, stones crawling up into his belly as he bared himself to the morning air. Some ten paces behind him, their little party stirred to life. What would Freyrík say to them this morn? Had he decided?

Ayden buttoned up and walked back to their little encampment in the middle of the meadow, boots crunching soft and wet in the snow. The Aegean on watch with Lord Vitr—Drengr, was he called?— nodded acknowledgment as Ayden ducked back into his tent.

Rík was awake, already dressed and packing. From the tents to the right and left of theirs he heard the sounds of men at similar work. Early start, then. Question was, where were they going?

Instead he asked, "Do you need help?"

Freyrík shook his head but said nothing, eyes fixed firmly on the furs he was rolling.

"Shall I tend the horses, then?"

Still no eye contact, just a soft, "Please do."

Ayden left to scoop far-too-meager portions from what little remained of their feed. He found the horses nosing in the snow, but they could not graze what did not exist. The poor creatures looked as thin and tired as his fellow travelers.

He fed them, then broke the ice on their water pails—no small layer; it went deep as the snow—that they might drink. By the time he'd finished, the others had struck the tents, but they'd not yet been packed away. So why was everyone standing round in a clump, doing nothing?

"What is this?" he asked, settling in between Rík and Lord Lini.

"*Your king* wishes words with us all, elf. Unless you'd care to keep him waiting some more?"

Your king. Not *our* king or even *the* king. Ayden did not like the sound of that.

Rík glared at the Aegean who'd spoken and said, icy calm, "That's enough, Lieutenant Herlid. I wish to thank you all for your sacrifice and your suffering in this difficult endeavor, but 'tis clear we've reached an impasse here, and I'll not see you dead one by one for a myth we've no means to verify, let alone pursue. We begin our journey home today."

Clear relief on the faces on Freyrík's men, outrage on the lieutenants'. Herlid took a large step forward and said, icy calm as Freyrík had been a moment ago, "Begging Your Majesty's pardon"— and wasn't that the jest of the century—"but we've not yet completed our mission."

"And nor shall we. Nor *can* we. Tell me, Lieutenant, where do we go from here?"

The man said nothing a long moment—he could no sooner answer that question than Ayden—but then said, "Again, begging Your Majesty's pardon, is that not *your* decision to make?"

"Indeed it is," Freyrík said, taking his own step forward to meet the lieutenant's near-sneering derision head-on. "And I've decided we go east, back toward Midr."

"Begging your—"

Freyrík's hand fell to the hilt of his sword. Lieutenant Herlid's eyes followed. "If you say 'Begging Your Majesty's pardon' one more time," Freyrík said, voice as low and dangerous as Ayden had ever heard it, "I will slice your tongue from your mouth. Now load the horses and speak to me no more; if I wish for your advice, I shall ask for it. Do you understand?"

Herlid bowed deep and said, "Yes, Your Majesty," to the top of his boot.

Ayden didn't believe him for a moment.

While the Aegeans packed the tents away and saddled and loaded the horses, Freyrík led Ayden into the forest under guise of scouting. As soon as Ayden could no longer hear the clamor and chatter of the men in the meadow, he turned to Freyrík and said, "The Aegeans will be a problem."

Freyrík touched his hand to his sword again, an absent gesture, as if unawares. "They do not wish to die here any more than you or I do."

"But they *would*, if they thought it mattered. Just as you would for your Aegis. Just as I would for the Republic." He stopped, peered out at the sunrise hazed behind a scrim of snow and fog. "*Do* they think it matters?"

Freyrík shrugged. "I do not know." And then, as Ayden began to walk again, "Where are we going?"

"This ridge runs north-south. If we're to travel east, we must find a safe path down. One the horses can manage."

Freyrík nodded, stumbled over a root buried in the snow. "Not too far, if you would. I do not wish to lose sight of the meadow."

Ayden didn't bother mentioning they'd lost sight of it already. The snow fell lighter through the trees, but still hard enough to white out the world at fifteen paces. He knew the way back. Besides, he had rather more pressing concerns. "So what happens next?"

Freyrík looked at him and tripped over another root. Tired. Hungry and tired, all of them. "How do you mean?"

"I mean I'll not return to High Court, and you shouldn't either."

Silence, long and loaded. Finally, "I don't know."

"If you kill the Aegeans, you can go anywhere. To Vaenn. Be safe."

"I'm not killing anyone."

"I am happy to do it for you." Freyrík stopped and stared, and Ayden turned to flash him a mouthful of teeth in case he wished to find Ayden in jest.

That was when he saw the slashes.

There past head height by a pace or two on the south face of a Douglas fir. *Five* slashes, not four, one opposite the others. Like a thumb and four fingers. Like a *hand*.

He shuddered, back muscles tensing against an invisible touch. "Ayden?"

Claw marks. A hand. Blood on the wind.

"Are you—"

Freyrík's gaze followed Ayden's, and he paled so quickly Ayden put an arm round his waist, meaning to catch him if he stumbled again.

"I have seen this," Freyrík whispered. He reached up with a shaking hand, toward the slashes on the tree, but then withdrew. Ayden felt quite certain Rík would rather die than touch them. "I have . . . In my . . ."

"Dreams," Ayden finished for him, and Rík nodded mutely, wide-eyed and frightened as Ayden had ever seen him. "Mine as well."

Sharing night terrors. For all the magic Ayden had seen in his life, he'd never seen *that*. And for all its terror, for all the dread the sight of the slashes evoked—half-forgotten fragments of blood and thunder, wind and hate—there birthed on Freyrík face the first true hope since they'd began this dreadful trek.

"Surely . . ." Freyrík breathed, grasping Ayden's snow-dusted shoulders in two shaking hands. "This is . . . But surely this is what we've come for! Look at it, Ayden." Freyrík shook him, but no need; Ayden could look at nothing else. "Look! We have found its trail again!"

Ayden plucked Freyrík's hands from his shoulders. "You want to follow it, don't you."

Freyrík nodded, and he was smiling, gods crack him, *smiling* at the thought of traipsing off through the snow in pursuit of shadows, of *death*, when they were *this close* to leaving this awful place.

And yet . . . *Something* had made those marks. And something had invaded their dreams—not just his and Freyrík's, he was sure of it, but *all* of them, for he'd seen them toss on watch, heard them cry out in the grips of their terrors. Dark elves, no, but something was out here. Something powerful enough to birth Ferals. Something they might just find a way to stop.

If it didn't kill them first.

Rík's excitement spread wide and deep as the fog—even Lord Lini, Ayden smiled to see, stepped into his saddle unaided—and within the hour the whole of their party was reined up beneath the tree. All eyes went to the marks. Even with his eyes closed, Ayden would have sensed the shiver that ran through the group.

"What if there are no more?" Lord Vitr asked.

"Where there is one . . ." Ayden said, but then said no more. His hand went to the collar round his neck, fingers curling round its edge. Tracking was so much easier when he could hear. "We'll spread out, form a net. This way."

Lord Vitr found the second set of marks not ten minutes later, in exactly the direction Ayden had pointed them, up a tree at the same height as the last set. Ayden studied them a moment, then set them out again in a more or less straight line. Lieutenant Varnan found the third set, and Freyrík found the fourth. It soon became apparent that whatever had left them was following what once might have been an elk trail, which was exceptionally—if suspiciously—convenient for them, for it took them over some of the gentlest slopes and levelest ground in the forested mountains. Almost as if these marks had been put here by some mischievous human to fool them.

On and on they went, the marks drawing them north-northeast, back toward the border with Farr—or at least where once it would have been before the dark beasts overtook the Myrkrs some three centuries past.

Eventually they outran the daylight and had to stop. The air was so dense with icy mist and the sky so swollen with storm clouds they barely noticed the sun setting 'til it grew dark. They built their sleeping nests in trees by scattered moonlight.

By morn it was snowing hard again, and the pigeons were growing restless. One made Lord Lini bleed when he reached into a cage to pick a carrier for Freyrík's latest report to the Aegis. Ayden did not miss the way Lieutenant Herlid hovered near as Freyrík dictated to his secretary. As if he wished to be certain Freyrík harbored no more thoughts of veering any further east than the claw marks led them.

Another day passed, and another, and another. The night terrors grew worse with the weather, until the horses were trudging through a foot of snow. Their compass stopped working. On the night of their sixth day following the marks, Ayden dreamed of broken bows drawn across tuneless strings, pulling him from bed and toward a darkening void. He dreamed of hate so raw and raging it ripped him from the inside, rent and broke him into something else, something terrible and new, all teeth and claws and fury, and he sank them into Freyrík's throat and *tore*, tasted blood flow on his tongue and down his gullet with pure white pleasure—

He woke screaming, and fell out of the tree.

Someone caught him by the wrist. Freyrík, of course, indomitably strong, hauling him back into their blind as if he were but a child.

Freyrík stared at him, chest heaving, face hard and hollowed in the narrow moonlight. He wasn't blinking enough, and what a strange thing that was to notice, but 'twas all Ayden could think of a sudden.

Until Freyrík lunged forward and kissed him, hands coming up and clutching hard in Ayden's hair.

"I dreamed I killed you," Freyrík whispered when they pulled apart, voice so near to cracking that Ayden couldn't help but hold him tight. He did not mention he'd dreamed the same; Freyrík was frightened enough already.

"But you woke and saved me."

Ayden drew Freyrík back beneath their furs, pressing up tight and throwing an arm and a leg round him. 'Twasn't sexual—he'd not felt so much as the slightest stirring of desire since they'd crossed the great crack in the earth—but the urge to *touch*, to feel life beating strong against his skin, he could not deny.

Silence, heavy and deep. 'Twas reassuring to feel Freyrík breathing against him, erasing the sense—memory but not memory, a thing he'd seen but *not* seen—of Freyrík not breathing, dead in his arms, ripped to pieces by Ayden's own hands.

"What do you think we'll find?"

Ayden shrugged. He'd been wondering that himself lately, more often than not. "Perhaps Nature has a face, after all."

"I pray not, for how does one stop such a thing?"

Ayden didn't have the heart to tell him you don't.

They were back on their mounts by first light, but by late afternoon, they were forced to admit they'd lost the trail. The marks had spaced thinner and thinner and finally just . . . disappeared.

"We are *lost,* Freyrík," Ayden said.

Freyrík shook his head. "No. *No.* We are not quitting now."

"Listen to your king, elf."

Ayden wheeled his mount round so quickly that Herlid's tripped back a step. "As you have listened to yours, human? Your blind adherence to your Aegis will get us all killed. The trail is cold; where would you have us go?"

"So ready were you to quit last week, and then we found the marks. We stay. We keep looking."

"*We*? 'Twas *me* who found the marks, not you, not any of you Aegean fools. And your king is the biggest fool of them all, for if he'd deigned to unbind me before he sent us here to die, I could have *listened* for what we seek and followed it that way. Now I am as impotent as you are."

If considerably less ugly and stupid.

The human opened his face-hole to spew more nonsense, but Lord Lini nudged his mount in between them and said, "Listened? How do you mean?"

Gods, why were they all looking at him like that, like if they could only crack him open, they'd find a map to their monster buried inside? "Whatever drives the beasts—whatever draws them, turns them Feral—my people call it the Hunter's Call. The beasts are drawn to it, powerless to resist. That is all I know."

"Who is the hunter?" Herlid demanded. "Is he elf?"

"How am I to know? 'Tis Nature, I suppose. The earth has many songs. This is but one."

The lieutenant scowled. It seemed he and poetry didn't get on well. "And does this . . . *nature* have form?"

Ayden shrugged again. He was far too cold and tired to stay angry at this fool. "If it does, I have never seen it."

"How do we find it, then?" Freyrík this time, voice so soft Ayden wondered if he'd meant to speak aloud.

"Unbind me. With the starfall gone, I'll hear it."

Lieutenants Herlid and Varnan actually *laughed* at that, but Freyrík's gaze was deadly serious.

"There must be at least one blacksmith in Midr who knows how to remove the collar," Lord Lini mused.

Lord Vitr nodded. "If we bird ahead, they can meet us at the border—"

"You *can't* be serious," Lieutenant Varnan cried. "You would hear strategy from a groom and a secretary, Your Majesty?"

"I would hear strategy from whomever speaks with forethought and wit. If ever you succeed in such lofty pursuits, then I shall hear strategy from you as well. Until then, hold your tongue."

He turned back to his own men, casting eyes from Lord Lini to Lord Vitr, and finally to Ayden. "'Twould take a week at least to ride back to Midr and another to return. By the time we get back, the trail would be even colder than it is now."

So that was it, then? Freyrík wouldn't even entertain the notion of setting his magic free?

"*But*, we've even less hope of finding what we seek as we are. We need Ayden's mind-ear." And oh, now he remembered why he loved this man. "We go back."

Instant clamor from the Aegeans, but 'twas hard to care when in a week, a single week, he'd be free of this starfall curse. To sing and hear song again . . .

Yet still the Aegeans argued on. 'Twas unnerving how long it took Freyrík to silence them this time.

"I will bird the Aegis our plan"—*if it will shut you up,* Ayden heard in the silence of a drawn breath. "If he does not approve, we will hear of it in Midr. If he does, the blacksmith will be waiting for us and we'll lose no time. Either way, we gather fresh horses and provisions and ride right back here. Lord Lini, paper and ink, if you would please?"

Lord Lini didn't bother to dismount, just rode up beside the proper packhorse and fished out his supplies. Freyrík ordered Lieutenant Varnan fetch the pigeon, and Ayden took no small pleasure from watching the man try to catch one without hurting it. The maddened creatures had no such compunctions about hurting him back. His hand was *dripping* blood, three fresh streaks of it on his forearm as one pigeon wormed out through the cage door via beak and talon and took off—

North. Not east, toward its roost. North.

It hears the call. We could follow it.

Or he could pretend he'd not noticed, and let Freyrík take him back to Midr and remove his cracking starfall.

Easy choice.

But one frustratingly—nay, *tragically*—taken out of his hands when Freyrík, eyes on the dwindling form of the escaped pigeon, said, awestruck, "It hears the call. We can follow it!"

But the bird was already a rapidly disappearing splotch of gray on gray after just a few seconds on wing.

Perhaps there is hope for unbinding yet.

"Quickly, how many birds are left?"

A long pause while Lieutenant Rekkr tried to count the birds. "Thirty-six, Your Majesty—no, thirty-eight. I think."

. . . And perhaps not.

Freyrík nodded, threw Ayden a quick glance and then turned back round, studying him in earnest.

"Pardon us a moment," Freyrík said, and though his eyes never left Ayden's, 'twas his lords and the lieutenants who clucked their horses some paces distant. When they were alone, Freyrík leaned in close and whispered, "You will do this?"

Ayden wanted to punch something, or scream, or maybe even weep for that hot cruel moment of hope, but instead he merely shrugged and said, "What choice is there?"

They both knew the lieutenants wouldn't listen to Freyrík now if he still insisted on returning to Midr. And they both knew just as well that Freyrík *wouldn't* insist. They'd been lost; now they weren't. They could move on. They could give meaning to General Vísi's death. They might even find what they'd come for.

"Yes," Ayden said into Freyrík's guilty silence. "I will do this."

Freyrík clasped his shoulder and flashed him a grim smile, then beckoned the others back. This time when Lieutenant Varnan released a pigeon, they were poised and ready to chase it.

Alas, it flew as it pleased, while they had to race it on the ground, over boulders and ridges, through roots and trees and fog the same color as the bird. No matter, though. They simply released another. And then a third, and a fourth, and a fifth, and on and on until, twenty-one birds and leagues and hours later, they nearly rode headlong into a whirling thundercloud.

The horses reared, and Lieutenant Varnan flew off his horse and right beneath the stomping hooves of another one. Howling wind competed for dominance with the neighing horses, but even over all that Ayden heard the man's ribs break. A hoof fell on the man's head and his screaming stopped. The riderless horse turned tail and bolted.

Good riddance.

"What beneath the shadow . . .?" someone said. Someone else was praying. Ayden wrestled his horse under control and reined in alongside Freyrík's mount, who was dancing and skittish but not trying to throw him. Freyrík's whole face had gone slack with awe, though there was no mistaking the fear in his eyes.

He leaned in and whispered something Ayden could not hear over the roar of the storm.

"What?"

"I said"—and now he was shouting, too loud—"what *is* it?"

"I do not know."

Except he did know, didn't he. He'd dreamt of it. They all had. 'Twas the Hunter, clear as water, and he did not need his mind-ear to confirm it.

"Why does it not attack us?" Freyrík shouted.

"I do not know."

"Mayhap it is weak, Your Majesty," Lord Lini yelled. "We are less than a full moon from the last Surge."

If this tree-ripping whirlwind, this . . . *raging power* was the weak face of the Hunter? Then Ayden was relieved beyond measure not to find it at full strength.

Or even half strength.

"Yes," Freyrík said, "but what *is* it?"

"Demons," said one of the Aegeans, and strange but how in the moment after that word tripped though his mind, Ayden swore he saw a face—no, face*s*—blurring through the churning cloud.

Yet what happened next was even stranger still. Three elf-sized bodies—three *very familiar* bodies, emerged from the storm, perfectly unscathed, and stood before it hand in hand.

Chapter Thirteen

The terror gripping Freyrík at the sight of this . . . roiling *monstrosity*—belching lightning and thunder, ripping limbs from trees as if the wings off a fly—dug far deeper than any battle fear he'd ever known. Even his first battle with the darker cougar hadn't left him so breathless, so blank in the mind, so near to paralyzed.

Spyrna danced beneath him, tuning into his panic or gripped in her own. He unsheathed his sword, but never had it felt so small and useless in his hands. However could he hope to fight this . . . this living breathing thundercloud on the mountaintop? How could one fell the very wind?

Yet there at the center of it all stood . . . what? Three beings, three *people*, the air so calm round them not even their hair whipped in the wind. Spyrna whinnied, bucked halfheartedly; he clamped his legs tight to her sides and muscled her back down. One of the beings took a single step forward. Then another, and another. A *woman*? Dressed in tatters of no discernable shape or color. A dark elf, surely. Freyrík raised his sword, fought for Spyrna's head, even as he knew with certainty he could no sooner charge the dark elf than the storm.

But then the woman took another step forward, and the other two moved to join her—men dressed in rags, their faces coalescing through the clouds and the wind—and beside him, Ayden made a little *whuff* of shock and turned white as the snow the demon-wind was blowing.

The elf slid from his saddle as if entranced.

"Ayden, what are you doing!"

The elf ignored him. Had the dark elves ensorcelled him too, turned him as they did the wild beasts? He flashed onto an image of

Ayden's face twisted in feral rage, the stuff of night terrors, of *his* night terrors, as Ayden took a step forward.

"Ayden, don't!" Freyrík lunged and grabbed Ayden's cloak. "Are you mad?" he shouted, tugging Ayden back so hard he sent the elf stumbling into his horse.

Ayden turned wide eyes up to Freyrík. "I know them. Let me go—I *know* them!"

When Freyrík refused to release him, Ayden simply unfastened his cloak and ran forward, leaving Freyrík with a fistful of empty fabric and a panic welling in his chest so hard and fast he found himself dismounting and chasing after the befanged fool.

"Missa! Skadi! Vesall!" Ayden shouted, even as Freyrík shouted, "Ayden! Stop! Gods beg you, stop!"

He didn't listen, merely shouted the three names again. The people he was calling to—assuming they *were* people—made no move, no response. Not even an indication that they heard or saw him. Yet *something* stopped Ayden cold: a great wet gusting wind like a churning fist lashed out and knocked him off his feet, threw him so hard he crashed right into Freyrík some five paces back. Freyrík had no time to get out of the way, wouldn't have even if he could have, for then who would have cushioned Ayden's fall?

They landed in a tangled, groaning heap, Freyrík's sword flying from his hand—and when had he unsheathed it?—slushy snow oozing through every seam and opening of his clothes. Ayden didn't move, but Freyrík could scarce afford to worry over that when that . . . *thing* might attack again, so he rolled the elf off him with a murmured apology and clamored to his feet, retrieved his sword and made ready. The three surviving lieutenants and Lord Lini were running toward him full bore, poor Lord Vitr left to manage eleven skittish horses.

When they reached him, Freyrík did the only thing he could—the thing he *must*: he gripped his sword in both hands and charged.

He felt more than saw his men fall in beside him, hardly saw at all the fist-like whirlwind that knocked them all aback five paces later. How odd, the sensation of flying—a moment's wonder, stillness, time frozen sure as the crusted snow . . . until the ground came rushing up and he tucked and rolled to meet it, landing hard anyway, every inch of him burning with pain and chilling on the trampled snow.

All round him, he heard the groans of his men as they too dragged themselves back to their feet. Lieutenant Rekkr, the coward, was running back toward the horses, screaming like a woman. Lord Lini threw Freyrík a panicked glance, scrambled to his side and seized his forearm. The man said nothing, just pulled, pulled harder, until Freyrík's own panic saw him yielding to Lord Lini's, and he ran after his secretary, arm still trapped in the man's iron grip. He could understand their terror; he felt it himself. But he'd have fought, gods befang it. He'd have stood his ground.

And been killed like a fool. All of us, killed.

He reined in Lord Lini just long enough to scoop up Ayden between them, but Ayden struggled, fought, shouted, "Let me speak with them! I can stop this!"

Except he couldn't, of course. He squirmed from Freyrík's grip and took but two steps back toward the storm-beast before its whirlwind fist lashed out again, and they *all* turned tail and fled, wind and ice and stones the size of apples pelting at their backs.

Somehow, miraculously, they reached the horses in safety. Freyrík fair leapt onto Spyrna, drummed his heels against her flanks and gave her free rein. The mare needed no encouragement; away they galloped, bent over their saddles like race-riders, until Freyrík realized the only storm raging in his ears was the drumming of hooves and the rasping breaths of man and horse alike.

He reined in on a wide patch of naked ground between trees and motioned them into a rough circle. All around him, people and horses panted and foamed. After the din of the demon-storm, the sound seemed a death rattle—a last, desperate gasp.

"Are you all well?" he croaked between breaths. "Vitr? Drengr?"

His groom seemed fine. The lieutenant was nodding despite the blood streaking down his face. Ayden he'd watched all along; the elf was moving stiffly but appeared unbroken.

"Lini?"

His secretary was holding one hand in the other, looking at it with dismay.

"*Lini?*" Freyrík called again.

"I've cut my finger," Lord Lini said, and for a moment Freyrík worried he meant he'd *lost* his finger, until he held it up for all to see. A mere scratch, a single drop of blood smeared at the edge.

"'Tis my *writing* finger," Lord Lini insisted.

Beside him, Lord Vitr let loose a braying laugh the likes of which Freyrík had never heard him make. Lord Lini joined in a moment later, and Freyrík after that. Shaky smiles bloomed on the lieutenants' faces.

Gods, they were alive. Surprisingly, impossibly *alive*.

Only Ayden remained sober, glaringly so, and one by one the men fell silent. Ayden turned his horse round, staring back the way they'd come.

Freyrík followed with his own eyes. Saw not even a trace of the demon-storm lurking beyond the trees.

"Ayden?"

The elf shook his head, eyes still firmly fixed upon the distance. Could he see beyond the fog?

A different tack, then. "Back there, you said you know them. What did you mean?"

Ayden turned to him and shook his head. He looked helpless, sick, utterly distressed, like in the hours following the binding or the *Blód Sekt*.

"I meant," he said, and then nothing else for several seconds. The urge to throttle the rest out of him was as powerful as it was shameful; Freyrík gritted his teeth and waited.

"I meant, I know them. Or rather, *knew* them. They are . . ." Ayden squinted, shook his head, and his fingers came up to his collar again, tugging unconsciously. "They are dead, you see."

No, he did not see. Did not see *at all*. "Are you saying they are spirits?"

Ayden shook his head again, shrugged. His mouth opened but no words came out, and again Freyrík forced down the urge to grab Ayden and *shake* until he spoke. He settled instead for a simple, warning, "Ayden . . ."

Ayden licked his lips and locked eyes with Freyrík. "Do you remember, at base camp during the Farr Surge, when I told you of the Great Betrayal?"

Freyrík nodded.

"And I told you three of our most revered elders were lured into the Myrkr Mountains by humans under false pretense and slaughtered there?"

Freyrík nodded again, quashing the urge to argue Ayden's version of events. If he did, they might never get answers.

"*Those* were the three elders. Skadi, Vesall, and Missa. They were— *are,* in fact, so old they have no ancestral names. No lineage. They are the *first*, do you understand?"

He didn't, but he nodded again anyway.

"And yet there they stand, three hundred years lost, dressed in rags in the dead of winter. Did you see? They did not even look to me when I called their names. 'Twas as if they were . . ." Another headshake, so bewildered. "As if they were *empty*. We felt them die, Freyrík. We *all* felt them die. What is this? What stands there before that storm?"

"I do not know."

"Are they the Hunter?"

"I do not know."

"We must get help."

On this, he could readily agree. "Yes, we'll ride back to High Court on the morrow."

Another long, blank silence. Except this time, 'twas no bewilderment or distress on Ayden's face—'twas incredulity, and anger, growing stronger by the second.

At last, Ayden said, slow and careful, "High Court."

"Yes. I would send bird from the nearest enclave, but we have all seen what happens to them now."

"The birds will fly true once out of hearing of the Call," Ayden said, each word its own sharp drop of ice, as cold as the fog through which they rode. "But that is very much not the point."

"Then I pray you educate me. What *is* the point?"

"What is out there"—Ayden flung his hand to the side, back toward the dark spirits of his ancestors—"is *our* concern, not yours. Those are *my* people. And 'tis my people who should know of it. We must go to Fornheim. To the Hall of Elders."

"Where they will welcome us with open arms, I'm sure."

"Freyrí—"

"No! We may no longer skirmish so very much, but our people are yet at war! And mayhap it has somehow escaped your notice, but by your own admission, the evil in these woods is *your own people*! The Dark Elves, Ayden. Right there, half a league distant, calling forth the beasts to kill us! What would your elders say, pray tell? Do you think they do not *know* what lives in these woods? Do you think they did not put it here on purpose?"

"No." Ayden's quiet intensity was a stark contrast to Freyrík's rage, and just when had he lost his temper so thoroughly anyway? "I do not think that. I do not think the elders know. And if anyone *put* them here, 'twas your own ancestors. Your own curse, your own dark magic. I do not know, Freyrík, but I know for certain you will find no answers in High Court. Only men-at-arms, and what good will that do you here?"

"I don't know!" And gods, but why was he still shouting? "But I cannot make this decision for the whole of the Empire, Ayden. I must get help."

"Then you go to High Court. I will ride to Fornheim."

Freyrík felt his stomach drop right down through his saddle. All round him, men put hands to sword hilts. But it wouldn't come to that, would it?

Would it?

Ayden thrust his chin at the Aegeans. "Would you have them stop me, Freyrík? I would fight. Could you watch that? Could you let me hurt them?" A pause, and then, "Could you let them hurt me?"

No. Gods, *no.*

But as he looked from one Aegean soldier to the next, he knew, clear as water, that these men were following orders higher than his own. "I do not think it is up to me," he said at last, shame stealing his words to whispers.

"Then you are a coward. We are four to three, and yet you would throw me to the wolves. *Again.*"

"No. That's not—"

"You have *never* laid your pride down, Freyrík. Not once, for me or anyone. You don't know what it means to give that up, even for a moment. And yet you ask it of me again and again and again! Tell me, Freyrík, what more can you wring from me? Have I not done enough for you to *trust me*, gods crack you?"

Ayden's chest was heaving, his hand clenched so tight round the reins his knuckles were white. His free hand, Freyrík realized, was busy with not one blade but two: those deadly little throwing knives with which he was so eerily proficient.

"I ride to Fornheim to get help that matters. Whatever is out there, whatever has happened to those poor elves, *my* people, not yours, will know how to fix it. Follow me or don't. I don't care. Three more dead humans—or six"—and the meaning there was so painfully clear the elf might have killed him anyway and caused no extra hurt—"it means nothing to me anymore."

Ayden kicked his horse, wheeled it sharply round. Lieutenant Herlid reacted nearly faster than Freyrík could think, spurring his own mount to cut Ayden's off. Ayden's horse reared, stumbled back on two legs and nearly toppled, and for one breathless moment Freyrík feared Ayden would share Lieutenant Varnan's fate.

But Ayden kept his seat, and his mount kept her footing; and Freyrík realized the Aegeans had drawn their weapons and boxed Ayden in, Lieutenant Herlid to the front and Lieutenant Drengr, gods befanged—he'd been respectful, even cordial to Ayden—to the rear.

"Stand down," Freyrík ordered.

No one took their eyes off their quarry. No one lowered their weapons. He supposed he could not blame them; they were good soldiers following orders higher than his own, and truly, not even he knew who he'd been talking to. Was he any more prepared to watch Ayden ride forever from his life than he was to let the lieutenants try to stop him?

He wrapped his own hand round his sword hilt. "I *said,* stand down."

Ayden, eyes still locked on Lieutenant Herlid, did something so complicated with the knife in his left hand Freyrík couldn't even track it. It came to rest along his raised forearm, hilt against his palm. *I could end you between blinks*, that little show said. The short sword held aloft in his right was no less threatening. "Get out of my way," Ayden growled, "or I will see you moved."

Lieutenant Drengr, still boxing in Ayden's rear, quietly raised his own sword, but some noise or reflection must have given him away, for Ayden thrust his little knife behind him without looking and said, "I will not miss, human."

Before Freyrík could second-guess himself, he nudged Spyrna between Ayden and Lieutenant Drengr and unsheathed his own sword.

"I will not say it again." A quick glance showed Lords Lini and Vitr at the ready, weapons drawn. A soft-looking groom and an even softer-looking elder secretary—the Aegeans would underestimate them. "You will respect my rule as law, or I will put you down as traitors."

Please, please *do not be foolish.*

Lieutenant Drengr grimaced, but did not sheathe his sword. "The *Lord Protector's* rule is law, Your Majesty," he said. He sounded almost apologetic about it.

"And as you so openly defy his law over an *elf,*" Lieutenant Herlid chimed in, "we cannot help but wonder: Has Your Majesty caught darker fever from the demon fog? Is Your Majesty's mind still sound?"

Oh, 'twas sounder than it'd been for weeks. For once out here in these cursed mountains, he knew *exactly* what he had to do.

"Final warning," he said. 'Twas small relief to see Lieutenant Rekkr apart from his fellows, eyes darting between them but hands holding only his reins, for the other two still defied him. He could give them no more chances, no matter how badly he wished to.

Instead he lunged forward in his saddle and sliced Lieutenant Drengr's head clear from his body.

He'd hoped—prayed—'twould be enough to make his point, and for Lieutenant Drengr it seemed to be. But Lieutenant Herlid lashed out, the befanged fool, and Lords Lini and Vitr set upon him before Freyrík could even dig his heels into Spyrna's sides.

The Aegean was dead in seconds, gods befang it. He'd longed to end the tensions between his men and the Aegeans for weeks, but not like *this.* They were good soldiers, following orders. And he'd made his groom and secretary complicit in their slaughter.

Worse, he'd have to execute Lieutenant Rekkr. For though the man hadn't lifted his blade—And why was that anyway? Cowardice?—he was of the Aegis and couldn't be trusted. He might mean to avenge his fellows.

It seemed his own men thought the same, for as soon as they'd made their kill, they closed in round Lieutenant Rekkr and held him still at blade-point.

"Freyrík."

Ayden. Eyes wide as he'd ever seen them, a thin rim of green round a pool of black. Clutching blades in both hands. Was he so hungry for human blood that he wished to make this kill himself? Freyrík swallowed his disgust and nodded. Let the elf do it; 'twas a duty gladly abdicated.

"Only make it quick," Freyrík said. "He deserves that, at least."

"Let him go," Ayden said.

"I— What?"

Ayden very deliberately sheathed his knives and said, in a voice more soft and even than Freyrík could credit, "There has been enough death today. He raised no arms against us. Let him live."

What beneath the shadow . . .

'Twas he who should be arguing for the lives of his men, not the elf who'd spent the last three hundred years dreaming of ways to kill every human he laid eyes upon.

And yet he would protect that elf at any cost. Protect the mission, as well. "We must sleep sometime, Ayden. We've no vigilance to spare here."

Ayden shook his head. "We are four to one. We must keep watch anyway. Besides, he believes the answers lie in Fornheim as surely as you do."

I do?

Yes, on reflection, he supposed he must, else why take the lives of his own men?

For Ayden, you besotted fool. For Ayden.

Ayden shook his head again, and the smile teasing at his lips seemed just this side of indulgent. "He did not let his comrades die for love, Rík; he let them die for the future of the Empire." Ayden lifted his chin toward the lieutenant. "Am I right, Rekkr?"

Lieutenant Rekkr held his empty hands up and slowly, ever so slowly slid from his horse. Lord Lini tracked his movements with the tip of his sword, but let the man fall unmolested to his knees. There Lieutenant Rekkr bowed deep, forehead to the muddied snow, and said, "My life to you, my liege. If we must walk into the maw of the enemy to end this darker scourge, I shall follow you there gladly."

Into the maw indeed. Freyrík prayed 'twas the right choice, and not one made merely out of love. Yet the gods remained as mute on this matter as they had on all the others.

Freyrík rode the afternoon in silence, trying to purge the guilt he felt over the Aegeans' deaths. 'Twas war, he told himself again and again. Regretful but necessary sacrifices. The fate of the Empire must come before the lives of two men.

Ayden said nothing, but rode near, meeting his eyes whenever Freyrík took them from the path ahead. No coddling—the elf wasn't capable of such—but firm, quiet support. Gratitude. Love. Trust.

All of which he showered on Freyrík in excess that night in their shared bed.

They set out the next morning due east, or as near to it as they could figure through endless cloud and fog obscuring the sky and a compass that would not work. Freyrík prayed each morning to cross the great crack in the earth by nightfall, but Ayden seemed blissfully unbothered by their long unpleasant trek. Such joy Ayden felt at the prospect of the morrow, of home; Freyrík saw it on his face in a thousand unguarded moments—a naked grin, a faraway gaze of remembered pleasures, a quiet endurance buoyed by the knowledge that his trials would be over soon.

Freyrík wanted that for him, wanted that for them both. Yet still the prospect terrified, for how could they be together once Ayden returned to his own people?

Unless, of course, the Aegis truly did wish Freyrík dead. 'Twas a possibility he tried not to dwell on. He did not believe the elves would permit him to stay in any event, even if he had nowhere else to go.

And gods, but that hurt most of all. Made him hunger for closeness more than anything, for surely it'd be over soon, and he'd have to learn all over again how to live his life without this maddening, astonishing elf in it at every turn. They did not speak of it, but surely by the way Ayden held him at night, made love to him, stared at him throughout the day, the elf was thinking the same.

They endured nine more days of haunted woods and anxieties for their future before they crossed the crack. When at last they did, they were in Farr again; they'd tracked further north than he'd realized.

They spent that first night in a shepherd's hut, where Freyrík agonized an hour or more over a bird-sized slip of paper and his pot of ink, wondering what to say. In the end he settled for as much truth as he could fit on the note; if they did not make it back, his people needed to know what they'd found in those mountains.

Yet he did not launch a bird, merely slipped the note into a saddlebag, where it would remain until the night before they crossed into elven lands.

They raided the shepherd's stores that night. He felt poorly for it, but their own stores had gone beyond thin over two weeks past, and between the hard riding and the bitter cold, they could ill afford to go hungry anymore. Nor could they simply ride into town to restock. Surely his dread over this was irrational, but he did not wish them to be seen. Not until their task was done.

So they ate their fill and stripped the hut of all but a few days' food. It wasn't much for the five of them, but 'twould hold them another three or four days, a week if they rationed. He pulled a ring off his finger and left it in the cupboard come morn. 'Twas a more than fair exchange for what they'd taken.

The food and shelter seemed a gift from the gods after all the deprivations of the past weeks, but they paled in comparison to what awaited them when they stepped outside: warm sun shining bright in a clear blue sky. Not a drop of fog, not a cloud in sight. The air was cold but still—no wind, gods blessed—and Freyrík tilted his head back to let the sun heat his face.

Ayden stepped out beside him, took one look at the sky, and laughed.

Then he too tilted his face up to the sun and cried, "And on a beam of purest light the gods fell from the skies."

"And in their clutched hands fires from the heavens, and on their tongues the song of the sun."

Ayden's head whipped round as Freyrík finished the verse, his brows drawn, his mouth open.

Before he could ask a thing, Freyrík grinned at him and said, "I still continue to surprise you after all this time?"

Slowly, so slowly, the smile crept back onto Ayden's face.

"Did I not once share with you my fondness for elven poetry?"

"You did," Ayden said.

"And let me guess—you did not believe me."

"No. I did not."

Freyrík turned, took a step, closing the distance between them. Though they had seemed this past week to be slipping from each other's reach, Freyrík reached for him anyway, laid hands upon Ayden's shoulders and slid them round the back of his neck. "Do you believe me now?" he asked.

Ayden blinked, licked his lips, leaned in ever so subtly. 'Twas not an invitation to kiss—at least Freyrík did not think so. No, 'twas something yet deeper, and entirely more intense. "Yes," he said, his face mere inches from Freyrík's, his eyes sharp and bright as cut emeralds in the sun. "Yes, I do."

Freyrík rarely thought himself a clever man when it came to Ayden, but 'twas clear as running water that they were no longer speaking of poetry.

"Good," he said, a mere whisper, his breath ghosting between them as his thumbs brushed up the sides of Ayden's neck.

Ayden's hands slid up Freyrík's flanks, shoulders, came to rest on either side of his head and tipped it forward until their brows met. "Good indeed. I would you kiss me now."

A request joyously granted. 'Twas a chaste affirmation, what with the men buzzing round them loading horses, but no less vital for it. A meeting on cherished ground, a promise that come what may, they would fight for what they had.

"Come," Ayden said when at last they broke apart. His fingers were still tangled in Freyrík's hair, gripping lightly, and Freyrík never, ever wanted him to stop. "We've still a long ride ahead of us."

Indeed they did. But his belly was full and his clothes were dry and the sun was shining and Ayden had *kissed* him, and for the first time in a month, absolutely nothing else mattered.

It took ten days to cross into Ingimárr Province. Only then was Freyrík willing to risk a trip to a town for supplies. They'd been able to hunt again, at least, and even with his magic bound, Ayden's masterful hand kept their bellies from shrinking.

They camped well on the outskirts of some small enclave, and he sent Lord Lini and Lieutenant Rekkr into town proper to procure supplies. They were desperate for horse feed, and Freyrík was fair confident his men would not be recognized this far from home.

They lost the day waiting on his men to return, and despite his itch to keep moving, he knew 'twas for the best. The weather might be better here—no more interminable fog, no more fire-quashing winds—and the night terrors had ceased the moment they'd left the darker forests, but they were still exhausted. Yet soon, gods permitting, they might celebrate victory with feasts and leisure, soft cushions and warm hearths, music and wine. He held on to that vision with both hands.

And to Ayden, as well, who he was ashamed to admit he clung to like some suckling babe at night. The elf didn't seem to mind, but always now he seemed distracted, as if carrying on some endless argument in his head to which Freyrík was not privy. Presumably about his future. *Their* future.

Freyrík would have rather liked a say in that, but even after slaying the lieutenants, he knew he had no right to one. He had made the choices alone for far too long, taken from Ayden far too much, and now 'twas Ayden's turn to decide their future.

They rode out with fresh horses and supplies, the moon waxing and then waning as they crossed north and east through Ingimárr toward Fornheim. Ayden's spirits lifted with each passing day, even as Freyrík's sank. 'Twas cruel injustice their happiness seemed always zero-sum.

He lost track of the days. 'Twas a monotonous drudgery of cold and snow, sore arses and hard beds, long leagues and creeping fear for the future.

And then late one eve the future came in the shape of the borderlands between Ingimárr and Fornheim.

They camped a hundred paces off the dirt road where they'd first encountered the warning sign—a faded old slab of wood and red paint shouting "Elven Border One League North, Do Not Cross" in letters the size of his hand. Somewhere out there would be soldiers on patrol, likely with dogs to assist. 'Twould be risky crossing into the border zone; they could not afford to be seen.

Ayden must have been thinking the same, for when he finished his meal—a cold one, for they'd risked no fire this night—he waved all the men in close and said, "We must speak of tomorrow."

The men gathered round to listen. Silent, respectful. "We cannot all cross; 'tis too dangerous. Rík and I alone will go. I will see to safe passage for Rík. He is an envoy; he'll be shown all due respect."

Lieutenant Rekkr held out a hand. "You are but a common soldier—"

Freyrík raised a warning eyebrow, and the lieutenant bowed his head.

"Apologies. I merely meant you are no more able to make such promises than I could promise for you. And I cannot let my king walk unprotected into enemy lands."

All frighteningly valid points. Yet Freyrík knew he had no choice in it. He would go tomorrow and beg their aid no matter what the cost.

But Ayden grinned at the lieutenant—a dark and feral thing— and said, "I am not quite so common as you may think. I will not swear an oath I cannot guarantee, but I *can* promise you this: I will protect his life with my own."

"Well," Freyrík said, even as his mind screamed, *You will die tomorrow, fool.* "That is good enough for me."

"I must voice protest, Your Maj—"

"Duly noted, Lieutenant." He turned to Lord Lini next, for though ever a taciturn man, he seemed especially so now. "And you, my dear lord? Would you protest as well?"

His secretary grimaced, but then ever so slowly shook his head. "No, Your Majesty." His gaze swept from Freyrík to Ayden, where it lingered long and appraising. "He trusted me with his dearest. I trust him with mine."

Ayden's grin at that was neither dark nor feral—no, 'twas beauteous, almost childlike in its pleasure. The elf would surely deny it, but Lord Lini had touched his heart.

"Thank you," Ayden said, and that too was sincere and pure. "Now Freyrík and I must rest. We will cross the border at dawn."

Ayden and Rík stole into the borderlands at first light, choosing foot over horseback for stealth's sake. 'Twould take thrice as long to cross the league between them and Fornheim, but at least they'd not be shot in the back on the way.

Ayden took the lead, not because he knew these lands but because he was the better hunter by far. 'Twas down to Ayden to keep them upwind of the guardsmen's dogs and out of the guardsmen's sights.

He knew from experience that where humans walked on one side of the border, elves walked on the other. Or perched up trees, more like, watching and waiting from the position of best advantage.

He also knew his people were not killers by nature. They favored fighting sticks and sleeper darts over short swords and foxglove. 'Twas beyond a border guard's purview to kill without reason—and trespass was *not* a reason. Muted as he was now by the starfall, he might sound like a human, but he and Freyrík were unarmed and of no clear threat. They'd survive the crossing, he was (nearly) certain of it.

Though 'twas likely they'd wake from it with cracking fine headaches.

They crouched low at forest's edge, the old dirt trading road some dozen paces to their right, the wide expanse of razed ground demarcating their lands directly ahead. 'Twas graveled and clear of grass or trees—a protection against both trespass and arson, for over the years, the humans had proven themselves above neither.

"Are you ready?" he asked.

Rík nodded. The fear in his eyes did not touch the stony set of his features, and gods but Ayden loved him in that moment as he'd never loved him before. He grabbed Rík by the head and kissed him, there and done before the man could even respond. If they lingered now, they might lose their courage.

"Remember: Walk, do not run. Hold your head up. And show your hands, do you understand?"

Rík nodded.

They made it four steps before Ayden felt the sting of a dart in the chest.

He woke with a splitting headache. No gradual rise to consciousness; he hurt too much for that. His back and his wrists were complaining, too, and being propped up against the rough bark of a tree wasn't helping. From the feel of it, he'd been dragged by bound wrists across a long expanse of forest floor. His hands weren't tied anymore—*how odd*—but he could see the rope burns.

"Are you awake?" someone shouted.

He blinked up at the sound of the voice, and saw some dozen paces distant a stunning female soldier with close-cropped yellow hair and a carved stick in each hand. At her feet lay Freyrík, bound hand and foot, unconscious but by all appearances unharmed.

"Yes. Is he well?"

She nudged Rík with the toe of her boot. "The human, you mean?"

He ached too much for sarcasm, so he said merely, "Yes."

"He is unharmed. Apologies for your own state, but it could not be helped. 'Tis quite unbearable to be near you, I'm afraid—we had to move you by a very long rope."

His hand went to his collar of its own accord—a habit he'd developed these last months against all attempts to quash it. "It's all right. I understand."

"You are Ayden *barn* Vaska, are you not?"

He felt a bit ridiculous shouting cross the forest, and anyway the sleeper dart had dried his throat, so he just nodded. 'Twas no great surprise to hear she knew of him. By now they probably all did, for as few who went missing these days and for all 'twas likely Ella had shared on her return.

She nudged Rík with her foot again, and Rík stirred briefly but didn't wake. "Is this your prisoner?"

"Not exactly? We must travel to the Hall of Elders. I will explain everything there."

The elf nodded. "I thought as much. I've sent up a signal cloud. An escort is on the way. In the meanwhile, I've food and water for you and your . . . *guest*, and some willow bark for your head if you wish it. And if I may be so bold, let me be the first to say: Welcome home, Ayden."

His grin nearly split his face in two. *Home.* Fallen gods praised, he was finally home.

Chapter Fourteen

The hours passed. He learned what he could while he waited. The soldier who'd taken them was named Atall, and Ayden outranked her, which went a long way toward convincing her to let him sit with Rík.

Rík woke some half hour after Ayden had, looking sick and uncomfortable and braced for the worst. Atall watched them from a distance, unable to bear proximity to the starfall round Ayden's neck. At least she kept her blowpipe at the ready. He'd have reported her otherwise; after so long in enemy hands, 'twas foolish to trust him absolutely.

The escorts arrived with horses in the early afternoon. Eight soldiers, armed to the teeth. He thought he recognized the one in the lead, a commander from Ayden's brief foray into espionage on the elven/human tall ships along the Meiri trade routes. He'd let the hair at his temples gray in neat streaks and his smile lines deepen—a strange fashion amongst his generation, mockery perhaps of human weakness, though Ayden had to admit some attraction for it. But surely 'twas the same elf.

Ayden stood to greet him, forgetting until the elf recoiled that he was poison now to all his people. "Commander Herra?" he called from some paces distant.

The elf nodded. "Captain Vaska."

So formal. Was he not to be trusted at all, then? He looked over to Rík, who'd climbed to his feet despite being bound tight at the ankles. The man was standing tall but not in challenge, the set of his chest and shoulders less to do with his pride than with his hands being tied behind his back.

Ayden turned eyes back to Commander Herra. "This man is King Freyrík of Farr, and he has come of his own volition, with peace in his heart, to have words with the first minister. In this endeavor I have sworn to protect him with my life. I know I am suspect and rightfully so, but I pray you not make my oath so costly."

Commander Herra cast dubious eyes toward Freyrík. "*That* is King Farr? That ragged little man?"

Ayden bristled, but he was suspect enough already, so he bit his tongue and said merely, "He is."

"And 'twas he who held you prisoner all this time?"

"Not exactly, sir."

The commander arched an eyebrow at Ayden. "One more riddle, I dart you both and let the Council sort it out."

"I only mean, sir, that while he is the man who held me at first, he later sought to release me at great cost to himself. As he did with Ella, who I'm sure has told the same story by now. Only circumstance was not so fortunate for me as for her. In any case, he returns me now, does he not?"

"You did not escape then and take him prisoner?"

"No, sir."

"All right, then. You"—he pointed to Freyrík—"can you sit a horse with your hands bound thus?"

Freyrík dipped his head, as much affirmation as a gesture of respect. "Indeed, Commander, if you'd grant me the privilege."

The commander turned to one of his men. "Free his legs and let him ride. Captain Vaska, you will ride ten paces ahead. I'm afraid none of us can stand to be near you."

Hah, Ayden thought, a wry smile twisting his lips. *Just like old times.*

'Twas a heady thing for Rík to realize that he was likely the first human to step foot in elven lands in three hundred years. So much so he nearly forgot to be afraid. Yet it looked no different than the human lands they'd so recently left, if perhaps a little wilder: forest and forest and more forest, game and foot trails winding through the trees. But for the sorcery by which the elves controlled his horse and the bright white glow about them all, he might have thought himself within the empire still.

Except of course for the female soldiers. Like the one who'd captured him, stunning in her beauty, yet fierce and competent as any man. Was that a race trait, this supremacy of the weaker sex? Or might human women hold some lost potential? Did it matter in any case, when birthing a brood of children held so much more value than lifting a sword ever could? Mayhap women warriors were a luxury only the elves could afford, for they need not fight to outrace extinction.

They rode for some hours—two, perhaps four; time passed strange in enemy lands. Eventually the road widened and the forest thinned, and they came upon a walled outpost carved from the woods.

All rode through but for Ayden and two escorts, who kept well apart but within darting range. "I'm sorry, Captain," the Commander called from the gate, "but we cannot remove the starfall here and mustn't have it in our midst. I will send out someone shortly with supplies. They will make you comfortable."

Ayden nodded and dismounted to stretch his muscles while he waited.

Inside the outpost were buildings of log and chinking, but it seemed a barrack was a barrack in any nation, and two formed an L along the back and left walls. Soldiers trained in the center square, and to the right, where they led Freyrík, was a stable and officers' quarters. Also a prison cell, which it seemed he'd be calling home for a time.

'Twas well appointed as prison cells went: four cots stacked two tall, mattresses, pillows, blankets. No hearth, but warmth drifted in from somewhere, and after so long outside in the bitter chill, Freyrík found himself sweating beneath his cloak. He shed it and paced the cell, not in search of escape but in simple curiosity. Two log walls, two of iron bars, the whole enclosure but four paces square.

On his second pass round, someone asked, "What do you call yourself? 'Your Majesty'?"

'Twas a female voice. She stepped into view before the bars, and he blinked at her elflight, at her beauty beneath. Tried very hard not to stare. "I call myself Freyrík," he said, "but others call me Your Majesty, yes."

She scoffed at that, hatred and derision flaring bright as her elflight. Would she have struck him then, if the bars were not between them?

Instead she disappeared, reappeared a moment later with a bowl in one hand and a mug in the other: porridge and water. "Here, *Your Majesty*. Your feast awaits." She thrust the food and water through a slot in the bars and turned her back on him before walking away.

The night seemed interminable. Freyrík spent it worrying about Ayden, yet stuck out in the cold, guarded warily by his own people. Every time he heard footsteps outside his cell, he thought, *This is it. They will come now and exact their revenge.* But they did not. By morning, when two male elves unlocked his cell and stepped inside, he was so certain of the inevitable beating he didn't even try to fight it when they hauled him from the cot he'd tossed the night in.

But they only stood him up, bound his hands behind him, and fastened his cloak back round his shoulders. And if they gripped him perhaps a little too hard and tied his hands perhaps a little too tight, well, at least that he understood.

They led him out into the bracing cold of early morn and onto a horse. "Wait here," they said, but it seemed they'd spoken more to the animal than to him. They left before he could ask where they were taking him next, or if Ayden was all right.

He found out soon enough, though. An escort gathered—the same eight soldiers from yesterday—and they led him through the gate. Ayden was mounted and waiting. He ended up leading the pack on their march toward the Hall of Elders, for still none could stand to be near him, and they did not trust him to ride behind. Did he realize his own fellows had weapons trained upon his back? If he did, it didn't appear to bother him.

Gradually the woods thinned and yielded to pasture and fields, stone shepherds' huts and sparse, modest homes made primarily of clay bricks and sod. They stopped the night at a lone log building set back from the road. Ayden slept outside again. For want of a prison cell, Freyrík slept shackled to a bolt in the floor.

Morning came between one breath and the next. After so many sleepless nights and long rides, he'd gone under like a man knocked on the head, and woke just as reluctantly. Someone shoved a waterskin and a hunk of bread at him. 'Twas strange stuff, permeated through with the taste of chestnuts, as if they'd been milled to flour along with the wheat. He decided he liked it, and was ravenous in any case; he ate it quickly before anyone might change their mind and take it from him.

Back on the road again. Midway through the day, they came across the first real town. They gave it wide berth, no doubt for any number of reasons. No one came to gawk at them.

The road out of town was graveled. By nightfall it had widened, and they'd passed two other enclaves and a number of crossroads. Another night in a lone log building, another day on the road. Country slowly yielded to town, which yielded to bigger towns. Not quite so human-looking anymore: Everywhere stood trees, gardens, wild parks. The air was sweet, the sewers out of smell and sight— underground perhaps. Animals grazed in unpenned yards, but almost never did he see their owners, or even a shepherd or herding dog.

They overnighted in a hall of magisters on the edge of a large town. There stood two jail cells, both four walls of stone, both empty. The elves escorted Freyrík into one of them and cut his bindings.

Despite the dungeon-like surroundings, 'twas nice as cells went. Little windows of iron and glass let in the last dying rays of sunlight. A lantern hung from the ceiling, and in one corner was a covered privy seat that smelled more of cedar than waste. The bunk beds were piled high with blankets, and on a shelf bolted to the wall near the door sat a pitcher of fresh water and a cup.

He went to pour himself some, and through the wall he heard the cell door beside him clank shut. Then a voice, muffled and distant: "Rík?"

He nearly dropped the cup in his haste to press his ear to the wall between the cells. "Ayden?" Gods, they'd not been permitted to speak to each other for *days*. "Are you all right?"

"I'm fine. You?"

"Yes. They have treated me far better than I'd expected."

"Fallen gods pray it lasts."

Indeed, he had prayed so each night to his own gods. "How do you come to be indoors tonight? Is the starfall gone?"

"Nay. But the others cannot hear it through the stone." He thought he heard Ayden laugh. "I never thought I'd be so glad of a prison cell. It is good to be warm."

"Indeed." Freyrík grinned, laid his forehead and palm flat against the stone between them. He imagined Ayden doing the same on the other side. Wished he could touch him, even if only for a moment. Soon, gods pray. Soon.

"Tomorrow we reach Fornheim and the Hall of Elders. I will stay with you if I can, but our ways may be parted by force. So tell me you love me and sleep well tonight; no matter what happens, you'll need all your wits about you come morn."

Of this he had no doubt. He only prayed his wits would be enough. "I love you, elf," he said, and prayed that would be enough too.

"And I you, human. Now rest."

"You as well," Freyrík called, for he feared Ayden would face trials of his own tomorrow.

When Ayden said nothing more, Freyrík tore himself from the wall, removed his boots, and climbed into bed. He lay awake beneath the covers, eyes closed, and prayed. *May the gods bless us both strong and wise.*

Something told him they were going to need all the help they could get.

Freyrík woke to a rooster's crow, the sound drifting through his glassed cell window along with the first dawn light. The elves came for him shortly after, brought him breakfast and fresh water and shackles that didn't chafe half so badly as the rope they'd used before.

The door to Ayden's cell was ajar as they marched him past it, the room empty; Ayden was waiting outside, already ahorse, by himself some dozen paces down the road. The guards helped Freyrík onto his own mount. No halter, no reins, just a saddle with low-hanging stirrups.

Others soon joined him. But for Commander Herra, the escorts were all new. One looked quite important, if the green velvet robe was anything to go by. Freyrík recognized some of the ancient elven symbols embroidered in silver thread upon the cuffs and hem: justice, balance, fairness, truth. The magister, mayhap? Or the governor of this place?

As they rode deeper into Fornheim, Freyrík committed to memory as many details as he could in the event his fate turned sour. They were not traveling a main road, if its emptiness was any indication, but it was paved here, and skirting nearly due north round ever-larger towns.

Though the whole of the land here was fairly flat, the road began to cant uphill sometime after noon. Of course it made sense to build your bastion on the highest ground, but the war had never spilled this far north, and the elves had never—at least not in recorded human history—fought amongst themselves. Why then the walled city on the hill?

'Twasn't quite so large as the Splendor, or at least it didn't seem so as they approached a little gate on the western wall. Their party went through without inspection, though Ayden and one guard waited well off to the side, the tall stone wall between his starfall and the tender-eared elves of Fornheim.

Freyrík watched him as long as he could, even found himself squeezing his horse's sides in unconscious attempt to stop it. It didn't work, of course; the beast was thoroughly enthralled to its elven masters. He'd managed until now to keep his fear mostly at bay, but as his horse passed through the gate and took Ayden from his view, panic spread like acid through his belly and chest and would not be quelled.

For you have no reason with which to quell it.

Indeed he did not. He was trapped here at their mercy, and Ayden nowhere to be seen—mayhap himself viewed as an enemy of the Republic, tainted, turned against his own as Jagall had been—

"Peace, King Farr. You upset your horse."

Indeed, he was squeezing its flanks so hard his legs were cramping.

"Breathe. I'd rather not have to have to haul you back up if you faint and fall."

He glared at the soldier who'd ridden up beside him. "Such kindness you spare. How do you bear it?"

He regretted the words the instant he spoke them, but the soldier only chuffed, more amused than irritated. And strange, but Freyrík *was* calmer, though there was no calling for it. Had the elf ensorcelled him as well as his horse? Soothed him as Ella had once done?

Panic was a weakness he could ill afford, but he resented the intrusion nevertheless. If they could sway him so easily, how could he trust anything he thought or felt here?

Gods, did Ayden too hold such power? And if so, had he ever—

No. Gods no. 'Twas Freyrík who had so doggedly pursued Ayden. Ayden would *never* . . . And 'twas surely but a mark of Freyrík's distress that such a vile thought could so much as waft through his mind.

He turned his eyes back to the cobbled street. From somewhere he heard water running, and realized of a sudden that the air was fresh. Like the forest, in fact, loamy and sweet and pitchy. Every façade was shaded, every block of row homes nestled in its own little copse of trees. 'Twas wild and ancient and wonderful—a time and place untouched by the hungry hand of man. No wonder the elves had left the shared ancestral lands the Empire had claimed in their absence.

Strange, how boorish and shameful that made him feel.

They crested a hill, and there in the near distance stood the Hall of Elders, or so he assumed, for a structure as magnificent as that must surely house the leaders of this land. 'Twas the size of his own palace, all polished white marble and glass, domed and spired like the crumbling old temples scattered throughout the empire's forests where the elves had once lived. Even in the dead of winter, splashes of color bloomed everywhere, tended no doubt by some magical gardener who sang his flowers warm in the chill. Several smaller buildings—still grand alone but not quite so by comparison—bracketed and segmented the grounds.

'Twas even more spectacular up close than from afar, though he had little time to look upon it before the elves helped him from his horse and tied a blindfold round his head. They led him indoors, the air blessedly warm and lightly scented with sandalwood—rare and precious to humans but grown in abundance on the elves' holy island of Svefn. Heels clacked on a hard floor. Marble as well?

They led him deep through the maze of halls, down a long flight of stairs and then another. The scent of sandalwood faded, a slight earthy mustiness taking its place. Belowground. Was it the dungeons for him, then?

They halted him. A door unlocked, and a hand between his shoulder blades urged him through it. Someone unshackled his wrists. Behind him, he heard the door close, the bolt throw. It seemed safe to take off his blindfold.

Indeed, 'twas a cell they'd put him in. Much like the one he'd stayed in the night before—clean and comfortable as cells went, neither too chilly nor too musty. 'Twas block stone through and through. No windows but the one on the heavy stone door, which looked out into a lantern-lit stone corridor and another stone cell across the hall. He pressed his face to the bars and saw a little stone shutter that could be locked across the window.

"Hello?" he called. He listened, heard nothing. Surely a guard must be standing watch somewhere. "Is anyone there? I must speak with the Council!"

Nothing. If life stirred down here beyond his own, it was keeping well to itself.

He pulled away from the door and paced the cell carefully, studying it for weapons, for means of escape, even as he prayed he'd not need them. Still, better to double-knot your laces than be caught with your cock out, as his brother was so fond of saying.

Berendil. Gods pray he was safe, wherever he was. Gods pray he might one day forgive Freyrík.

Freyrík sat down on the cot, unlaced his boots, peeled off his socks and wiggled his toes. The cool fresh air felt grand against his overheated skin. He stretched sore muscles one by one, then lay abed and closed his eyes.

He allowed himself to count his lost kin in his prayers, but when he was finished, he thought only of what the morrow might bring, and how best to meet it on both feet.

Ayden was starting to feel like he'd never come home. 'Twas all still prison cells and wary stares. Nobody would come near him. Nobody would give him a chance to explain himself. They'd taken

Rík from him at the city walls several hours past and still hadn't told him what they'd done with him or when he might see the man again. They'd not told him when he might have audience with the Council, or at least with elves who might take his message to them. They'd not told him *anything*.

He paced his little stone cell for the hundredth time. The door was unlocked, but 'twas naught but a courtesy illusion: guards stood in the corridor, ready to dart him unconscious if he tried to leave.

And worst of all, he was still deaf.

But they would fix that soon. They'd promised him.

He sat on the cell's only cot, changed his mind and stretched out flat. Sleeping would pass the time. Besides, he faced a long inquiry when the collar came off. 'Twas unlikely it'd be hostile, but best nevertheless to be rested and sharp. Freyrík's life might well depend on it.

He woke to the sound of his cell door opening, and was on his feet before anyone had entered the room. Such caution was likely unwarranted, but he'd been through too much this year to take needless risks.

He saw the robe before the person—a hem of green and gold, pure silk velvet draped across a boot-clad calf—and stiffened to attention. Surely the Council was not meeting him here in some tiny stone cell? Surely it couldn't be that easy?

No, not so easy after all. 'Twas but two councillors, one Father and one Mother of the Republic in full ceremonial regalia. He thought he recognized them both: Mother Megin, first representative of Vaenn for nearly fifty years now. He'd voted for her, in fact. Planned to again if he and Freyrík survived this mess. The Father was likely Krellr, second representative of Vaenn.

He forced himself not to accost them physically, but could not stop himself saying, "Councillors, please. I must speak to the Council in—"

"Quiet, soldier." A glowering male in the field dress of the Defense Ministry—a colonel by the insignia on his sleeve—shoved into the room and placed himself between Ayden and the councillors. Not threatening, exactly, but no mistaking that he could if he wished it.

Behind him, two females in the blue and green robes of the Academy of Sciences filed in. One was carrying a stone box the size of his forearm, another a bundle of clothes. The door closed behind them, and they formed a semicircle, hemming him in. If his starfall caused them pain, they showed no indication—truly, such grand power in their old age.

Mother Megin stepped forward. "I am Mother Megin. You will forgive us for our curtness, but the starfall causes great distress. We have come to remove it. Please, lie down." Mother Megin waved him toward the bed, and though he did as asked, he could not help but think of the day the collar had gone on—how they too had told him to lie down, and why it had been necessary.

Perhaps Mother Megin sensed his fear despite the starfall, for she added, "This will be very loud. 'Tis fortunate you are deaf for now. Even still it may not be pleasant, but 'twill be over quick."

Ayden nodded his permission—*as if they'd need that anyway*—and closed his eyes. He realized he'd fisted his hands in the sheets, even though he felt nothing yet. Heard nothing, either. Why wouldn't they just get *on* with—

The collar began to vibrate. It tickled, itched. He touched a hand to it to stop it and felt the buzz all the way down to his elbow. It was starting to hurt. And grow hot. The cracking thing was round his *neck*, not a tree limb; did they not realize they needed to leave what lay beneath it in one piece?

"It's burning." The collar's vibration infected his words, made him sound as if he were speaking into a strong wind. "Is it supposed to be burning?"

No reply. He raised his head from the pillow to look at the councillors. The motion left him dizzy. His temples throbbed. The councillors and scientists had their eyes closed, brows furrowed. They were sweating, all of them, despite the cool air. One had fisted his hands as if in strain.

Ayden let his head fall back. The vibration grew stronger, made his teeth hurt, his eyes ache. He wrapped fingers round the collar but pulled them away an instant later—one councillor barked, "*No*," and besides, the metal burned his fingertips. 'Twas also burning his neck. He gritted his teeth against it, felt a scream welling up in his throat, shaken loose by—

The collar fractured into pieces round him, and everything went still and silent. He sat up, put both hands to his neck and felt skin, only skin.

"Put the pieces in the box, if you would."

He took the box with shaking hands. 'Twas heavy, thick, the lid held shut with two sturdy latches. He undid them, plucked the collar pieces from the bed—still so hot he had to use the hem of his shirt to protect his fingers—and secured them inside.

When he'd gotten the last and latched the lid closed again, 'twas as if he'd shut away all the tension in the room. Well, excepting the colonel, but he'd not expected the soldier to relax like the councillors did. Mother Megin sat beside Ayden and put her hands to his burning neck. The pain disappeared. And he realized . . .

"I am still deaf." Cold panic seized his chest, left him dizzy, breathless. He clutched at Mother Megin's hands. "I am still deaf! Why am I still deaf?"

"Shhh," she said, and only then did he notice the colonel had advanced a step, was falling back at the shake of her head. She pried a hand free from Ayden's, brushed it across his temple. Gods, but she reminded him of his own mother, of curling in her lap and being soothed to sleep. He leaned into her touch, felt the anger and panic drain from him even as he wished to keep it . . . and just why was that happening anyway? Why was he so calm of a sudden?

And then he realized . . . *She is singing you down.*

"Stop," he begged, twisting out from beneath her touch. They weren't supposed to do things like that to each other. It was wrong, too intimate, a violation between strangers absent permission. He'd had enough of that in the human world; he could not bear it now he was home. "*Please*. Don't."

"Apologies." Mother Megin looked sheepish, even guilty, and Ayden felt the fear crawling back, cold and thick. "You were so distressed; I only meant to help." He nodded, understanding but not quite yet ready to forgive. "Your hearing *will* return. But the starfall has harmed you, here"—she touched a gentle fingertip to the space between his eyes—"where the song is so complex we daren't try to right it. It will right itself soon enough. We have seen this many times with others like you."

Soon enough? "How soon?"

Her look of sad sympathy was as sure an indication as any that he'd not like her answer. "A season, perhaps two."

Fallen gods cracked, so long?

"Some recover faster," she added, taking his hand in hers. Strange how he didn't mind the touch after all he'd been through, after what she'd just done. But he felt quite certain she wasn't doing it again; this was all him. "'Tis not so very long in the scheme of things, no?"

Perhaps not for someone who'd passed millennia on this earth, but for him? For as long as he'd endured a soundless world already?

"I promise, Ayden: Soon you'll be back to your old self. 'Twill be as if you'd never been in human hands."

Human hands. Rík. "I must see Freyrík," he said, then quickly corrected, "King Farr. And the Council. I must speak with them."

She squeezed his hand, smiled at him like she'd cared for him a thousand years. He found he didn't mind that, either. "Rest easy, child. Your human friend is safe for now. As for the Council, that will come in due time." She stood, disentangled her fingers from his own. "For the moment, Colonel Frétta will hear your story."

Ayden jumped to his feet, reached for her hand again. "Nay, Mother, you must hear me! I need audience with the Council, not an interrogator!"

"I assure you, he is not—"

"I have seen the Grand Elders in the Feral woods!" Ayden shouted, and though he'd not meant to say such in front of so many of so little import—*outrageous*, they would think, *he is mad*—at least it caught their attention.

He felt Mother Megin's eyes bore through his, even thought, for a moment, that he heard the burrowing hum of her song reaching out for his, seeking truth. But of course he hadn't; he was *still deaf.* "What did you say?" she whispered.

Ayden swallowed, self-conscious of a sudden. They already thought him compromised. Would they think him insane now too? "The Grand Elders. Skadi, Missa, Vesall. I have seen them." He seized

Mother Megin's hand again, and this time the colonel made no move to stop him. "Please, I beg of you. I must address the Council."

Another long stare, a sensation like fingers on his skin, combing through his head. They weren't supposed to do *that* to each other either, but he understood the necessity of it, was grateful for it even. Let her hear the truth in him, if she could.

Yet he was mute still as well as deaf, with no song to hear.

Despite that, Mother Megin nodded at last, then stood, his hand still in hers, and pulled him to his feet.

"Yes," she said. "Yes. I think that would be wise indeed." She turned, and one of the scientists mutely extended the bundle of cloth in his hand. "Oh, yes. Do change your clothes first. You are . . ."

"Filthy?" Ayden suggested.

Mother Megin smiled wanly and nodded her head, and Ayden took the clean clothes—the winter field wear of an elite fighter—with a heartfelt "Thank you." Thirty seconds—he could spare that much to make himself presentable now he knew they would hear him at last.

He turned to lay the clean clothes on the bed, stripped down and re-dressed as quickly as he could, and turned back round to find everybody staring at him.

He didn't need his mind-ear to hear their shock. "What?" he asked.

The stares hardened. Not just the shock and disbelief of a moment ago, but now anger, disgust. Fury. What could he possibly have done to offend them so between one breath and the next? Had they heard something?

"What?" he asked again. Demanding this time. Defensive.

Mother Megin, still standing beside him, laid a hand on his shoulder. "Ayden," she said. No "Captain" this time. Despite the overfamiliarity, she sounded as if she were forcing the word through clenched teeth. "Who hurt you so? Was it your human *friend*?"

The hand on his shoulder slid to his back, and his heart sank right down to his feet. How could they concern themselves with such petty things after what he'd just told them? "Don't hurt him," he demanded. "You must promise me you won't hurt him."

"It was him, then?"

"It was *me*."

Father Krellr stepped forward, arched a brow. "You're saying you flogged *yourself*?"

"No, I— I mean, sort of?" He pushed past Mother Megin, anxious to move beyond this pettiness and have his audience with the Council. "This does not matter now. Please, I will explain everything, I promise. But you must trust me. I have served this nation at arms for over six hundred years; have I not earned that much? Promise me you'll not harm him."

The councillors conferred with each other, not in silence but still silent to Ayden's damaged mind-ear. 'Twas a strange thing to witness—this long unspoken series of nods and shrugs, shakes and scowls—when he could follow nothing of their meaning.

At last Mother Megin turned back to him. "Peace, Ayden. We'll make no decision without hearing your story in full. Come now. The Council waits."

Freyrík woke to his cell door unlocking. There was no time in this windowless underground prison, but he'd not been here so long that his body had forgotten its rhythms. He felt sleep-fogged and fairly certain 'twas the middle of the night, or at least very early in the morn. Why had they come for him now? He sat up, shoved the covers back, swung his legs over the edge of the cot.

Two elves stepped into his cell—a man and a woman. 'Twas jarring afresh to see curves and full breasts beneath heavy leathers. She carried carved sticks in both hands, nearly identical to the ones Ayden so favored. As if she were expecting trouble. The male elf was carrying a shallow bowl.

"Is it morning already?" Freyrík asked. He wanted to stand, face them on his feet, but he held perfectly still. Best not to give the female any reason to use her weapons, for by her expression, she was looking very hard for an excuse.

The male stepped forward, within striking distance, and held out the bowl. 'Twas only porridge, but he was hungry enough not to care. He opened his hands for it, but let the guard come to him.

Just as the bowl touched his fingertips, the guard upended it with a sharp flick of the wrist. It hit the floor, shattered. Porridge oozed everywhere.

"Oops." The guard grinned, cold and nasty, baring his teeth. "Apologies, Your Majesty."

Freyrík clenched his jaw against sharp retort.

The female stepped forward, prodded his chest with a stick. "Aren't you going to eat your breakfast, Your Majesty?"

Freyrík looked to her, to the porridge spilled across the floor, to her again. Said, polite and demure, "Thank you, no. I'm not hungry."

She looked to the male and shook her head, then prodded Freyrík with a stick again. "Such ingratitude. Eat it."

Freyrík was willing to cede a great many things here for the good of his people, but licking porridge from the floor was not one of them. Not for some petty guardsmen, at least, who held no power to help him, and likely no power to hinder him either.

Another poke with a stick, to the shoulder this time, hard enough to rock him. "*Eat it.*"

When he didn't drop immediately to the floor, she spared him the trouble of concocting a suitable reply by cracking her stick across the side of his head.

He fell hard into a puddle of milky porridge and clay shards, forgetting where he was or why his head hurt so much until the elves set upon him and it all came rushing back. He'd no time to defend himself. Someone sat on his legs, someone else on his neck, pressing him to the cold stone floor.

Others must have rushed in at the noise, for he heard shouting, laughing, felt far too many hands upon him. Someone stretched his arms out in front of him and pinned his hands. Someone rucked his shirt up to his shoulders. Booted feet drove into his flanks. They held him so fast he could barely even squirm.

"Please don't do this!" he shouted, for though he knew it would not stop their vengeance, he was not above begging to live long enough to secure the elves' help against the dark beasts.

He was answered with another kick to his flank, hard enough to snap a rib. He shouted, gagged round the pain, fingers clawing at the floor. He couldn't even curl to protect himself.

"How do *you* like it, *Your Majesty*? Huh?"

Pain seared across the small of his back, a stripe of noise and fire quickly followed by another, and another, and another. Someone's belt, metal buckle and heavy leather, lashing like a whip. A second joined it across his shoulder blades, trebling the pain. He screamed, struggled to no avail. They beat him until his voice cracked. Until he stopped moving.

"Enough," someone said. He could have wept. Might have. 'Twas all agony so fierce he could hardly tell they'd stopped. Was only distantly aware of hands landing on his arse, curling round the waist of his breeches and tugging. 'Twas enough to set him struggling again, to moan a broken, "No."

From somewhere above him, another laugh. "Leave it. If you stick your cock in that, it'll wrinkle and die in thirty years." More laughter, raucous. The hands stopped tugging.

"Better clean him up."

Hands on his back, pain like a bright white blast of light. He twitched beneath the weights atop him, felt another "Please, no," claw its way up from his throat. Strange warmth in his back, tingling, nothing like the fire dancing cross his skin. The pain lessened. A wet cloth, blessedly cool but far too rough, wiping away the blood. Hands on his head, the pain there fading as well. Yet this was an especial cruelty, for so too went the obscuring fog of semiconsciousness, and all his body's complaints grew louder of a sudden by a factor of ten.

The elves straddling his neck and thighs stood away, and he curled without thought onto his side, gasping for air and hugging tight to himself. The room fell silent, empty. He'd not even heard the door close.

A shard of pottery was digging into his hip, but 'twas too much bother to move. Nothing seemed broken or bleeding anymore—gentle exploration with fingertips revealed the cut on his temple had been mended as if it never were, and it felt as if they'd done the same with his back. Hiding their traces? Had this attack been unsanctioned, then?

No matter. He'd known it was coming from the moment he'd stepped foot across the border. Deserved it, even.

At least it was over now, though they'd left him with reminders aplenty: he could feel bruises blooming right down to his bones. All he wanted to do was sleep.

And why not? The cool stone floor kept the fire in his back from raging, and gods knew he'd need all that remained of his strength for the fight ahead. The only question now was which opponent he'd be facing: the dark elves, or the corporeal ones?

Chapter Fifteen

Ayden hadn't talked this much in centuries. Hours upon hours. 'Twas not enough just to tell his story—he'd known it wouldn't be. The Council had questions. The ministers had questions. His commander and the generals had questions. Worse, they had *doubts*. Of course they would—who among them would wish to believe they'd been wrong for three hundred years? Who among them would wish to believe they'd left their elders to untold suffering all that time?

Fallen gods forbid they point their outrage inward, so of course they expended it on him. Called him compromised. Three seasons in enemy hands, the scars of brutal tortures stark on his skin. They could not hear the truth in his song, *would* not hear the truth in his words no matter how often he repeated them. Besides, he'd committed a cardinal sin: he'd fallen in love with the enemy. And so began another round of tiresome inquiry.

"What you ask of us," said the Minister of Defense, "seems the selfsame trap that took our Grand Elders' lives."

Oh fallen gods crack him! "But they did *not* die! I saw them with my own eyes! I would take the risk myself, sir. *I* would go. King Farr would stand at my side. Is that not assurance enough?"

"King Farr, yes. The man you claim to love." The Minister of Defense couldn't even say the words "man" and "love" in the same sentence without his upper lip curling. "The man you say tortured you."

This again? "Only briefly," Ayden growled for the thousandth time. "The first day. And I told him nothing—he quickly realized the futility of that tack."

"And so he had you whipped half to death in front of his entire kingdom?"

Ayden stood from the speaker's chair at the center of the rotunda, just barely restraining himself from storming the ministers' dais and choking sense into that cracking self-righteous elf. "I already told you—"

"That you 'volunteered' for that yourself, yes. Sit down, Captain, and kindly refrain from shouting again."

Ayden sat. Took a sip of water someone had left on the table beside him. He must not let them rile him.

Well, not any more than they already have.

"My apologies, Minister. I merely pray you understand I am not tainted. I was not swayed by pain or fear. Every nerve in me wanted to hate him, but I could not, not when I saw his true person. You claim this love eased my imprisonment. I say it has done anything but. It brought me comfort, yes, but also equal parts scrutiny and danger. Trust me, Minister, it would have been much easier to hate—as you so obviously do."

The Minister of Defense stared down at him from his seat on the ministers' dais, stony-faced and silent. Did he believe Ayden at last? And what of the others? The councillors, the First Minister? Fallen gods pray they did, for he could think of no more to say that might convince them.

Well, perhaps one thing.

"Bring King Farr to the chamber. Hear him. He is without guile. You will know the truth." Not that it would change a thing about their need to help the "dark elves," and he'd lost count of how many times he'd said that. "Whatever happened to our Grand Elders, we can help them. *You* can help them. Put end to their possession. And if it puts end to the Ferals as well . . . well, I have learned these last seasons that might be for the better too. Speak with King Farr and you will see for yourself—this is *not a trap*. Further, with a man such as Freyrík on the throne, we could know peace again."

Still the Minister of Defense remained stolid. "Yet you yourself said the Aegis sent King Farr into the wilds to die. What power over peace could such a man possibly have?"

"With respect, Minister, does it even matter?"

Mother Megin. Ayden could have kissed her.

"If Captain Vaska speaks the truth of our elders, then whatever he saw—whatever's become of them, whatever King Farr can or cannot achieve toward peace—we must help our Grand Elders if we can. We must speak with King Farr; we will hear the truth or lie in his story."

Murmurs from the Council, nodding heads. The defense minister did not agree aloud, but 'twas his job to be suspicious, after all.

"As for Captain Vaska, we should be honoring his suffering and sacrifice, not raking him over coals. And if he speaks true—and I believe he speaks true—then each hour we spend here debating the merits of his affections is another hour our true Mother and Fathers wander lost and alone in the Feral woods."

More murmurs, more nods of agreement. The defense minister seemed to consider this, and at last said, "Very well. With the First Minister's permission, let us break for the evening meal and return after to hear the human's tale."

The defense minister raised a questioning eyebrow at the First Minister, who nodded. Ayden thought it strange she seemed so unbothered by a cabinet member's takeover of such potentially life-altering proceedings. Would she not voice her own opinion in this matter? Or was she merely waiting to hear Freyrík's story too?

She stood. As per protocol, so did everyone else. They waited as she left the chamber. The ministers followed. Then the Council. Those few who remained—Ayden, officers, secretaries, assistants, some guards—filed out last. He stood in the broad marble hallway and watched everyone walk away but for two guards at respectful distance from himself.

Hours at debate, and still the Council did not trust him. Crack the cracking fools. 'Twas hard not to hate them for it—

"Bitterness does not become you, brother."

Ayden whirled at the sound of a much-missed voice, just in time to catch Ella mid-leap as she threw her arms round him. He hugged her back with equal fierceness, all the strain of the day washing clean in the joy of surprise. And a second surprise, as well, for standing there behind Ella, patient and smiling, eyes bright with tears, was his mother.

He opened his arms and brought her into the hug, asked on a laugh, "What are you two doing here?"

Ella pulled away, that old familiar mischief sparkling in her eyes. "I came to see Freyrík, of course."

Their mother swatted her good-naturedly. "We came as soon as we heard. We did not know . . ."

Even deaf, he could tell from the way her gaze flicked to the floor, from the way her mouth pinched, how that sentence was to end: *if you'd be whole. If you'd need us.*

He slung an arm round her shoulder and pulled her in close, kissed the top of her head. She'd cut her hair short in mourning. For him? "I'm fine, Mom."

Ella looked him up and down. "Better than fine. You're in love."

"You're so thin," his mother said, as if Ella hadn't just made such a grand declaration.

"We traveled hard. It's nothing some home cooking won't fix."

Ella took his hand, pulled him down the hallway in the direction the others had gone. To the mess, he assumed. "I told them all I knew," she said. "When I came home. They sent Afi Kengr to try to retrieve you, but you'd already gone. He brought back . . ." A pause, long and miserable. "Stories." She stopped walking, spun him to face her and grabbed his other hand. "Tell me Freyrík didn't—"

"He didn't. 'Twas my choice. And as for High Court . . . well, that was nobody's choice. At least not his or mine."

It seemed good enough for her. She started walking again. His mother grasped the hand Ella had let go. He squeezed her fingers, praying she didn't know what Ella was talking about.

But of course she did. How could she not?

He looked to her and tried to smile. "Promise me you'll think no more of it."

She made no attempt to smile in return. "You have said that to me too many times since you joined the army."

"Mom—"

"I know, you do not wish to argue." She pulled her hand from his, swiped at her eyes, took his hand again. Squeezing hard. "Nor do I. Come, let's eat. Gods know you could use a good meal."

Improbably, Ayden laughed, pleased to find at least one thing they could all agree on.

When the guards came for Freyrík again, he was ready. Well, on his feet, at least, and steeled against enduring whatever humiliations they might inflict. Ayden thought him unable to lay down his pride, but the elf was wrong. He would say or do what he must, *anything at all*, to stay fighting fit against the dark elves.

Or so he'd convinced himself, at least. Gods thanked he had no call to test the theory, for the guards merely opened the door and gestured him into the hall.

"The Council awaits you," one of them said.

He stepped out, wary. The guard who'd spoken tied a blindfold over Freyrík's eyes, curled a hand round his arm, and led him away unharmed.

Freyrík tried to map the route, but it seemed deliberately circuitous. Up stairs and down, left and right, forward and back, over and over again. At last they entered a room, large by the sound of the guards' heels on the hard floor. They sat him in a wooden chair and pulled off the blindfold.

Freyrík blinked against the brightness, a thousand candles like sunlight gleaming on the clean white marble walls. 'Twas a large room, rounded and domed, the ceiling painted like a perfect summer sky. Tiered bench seats encircled the room—a commoners' gallery, mayhap?—and some four or five paces before him sat two elevated marble platforms like box seats at a theater. Before the platforms ran a long, low table with six chairs and as many stacks of documents, quills, and ink pots. The secretaries' space?

In short order, a whole great glowing mob of elves filed into the chamber in a rush of noise and energy and light. Indeed the low table was for scribes or assistants, for the six seats filled with five men and a woman dressed all in fine but plain gray robes, youthful faces studious, fingers ink-stained. They sat, shuffled papers, armed themselves with quills and waited.

Freyrík counted twenty-four men and women take seats in the box on the right, thirteen in the box on the left. Not a one in the right-hand box looked older than forty, yet to a man—*and* woman, *Freyrík, more women than men, even*—their hair was white. 'Twas a stark and beautiful contrast to their unblemished skin, to the green and gold robes they all wore.

The men and women in the left-hand box wore the same white hair but different clothes. Three were in full military regalia, nine in robes of blue and silver. The last woman, sitting slightly apart from the others, wore a robe of bright red silk velvet. Freyrík knew it from the history books: 'twas the heart of the Elven Republic, the uniform of the First Minister.

A woman.

She looked right at him, brows arched, and said, "Is it truly so surprising, Your Majesty?"

Oh gods, could she read his thoughts? Ayden denied such power, but he was young for his people, his magics mayhap yet undeveloped—

"Peace, King Farr. We must all obey the laws here, myself included. Your mind is sacrosanct." A small tilt of the head, a hint of a smile. "Your emotions, however, you shout for all to hear."

Laughter from the gallery, some demure, some snickering. He looked at the benches behind the box seats, scattered here and there with people. Not many, certainly nothing compared to the crowds that gathered at audience in his Great Hall. Still some trickled in, eyes upon him as they took their seats. Like a beast in a cage. Mayhap that's how they saw him.

He met their gazes, and did not falter.

Until he sensed . . . *something*. Warm, familiar, calm. Near the doors to his left. He glanced round, and there he spotted the one person he'd hoped to see more than any. No, make that *two* people. Ayden *and* Ella.

Ayden caught his eye and nodded, asking without asking if he was well. He nodded. Ella grinned at him, bright and pleasing as a sunbeam. He smiled back, watched them take seats on a middle bench. Ayden looked tired. And something else, something it took a moment for Freyrík to place. The elf was glowing again—so faintly as to pass nearly unnoticed, but there nonetheless. Gods thanked, the starfall was gone from his neck.

The last of the observers filed into the hall, and the great doors *clunk*ed closed with such solemn finality that Freyrík wondered if he'd ever leave this place again.

So maudlin. Do not be a fool.

The secretary at the far end of the low table picked up a handbell and rang it for several seconds. The hall stilled, quieted, and the First Minister rose from her chair.

"I am Styra, First Minister of the Elven Republic." She gestured to the men and women sitting nearest her, one at a time. "My Second Minister, Annarr. Our Ministers of Defense, State, Treasury, Foreign Affairs, Citizenry, Justice, Science, and Trade." She gestured next to the man and two women in uniform. "The First Generals of War, Defense, and Intelligence." Last she waved to the second platform. "The elected council of the twelve territories of the Republic."

Freyrík knew not the protocol for such grand introductions. He thought to bow, but rose no more than a finger's width from his chair before a guard laid a hand on his shoulder.

"Please, King Farr, sit. No person kneels before another here."

He bowed his head, wondering if she'd meant that as the insult he took it for, despite the lack of judgment in her tone.

"Now if you would, King Farr, start at the beginning. The Council would hear your story."

Freyrík breathed deep—this was his chance, the moment he'd been waiting for; why was he so nervous now? Every eye in the chamber was upon him, and every ear as well, he felt quite certain. Mind-ear, had Ayden called it? Was this some test? Some magic performed in the silence? He very carefully did not shift in his chair, or drop his gaze as a guilty man might. If they could read thoughts, then let them. Let them hear the purity of his intentions. Let them hear all he would sacrifice for his people. For one of their own people.

Let them hear his story.

He started with the day his soldiers had brought him Ella and Ayden. And talked, and talked. And talked. Uninterrupted, to utter silence, to such scrutiny as he'd never known, not even before the Aegis in the aftermath of the failed coup. 'Twas as if they were staring straight through to his mind, sifting through his thoughts without him. As if they didn't even need to hear him speak.

At last he reached the critical moment of choice: Ayden's insistence on returning to Fornheim, Freyrík's decision to trust him, to slay his own men in service to the cause. "Ayden believed you would help with the . . . with whatever spirits lurk in the darker forests. If this is true, I would offer you all within my power to offer. My life, even, if such were your price."

The First Minister cleared her throat, the only sound any but him had made in what seemed like hours. "Your life is poor price, King Farr. We will go with you into the Feral woods." They would? They *believed* him? "But we *do* ask for lives in return: the lives you've taken from us."

The lives *he'd* taken? "Begging your pardon, madam, but we are not the magicians of this world. We've no power to raise the dead."

"Nor we, sir. Magicians you may not be, but slavers you are. Fifty-two prisoners. Fifty-two citizens of the Republic, held in cruel bondage at human hands. Return them to us, and we will speak again of what lives in those woods."

Gods befanged. Of all the things they'd ask . . . "I've no power in that matter either, I'm afraid."

As if by silent cue, one gray-robed secretary stood from the table and approached Freyrík with a writing tray. He placed it on the table beside Freyrík's chair, then retook his seat.

The First Minister gestured toward it. "If you would, please, Your Majesty. You are a king. A valuable hostage. Surely the Aegis would trade slaves for you."

He shook his head again, half against the faulty assumption, half against the despair digging claws into his breast. "Nay, madam. The Aegis does not wish me ever to return."

"And you know this how?"

"I told you: He sent me off to cursed lands in the dead of winter to find a thing he did not believe existed. A fine solution for a man he no longer trusts but cannot simply execute."

"I would suggest, Your Majesty, that Captain Vaska was in error in this supposition. That the Aegis lied to Captain Vaska about his beliefs in order to enlist his assistance. That he knows full well something dangerous dwells in the Feral woods, and that he meant your quest as the test of loyalty he said it was. In which case you have proven yourself, and his own lieutenant wrote in great detail of what you found." Lieutenant Rekkr had done *what*? Had the elves intercepted his bird? "Your Aegis will believe you, and furthermore he will wish to reclaim you for his own. He will accept the conditions of our assistance and your release."

Such confidence! Or was it simply arrogance? 'Twas a hope he held secret in his own heart as well, but he dared not believe it true. And yet . . . What if it were? He'd nothing to lose by trying—*except hope, of course*—and so very much he might gain.

He fingered the quill, the fine white paper.

"Write the letter, Your Majesty. When you've done, I'm afraid we must return you to your cell until your master replies. But we are not barbarians; you shall be treated well."

Well as in his first days here, when they'd fed and watered and warmed him, or *well* as in last night, when they'd—?

No. He would not dwell on that. Besides, what did it matter to anyone but him? He'd spoken his piece—or rather, Ayden had done it for him, it seemed—and the Council had heard all they'd needed to hear. Whatever test to which they'd subjected him, it seemed he'd passed. Now if only he could convince the Aegis of the danger, of the *need*, then the elves might help them end the darkers forever. Whether they were right or not about where Freyrík stood in his *náungi's* eyes hardly even mattered, for 'twas not his own life the Aegis must trade for, but the lives of every son of the Empire, present and future.

Freyrík closed his eyes, breathed slow and deep to still his mind, picked up the quill and dipped it, knowing full well his next words would be the most important of his life. Of every human's life.

May the gods bless him as strong and wise as ever he'd been.

When the First Minster left the chamber, Ayden just barely resisted the urge to rush her, halt her, bombard her with questions. Still he found himself shifting to the end of his bench, near the door, itching to call her name. Someone took his hand, held it tight. He turned round and saw his mother shaking her head.

The Council filed out next, two and three at a time through the broad double doors. He watched them go, wishing he could hear a cracking thing, wishing he could make them see reason. The Aegis would never trade the slaves for Freyrík.

Mother Megin caught his eye as she walked past. She slowed. Stopped. Backed up two steps to stand beside him. "Walk with me, Captain," she said, hooking her hand round his arm.

He nodded, stood. Went to excuse himself from his family, but Mother Megin said, "It's all right. Let them come."

He followed her from the chamber, Ella and his mother in tow. Ten paces down the corridor, he realized his mother was still holding his hand.

He stopped, disentangled himself as gently as he could. "Perhaps we could speak in private, Mother Megin?"

She looked to him, to his mother and sister, to him again. 'Twas she who'd asked him to walk, not the other way round. Why hadn't she spoken yet?

"If you wish it, Captain. Only I had the sense you were ready to confront the First Minister in the middle of the Council chamber." Her lips quirked at that, softening her words. "I believe I have answers to the questions burning your tongue." She started forward again, gestured him along with an open arm. "Come. This way."

She veered toward a plain, unmarked door, one of many along the marble-tiled hall. A simple meeting room, table and chairs and darkened candles she sang lit, easy as breathing. Gods but he envied her for it.

He realized, of a sudden, that no guards had followed him inside. Which could mean only one thing: They no longer thought Ayden tainted. They *believed* Freyrík, fallen gods thanked.

"It's late," his mother said as he and Mother Megin took seats. It wasn't, not really, but he supposed it'd been a long day for them all. "We're staying in the guest rooms in the east wing, second floor. Last two at the end of the hall. Come say good-night when you're done here."

She leaned in for her old familiar hug, arms slung round his neck from behind, lips pressing to the crown of his head. It turned lingering, and he crossed his arms over hers, waited for her to take her fill of him. "Good night, Mom," he said—prodded, really—when things had gone on long enough to be awkward for a soldier. "I'll see you soon."

Mother Megin looked on warmly as he and his mother exchanged affections, as his mother took Ella's hand and tried to pull her from the room. Ella, stubborn mule she was, plunked down in a chair and folded her arms over her chest. "I'm not tired."

Ayden ground his teeth, but nodded. She was as much a part of this as anyone, and if she meant to stay, it wasn't as if he could stop her. Gods knew their mother knew that; she chose not to argue, and made her graceful exit while she could.

"My apologies," he began, but Mother Megin cut him off with a wave.

"Nonsense. You've been gone behind enemy lines over half a year, and she heard . . . stories." Ayden resisted the urge to squirm before the glance she threw him. It stripped him open, naked. "A mother's allowed to worry." Another glance, shrewder than the last. "As is a lover."

Did she mean to chide him for that now? "My love does not offend?"

She shook her head. "Love never offends, Captain, unless one objects to the building of bridges. Though I must admit some among us *do* object."

"I have seen these humans at work. There will be no bridges. And there will be no prisoner exchange. If you mean to wait for the Aegis to come round, Rík will die of old age here while Grand Elders Skadi, Vesall, and Missa yet wander lost through the Feral woods!"

"Skadi, Vesall, and Missa *are* the Feral woods. Hush, boy"—she held up a hand before he could argue or question—"and listen to me. There is much dissent among the Council and the ministers, true, but we need not all agree to move forward. A group has volunteered; we leave on the morrow. We claimed delay only to compel King Farr to make the strongest possible case to the Aegis."

Ayden's first instinct was to rail at the hypocrisy, the deceit, the utter lack of faith and trust in his judgment, but he swallowed it down. In all honesty, he could see her point. Fear had its uses, after all. And if they didn't trust his judgment, well, he supposed he could understand that too.

"You know the story of the Great Betrayal, yes?"

"Of course. The human Council of Eight lured our Grand Elders into the Myrkr Mountains under guise of shared discovery, and there they shackled them with starfall and slaughtered them out of jealousy and fear for the magic they tried to take but could not. We all felt it. The very earth cracked open and wept molten tears. And Nature in her vengeance made the Ferals."

Mother Megin nodded slightly, as if to herself, her lower lip pinched between her teeth. "So we've always thought," she said. "But what if they did not die? What if, in trying to steal their magic, the humans trapped them somehow between life and death? If our Grand Elders' songs had been ripped from them, but could neither become one with the earth's song nor rejoin their bodies? Would they not seek forever to reclaim what they'd lost? Would they not seek revenge for their fates? Would they even be elven anymore, or merely some essence, some great churning crescendo of rage, betrayal, power unchecked and unfurled."

Fallen gods thanked she expected no answers, for those questions were too big to fit his mind round. Too big for Ella as well, if her stunned silence held meaning. She'd been but a girl when the Grand Elders had died, but he remembered clear as running water. The shock and pain of it, the certainty, the *finality* of what'd been done.

"Are you saying . . ." He shook his head, rubbed at one aching temple. "Did you glean all that just from what I saw?"

"Among other things. Work in fact you did some three centuries past, when you spied for us on the elven/human trade ships."

Ella cast him a sharp look. He'd never told her about that chapter of his life, secretive by necessity as it'd been. Had simply let her think he was on his *Foldfara,* seeing the world as many young elves were wont to do.

And just what about the information he'd brought back then could possibly matter so now? He burned to ask, but 'twas clear from Mother Megin's closed expression that she'd say no more about it— that she'd likely already said too much.

"In any event, given what we believe, of course we must go. We'll not wait for the Aegis's reply; we leave on the morrow. You will come with us, of course?"

He thought that less an order than an assumption, but it suited him fine either way. Of course he'd go. How could he not? He nodded.

"Good. Then the only question left in the balance now is the fate of King Farr. You have experienced firsthand the conditions in which our missing sisters and brothers are kept. If they are not released . . ."

"You'll kill him," Ayden said flatly.

Mother Megin touched her hand to his. It took everything he had not to smack her fingers away. "Let us hope it will not come to that."

Chapter Sixteen

Freyrík lay awake long into the night, wondering if he'd done enough, said enough, to convince the Aegis to help. At some point, his worries carried him off to sleep, to dreams of cold fog and raging ghosts, of teeth and claws and human blood. He woke gasping, flailed out of bed and landed, somehow, on his feet. He realized he was not alone.

Four guards. One held a bundle of cloth in his hands, another a bowl of porridge. The other two held sticks at the ready.

The one with the bundle tossed it at him and said, "Change. Eat. You leave in ten minutes whether you're finished or not."

They were out the door before he could ask where they were taking him.

He shook out the bundle. Fresh clothing, heavy and clean. Undergarments, breeches, shirt, and coat in the elven styling, coarser than his own fine silks and yearling wools, but at this point he'd take anything that didn't reek of blood and old porridge and sour milk. He spared some water from his pitcher to scrub himself before he donned the clean clothes, then set to his breakfast.

But 'twas a councilwoman, not the guards, who came to his cell as he was scraping out the last of his porridge with a wooden spoon. He stood hastily, put the bowl down on the bed, bowed his head.

She bowed back. "I am Mother Megin. Do you remember me from last night?"

He nodded. "Yes, Mother, by face if not by name." When she said nothing, merely studied him as if a particularly vexing chessboard, he added, "Can I be of some assistance to you, madam?"

Another long moment of studied silence, and then, "You were beaten very badly in this room last night."

Not a question. She knew. Had it been sanctioned after all? "Yes," he said, a sick ache in his ribs just *thinking* about it. He swallowed it back.

Mother Megan grimaced. "I am sorry. 'Tis not our way."

Except for when it was, apparently.

A wan smile on the elf's lovely face. "Or rather, 'tis not the way to which we aspire. Why did you not call them out? Accuse them? If you'd have spoken at Council, we'd have found and punished those who'd abused their—"

She silenced herself when Freyrík shook his head. "Nay, Mother. That was personal, and well within their purview. But *this*, this . . . mission, this quest, is bigger than me or them or all of us. There is no room for pettiness here. No room for tattling or inquiries. Besides," he added at the look of . . . what? Wonder? Nay, *respect* dawning across Mother Megin's face, "Ayden has done the same for me and more, and for a much less noble cause than the one we now face."

"Indeed." Mother Megin nodded slowly, face still slack with a look he knew well among leaders of men: relief born of a difficult choice made wisely. She stepped forward, slid a hand up his arm and squeezed his shoulder. "A noble cause indeed."

Then she turned to open the cell door and said to the guards in the hall, "He is ready now." Back to Freyrík, she said, "I shall see you again shortly, Your Majesty." And then she was gone.

The guards came in as she left, blindfolded him and led him away. He stopped asking where they were taking him after the third ignored request, and simply opened his senses instead, trying to hear or smell or feel something that might clue him in. Upstairs, the air grew warmer, and the faint scent of sandalwood returned. The tiles beneath his feet felt like marble again. He heard voices echoing down the corridor, and then two louder ones, quite distinct: Ayden and Ella.

". . . a military mission." Ayden. Exasperated, even angry.

"No, it's a *diplomatic* mission."

"It's *dangerous*. You're not going."

"I am not yours to command, brother."

Strange how their bickering made him grin.

"Perhaps you don't recall what happened the last time you said that to me."

That seemed to stop Ella cold, seemed to make the very *air* cold. The smile fell from Freyrík's lips. Bickering like children they might be, but Ayden had clearly touched a nerve.

Sliced right through it, more like. Ella blames herself for Ayden's suffering.

Her voice was soft, tremulous as she replied. "Which is exactly why I must go now. Let me help you. Let me right these wrongs if I can."

"She may have a point, Captain." A female voice, not entirely unfamiliar, but nor could Freyrík place it. "She is young, gods know, and untrained. But she is possessed of extraordinary talent—such song as I've rarely heard in all my many years."

"I know." Ayden. Reluctant, grudging.

Freyrík could picture the scowl on the elf's face, the arms folded across his chest. He'd drawn close enough to sense the elf, just out of reach. His escorts halted him, took off his blindfold.

And sure enough, there was Ayden some few paces distant, scowling, arms crossed. Ella's posture mirrored his. A white-haired woman dressed in a green and gold robe completed their little triangle. She was the only one who didn't look ready to hit something.

"We could use her," the woman said. "Gods know what magic binds the Grand Elders' songs yet to the living realm. What magic we might need to unbind them."

Ayden's scowl deepened, but Freyrík could see him caving. "Fine. But if anything happens to her . . ."

"I can make no promises, you know that. But I hear her brother is one of the finest warriors in the Republic. I trust he'll keep her safe."

She clapped him on the shoulder and turned, catching Freyrík's eye from cross the hall and nodding at him before striding off. Freyrík thought to step into the spot she'd vacated, but his escorts still had a hand on each arm, keeping him in place.

No matter. Ella knew he was there. She took three steps forward and conjured up a smile. "Sir Prince."

'Twas said with a spark of mischief, and he laughed at it, bowed as much as his escorts would permit. "Lady Daell."

Ayden started at his voice, turned his gaze from its contemplation of the floor to Freyrík. The anger dropped clear from his face, replaced with worry, pleasure. He strode over, nodded to the guards. "He's not going anywhere," Ayden said.

The instant they let Freyrík go, Ayden stepped in to fill the void, wrapping him in a fierce hug, joyfully reciprocated.

When Ayden let him go and he could breathe again, he asked, "What is this? Surely they can't have heard back from the Aegis already."

Ayden pulled him aside and set to explaining the situation. He seemed angry at the deception, but to Freyrík it made simple sense. He'd argued for the slaves as if the whole of the Empire was on the line; could he have done so well if he'd known the truth? Might the Aegis—who knew him better than most—have seen through him if he'd known the truth? And anyway, his relief at knowing the truth left no room for anger. The elves were rushing to help, and soon the darker menace might be gone from them forever.

Only he wished he weren't walking Ayden and Ella into danger yet again.

Ella squinted at him, touched his arm. "None of this is your fault, you know."

He nodded, but knowing that changed nothing of how he felt.

They mounted up and rode out as the sun was cresting over the eastern wall of Fornheim. 'Twas a smaller crew than he'd expected, an even dozen consisting of himself, Ayden, Ella, the commander who'd escorted them through elven lands, a general he recognized from the council chamber, four soldiers under the general's command, the green-robed woman who'd been speaking with Ayden earlier this morning, and a male and female elf he'd never seen before, both dressed in long cloaks of navy blue. Freyrík rode in the middle of the pack, his reinless horse following orders not his own. Ayden rode beside him, Ella next to Ayden. Ella kept up a light stream of chatter that washed over them both like a warm breeze, though neither Freyrík nor Ayden said much in reply. She seemed content with that.

'Twas clear Freyrík was still a prisoner, though they treated him gently, if not quite with respect. He rode unbound all day—where would he go, after all, on a horse bespelled?—though they locked him in a stone room when night fell.

He slept like the dead. No night terrors. When they woke him come morn, he felt rested for the first time in weeks. 'Twas likely he was marching to his death, that even if he survived the dark elves he'd not survive their corporeal cousins, and yet he could not recall the last time he'd felt so at peace.

No . . . not quite peace. Something else, something strange and wonderful lodged almost painful in his chest: Hope. For the future of the Empire. For his sons. For *everyone's* sons.

For himself? Not so much. But he was unafraid. Whatever came after this life—the Warrior's Rest or a long dark sleep—mattered not, for he could think of nothing more noble than death in service to the Empire's future.

They rode long, but not as hard as they might have were it not for the scientists and Mother Megin. Three days in, they overnighted in a midsized town on the edge of Fornheim, and found three familiar humans in the jail there when they went to lock up Freyrík for the night: Lord Lini, Lord Vitr, and Lieutenant Rekkr. They looked unharmed and quite pleased to see Freyrík alive.

"My troops took the liberty," Commander Herra said to Freyrík, "of fetching them from the borderlands when the Council made its decision."

Ayden said nothing of their presence to Ella, wishing Lord Lini to be a surprise. 'Twas a testament to the sharpness of her mind-ear when she stiffened at the communal table where the elves in their party were breakfasting, turned to him and smacked him on the arm with an indignant, "Why didn't you tell me!" The inn was at least thirty paces from the jail, yet clearly she'd heard Lord Lini's song the moment he'd been let from his stone cell.

He shrugged, smiled, went back to his food. The humans and their elven escorts arrived, and Ella stood from the table, ran to Lord Lini and threw her arms round his neck. He scooped her right off the ground and held her a moment, then put her down as if his back ached.

Maybe it did. Gods knew he wasn't young for a human anymore, and the last months had been ruthless on them all.

Ella took him and Freyrík both by the hand and led them to the breakfast table. Freyrík slid in beside Ayden, inched over 'til their bodies touched. 'Twas all the affection they dared show in current company, but 'twould do for now.

They rode another week, crossing in and out of small towns and large stretches of forest, overnighting at inns if they were lucky and under the stars if they weren't, before crossing the border into Vaenn. Slowly, their group grew to know one another. The ranking officer was the Second General of Defense for the Republic, over two thousand years in service and skilled as any Ayden had ever known. He'd handpicked the others: two were scouts, no doubt spies; one a long-distance signaler; the fourth in service too secretive to discuss; the fifth, Commander Herra, an elite forces trainer, which was how he'd met Ayden so many years past.

Their nonmilitary company was no less distinguished. Ayden's respect for Mother Megin grew each day as she conversed with Rík and Lord Lini. 'Twas clear she wished to learn all she could of how human culture had changed in the centuries since the war. This made both diplomatic and strategic sense, but Ayden thought it more than that. Quite frankly, she seemed to *like* Rík and his men, or at the very least to respect them. 'Twas hard to believe she could turn them over to death if the Aegis failed to release the elven slaves.

The land grew steeper, colder, and wetter as they crossed through Vaenn, but Ayden didn't mind it, even if he still couldn't sing himself warm. Ella stayed close and made heat for them both, and anyway Vaenn was *home*—not just his Republic but his territory. Familiar terrain, familiar red cedars straining toward the sky, familiar wildlife and rivers, roads and towns. One night when the snow fell particularly heavy, they sheltered in the empty heritage home of an old family friend. 'Twas warm in a great many ways, and as he sat by the hearth with Freyrík, sharing supper off the same plate, he couldn't help but think, for a moment, *I don't ever want to leave here.*

'Twas nonsense, of course. But he was young yet, and weary beyond words; he was entitled to the stray childish thought every now and then.

He soon lost count of the days, resigned himself as soldiers do to the grind of *wake, ride, eat, sleep, start all over again*. 'Twas easier to think of nothing, to take what pleasure he could from Freyrík's company and give no consideration to the cold wet miseries of the present, or worse, to the future. For all that lay there were uncertainties and fears. He could envisage no world in which he and Freyrík might be together once the spirits of the Grand Elders were freed, so 'twas best not to envision anything at all, lest he lose his nerve when the time came.

Ayden had gone strangely quiet these last many days. Thinking of the future? Or mayhap simply disappointed with his ongoing deafness; gods knew the news had crushed the elf when he'd heard it, try as he might have to hide that fact.

Mayhap tonight would be different. Tomorrow they'd cross back into darker lands, but tonight they'd sleep at Ayden's outpost, amongst Ayden's comrades-in-arms: men and women who knew him, who he'd not seen in half a year. If that wouldn't lift his spirits, Freyrík knew not what could.

They arrived in the late afternoon, in plenty of time for a hot wash and a hot supper. Ayden was fair mobbed before he could even dismount, and his bark of laughter at the dozen men and women literally pulling him from his horse seemed real. Blessedly unfettered. He was grinning wide, exchanging hard hugs and friendly slaps. Everyone jostled to be near him.

Freyrík watched from afar, quite content to see him happy. He had no desire to spoil the joy of the moment by smearing it with his humanness.

Sobriety came all too quickly anyway, in the form of a birded message from the Council. No word yet from the Aegis, it said. How long had it been? Two weeks? More? A bird should take but three days, mayhap four, to transport a message from the Hall of Elders to High Court. Which meant the Aegis had sat on Freyrík's letter at least a week, assuming it had arrived. And Freyrík had seen the elves' dominion over animals; he had no doubt the bird had delivered its message. So what beneath the shadow was the Aegis waiting for? 'Twas true his silence would not impact their task, but the Aegis didn't know that.

Besides, Freyrík could not be blamed for wishing to know his fate.

Of course, 'twould all be for naught if he failed to survive the coming encounter. Which he had to admit seemed likely. Even with the elves' help, how could they fight such a thing?

He felt on the heels of this admission a desperate hunger to taste life once more before they entered the forest of the dead. Yet he quashed that too, left Ayden to his meal and his comrades and the birch ale that flowed with a tacit wink from the officers until long past sunset.

He didn't touch it, though Mother Megin herself brought over a mug and tried to lure Freyrík to the fire. This revelry wasn't for him, and despite Mother Megin's pretense otherwise, he wasn't wanted there.

He found Ayden's quarters instead, small but serviceable—a bed, a hearth, a desk, a cedar trunk, a dresser of three drawers, all crammed into a room four paces by four in the officers' wing of the outpost. Moonlight spilled in through a window. Above the desk hung a masterful oil portrait of a smiling man with a small girl in his lap. The girl was obviously Ella, all red hair and freckles and big-toothed grin. The man was just as obviously Ayden's father, dark-haired and green-eyed, the same full lips, the same high cheekbones. More handsome than pretty—Ayden had gotten that from his mother. And the painting too; in the lower left corner in artful white letters was the artist's signature: Vaska.

The bed was small, barely large enough for one. But it was comfortable, and warm. He added wood to the fire and crawled beneath the covers, waiting for Ayden to join him.

The elf was not so long in coming. He closed the door, stood at the foot of the bed and gazed on Freyrík in silence. His eyes glimmered in the firelight, sharp and free of the influence of drink.

Freyrík propped himself on his elbows and gazed back, waiting for Ayden to say something, do something. A knot popped like flashpowder in the fire.

"Did you not wish to stay with your friends?"

Once, slowly, Ayden shook his head. His hand went to the cloak clasp at his left shoulder, flicked it open. The cloak puddled at his feet. His shirt followed seconds after, and his heavy wool undershirt seconds after that. Never did he take his eyes from Freyrík.

Freyrík, however, found holding Ayden's gaze quite the challenge in the face of all that pale muscled flesh, angles and shadows in the firelight like a hidden promise. So too were Ayden's fingers on the strings of his breeches, deft and deliberate, peeling back fabric to reveal the skin beneath with all the sultry finesse of a consort.

Freyrík licked his lips, swallowed hard, already tasting Ayden upon his tongue, breathing his scent in deep. He was wearing too many clothes of a sudden, couldn't get rid of them fast enough. He threw back the covers, nearly ripped his shirt in his haste to remove it. He burned. *Burned*.

Ayden took a step toward him. Another. So controlled—the ring of stones round Freyrík's fire, and the fuel within it too. Naked, perfect. His.

Ayden laid his hands on Freyrík's bare shoulders, leaned in close and kissed him. So gentle in the face of so much heat—almost chaste. "This will not be our last," he whispered against Freyrík's lips. "I'll not let it be."

How Freyrík wished he could share Ayden's confidence. But in its absence he'd settle for sharing Ayden's breath, Ayden's taste, Ayden's touch. In truth, 'twas no settling at all. 'Twas everything that mattered.

Everything.

Chapter Seventeen

Freyrík made his second crossing into darker lands with no less trepidation than the first. He'd thought himself over the fear—gods knew he'd long resigned to dying out here, long accepted the value of it—but each time he looked at Ayden, each time he thought of his sons, he was overcome by such powerful longing to survive that he found himself scheming to flee in the night. He'd missed so much already, had spent what seemed like lifetimes apart from his loved ones. Had Lady Drífa borne their newest child already? Surely he'd been gone long enough. If he lived, would he return home to find himself the father of the little girl he'd so long wished for? Would but the gods bless him so.

Their odds of surviving the darker woods were better now with so many elves of such great power leading the way, but defeating the dark elves still seemed an impossible thing. Even these ancient and powerful beings seemed . . . *unsettled* by the evil here, traveling in tight ranks, speaking in hushed tones as if in fear of disturbing the dead. They kept four on watch at all times. They pushed harder than they probably should have, traveling blind—or was it deaf?—in the general southwesterly direction where the dark elves had been before. Gods pray 'twas the right stratagem.

The demon wind returned first, and then the strange sickness, and then the endless icy fog. Both wore at their spirits, but the elves, at least, could hold a fire. They built shelters at night—not up the trees as Ayden had done, but in lees of their lowest branches, for their magic lent them confidence against tramplings—and warmed the air inside with songs Freyrík could not hear. 'Twas all told much more comfortable than before, but still the body wearied and the spirit feared. He wanted done with this. Done with all of it. Which was why 'twas such thrilling—if terrifying—relief when, midway through one dreary, snow-touched afternoon, the elves froze as one atop their horses, and someone said softly, almost reverently, "The Hunter's Call. We are close."

Freyrík's hand went to his sword hilt. "How close is close?"

The strongest magician among them, a scientist named Kenna, cocked his head and closed his eyes a moment. "Hard to say. Thirty leagues? Maybe fifty?"

That was the elf's idea of close? Freyrík relaxed his grip on his weapon. Behind him, he heard the hiss of steel sliding back into its sheath—no doubt Lieutenant Rekkr. "You can guide us there?"

Kenna nodded, but General Sókn tossed him an ugly glare. Freyrík wasn't fond of the hostility, but he certainly understood it. General Sókn was second in charge of defense for the whole of the Elven Republic; he was used to taking charge, not ceding leadership to some human who'd lived fewer years than his toenails.

Freyrík bowed his head. "Apologies, General. I did not mean to usurp your authority; only I am used to making decisions." Best not to upset the elf, after all. If the Aegis wouldn't ransom Freyrík, his only hope of surviving the winter was to make these elves his allies.

"Your task is finished now we hear the Call," the general said, even as Mother Megin waved the elf silent and said, "That's quite all right, King Farr. We are all free to ask questions here."

Well, one ally was better than none, he supposed.

Ayden woke sometime in the night with a familiar ache behind his eyes and in his jaw, and thought he'd never been so grateful for pain in his life. 'Twas the Call, of course, and though he could hear it only barely, he *could* hear it. He could *hear*.

He sat up in the tangle of blankets and furs he shared with Freyrík in the shelter of pine boughs they'd built for the night, and poked his head through the opening. The fog outside was thick; he could see nothing but the dying embers of the fire Commander Herra was trying to nurse. He couldn't hear the elf. Couldn't hear anything but the whisper-faint scritch of the Call in his head. He tried not to let that disappoint him.

Across the sickly fire, Commander Herra winced and pressed the heels of his hands to his temples.

Maybe 'twas best he could barely hear, after all.

The commander pried a hand from his head and waved Ayden over. "They're coming," he said when Ayden drew close.

Ayden took a long look round the little clearing in which they'd bedded down, but could see nothing beyond the pale reach of the firelight. "When?"

"By sunrise, I'd say." He rubbed at his temples again, squinted up at Ayden. "Truly, it does not pain you?"

"Not very much. But I know what it's like."

"I have never heard it so strong. So close. You and your human friends will have the advantage if it comes to a fight."

"Do you think it will, sir? The Ferals have never attacked an elf before."

Commander Herra shrugged. "Who knows what remains of our elders' minds. If it is as the scientists think it, there may be nothing left but fury—formless, unthinking. We will do what we can to give them peace, but they may not wish for it. They may fight us."

Ayden couldn't fathom how to fight back against such a thing. The commander must have heard this over the din of the Call, for he said, "You take care of the Ferals, and leave the Grand Elders to us. Now go rouse the camp. We must be ready when they come."

When they did come, 'twas clear to Ayden how laughable the idea of readiness truly was.

It began as a storm, fog coalescing into clouds so thick and black they blotted out the rising sun, rending the sky with lightning and thunder. Snow whipped blinding thick in howling wind. Somewhere near, a mighty crack split the air as a tree toppled. Then another. Sounds like a stampede rolled in from nowhere, everywhere—if they weren't actually surrounded by Ferals, the fog certainly made it sound so. Everyone with weapons to draw brought them to the ready.

"Circle up!"

The pain in Commander Herra's voice was palpable. Even Ayden, still almost entirely deaf, reeled from the pressure in his head, the unsettling feeling that his teeth might shake right from his gums. There'd been no such sound in the last Surge; the Ferals had been gathered and the Call gone silent. But now . . .

"Move! Now!" Commander Herra shouted. The elves were slow to position, but Freyrík and his men hustled, herding Mother Megin, Ella, and the two scientists into the middle of the field and forming two rings round them facing out: an inner ring of six singer-warriors, and an outer ring of human and elven soldiers.

Ayden quickly found his place in the outer ring between two humans—Freyrík to his left and Lord Lini to his right—in case the Hunter's Call drove him to his knees, helpless. In case it drove the humans to madness and they need be struck down.

Dire precautions aside, there were no two men he'd rather have at his back.

The storm tore like fingers at his clothes and small debris pelted what little skin he'd left exposed, but no fists made of wind came to strike them down, and no Ferals either. Yet. He dared a glance behind him, saw General Sókn gripping a sword in each hand but no doubt twining songs Ayden couldn't hear with the other elves. The pressure in his head seemed to ease a touch, as if their songs were somehow canceling out the Call.

A shouted warning—he turned back in time to see the first Feral beasts rushing in from the fog: a lone wolf, a coyote, a whole cracking flock of pigeons—their *own* pigeons, the ones who had originally led them here—grown to the size of hunting hawks, with twisted beaks and outstretched talons.

The coyote lunged, sloppy with rage, and Ayden struck high with both swords. He caught the creature on the underbelly, bore it down to the ground. Only then did he realize it had tried to leap clear over him. Not attacking Freyrík or Lord Lini. Not aiming its rage at a human, not even at his muted self.

No, straight at the elves behind him.

The spirits know, then. They know we have come to free them, and they do not wish to go.

He'd no more time to contemplate that before a large gray blur tried to leap past him; it took the combined efforts of himself and Lord Lini to ward the wolf off. Lightning split the sky, momentarily blinding him, and the thunderclap that followed left his ears ringing.

Something raked across his left biceps, taking skin and flesh with it, knocking one sword from his grip. He staggered back, a scream he couldn't hear burning in his throat, and frantically blinked the spots from his eyes. The wolf. Denied its intended prey, it had turned its rage on Ayden, muzzle overfull with teeth rushing at his throat.

He twisted aside and drove his right sword through the beast's rib cage. Still it fought, pinned and struggling. Ayden fumbled with blood-slicked fingers for a dagger to replace the sword he'd dropped, even as the wolf thrashed and snapped, working his way up the blade to Ayden's arm—

And then squealed and fell still, Lord Lini's sword thrust through its neck.

No more beasts to avenge it—at least not yet. Ayden dared a look back to the singers at the inner circle, heads bowed and huddled tight. An elf in the second ring staggered, opened his eyes, looked round as if he'd forgotten where he was.

"Be quick!" Ayden shouted. "We can't hold them back forever!"

The elf blinked, nodded—

"Look out!"

Ayden whirled back at Rík's shout, saw a bighorn sheep with its head down charging straight at him. He moved to dodge it—then froze. There were innocents behind him, *Ella* was behind him, and if they were lost, so was everyone else.

"Rík, brace in! Switch with me!"

They crossed positions in the blood-slicked snow. Ayden sensed more than saw Rík kneel to brace his longsword, and that was nearly the last thing he *ever* saw; a massive talon swiped at his eyes, and only a frantic jerk of his head saved his vision. He batted the Feral pigeon from the sky, and its flockmates swarmed him.

He cut one in half, chased after a second as it attempted to swoop at the inner circle. Behind him came a Feral scream overtop a human shout. Wet snow sloshed over him in a wave, but he could ill afford to check on Freyrík: a third pigeon and a fourth, then a fifth, streaked overhead, clumsy in the wind but strong in their rage. He cut them down one by one.

Another blinding lightning bolt, another crack of thunder. The wind whipped so hard it pelted them with branches and stones. One struck Ayden's temple; he stumbled to his knees. A warm, strong hand on his elbow helped him to his feet, and he looked into Freyrík's worried face. The man was shouting something at him. Even a handspan away, Ayden couldn't tell what.

Another lull in the Feral battle, and Ayden glanced again at the elves behind him. The sight spread despair like poison in his chest: The outer circle of singers was in shambles, and the storm, clearly out of their control, was growing fiercer by the second. The singers of the inner circle—even Ella, so raw with power—were leaning heavy on each other, faces red with strain and streaked with frozen sweat.

He turned back, squinted into the heart of the storm. The three Grand Elders stood impassioned and cold, watching, waiting, while around them Nature bent to their bidding, churning with the hatred of centuries.

The darker beasts lulled, and Freyrík bent over double, leaning heavy on his sword. More lightning cracked overhead, thunder rattling his bones near as hard as the winds and the blinding snow. He made the mistake of looking up and saw . . . well, he knew not quite what he saw, but 'twas paralyzing, breath-stealing. If his night terrors had a visage, that was it, molded from the clouds looming livid in the sky.

It glared down upon them and roared. A living face a hundred paces wide—no, two faces; three?—metamorphosing one into the next, twisting and writhing. It opened its ever-changing maw, and for a single, horrifying moment, Freyrík was certain it would swallow them all.

Then from the mouth came sound and wind like a thousand dying beasts, and next he knew, he and everyone near him were flat on their backs. Only the elves in the center remained on their feet, huddled shoulder to shoulder, a single blazing beacon of light so bright he daren't look at it direct. The beast-cloud raged over their heads, at their heads. Yet for now, at least, it seemed it could not harm them.

Movement in his peripheral vision. He rolled from it, bringing his sword round, before he realized 'twas just Ayden, arm outstretched to help him to his feet. His leg throbbed where he'd braced his sword against the ram. Not the wisest choice, mayhap, but the ground was slick and frozen and would not have held. Ayden was bleeding like a gutted stag from the slashes on his arm, his whole sleeve red, his fingers dripping with it. He didn't seem to notice. Freyrík pulled him near, cut a strip of cloth from the bottom of his cloak, and made hasty work of binding the wounds. They could ill afford Ayden fainting on the battlefield.

The face in the cloud opened its tree-sized maw once again, and the wind buffeted them all back to the frozen loam. Yet still the elves in the center remained on their feet, glowing like miniature suns come down to earth to chase away the darkness.

Gods pray they could.

From the opposite side of their line he heard a scream, the unmistakable sound of blade cleaving flesh, an animal roar. More dark beasts come to fight their way past them, to fell the elves before they could work their magic.

Flashes of movement near the tree line, difficult to discern through the fog, the blowing snow. He hefted his sword, resisting the urge to charge the beasts. They must hold the line, protect the elves in the center at all costs.

One figure emerged: a woman, half-naked. Dark elf. Another one step behind her, male. A third, also male. They looked . . . empty. Lost.

Yet they were causing this, surely they were. If he slayed them, it would end. He turned to Ayden on one side, Commander Herra on the other. Shouted, "Close ranks!" above the wind, and rushed forward, trusting them to fill the gap he'd made.

He took not two steps before being knocked off his feet once more. Except this time 'twas not the great churning beast in the sky. This time, 'twas Commander Herra.

"You mustn't!" the elf cried. "They are not the cause of this!"

Freyrík rose to his feet and snatched up his sword, throwing the commander a glare that said, clear as words, *Are you quite serious?*

"They are but empty vessels," he shouted above the wind. "*This* is what remains of their song." He pointed toward the monstrosity raging above their heads, joined to them now by a great funneled cloud of wind and light. "Souls ripped clear from their flesh, victims to their fate as surely as we! 'Tis the *magic* we must end. Kill their bodies and risk their song raging all the more—ripping all the world apart!"

"Then what do we do?" Freyrík shouted back, but had no time to hear the answer, for the second wave of dark beasts was closing in. A darker bear the size of ten men lumbered out of the forest, roaring fit to compete with the malevolence above.

Freyrík watched with horror as Ayden dug his heels in and raised his swords, clashed them together to draw the beast's notice. It swung its great head round and roared anew, took one step toward Ayden, another, gaining speed like a runaway carriage down a hill. Ayden held his ground, the befanged fool; he couldn't hope to fight such a monster on his own.

Freyrík crept round to flank the bear, caught Ayden's eye and nodded. Ayden nodded back, fingers tightening round the hilts of his raised swords. The bear failed to notice. Like any dark beast in its rage, it had no head for strategy, no eyes for any but its target. And Ayden was standing in its way.

It charged in and swiped at Ayden, its massive paw long outreaching Ayden's swords. Ayden ducked, rolled, came up swinging and drew blood with twin slashes across the beast's chest. Alas, not very much blood—the beast's hide was so thick the swords made but a scratch.

Ayden moved in for another strike as Freyrík lunged for one of his own, but the beast evaded, rearing up on its hind legs with a roar. 'Twas foolish of it to expose its underbelly like that, but Ayden couldn't get near to take advantage; his next strike was met with a paw like a blacksmith's hammer crashing across Ayden's blade, and the sword went flying from his hand.

Freyrík didn't wait to see what would happen next. The others were consumed with their own fights, the line round the elves barely holding. He couldn't flank from the side without being seen, and it seemed doubtful they could fell the beast with anything short of a slit throat or a pierced heart. Alas, both organs were currently some five paces off the ground.

Before Freyrík could second-guess himself, he took a running leap at the beast and launched onto its back.

The bear lurched, roared, whirled round and nearly threw him. 'Twas like trying to cling to a shaking wall, so broad was its back, and his grip was tenuous at best between the longsword in one hand and the lack of purchase for his feet. He spread his knees and clung with his thighs as if to a bucking horse, reached up to grab a fistful of coarse fur round the hilt of his sword, and hauled himself up toward its neck. Still the beast spun and swiped, but couldn't quite reach him or throw him. He hitched his legs up, shimmied a handspan higher.

The bear stumbled back a step, another and another. Freyrík dared a glance over his shoulder and saw the trees at forest's edge closing in at alarming speed. The beast would crush him up against one if he didn't stop it soon.

And where beneath the shadow had Ayden gotten to? Why hadn't he made use of the distraction?

Ah well. Freyrík would simply have to do it himself.

He pried his sword hand free of the beast's fur, clung for life with his remaining limbs. Gods befanged, no room to maneuver a man-sized blade. Though his every instinct screamed against it, he dropped his sword, pulled a dagger instead and drove it into the beast's back.

If the creature had been enraged before, 'twas nothing compared to now. It roared, whirled, nearly toppled over backward, gods help him, but then righted itself and came crashing down on all fours. Freyrík took advantage of the new position, wrenched the dagger from the beast's back and scrambled toward its head, driving the blade in through the side of its neck. Before it could drop and roll him, he pulled a second blade and drove it through the other side.

Blood spurted hot and foul across his face, in his eyes, all over his hands and down his arms. He tasted it on his gritted teeth, spat it away even as he clung to both knives for life, screaming fit to drown the darker's dying roars.

The beast dropped to its knees. Freyrík pulled the blades free and blood gushed afresh, painting his clothes and the bear's matted fur and the grass at their feet. He leapt free, wary still of tooth and claw, and came to his own panting stop upon the frozen earth.

He realized only then how still the battlefield had become, even as the dark elf storm above them raged and raged.

A lull from the beasts, but not from the monstrosity in the sky. The soldiers watched the trees, waiting. Holding the line. There were fewer of them now; it seemed *all* the elves, even the warriors, had moved into the center of the ring, leaving only humans to guard it. Well, humans and Ayden. If 'twas extra magic they needed, Ayden could lend no voice to their chorus now.

Freyrík wiped his hands in the grass, cleaned his blades against the leg of his breeches, retrieved his sword and limped back into place beside Ayden. His leg hurt more than it had before. He looked down, saw fresh blood on his calf, bright red, clearly his. When had that happened?

His men had drawn in tight to cover the spaces left vacant by the warrior elves, so tight they were almost back to back with the elves working their magic. The proximity worried him. If a large beast came charging, could they stop it in time to protect the magicians? No dark beasts in sight now, but from across the meadow, the childlike husks of the dark elves looked on, watching him, watching them all.

Empty. Victims as much as we.

And on the heels of that revelation, a second one, so startling he'd have stumbled, even without the wind to push him down: There were indeed no dark elves, never had been. The only darkness here was what had been done to the Grand Elders.

A scream carried over the wind, not from dark beast or soldier but from behind. A female.

Ella.

Freyrík whipped round and saw that Ayden had too, one eye on the forest, one eye on his sister slumped unconscious—*dead?*—in the midst of their circle, clearly torn.

Mother Megin met their gazes but a moment and said, tight and strained, "She lives." Lightning and thunder followed, as if raging against her proclamation. A branch hurled by the wind struck Freyrík in the shoulder, nearly sent him to his knees. "We cannot—" She cut off, panting for air. Gods above, she sounded as if she were dying. Mayhap she was—mayhap they *all* were—locked in some strange mortal combat with the spiritbeast.

"The song of the fallen is too strong. We must retreat!"

Another bolt of lightning, and another and another in rapid succession, close enough to raise the hairs on his arms, heat his skin as if burnt by the sun. That it did not strike them directly he credited to the elf-singers, but clearly there were limits even to their grand magics.

"I do not think it will let us," he shouted over the endless peal of thunder that followed.

"You must try!" Mother Megin shouted back. "We will hold back the storm as long as we can—"

She may have said more, but Freyrík had already turned back round to face the forest again. He would *not* hear suggestion of his own retreat on the trampled backs of these brave elves.

No, he knew exactly what he need do, and retreat played no part in it.

He sheathed his sword and took a step toward the Grand Elders. The wind buffeted him back, but he squinted against it, leaned into it, took another step. And another—

Ayden's hand fisted round his arm and yanked him back to the line. "What are you doing?" the elf cried.

Freyrík turned to him and smiled. Strange how calm he felt of a sudden, now he knew what must be done. The eye of the storm. The peace amongst the rage.

He laid his hand over Ayden's where it clutched at his sleeve, and raised his voice to be heard above the maelstrom. "'Tis fury unbound. It cannot be reasoned with or soothed. Nor in all its terrible focus can it be overpowered. But mayhap it can be surprised. Confused. Distracted."

Ayden glared at him as though certain Freyrík was about to do something terribly, irrevocably foolish.

Mayhap he was.

"If I fail, use the moment to best advantage; lead our people to safety."

Ayden shook his head. "Freyrík, don't—"

"There is no choice," he said, tugging free of Ayden's hand.

But Ayden just grabbed him again. "There is *always* a choice."

Freyrík's heart swelled with pride, and sadness, and so much love. "Then I have made mine." He gripped Ayden by both shoulders, pulled him close, and pressed a kiss to the hard line of his lips. "I love you," he said, and then kissed him again, there and done in an instant. "I *love* you."

Before Ayden could reply, or argue, or even return the sentiment, Freyrík whirled round and pressed forward against the storm, against sanity, against reason. Toward the Grand Elders.

For at last the gods had whispered in his ear, and he was unafraid.

Twenty paces. A rock clipped his shoulder.

Fifteen. The wind howled and gusted and forced him to the frozen earth. He bent his head and crawled on all fours.

Ten. Eight. A bolt of lightning like a mortar, splitting the earth before him in a hail of mud and stones and fire. He snatched back his outstretched hand, bloody and burnt. Sickening pain in his ears, wetness trickling down the sides of his neck. All the world went suddenly, strikingly silent, though it raged and raged all round him.

Seven paces. He canted, dizzy, but pressed on.

Five paces.

And all the while the Grand Elders watched him, faces blank and unblinking.

Four paces. The storm cloud seemed to coalesce over his head, grow darker, more menacing. A wall of detritus flew at him faster than an arrow, and he threw up his hands to protect his face but the impact never came. Knocked away by a countercurrent—the elf-singers, surely the elf-singers saving his arse.

He levered himself onto his haunches and looked from the empty faces of the Grand Elders to the shifting visages in the storm clouds above.

Matching. Gods above, matching faces.

"I pray you hear me, honorable elders!" he cried to the raging whirlwind. Strange, to shout and not hear oneself. Not hear *anything*. "I am King Freyrík of Farr, and I come to offer tribute!"

Behind him, the countercurrent grew stronger, the elf-singers' light so bright it hurt his eyes, even from behind. Had he won them the distraction they needed to flank this fury?

He fought his vertigo to climb to his feet, threw his arms out to his sides, well away from his weapons.

"My people betrayed you, perpetrated a great injustice upon you. I have come to make amends!"

For a moment the storm overtook the countercurrent, and the wind knocked him flat to the earth. For a moment he knew not which way was up, but then he did and he was clawing back to his knees, humble and prostrate before the Grand Elders' husks. "I know I cannot return that which you have lost. I am sorry for that. But I offer my life in return." Again he threw his arms out, tilted his head back to the sky. "Take me. Do with me as you will. Assuage your anger upon my flesh!"

Behind him, the singers' elflight grew brighter still, and though he was deaf as the dead he could *feel* Ayden shouting *No!*, and then he felt the shift in the air, the storm twisting round, the static charge and sharp smell that presaged a hard rain. It fell upon him like a runaway horse, like a darker horde, all howling winds and flying debris and fury, *fury*, blistering raw and arterial red, sheeting out his senses. There was heat, and pain, breathless burning and a terrible noise inside his head and the knowledge, the *peace*, that he had done what he'd set out to do, had bought the elf-singers enough distraction to finish their work, to put end forever to this menace, to the hatred of the wronged—

And then he knew only darkness, and silence, and the cold of final sleep.

Chapter Eighteen

mazing how a mere six months and several rounds of treaty talks could change the world. The animosity was still there between their people, of course, no doubt would be for a good long while yet. Ayden himself still felt that gut reaction—*Cruel children, destructive fools*—when he looked at humans sometimes. It did not help to be standing by the back stairs to the very pavilion where they'd spilled his blood with such ferocious intent, cheering every lash as if his torture were some wild entertainment, some traveling show.

But those days were behind him now. Behind all of them, fallen gods pray.

"Would you like to hold her?" Rík asked. He gestured with his chin toward the cooing bundle in his arms.

Ayden needed no more invitation. He plucked up Rík's newest spawn and swung her round, cooing right back. She giggled and stuck her fingers in his eye. "Ow," Ayden laughed. "When do they stop doing that?"

Rík grinned and shrugged. "By the time they're twelve, mayhap? So . . ." He peered up at the sun as if gauging the time. "Eleven and a half years to go?"

Ayden snorted and handed her back, but a wet nurse swept in with an "Allow me, Your Majesty," and stepped away to feed her.

Rík watched, song and expression solemn of a sudden. Serious. "I wanted a girl for so long," he said, watching as the baby latched toothless mouth to bosom, "because sons die. Fight, and die. Always."

Ayden slung an arm round Rík's waist and pulled him close. "Not anymore," he said.

"No." Rík rubbed his cheek against Ayden's shoulder, placed a lingering kiss there. "Not anymore."

Silence then for a time while someone made a speech on the pavilion above their heads, while Rík's youngest child fed at the breast. They stood hip to hip and shoulder to shoulder, companionable, happy.

"Did you know," Rík said, eyes still on his baby girl, "that the Aegis wants me to marry now?"

"Very well," Ayden sighed, "but I have seen the human tradition in these lands. *You* shall have to wear the dress."

Ayden thought his comment rather clever, but Rík didn't laugh. Turned instead to face Ayden, the barest hint of a smile gracing his lips and his song, and took both of Ayden's hands in his own. "I told him no."

Ayden's shock must have shown on his face, for Rík added, "Being the hero king has its privileges, you know." He shrugged, still holding Ayden's hands. "I've enough heirs in any event. Five sons who all may live now to decrepitude, gods willing."

"Gods willing," Ayden repeated, and leaned in to kiss him.

They were halfway to sheer indecency when a page scuttled forward—Ayden heard his nervous twang long before he heard his footsteps over the hubbub on the great lawn—and cleared his throat. "Begging pardon, Your Majesty, but the Aegis is ready for you."

Rík nodded, stole one more kiss, and asked Ayden, "Are *you* ready?"

Rík reached out a hand, and Ayden took it in his own. They climbed the last few steps up to the pavilion together, waited there beneath the warm summer sunlight as the Aegis finished his speech-making.

"And now"—the man's voice was so bold, so confident and powerful, it carried round the whole vast lawn as if the loudest elven song—"I present to you the heroes of the day, of the year, of our lifetimes and our children's lifetimes and *their* children's lifetimes, the great champion king and the warrior elf who braved the darker forests to put end to our three-century curse . . . King Freyrík Farr and Colonel Ayden *barn* Vaska!"

Ayden stepped out with Rík to the roar of the crowd, the heels of their dress boots clacking loud against the wooden floor. Strange thing to hear over the wild cheers, the songs of adulation and gratitude and hope, gods, so much *hope*. Yet with Rík's hand in his, Rík's shoulder pressed warm against his own, the world seemed always a private, quiet place. They might not be standing together against the world anymore, but they were standing together nonetheless. That much hadn't changed.

They were standing together now before the whole of Rík's kingdom, or so it seemed, joined hands raised in triumph. He felt the soft, sure presence of Mother Megin, new elven ambassador to Aegea, on the pavilion behind them, and sent a gentle trill of *gratitude-warmth-adoration* tickling past her mind-ear. He'd be standing on this stage alone today had she not acted so quickly when Rík had offered himself in sacrifice, and the Elders' lightning had cut him down. She'd risked not only herself but the entirety of their mission to sing the steady beat back into Rík's heart, and for that he would ever love her in ways he could not express with words.

From beside her, enthroned on the raised dais, came the thrumming refrain of the Aegis himself, paternal and proud, grateful and loving. Ayden was elf enough to admit he'd misjudged the man.

Crack "misjudged," Ayden; you were wrong, *utterly wrong.*

Yet he could hardly be blamed for having thought the Aegis had wished Freyrík dead. Nor blamed for disliking him still, even if he had exchanged all the elven slaves for Rík's freedom and a chance at peace. Even Jagall. Even Simi, the poor child, may she one day learn to live for herself again.

Ayden shut those thoughts and the Aegis's song from his head and focused only on the crowd, the ambassador, the warm solid press of Rík's hand in his own, the grand untamed chorus of ten thousand songs washing over his mind-ear. Looking out at that press of bodies, that sea of joyous faces, he could indeed believe there would be lasting peace again.

And fallen gods help him for thinking so, but perhaps that wasn't such a bad thing after all.

Ayden looked to Rík, saw the same runaway smile on his lover's face that he felt on his own. Rík was waving to the crowd like the king he'd become, and though Ayden felt a bit foolish, he did the same. Down in the front rows below the pavilion, men crushed forward against the line of guards, thrusting out fists clenched round wooden address markers, tossing them onto the stage. The men's intent washed high and clear across his mind-ear, and he started so hard he knocked Rík off-balance. The markers were not meant for Rík—of course they weren't; a commoner couldn't give his daughter to a king, not even as a consort—they were meant for *him*.

His smile slipped a little, but in truth, he supposed this meant progress. The men would no doubt rescind their offers when they learned he couldn't give a human female children, but the fact they'd made them at all was remarkable.

Rík grinned at him again, knocked his shoulder with gentle mischief. Ayden scowled, but couldn't hold it long. His own grin forced its way back onto his face.

He stood there some many moments longer, smiling and waving like a simpleton, until at last the small scrape of the Aegis's impatience cut across his mind-ear and the crowd before them fell silent as if struck down by some massive hand. In a way, they had, for the Aegis had risen to his feet, holding out his arms in a gesture of silence. When the Aegis nodded at them, he and Rík made good their escape.

Their speeches would come later, just before they lit the bonfire and tapped the ale casks and uncovered the commoners' pit roasts. But for now he put the thought of it from his head and followed Rík down the stairs. Then through the gate, across the bailey—running now, the both of them, headlong and laughing, into the keep.

They'd but crossed the first threshold when Rík seized him by the shoulders, whirled him round, and slammed him against a convenient wall. He tasted wine and honey on Rík's lips, parted his own to make way for demanding tongue and teeth. Rík's fingers were already worming their way down the collar of Ayden's dress clothes, tugging impatiently.

"We've only an hour," Rík said, though what Ayden heard behind all that hunger and frustration was *Why aren't you undressing right here in the corridor?*

Ayden chuckled, snatched up Rík's hands in his own and kissed his knuckles. "Nonsense. We've a *lifetime*. I've over sixty years of leave saved."

Rík tried to reclaim his hands, and when he realized he couldn't, he simply started down the corridor toward his rooms, tugging Ayden behind him. "Like you could sit still for sixty years."

Another laugh, from both of them this time. "Who said anything about sitting still? I plan to wear you ragged, human."

Rík's walk turned into a run, and Ayden turned the run into a chase, herding Rík down half a dozen halls and through their apartment doors before tackling him onto the rug by the drawing room hearth. 'Twas all hands and lips then, grappling limbs and tearing clothes, tongue and teeth on freshly bared skin and the aching twine of song and flesh.

Later there would be feasting and speeches and ceremony, music and dancing and plays. Later still there would be debates and accords, setbacks and agreements, long years of seeking—and if they were foolish, burning—common ground. But for now there was only him and Freyrík, bridging the gap between their two worlds not for peace or politics or their people, but for themselves alone. For joy, for music.

For love.

Revisit the Song of the Fallen from the
beginning with *Counterpoint.*

Dear Reader,

Thank you for reading Rachel Haimowitz's *Crescendo*!

We know your time is precious and you have many, many entertainment options, so it means a lot that you've chosen to spend your time reading. We really hope you enjoyed it.

We'd be honored if you'd consider posting a review—good or bad—on sites like **Amazon, Barnes & Noble, Kobo, Goodreads, Twitter, Facebook, Tumblr,** and your blog or website. We'd also be honored if you told your friends and family about this book. Word of mouth is a book's lifeblood!

For more information on upcoming releases, author interviews, blog tours, contests, giveaways, and more, please sign up for our weekly, spam-free newsletter and visit us around the web:

Newsletter: tinyurl.com/RiptideSignup
Twitter: twitter.com/RiptideBooks
Facebook: facebook.com/RiptidePublishing
Goodreads: tinyurl.com/RiptideOnGoodreads
Tumblr: riptidepublishing.tumblr.com

Thank you so much for Reading the Rainbow!

RiptidePublishing.com

ALSO BY

Rachel Haimowitz

Anchored (Belonging, #1)
Power Play: Resistance, with Cat Grant
Power Play: Awakening, with Cat Grant
Master Class (Master Class, #1)
SUBlime: Collected Shorts (Master Class, #2)
Counterpoint (Song of the Fallen, #1)
The Flesh Cartel, with Heidi Belleau
Break and Enter, with Aleksandr Voinov

Coming Soon
Where He Belongs (Belonging, #2)
The Burnt Toast B&B (A Bluewater Bay novel),
with Heidi Belleau

ABOUT THE *Author*

Rachel is an M/M erotic romance author and the Publisher of Riptide Publishing. She's also a sadist with a pesky conscience, shamelessly silly, and quite proudly pervish. Fortunately, all those things make writing a lot more fun for her . . . if not so much for her characters.

When she's not writing about hot guys getting it on (or just plain getting it; her characters rarely escape a story unscathed), she loves to read, hike, camp, sing, perform in community theater, and glue captions to cats. She also has a particular fondness for her very needy dog, her even needier cat, and shouting at kids to get off her lawn.

You can find Rachel at her website, rachelhaimowitz.com, tweeting as @RachelHaimowitz, and on Tumblr at rachelhaimowitz.tumblr.com. She loves to hear from folks, so feel free to drop her a line anytime at metarachel@gmail.com.

Enjoy this book?
Find more fantasy romance at
RiptidePublishing.com!

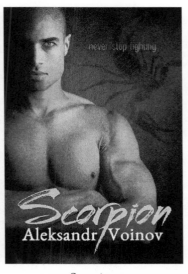

All My Crimes
ISBN: 978-1-937551-93-3

Scorpion
ISBN: 978-1-62649-014-7

Earn Bonus Bucks!

Earn 1 Bonus Buck for each dollar you spend. Find out how at RiptidePublishing.com/news/bonus-bucks.

Win Free Ebooks for a Year!

Pre-order coming soon titles directly through our site and you'll receive one entry into a drawing to win free books for a year! Get the details at RiptidePublishing.com/contests.